BOUGHT AT HILLMORTON BOTTOM
LOCH, CANAL BOAT HOLLDAY
2017

W0009884

THE BEST OF
WINTER'S
CRIMES: 2

THE BEST OF WINTER'S CRIMES

A selection from Winter's Crimes 1–17

VOLUME 2

Anthony Lejeune to
P B Yuill

Edited by GEORGE HARDINGE

GUILD PUBLISHING
LONDON

All rights reserved. No reproduction, copy or transmission of this publication may be made without written permission. No paragraph of this publication may be reproduced, copied or transmitted save with written permission or in accordance with the provisions of the Copyright Act 1956 (as amended). Any person who does any unauthorised act in relation to this publication may be liable to criminal prosecution and civil claims for damages.

This edition published 1986 by
Book Club Associates
by arrangement with
Macmillan London Limited

Typeset by Wyvern Typesetting Ltd, Bristol,
in Linotron 202 Bembo

Printed and bound in Great Britain by
Anchor Brendon Ltd, Tiptree

ISBN: 978-0333424971

CONTENTS

EDITOR'S NOTE

I did not attempt to compile from memory my selection for this omnibus anthology of the *Winter's Crimes* series which my colleagues have encouraged me to publish, though it is something of a self-indulgence. The choices have been made from the annual volumes spanning seventeen of the eighteen years' full-time service I am due to complete with Macmillan. I founded this series and edited all the volumes except for *Winter's Crimes 5* edited by Virginia Whitaker and *Winter's Crimes 8, 10, 12, 14* and *16* edited by Hilary Hale, formerly Hilary Watson.

I owe many debts, one of them (once again) to my friend Julian Symons. At the very start he acted as an unpaid and more or less unthanked adviser: the concept of the *Winter's Crimes* series was worked out with his help in the bar at the Charing Cross Hotel many years ago.

Among other acknowledgements that are due the help given by my friends Virginia Whitaker and Hilary Hale obviously comes very high. But of course the whole Macmillan publishing machinery from production to sales has been needed to bring the book into being: and is needed again now that this comprehensive anthology is going to the printers.

To make my choices I have re-read all of the one hundred and ninety-three stories that appeared in the annual volumes referred to above. Coming again to these stories I found myself in an absolute Aladdin's Cave of marvellous things. If I had really been the editor who sponsored and conjured so many wonderful gems of invention and craftsmanship into being, had I not something to be proud of?

The real answer, I think, is luck: luck in having such support from an immense range of authors including many who have been and mostly still are personal friends. And already some of these friends who have had more than one story in the series have been pointing out to me, in the kindest possible way, that I have chosen the wrong one. They may well be right; these are subjective questions.

Obviously all these stories have been published before, some more than once and in different media. But they have not been published together, and I am going to have the temerity to suggest that this is an absolutely stunning compendium of crime short stories: the authors' names are a roll-call of distinction and success in crime-writing in the second half of the twentieth century, and in their inventions for the *Winter's Crimes* series they have often reached the height of their powers.

I hope many readers new and old will come to share the huge pleasure I have derived from re-reading these stories.

George Hardinge

Collection © Macmillan London Limited, 1986

The stories are copyright respectively:
© Anthony Lejeune 1979
© Michael Z Lewin 1984
© Audrey Erskine Lindop 1973
© Ivor Drummond 1974
© Peter Lovesey Limited 1985
© Desmond Lowden 1981
© Sabensa Gakulu Limited 1985
© Ellis Peters 1985
© Anthony Price 1979
© Kingsmarkham Enterprises Limited 1977
© Maurice Richardson 1975
© Geoffrey Rose 1972
© George Sims 1980
© Jean Stubbs 1971
© Julian Symons 1979
© Miles Tripp 1971
© Michael Underwood 1983
© John and Avis Wainwright 1985
© Ted Willis Limited 1975
© P B Yuill 1977

THE BEST OF
WINTER'S
CRIMES

VOLUME 2

SOMETHING ON EVERYONE

Anthony Lejeune

John Deakin's voice, normally a controlled and confident instrument for speech-making, trembled on the verge of a stammer. 'As I told you on the telephone,' he said, 'I'm in rather a jam.'

'All right,' said Lord Frane, 'let's have the story.' It was lucky, he thought, that the Great British Public – the voting public – couldn't see Deakin now. The man was shaken and scared in a way that Frane had seen several times before in his long political experience; the way of hitherto unblemished success which suddenly hits trouble; the way of a much-praised rising politician before whose feet a gulf has opened which threatens to swallow up everything he has achieved and hoped to achieve.

Deakin's fears, whatever they were, might be exaggerated. People generally did manage to get out of their troubles somehow, particularly if they had sophisticated and powerful friends. But, of course, not always. Frane could remember one or two sad cases . . . He didn't really like John Deakin very much, but the Party had great hopes of him. He looked good on television – which is what mattered nowadays. If he came unstuck, it would be not only a personal tragedy but damaging: and Frane's job was to see that the Party didn't get damaged.

The other two people in his drawing-room were very old friends: George Liddle and Sir Peter Farmiloe, sound Party men both, who knew the world and knew Westminster. Frane had asked Deakin if he minded their being present; their advice might be useful, he'd said.

Deakin swallowed a little more whisky. 'I got this letter a month ago,' he said. 'It was from a man I once knew, called Derek Shee. You might have come across him. He was interested in politics. I think he was on the Candidates' List for a while. Anyway, this letter referred to something which once happened to me, and said that, if I wanted to talk about it, I was to put an advertisement in the personal column of *The Times*, consisting of just one word – 1968, the year 1968, which is when the thing happened.

'So I did that. I put the advertisement in. And late in the afternoon, when it appeared, Shee telephoned me at my office in the City. He wanted me to meet him at a pub that evening. I went there. And he asked me for money – to keep quiet, though I'm not sure he ever put it so crudely. But the implication was that, if I didn't pay, he would sell the story to a newspaper. He didn't ask for a great deal, only the equivalent, he said, of what a newspaper might pay him. Five hundred pounds. I agreed. I got the money out of the bank next morning, and delivered it to him at another pub.

'It's odd. I knew as well as anyone else that when you pay off a blackmailer you don't get rid of him. He's likely to come back for more. I've heard that, and read it, a dozen times. And yet I believed, or I convinced myself, that I was getting rid of him. He telephoned again this morning, wanting another five hundred. When I hesitated, he began putting on the pressure, hinting at what would happen to my career if the facts became known. Only hinting. He was obviously being careful not to say anything too explicit on the telephone. He told me to be at the same pub tomorrow evening at six-thirty. I said I'd think about it, and hung up.'

Deakin paused, and looked at the others for their reaction.

'Did you consider going to the police?' asked Frane.

'Of course I did. But I can't.'

'Because you don't want to tell them – whatever it is that Shee knows?'

'Partly that. And partly because it wouldn't be safe, would it? That's one of the things I wanted to ask your advice about. I mean, if there was a prosecution, I might appear as "Mr X", but surely the chances are it would leak? There would be gossip in the Temple or in Fleet Street, and then in the City and at Westminster. And I'd be done. Isn't that likely?'

Frane nodded. 'I must admit it is. At least, there would be a danger. And this is something you absolutely can't risk?'

Deakin took another drink of whisky. The only sound in the room was the soft ticking of a handsome clock on the chimneypiece and a faint murmur of traffic, deadened by good double glazing and heavy velvet curtains. At last Deakin said: 'I think I'd better tell you.' He glanced at Farmiloe and Liddle. 'I know I can trust all of you to keep quiet about it.'

From his inside pocket he produced an envelope. 'First,' he said, 'here's the original letter.'

The address on the envelope and the letter inside were typewritten, rather badly. Frane read it in silence, and then handed it to the others.

It said: *Dear Mr Deakin, It's a long time since you heard from me, but I've been hearing about you. As one of your supporters, I've been shocked by what I heard. It's about the poor little girl and the cover-up. At the moment I'm the only one who knows, apart from those who were involved. But if the facts were ever published, it would do great harm to the Cause we both believe in, and it would ruin you. I need reassurance. If you are willing to talk about it, please insert a small ad in* The Times, *just saying '1968'. Meanwhile I don't think you should tell anyone else about this letter. Yours very sincerely, Derek Shee.* There was no address or date.

Having read it, Farmiloe handed the letter back to Deakin. 'Quite clever,' Frane said. 'You couldn't exactly call it a blackmailing letter.'

'While making the intention fairly plain,' added Farmiloe.

Deakin took a deep breath. 'What he's referring to happened in my last year at London University. There was a girl. Not a student, just a girl I met at a party. She became pregnant – and that's when I found out she was only fifteen. Only fifteen! My God, in many ways she was far more sophisticated than me. My father and her father fixed it up between them. My father paid, quite a lot. I lived in a nightmare for several months, in case something went wrong. But nothing did, and the girl kept quiet. I never saw her again, but a few years later I read about her in the papers. She'd killed herself. Sleeping pills and drink.

'I'm not proud of that story, but, looking back, I can't see myself as a villain. If it hadn't been me, it would have been someone else. The father was a drunk. Her mother was dead, and there were no brothers or sisters. That's how we were able to hush it up. Eventually I really had almost forgotten about it. It seems like something which happened to someone else.'

'How did Shee come to learn about it?' asked Liddle.

'From the girl's father, when he was in a maudlin condition one night. He swore Shee to secrecy, and said he was going to tell him a family secret he'd never told anyone before. Well, that's the size of it. What do you think?'

Frane poured whisky. 'It's not good. I've no idea if the police would prosecute after so long. Probably not, and I could make discreet enquiries about that. They might feel they had to if it became very public. But that's not entirely the point, is it? How do you think your Constituency Association would react?'

'Some of them might be sympathetic. But they'd sling me out. And then my job, which is really just a way for the bank to sponsor an MP, would go too.'

'So at all costs it must not become public. I think I agree; it would be too risky to go to the police. John, I'd like to mull this one over. Could you bear to go home now, and let Peter and George and me talk it out and see what we can come up with?'

Two hours later they hadn't come up with much. Farmiloe had begun by wondering if the matter was actually as serious as Deakin thought. 'It's a long time ago, and he wasn't responsible for the girl's death.'

'If that's all there is to it, I'm inclined to agree with you,' said Liddle. 'But is that all there is to it?'

Frane shook his head. 'I doubt it. You know Deakin's reputation. You've seen the gossip columns. He likes girls, and very young girls too. If once this can of worms is opened, who knows what may crawl out?'

'So you think that's really what's worrying him? Nice man, our promising young colleague.'

'We don't *know* there's anything else,' said Farmiloe.

'There's always something else,' replied Frane. 'He's not my favourite man, but nor am I inclined to throw first stones. The remarkable thing, surely, isn't when somebody gets found out but that most of us never do. If our lives and careers were extended indefinitely, we should all come a cropper sooner or later.'

'Speak for yourself.'

'Oh I am, I am. But the point is, we've all seen political scandals. Several in the past few years. And once they start to unravel, it's very difficult to stop them – particularly if the press has got wind of the story.'

'In most of the cases you're talking about, the best policy would have been to make a clean breast of it straight away. Trying to cover up was what did the real harm.'

'Making a clean breast of it might have been a very fine gesture,' said Liddle, 'but it usually wouldn't have saved the chap's career.'

'The art of covering up has always seemed to me an essential part of politics,' said Frane. 'The problem is to make the covering up stick. In Deakin's case, how do we persuade Mr Derek Shee to keep quiet permanently?'

'Threaten him with the police? I agree that an actual prosecution would be risky, but perhaps we could scare him.'

'We might scare him off demanding any more money, but that wouldn't prevent him from sending an anonymous letter to some newspaper. Rather the contrary indeed. He'd probably want to get his revenge.'

'Just think what Fearless Fred would do with it in the *Daily News*,' said Farmiloe.

'I must confess I take that rag purely for Fred Mandeville's column,' said Liddle. 'He can be bloody funny.'

' "Scurrilous" is the old-fashioned word,' Farmiloe retorted.

'Well, a power in the land anyway,' agreed Frane. 'So we must keep his nose out of young Mr Deakin's past if we can. Any suggestions?'

'A private detective,' said Liddle, 'who might get something on Shee?'

'It's a thought, but I'm not very keen on bringing in someone else. We know where that sort of thing can lead, don't we?' Frane knocked the ash off his cigar, then said slowly: 'I think I might talk to Mr Shee myself.'

'Is that wise?' asked Farmiloe. 'Wouldn't it be exposing the Party, an admission of vulnerability?'

'Oh,' said Frane cheerfully, 'I'll go in disguise.'

And so, in a sense, he did. He arranged to go with Deakin to the rendezvous in the pub. 'Just introduce me as a friend. I can be Mr Robinson.'

'He's not going to say anything in front of a witness,' objected Deakin. 'He'll probably think you're a policeman.'

'If he believes that, he'll believe anything. My grey hairs should convince him I'm not. But let's see what happens. I want to size the fellow up myself.'

He indulged himself in the agreeable notion of disguise to the extent of wearing glasses, which he never normally did except for reading, wrapping a muffler round his neck and pulling an old tweed hat down over his eyes. 'Pretty sinister,' he said to his image in the looking-glass.

The pub was quite sinister too, in an alley off the Strand. Shee had probably chosen it because nobody could be watching the entrance without being seen, and the bar, at that time of the evening, contained only a couple of regulars – the stage doorkeeper from an adjacent theatre and a newspaper-seller who had just finished peddling his wares. Later there would be some theatregoers, fortifying themselves before the curtain went up and restoring themselves in the interval: but not yet.

Arriving at exactly six-thirty, Frane and Deakin bought drinks and took them to a table in the corner. Five minutes later Shee pushed open the door. He froze for a moment when he saw Frane, but then walked over to them grinning.

14

Neatly dressed, podgy, somehow too confident – Frane wondered if it was only knowing that he was a slippery villain which made him look like one.

'This is a friend of mine,' said Deakin, 'George Robinson.'

'I'm honoured,' said Shee. 'Don't I remember your friend from my political days? Not that we ever met. I was much too unimportant. But, of course, I've seen his picture in the papers. "George Robinson" – that's a good one.'

'I've heard about you too, Mr Shee,' replied Frane. 'Let me get you a drink.'

While he did so, Deakin and Shee sat in silence. When Frane had rejoined them, Shee said to Deakin: 'You decided to come then.'

'You asked me to.'

'So I did. Just for a friendly chat – since we have so many interests in common.'

'May I ask what those interests are?' said Frane.

'Oh, the good of the Party. And old times. I'm still very keen on politics, you know. I read the newspapers and I've a lot of friends in Fleet Street. I was thinking only today that I ought to get in touch with my friends in Fleet Street. Perhaps I will. Very soon.'

Deakin had already emptied his glass and was looking at it fiercely. 'For God's sake, man,' he muttered, 'say what you mean.'

'Mean? I don't mean anything in particular. But I had hoped for a quiet talk, just you and me. If you'd like that, perhaps you'd get in touch with me. The same way you did before. Shall we say within the next week? Now, if you gentlemen will excuse me. I'm afraid I can't afford to buy you a drink. I'm a little short of funds – temporarily: but that's a condition I hope to relieve. One way or another. Good night, Mr Deakin. Good night, Lord Frane.'

He grinned at them, and was gone.

'He thinks he's very clever,' said Lord Frane.

'Slimy bastard!'

'Oh yes. But a dangerous slimy bastard. I think we'll have to buy some more time.'

'You mean I'll have to buy some more time.'

'Insert that notice in the paper again. Say, two days from now. Then he'll presumably telephone you to arrange another meeting. Let me know. Meanwhile, I'll put my thinking cap back on, now that I've met him. Give me your glass. We need another drink.'

'Oh, let me,' said Deakin bitterly. 'It is my round.'

Frane was still sitting at his breakfast table, surrounded by newspapers, opened envelopes, coffee cup, marmalade and toast crumbs, when Liddle marched in, three days later.

'Richard,' he said, 'here's a turn-up for the books. I got a letter this morning.'

'Somebody loves you.'

'Somebody doesn't. Here, you'd better read it.'

Frane took the letter, examined the envelope, then the single sheet of paper inside. It was typewritten, rather badly. There was no address.

Dear Mr Liddle, it said. *You don't know me, but I have followed your political career with admiration for many years. It would be tragic – for you and for the Party – if anything were to damage your reputation now. I've recently learned certain facts which worry me very much, and if they were published I feel sure they would worry other people too. Need I say more than that they concern a house in St John's Wood? If you are willing to discuss this matter with me, please insert a small ad in* The Times, *just saying 'Thanks to St John'. Meanwhile I don't think you should tell anyone else about this letter. Yours very sincerely, A Well-wisher.*

'The style seems familiar,' observed Frane.

'Doesn't it? You know what he's talking about – the house in St John's Wood?'

'I remember there were rumours . . . '

'The point is, they were wrong. The Special Branch were watching that house, for reasons we all know, and they saw my car parked outside. But I was actually visiting a lady next door. I explained that to the Prime Minister at the time. I couldn't deny the rumours publicly without bringing her name into it, so we agreed to make no statement and just let the rumours die down. Which they did. But if any paper trotted that old story out now, I'd slap a writ on them quicker than you could say knife. The lady in question is divorced now, and it doesn't matter anyway. What Mr Shee seems to be doing is relying on out-of-date political gossip. With Deakin it worked. But he's picked the wrong man this time.'

'Two wrong men.' Frane picked up one of the opened letters from beside his plate and tossed it over to Liddle. 'Snap.'

Liddle glanced at it. 'You too?' he said with astonishment.

Frane nodded. 'Mr Shee appears to have launched on a new career. Or perhaps – more probably, come to think of it – Deakin wasn't the first, just the first we've heard of. Now he seems to be trawling, to see what he can catch. But I'm glad to say he's got my little affair slightly wrong too. I was used by those whizz-kids in the City, and the ice was thin. My fault; one shouldn't stray too far outside one's own territory. Anyway, I'm not worried now about what he's hinting at. The ice held, that's what matters.'

'So he hasn't really got anything on you either?'

'Not really. I can see why he might think he had, and I wouldn't be specially pleased to see the story revived in the City pages – or in Fearless Fred's column. But, like you, I wouldn't mind waving a few writs in the air.' He chuckled. 'Come to think of it, I wouldn't mind collecting some tax-free damages. At my time of life I'm quite willing to be libelled if the price is right.'

'It shouldn't come to that,' said Liddle. 'We're not as vulnerable as Deakin, so we should be able to nail Mr Shee. Shall we go to the police?'

'Not yet. We couldn't explain about Shee without telling them about Deakin. And the reasons for not doing that still apply. I'll tell you what – you give me a photostat of that letter, and I'll have a private word with my friend, the Assistant Commissioner. Then we'll see what we'll see.'

★ · ★ · ★

Later the same day, Deakin telephoned Frane to say that Shee had called, and that a new meeting had been arranged for the following evening in a different pub. 'He said I'd bloody well better not bring anyone with me this time. And he said – or rather implied – that I had better bring the money.'

'I'm afraid you'll have to pay him again,' said Frane. 'But cheer up. The US Marines may be on the way.'

'It's no joke to me,' said Deakin. 'And I can't say you've been much help so far.' He hung up.

Frane grimaced. No, decidedly he didn't like Deakin. He had made a note of the time and place of the new meeting with Shee. For a minute he was tempted by the notion of disguising himself properly – perhaps even a false beard? – and watching from a distance. Reluctantly he abandoned the idea and buzzed for his secretary. Her name was Carole. She was an inconspicuous sort of girl at first sight, but, Frane thought, distinctly attractive at second or third glance. He wouldn't have employed her otherwise.

The pub this time was in Earls Court. Again Shee arrived a few minutes after Deakin. He looked round suspiciously, making sure Deakin was alone before joining him.

'Left your friend at home?' he said.

'I came alone. That's what you told me to do. I've got some money.'

They both spoke quietly, and the room was noisy. No one could have overheard them. But Shee was wary. His eyes kept running round the room. 'How much?'

'Five hundred pounds.'

'In cash?'

'In ten-pound notes.'

'All right. This is what I want you to do. In a minute I'm going over to the bar to buy a drink. I'll leave this copy of the *Evening Standard* on the seat beside you. Slip the notes inside it and fold them in tightly. After I've come back, wait a minute, then say goodbye naturally and leave. Take the paper with you. There's a litter basket attached to the lamp-post immediately outside the door. Put the paper in that. Then go away.'

'I haven't told the police,' said Deakin. 'There's no one watching.'

'Just do it.'

He's nervous, thought Deakin while Shee was at the bar. I only wish he had more reason to be. He doesn't want anyone to be able to testify that he saw something pass between us.

His hand concealed by the table, Deakin carefully folded the paper so that the notes couldn't slip out. Shee returned. For a couple of minutes they made desultory conversation about the weather.

'All right,' said Shee. 'That's enough.' Obediently Deakin rose, nodded goodbye and went out, taking the paper with him. Shee watched through the window as Deakin deposited the folded paper in the litter-basket. He forced himself to wait another full minute, fearful that some passing tramp might fish the paper out of the basket. He felt reasonably sure, though, that Deakin had been speaking the truth, and that there was no one in the room who seemed in the least likely to be a detective.

Finally he put down his glass, left the pub and retrieved the newspaper, going through a little pantomime as though something in the headline which protruded from the basket had caught his eye. He walked away reading it.

He didn't notice the girl and her young man who came out of the pub almost on his heels. He had, after all, been quite right. They weren't detectives. But they followed him.

It was just about twenty-four hours later when Peter Farmiloe arrived at Frane's house in a state of some excitement. 'I've been at the club,' he said. 'Bill Broughton was there and that rather pompous City fellow, Wysard. They were talking to each other in the bar, and I gathered from what they were saying that they'd both received blackmailing letters during the past few days. Almost identical letters. And they sounded to me very like the letter which Shee sent to Deakin.'

'Oh really? Well, if they were talking about it in loud voices, they must have been rather less scared than Deakin was.'

'They were. Wysard had already been to the police. Actually, they were being slightly cagey about just what was in the letters – though I bet you I could guess in Wysard's case – but they both said that whoever wrote the letters seemed to know something about them but got his facts all wrong. You don't seem very surprised. Had you heard about this?'

'I know that George Liddle received a letter like that a couple of days ago. And so did I.'

'My God! The fellow's running amok. Has he got something on everyone?'

'Almost everyone. He's nothing on you, has he?'

'Certainly not.'

At that moment Frane's Filipino butler came in. 'Mr Mandeville here, sir.'

Farmiloe practically shot out of his seat. 'Fred Mandeville? Fearsome Fred? He's on to us. What are you going to say?'

'Calm yourself. I asked Fred Mandeville to come and see me.'

'You asked him? Why?'

'I thought I could put him straight about one or two things. A pre-emptive strike, you might say.'

'He'll bite your fingers off.'

'No, he won't. Journalists very rarely bite the hand that feeds them. Anyway, he's rather a nice boy. He was at school with my son. Do you want to meet him?'

Farmiloe didn't, though he glanced curiously at the soberly suited, bespectacled young man who was waiting in the hall.

Frane and Fred Mandeville were closeted together for nearly an hour. When Mandeville had gone, Frane looked at his watch and thought that, with a bit of luck, his friend the Assistant Commissioner (Crime) should be at home by now.

He telephoned him there, and they had a very private conversation. Afterwards he made another telephone call, no less private.

'Carole,' said Lord Frane around teatime the following day, 'I am now going to call on Mr Shee at that address to which you so kindly followed him. I shall take my swordstick.'

He didn't really think Shee was the dangerous type, but the swordstick made Lord Frane feel dangerous, which appealed to his romantic – or melodramatic – soul. A taxi deposited him outside a rather shabby Victorian house in South Kensington, which had been converted into flats. He pressed the buzzer beside the Entryphone.

Shee's voice said: 'Who is it?'

'Lord Frane. I want a word with you.'

'What about? I've nothing to say to you.' Frane was pleased to detect a note of panic.

'I've something to say to you. Let me in, unless you want another visit from the police.'

Silence. Then the door clicked open.

Frane walked up three flights of stairs. The door at the top was open. Shee was waiting there in his shirtsleeves, tie loose, hair unkempt, obviously a shaken man. Frane brushed past him into the sitting-room, then turned on him, standing rock-firm in front of the fireplace as though he owned the house.

Shee started to say something, but Frane cut him short. 'When the police came here this morning they took away a typewriter. Certain letters were typed on that machine.'

'That typewriter wasn't mine. And I never wrote the letters they were talking about. I'd never seen them before.'

'Of course you didn't,' said Frane cheerfully. 'I wrote them. And you might – I say you *might* – be able, eventually, to convince the police that you are innocent. Innocent of writing those letters. But in the process your little transaction with John Deakin is going to emerge, don't you think? And how are you going to explain that away? Are you with me so far?'

Shee tried to speak but proved literally speechless. Frane grasped his sword-stick more tightly for a moment. It wasn't necessary though. Morally and even physically he felt in command, dominating the wretch who now sat down, almost collapsed, on to the sofa.

Frane was enjoying himself. He went on: 'The police came here today at my suggestion. They are presumably now examining the typewriter and the letters. The type-face will match. They will also examine them for fingerprints. They won't find your fingerprints, but I can assure you they won't find mine either. They haven't – yet – seen your letter to Mr Deakin, which of course was written on a different machine. But you can hardly tell them that, can you? There will, therefore, be an element of doubt. Further investigation will be needed. Somebody, I imagine, will come round again tomorrow to interview you. Very nasty, that sort of interview, very embarrassing. Now I might – mind you, I say

19

I might – be able to persuade my friends at Scotland Yard to take the matter no further, if, when the detectives come here tomorrow, they find that you've gone. Really gone. Left the country, without making any further nuisance of yourself. You've got funds – a thousand pounds which Mr Deakin gave you. I'm not asking for that back. You have a passport, I hope? Otherwise it'll have to be Ireland, to begin with. What do you say?'

'I really think we deserve this,' said Lord Frane, easing the cork out of the champagne bottle. He filled three glasses.

'How did you manage to plant the typewriter?' Liddle asked.

'I have useful friends in low places. I met this one long ago in the army. Locks speak to him: or rather he speaks to locks – and they open. It's his *métier*.'

'You mean he burgled Shee's flat?' said Farmiloe.

'I'm afraid so. Are you shocked? I've been wondering – purely as an academic question, you understand – whether I have actually committed any grave crimes. I caused that flat to be broken into – yes: but we didn't take anything, on the contrary we added something – *viz*, one typewriter. I issued a number of letters containing nasty insinuations: but I didn't demand any money. All round, I reckon I'm innocent. Pure as the driven snow.'

'While you were investigating nasty insinuations about me,' said Liddle, 'you might have invented something I could have let leak out publicly to please my constituents. You could have said I was the father of sixteen illegitimate children or something like that. I'd have increased my majority at the next election by thousands.'

'I hope some of your other victims don't find out who wrote those letters,' said Farmiloe, 'or you won't be at all popular.'

Frane chuckled. 'It was great fun. I'm tempted to go on and touch a few more of our friends and colleagues on sensitive spots – just to see them jump. One can do it to almost anybody. Except you, dear Peter. You're the unblackmailable man.'

'Hm. I wish I felt you intended that as a compliment. But what were you doing with Fred Mandeville the other day?'

'I was giving him a friendly tip. I told him that there was this man with a grudge against the Party who had been trying to blackmail several of its senior members. You may hear rumours, I said, about some of the stories he's got hold of. Somebody may even show you one of the letters. But be careful, I said. You'll be walking into a minefield of libel actions. This jolly blackmailer gets all his facts wrong. I suggested that, if Fearless Fred wanted a story, he might do one about The Incompetent Blackmailer.'

'You hid the leaf in the forest,' said Liddle. 'I hope friend Deakin is grateful.'

'I telephoned him. I just told him we'd got Shee off his back. He was moderately grateful. You know,' said Frane, emptying the bottle and starting to remove the wire from another, 'he really won't do. Not the right type at all. I must drop a word in a few ears . . .'

THE RELUCTANT DETECTIVE

by Michael Z Lewin

It started as a tax fiddle. Well, paint on a little semantic gloss: call it a tax avoidance structurisation. Uncle Edward would have preferred that, I think.

It was Uncle Edward who was responsible for my coming to England in the first place. I am American by birth and by upbringing. So was he, but some time in his relative youth he moved over here – I don't know what brought him – and he stayed. That was a long time ago, his moving. Before I was born. I'm twenty-six now. And I never actually met him, though I wrote to him often. Not letters exactly, because what we did was play postal chess. We did that over a period of more than ten years, so while I didn't know him at all, I felt I knew him fairly well. You get a sense of people by their chess games. Look at Anatoly Karpov's style on the board and you'll see a map of his face. No expression in either.

But that's by the by. I was Uncle Edward's only child-age relative – he never had kids of his own – and from the time I was born he kept in contact. He was quite close to his sister – my mother – and I always got a present on my birthday and at Christmas. It added a certain cosmopolitan touch to these occasions. And then he wrote direct to me when he heard from Mom that I had begun to play with the chess set he sent. We took it from there, playing by post till he died. Even during my years in college we kept it up. And afterwards too, when I was realising I didn't want to be a lawyer, no matter what Dad said about it being useful to fall back on even if I didn't know what I *really* wanted to do.

When Uncle Edward died I was sad. He was one of my few fixed points, a focus for a little contemplative time no matter where I was or what a shambles I was making of the rest of my life.

When I learned that Uncle Edward had provided for me in his will, I was astonished.

What I inherited was a house over here. Also a small income to be sent to me every month from the States. Just about enough to live on.

At first I didn't know what to do. Sell the house, or what. But when I thought about it, it occurred to me that if I thought I could tell about Uncle Edward from our chess games, maybe he could tell about me. Perhaps he was suggesting that it would be good for me to live in England for a while. I'm sure he knew from Mom that I was kind of at loose ends anyway because they wrote to each other. Actual letters, I mean. She only ever quoted to me from one once. When I asked her why Uncle Edward lived in England. She said he had written, *Britain is the closest thing there is left to a civilised English-speaking country.* 'He was never very good at languages,' she said after. The more I thought about it the better an idea it seemed. So I decided to give it a try, and over I came.

★   ★   ★

The tax fidd . . . tax avoidance structurisation didn't come up till I had been here a year or so. In fact, it was Dawn's idea, so in a way everything that's happened is down to her.

Dawn is the lady friend I've made. She is very civilised and if she is what Uncle Edward meant, I understand better why he spent his life here. It could happen to me, though that's not something I think about a lot.

Dawn agreed to move in after I'd been here about six months. We live in my house, and on my income. It gives us a lot of time to enjoy life. And think about things. We're not quite what they call drop-outs back home, because we intend to get into careers when we're sure what we want to do. But if we have no need to rush a decision . . . well, we didn't make the rules.

I see I'm already talking as if I am staying forever. Well, there are worse fates.

And, it turns out, we've already done something along a career line, even if it was strictly by accident. That's what this story is about.

OK, get the picture. I come over here to my house and an income. After six months Dawn and I are friends enough to live together. After six months we realise that comfortable as my income is, maybe there are things it would be nice to do if there were a little more money around.

Get a car for one. Nothing flash, but some wheels to see some of the rest of the country with.

Have I told you where I am? It's a little town in Somerset called Frome. (They pronounce it to rhyme with broom, by the way.) And it is pretty enough and in a lovely part of the country. But there are other places to see. Yes, it was considering getting a car that set us thinking in the first place.

Or set Dawn thinking, actually. She is the one who cooked it all up.

The idea was this. If I set up in business, as a self-employed person I could save money in taxes by deducting a lot of what we spent as necessary commercial expenses. Part of the house as an office; proportion of rates and heat and repairs and insurance; even a salary to Dawn as my secretary. And all the costs of my business vehicle.

Dawn worked it all out, and there was no question, it would pay for the car. And maybe a little bit more as we went along.

Then the question was what kind of business to supposedly set up in. That was Dawn's idea too. Well, not all ideas are necessarily bright.

I set up as a private detective. See, in Britain you don't need a licence of any kind. And, I have to admit, we yielded to a certain pleasant absurdity attached to the notion. I mean, a private detective, in Frome!

As well, the chances of anybody coming to us for business were, of course, nil.

Which was the idea. We didn't want the business to succeed, or, indeed, for there to be any work at all. What we wanted were the deductions. It was a tax fiddle. As I've mentioned.

So, I bought a notebook and pen, and a small sign to put on the front of the house. It gave my name and said under it *Private Inquiry Agent* which is what they call private detectives here.

And that was it.

No advertisements, no listing in the Yellow Pages.

And no business.

We bought a little yellow Mini. Life as planned. It worked like a charm.

For a while.

It was a Tuesday, I remember, because I was reading the basketball column in *The Guardian* – I try to keep up with some of my old interests from the USA – when the doorbell rang. It was about ten o'clock. I thought it might be the gas man. Dawn was out visiting her mother – she's got as many relatives here as I have none, so to speak. A lot is what I am saying.

At the door was a sallow-faced little man – well, I suppose he was about average height, but I am awkwardly tall, about 6' 5", so I have a distorted perspective on people. He had a jacket and tie on and he looked unhappy.

I thought, not the gas man but maybe a local government official.

'Are you Mr Herring?' he asked.

'Yes.'

'May I talk to you?'

'What about?' I asked.

He looked momentarily at the sign on the house by the door. It's so small you can hardly see it even if you know it's there. 'Are you the Mr Herring who is a private inquiry agent?'

And I suddenly realised he had come on business. I was stunned. I began to shake, though I don't know if he noticed.

'Yes, yes, of course,' I said. 'Fredrick Herring. Do come in.'

I led him to the living-room. It wasn't much to look at. Not for a detective's office. It was just a living-room, and lived in at that.

I sat him down. I didn't know what to say. But he made the running.

'My name is Goodrich,' he said.

'Hi.'

'I don't know whether I should even be here.'

'It's not a step to take lightly,' I said.

'I'm not,' he said. 'I'm not.'

'Oh.'

'I am a solicitor with Malley, Holmes and Asquith, but I need someone to make some inquiries for me on a private matter.'

'I see.'

'Well, you do that kind of thing, don't you?'

He looked at me. There was something devious in his eyes. And I had a sudden shock of suspicion.

You see, Dawn and I had talked about what to do if someone did actually come to us for work. We would just say that we were too busy to take the case on. But there was something about this man. The same thing that made me think he might be a council official. I got this idea that he was from one of the tax offices and that he was checking up on us.

It's just that on all these tax forms we'd been sending in we always had expenses listed, but never any income. It looked funny, of course. But economic times are hard and we assumed out amounts were so small, relatively, that nobody would notice.

But when you think you are being checked on, you suddenly feel the cold draught of accusation, prosecution.

'Of course,' I said.

Dawn was not pleased when she returned to the house and found that I had taken a case. But I explained my worries and she accepted the situation as a fact.

'It's about his brother-in-law, a guy named Chipperworth, who is a crook,' I said.

'Chipperworth . . .' Dawn said. She was thinking. She's lived in Frome all her life and knows a lot of people.

'He has a company that manufactures beds, up on the trading estate. The brand name is Rest Easy.'

'Ah.'

'You know it?'

'Rest Easy, yes.'

'And this man Goodrich says that Chipperworth set fire to a warehouse next to his factory up there and collected the insurance for it.'

'I read about the fire,' Dawn said. 'But not that it was on purpose. How does Goodrich know?'

'He says Chipperworth was bragging yesterday that he had just collected a cheque for over three hundred thousand pounds and it was for beds he wasn't going to be able to sell.'

'Good heavens,' Dawn said. 'But why doesn't Goodrich go to the police?'

'Because that's not what he's trying to sort out.'

'Oh.'

'What he's worried about is his sister. That Chipperworth is a crook, and he's dangerous. He wants his sister to divorce him.'

Dawn cocked her head.

'But his sister doesn't believe the stuff about the insurance fraud.'

'What are *we* supposed to do about that?'

'Goodrich wants us to prove Chipperworth has a woman on the side. If we can do that then the sister will divorce him and will be safe. Goodrich is sure that his sister will get a divorce in the end anyway, but if he precipitates it at least she'll be well off financially. If he waits till Chipperworth's activities catch up with him then it might ruin the sister too.'

'Oh,' Dawn said.

'I agreed to try.'

She nodded. Then she looked at me.

And I looked at her.

We were thinking the same thing.

I said, 'What the hell do we do now?'

Well, we had to go through the motions. The first motion was to find Chipperworth and identify him.

That wasn't hard. Mr Goodrich had given me a photograph and we decided to wait outside Rest Easy Beds toward the end of the work day. Rest Easy was not a big company. We counted about twenty people coming out after five-thirty. Chipperworth was the last and got into a new Sierra.

'OK,' Dawn said. 'There he is. What do we do now?'

'Drive along after him, I guess,' I said.

So we did. He went straight to a house on the Prowtings Estate. He pulled the car into the driveway. Got out. Went to the front door. Was met by a woman at 5.48 p.m. Then Chipperworth went into the house and closed the door.

That would have wrapped the case up if the woman hadn't been his wife.

Dawn and I sat.

'At least we know the registration number of his car now,' I said after ten minutes.

But we were both sinking fast.

After half an hour Dawn said, 'This is no good. What are we going to do, sit out here all night without any food or anything?'

And after some consideration of the situation, we decided to get fish and chips from Pangs. Even detectives have to eat.

When we got back, Chipperworth's car was gone.

Solicitor Goodrich rang up at nine the next morning. He seemed annoyed that I didn't have anything to report.

I explained that progress is not always rapid, that we'd had less than a day on the job.

But Goodrich knew that Chipperworth had been out the previous night. He'd called his sister and she told him.

'If you want to do the surveillance yourself,' I said, 'please say so. Otherwise, leave it to us.'

He took a breath, then apologised – rather unconvincingly I thought – and we hung up.

I told Dawn about the call.

'If we don't sort this out quickly,' she said, 'it's going to mess up our lives for weeks.'

'I know.'

'I'm going to see a couple of my cousins.'

I looked puzzled.

'Nigel is a telephone engineer,' she said. 'He's a nut case and would probably be willing to work out a way to tap the Chipperworths' telephone. And Paul works in the photographic section at Valets.' Valets was one of the local printing firms. 'He's a camera buff. He'll lend us a camera with a telephoto lens.'

'Right,' I said.

'We may have to borrow another car too, so we can cover Chipperworth the whole day. If it goes on for long we'll have to do shifts. I ought to be able to use Adele's Reliant. You remember Adele?'

'No.'

'She's the small one with the big—'

'I remember now,' I said.

Biggest feet I'd ever seen on a woman.

'I just wish I knew someone who could lend us a two-way radio.'

'There's your Uncle Mike,' I said.

'So there is,' she said. Then made a face. 'But he pinches and pokes whenever I get close enough and what he'd want for doing me a favour . . .'

'We'll get along without,' I said firmly.

In the end it only took a day.

It was the afternoon of my first shift. I was rigged up with a thermos, sandwiches and a radio. Even a specimen jar – from Dawn's friend Elaine, the nurse – in case time was short and need was great.

When Dawn and I get down to it, we're impressive.

I took the afternoon shift because Dawn had to see her Auntie Wendy who was having troubles with a neighbour's boy picking on her son Edgar.

The camera was one of those instant print jobs. We'd talked it over with Paul and he figured that would be best. No time waiting for the film to come back from the developers. 'And,' he said, 'considering what kind of pictures you may get, a commercial firm might not print them.' Does a great leer, does Paul.

He also gave us a foot-long lens for the thing. 'It'll put you in their pockets,' he said. 'If they're wearing pockets.'

Cousin Nigel jumped at the chance to plant a tape recorder up a telephone pole to tap the Chipperworths' home phone. He volunteered to do the company phone too. Well, you don't turn down offers like that.

It's always struck me that all of Dawn's family are just that little bit shady. I offer it as an observation, not a complaint.

Anyway, after an hour's lunch at home, Chipperworth didn't go back to his office. He drove instead to Marston Road and pulled into the driveway of a detached brick house just beyond the end of speed restrictions. I drove past but parked immediately. I left the car and got the camera aimed and focused just in time to see Chipperworth open the door to the house with a key.

The picture came out a treat.

I stood there in the road looking at it. And wondering what to do next.

But Dawn and I had talked it through. First I made a note of the time, date and location on the back of the photograph. Then I set about trying to find out who lived in the house.

I went next door and rang the bell and had a little luck.

A tiny old woman with big brown eyes answered it. I said, 'Excuse me. I have a registered letter for the people next door but nobody answers when I ring.'

26

'That's because Mrs Elmitt has her fancy man in,' the old woman said. 'And she wouldn't want to be disturbed now, would she? Some of the things I've seen! And they don't even bother to draw the curtains.'

Old women can do pretty good leers too, when they try.

Dawn was pleased as punch with me. I was pretty pleased myself. It meant that the wretched case would soon be over and we could get back to life as usual. I resolved to try to arrange for my income to arrive from America as some kind of retainer so that it looked like proceeds of the business. Then we wouldn't have to worry about being inspected by the tax people. Worry is a terrible thing.

But just about the time that we were getting ready to be pleased with each other, Cousin Nigel showed up at the front door.

He punched me on the shoulder as he came in, and gave Dawn a big kiss. A hearty type, Nigel.

'I've got your first tape,' he said jovially. 'Went up to see if it needed changing and blow me if there hadn't been a lot of calls. Thought you would want to hear them sooner rather than later, so I put another cassette in the machine and brought this one right over. Got any beer while we listen to it?' He dropped into our most comfortable chair. 'Hey Dawnie, how about something to eat? Egg and chips? Hungry work, bugging telephones.'

The tape was a revelation.

Right off, the very first phone call had things like the man saying, 'Darling, I can't wait until I see you again.'

And the woman: 'I don't know whether I'll be able to bear not being with you all the time for very much longer.'

'It will be soon. We'll be together, forever. Somewhere nice. Away from your wretched husband.'

'I don't know what will become of me if our plan doesn't work.'

'It will work. We'll make it work.'

'Oh darling, I hope so.'

And on and on, that kind of mushy stuff. There was a lot of slobbering sounds too. I would have been embarrassed if I hadn't been so upset.

'Wow!' Nigel said. 'All that kissy-kissy, and before lunch. They must have it bad.'

Dawn said, 'Isn't that great! We've got all we need now, Freddie, don't you think?'

But I was not happy, not even close.

Because, unlike my two colleagues, I had recognised one of the voices. The man's. The conversation was not between Mr Chipperworth and Mrs Elmitt. The man on the telephone was our client, Mr Goodrich, and the object of his affection was, presumbly, Mrs Chipperworth, his 'sister'.

We got rid of Nigel before we talked it out.

'I guess this means that our client was not being completely open and frank with us,' Dawn said.

There was no law that a client had to tell us the truth. But neither of us liked it.

'But what do we do?'

We had a long chat about it.

What we did was go the next morning to Dawn's Uncle Steve, who is a police sergeant. We asked him about the fire in the Rest Easy Beds warehouse.

'Always knew it was arson,' Uncle Steve said. 'But we couldn't prove who did it. The owner was the only possible beneficiary, but he had an airtight alibi. Not quite as good as being out to dinner with the Chief Superintendent, but he was at a function with the Mayor and he was at a table, in full sight, the whole evening.'

'I see,' Dawn said.

'I interviewed Chipperworth myself,' Uncle Steve said, 'and he was quite open about being delighted about the fire. Business wasn't very good and he was having trouble moving the stock that was destroyed. Personally, I don't think he *did* have anything to do with it. I've been at this job long enough to get a good sense of people and that's the way he came across.'

'I see,' Dawn said.

'But we never got so much as a whiff of any other suspect. Checked through all current and past employees for someone with a grievance. Sounded out all our informants in town for a word about anybody who might have been hired to do the deed or who heard anything about it. But we didn't get so much as a whisper. It's very unusual for us not to get some kind of lead if something's bent and we try that hard. In the end, it was written off to kids. There are so many around with nothing to do these days that we're getting all sorts of vandalism.'

'Thanks, Uncle Steve,' Dawn said.

'Helps you, does that?' he asked.

'I think so.'

'If you know anything about the case, you must tell us. You know that, don't you?'

'Yes, Uncle Steve.'

He looked at her and shook his head. Then he said to me, 'Young man, there is a look in her eye that I don't like. There's something tricky about all her people. You watch yourself.'

He was right, of course. Dawn was cooking something up, and it wasn't chips.

When we got home we sat down over a nice cup of tea. She hadn't said a word during the whole drive.

I couldn't bear it any longer. I said, 'All right. What *is* the significance of that funny look?'

'I've decided we're going to get Mrs Chipperworth that divorce our client wants after all.'

'We are?'

'It's what we were hired to do, isn't it?'

★   ★   ★

I called Solicitor Goodrich to tell him that we had had success in our investigation and did he want our report.

He did. He was with us within twenty minutes.

I explained what I had seen the previous afternoon. I gave him the photographs I had taken of Chipperworth entering Mrs Elmitt's house with a key and, later, adjusting his flies as he came out. I reported what the neighbour had told me.

'She is willing to testify to what she's seen in court, or to swear out a statement,' I said. 'But she would like some money for it.'

'I think that can be arranged,' Goodrich said.

A little ready cash might help the old woman get some curtains for her own windows.

Goodrich wrote out a cheque for our fee and expenses on the spot.

'Of course, if *we* have to testify,' I said, 'there will be an additional bill.'

'I don't think it will come to that,' Goodrich said.

After he left I rang Rest Easy Beds.

I explained to Mr Chipperworth that we wanted to come over to speak to him.

'What is it that is so urgent, Mr Herring?' he said.

'We wanted to tell you about your wife's plans to sue you for divorce,' I said.

As soon as we arrived we were ushered into Chipperworth's office.

'But she's known about Madeleine for years,' he said when I explained what we'd been hired to do. 'It's an arrangement we have. She doesn't like *it*, you see. So Madeleine keeps me from making . . . demands.'

'She doesn't seem to mind the demands of her lover,' Dawn said.

'Her *what*?'

'Why don't you ask her about her telephone calls recently,' Dawn suggested. 'We have to be going now. Ta ta.'

We stopped at Nigel's and then we went on home.

We didn't have long to wait.

A few minutes after noon the bell rang. Before I could get to it, pounding started on the door. When I opened it I faced Solicitor Goodrich, in a fury. He swung fists at me.

For the most part being as tall as I am is an inconvenience. But at least I have long arms and could keep him out of reach. When he finished flailing, he started swearing. The rude language seemed particularly unseemly for a member of the legal profession. I would have been very embarrassed for Dawn if I hadn't heard as bad or worse from her family. But they are foul-mouthed in a friendly way. Goodrich was vicious.

Also defamatory. He claimed that we had sold information to Mr Chipperworth.

I was about to deny it when Dawn said, 'What if we did?'

'I'll have you for this,' Goodrich said. 'It's illegal. I can put you in gaol.'

'That's fine talk from somebody who set fire to a warehouse.'

29

Goodrich was suddenly still and attentive. 'What?'

'You're the arsonist responsible for the fire at Rest Easy Beds.'

'That's silly talk,' Goodrich said. But he wasn't laughing.

'The idea was that when Mr Chipperworth collected the insurance money Mrs Chipperworth would start divorce proceedings which would entitle her to claim half of it. With your help she could probably settle out of court and between the insurance cash and her share of the rest of the joint property, you and Mrs Chipperworth would have a nice little nest egg to run away on.'

'Prove it,' Goodrich said.

'Oh, I think it's a very clever plan,' Dawn said charmingly. 'I suppose you have an alibi for the night of the fire?'

'Why should I need one?'

'Well, if we went to the police . . .'

'Why the hell should you do that?' Goodrich burst out.

'Ah,' Dawn said. 'Now we're getting down to the serious questions.' She batted her eyelashes. 'We never actually gave our evidence to Mr Chipperworth, you know, and as long as Mrs Chipperworth has denied everything . . .'

'You want money, I suppose,' Goodrich said.

'Well, poor Freddie is terribly tall, and a bigger car would be so much easier for him to get in and out of.'

'All right,' Goodrich said. 'A car.'

'And there are so many little improvements that ought to be made on this house.'

'How about just getting to a bottom-line figure.'

'I think thirty thousand would come in very handy, don't you Freddie?'

'Oh, very handy.'

'Thirty thousand!' Goodrich said.

'Yes,' Dawn said. 'See how reasonable we are?'

When the trial came along it was plastered all over the local papers. Frome is not so big a town that we get serious court cases involving local people every week.

Especially not cases involving solicitors and arson, not cases with a little titillation in them. Goodrich pleaded guilty, but the local reporter, Scoop Wall, tracked down Mrs Elmitt's neighbour who was photographed pointing to some of the uncurtained windows through which she had been forced to witness indescribable acts. Well, the descriptions didn't make the papers anyway.

Uncle Steve was not pleased at first when he heard what we had done.

Heard is the operative word because we had tape-recorded the entire conversation with Goodrich on equipment we borrowed from Cousin Nigel.

But Dawn explained. After all this time the only way Goodrich's arson would be proved was if he confessed to it. But the police couldn't have used the threat of exposing his relationship to Mrs Chipperworth the way we did because that would have transgressed legal niceties. 'So it was up to Freddie and me,' Dawn said.

Eventually Uncle Steve laughed.

'I warned you about her,' he said to me.

But it worked out all right in the end.

Except . . . Scoop Wall tracked down Dawn and me too.

We begged her not to put anything about us in the paper.

But she refused. We were key figures in bringing a dangerous solicitor to justice. It was news. And besides, Dawn has good legs and photographs well.

It's not that we weren't proud of what we – or let's be fair – what Dawn had done.

But it meant that the Fredrick Herring Private Inquiry Agency burst from its quiet and planned total obscurity into the glare of public attention.

We started getting calls. We started getting visitors. We started getting letters. Find this, look for that, unravel the other.

And it wasn't actually the attention which was the problem.

The problem was that we found we quite liked it. See, some of the cases we were offered were pretty interesting. Rather like chess problems . . . So, we decided, maybe one more. Or two.

THE MISTAKEN SMILE

by Audrey Erskine Lindop

When Laura first told me that she thought Robert was trying to murder her I laughed; the second time I repeated the story to Robert, but on the third occasion we both told her doctor. He advised a holiday, a wise if rather obvious prescription.

No woman likes to hear her husband say, 'My dear, I'm delighted you're leaving me. It'll save me pretending I want to sleep with you.' Much as she had come to detest Robert, it was not very flattering to know that she could not even satisfy a country parson.

As a solicitor I had acted for the Vinces for many years, and because I was their nearest neighbour I saw plenty of them.

I confess that I dreaded Laura consulting me professionally. Her absurd fears irritated me, almost as much as they seemed to irritate her; but Robert's personality had the opposite effect. It never failed to soothe me and bolster me up. Quite frankly I suspected Laura's complaints about him as being nothing but the ramblings of an over-excited mind. I still blame myself for my lack of perception. I have heard that there is no more cruel emotion than remorse and I have certainly had my share of it.

Laura Vince was a research worker and lecturer. She was a keen observer of life, and in spite of her apparent independence had a deep need for human company and affection.

Robert was an Anglican parson. They had met at Oxford and in the tumultuous unawareness of youth had thought themselves twin souls. But they were not, and it took marriage to prove the fact.

Laura was convinced that in his heart, Robert Vince knew himself to be a militant phoney – this he could at times hide from himself but he suspected that he could not hide it from Laura, no matter how hard she tried not to show it.

It was ironical, she always thought, how popular he was with both young and old parishioners. His was one of the few well-attended churches. He let the conventional believe him to be conventional, and the unconventional that he was 'way out'. Laura thought he should have been an actor. He gave an admirable daily performance and no one but she could have guessed at his narrow and hypocritical spirit. It was hard for her at times to sit and listen to his warm and entertaining sermons when she remembered the hours of rehearsal, the pauses for possible laughs, the studied effect of geniality expertly timed to switch into sincerity, humility and piety. Even his smile, the pitch of his voice and his gestures were worked out and timed. Nothing, she assured me, came from his heart. His easy charm was also practised in front of a looking-glass down to its smallest detail. She was sad because she had loved him once.

She was sure that he intended to become a bishop and she was also sure that she gave him a guilt complex. He felt that she would see through him and the mere sight of her sitting dutifully in a pew undermined his confidence.

What hurt her most was that even in their bitterest moments he could not forget the charm. It was as if he were trying to show her that however unlikeable she might be he was incapable of being objectionable. She would rather he had shouted his insults at her but he delivered them sulkily with the daily perfected smile. She might have been one of his parishioners.

Before they gave their dignified little sherry parties he would say, 'Don't forget, please, not to cap my stories – there's room for only one wit in this house, and don't try to entertain people by showing how greatly you've benefited from an academic education. Few things can be more boring.' And he said it as if he had paid her two loving little compliments.

It was the same when the party actually took place. Whilst warming the hearts of his glowing devotees he found time to pay chivalrous attention to his wife, sending her soft glances of affection and appreciation, apparently unaware that she received them stonily. She had few friends in Elstead. Everyone had come to see Robert and anyone who had not she rebuffed. She thought she was being patronised.

There were few women in their parish who did not envy lucky Mrs Vince, and they mistook her shyness for haughtiness.

I simply thought her dull and gauche but that, of course, was before I fell in love with her.

I am ashamed of my behaviour at those morbid little social gatherings at the Rectory with poor Laura circling stiffly round with cocktail snacks, hardly acknowledged by her guests whilst from her husband's corner there came nothing but warm laughter and obvious adulation.

Laura, failing in her efforts to hold anyone's attention for longer than strict politeness required, tended to attach herself fiercely to me. I did my utmost to shake her off and join the audience who were so appreciating Robert's witty anecdotes, but at the time I simply thought her a tiresomely neurotic woman and suspected that most of her troubles with Robert were due to jealousy over his popularity.

She was forever telling me how plain he made her feel and yet to me he praised her beauty. He said, 'Peter, don't you think Laura's got lovely features? They remind me of a Botticelli.'

'Why don't you tell her?' I snapped. 'It might make her less of a self-pitying bore.'

'I do,' he sighed. 'But it makes her worse. She simply thinks I'm making fun of her.'

'Did you,' I demanded, 'actually say to her that it would be a relief not to have to sleep with her?'

He sighed again. 'Yes, and it is. You've no idea what we go through on those occasions. She's moved to another room now. She's convinced I'm going to smother her in her sleep.'

33

I realise now that however ridiculous I might have thought it I should have shown Laura sympathy. Those fears were very real to her.

I told Robert that I would prefer Laura to get another lawyer, but he begged me to keep her on as a client. He said, 'For God's sake Peter, do let her come and let off steam. Please put up with her nonsense. I simply can't have a stranger listening to all that rubbish.'

Out of friendship for Robert I agreed, but I must confess that when I heard her shouting at my secretary in the outer office I felt like leaping out of the window.

'I *must* see Mr Cowles!' she was shrieking. 'It's terribly terribly urgent.'

My unfortunate secretary was doing her best to protect me, being well aware of my aversion to Laura and her lunatic suspicions, but she failed. Laura burst into my office.

'Peter, please help me! Something really frightening has happened!'

She pulled up a chair and sat panting in it. Oddly enough, it was at that moment that I realised that she had an eerie shell-like type of beauty. Her black eyes had a warm glow and her figure was really all that a man could ask for. But she was shouting at me as if I were in the spring-time of my senility and it was vital to catch me before I reached the autumn. I could have murdered her. Not a very happy thought in the circumstances.

I managed to calm her down with the aid of a spot of brandy out of my filing cabinet and said, as patiently as I could, '*What* has happened, Laura?'

She swallowed the rest of her brandy and said, 'Robert *smiled* at me.'

I laughed and she must have wept for a good five minutes whilst I sat and stared at her. Then she whimpered, 'You *must* believe me. I shall go mad if you don't. I simply have to get away from him. I tell you he actually smiled at me.'

'He smiles at everyone.'

'Yes, yes. Everyone but *me*. He's thought of something. He's thought of a way of getting rid of me. It wasn't his usual smile.'

'Which is notoriously charming.'

'I know, but this wasn't. This was sort of serious and dangerous – as if he had found himself out and wanted to dispose of anyone else who might have done the same.'

In desperation I said to Robert, 'For God's sake give us both a break and pack her off somewhere she can relax!'

He chose Provence and he rented a house called 'Le Bois des Papillons' in the village of Vallon. As its name suggested it stood in a wood full of butterflies. It was exceptionally cheap and the agent was completely honest about the reason. The house had once been the headquarters of members of the resistance and their chief had been tortured to death there. It was not everybody's idea of a happy villa. With true French logic no one suggested that it was haunted. Ghosts they said would keep away from a place like that with its sunny woods and gay butterflies and its fearful memories. But there was a persistent rumour that the resistance had buried their funds somewhere in the house. Now and again fools, chiefly foreigners, got wind of this little tale and broke into the house searching for the hidden treasure. None of the locals really believed there was any money there, but the agent suggested that it would be safer for Madame Vince to have a companion, just in case some bullion hunting enthusiast should break in again.

Laura was persuaded to take with her a friend called Ellen Cook. Miss Cook had a small mind and a narrow nature, but great physical strength. She would have been enough to frighten any treasure hunter.

But in spite of this Laura was not satisfied with the arrangements. She mistrusted anywhere Robert chose for her, and she wanted more than a holiday from him; she wanted a divorce. She told me that he could shatter her nerves to such an extent that she felt as if she was going out of her mind, but of course no one would take her word against his, not even her doctor who had only seen Robert as his charming self and apparently devoted to her.

I tried to be as patient as I could for Robert's sake and as he had asked I allowed her to 'let off steam' at me. She told me that during a quarrel he could remain reasonable and low voiced whilst she shrieked like a demented fishwife. When attacked in those soft clerical tones she lost all control. His constant taunt – 'My dear, you mustn't forget you're an intellectual. You have every advantage over a country parson. Please don't make a fool of yourself.'

Divorce, he told her, was out of the question. It would affect his career. He could afford no scandals.

He spoke in his most pleasing voice, 'If it will comfort you I can tell you that nothing would give me greater pleasure than to be rid of you. Your supercilious little face infuriates me – you're not the only woman to have obtained an MA or given lectures or done research work and written pamphlets – most women have done rather better and still remained feminine.'

She had to clench her fists to keep her nails out of his face. 'How could anyone be feminine with a megalomaniac like you? You're a Victorian sadist – you're such a master at it. But I'll divorce *you* – I'll divorce you for cruelty—'

His laugh was even more well-modulated than his voice. 'My *dear*! On what grounds?'

'I'll bring up mental cruelty.'

'Bring it up. Who in the world is going to believe you? My adoring parishioners? They all think I'm badly done by through my so-called intellectual little wife – with the only MA in the world after her undistinguished little name!'

In her temper she threatened him.

'You may despise my degree and hate me for it – but I'm still a woman and I have feelings. For you they cover every form of hatred. I shall follow no Christian ethic such as you're supposed to have. I'll do everything in my power to discredit you. I'll let your adoring flock know just what their beloved shepherd is really like. Every besotted spinster, every worshipping matron – they'll all know. I'll tell them that you're using the words of Jesus Christ to further your own ambitions.'

That was when he smiled at her and she came running in to me. I said, 'Yes, yes, yes. Now Laura, take the pills the doctor gave you and pack your things for France. Oh, and incidentally, "Le Bois des Papillons" is in mountainous country. Did you know? It's in the south of France, but Vallon is very high and can sometimes get as misty as Dartmoor, so put in some little woollies.'

She said, 'Oh, thank you,' and as she said it she reminded me of one of those forlorn little butterflies which get stuck in a house for the winter, and who creep out with faded wings and no hope of ever being able to fly happily in the outside world again.

She had nothing to thank me for and she knew it. I was just trying to get her out of the way for Robert's sake. It seemed so wrong that someone who was doing so much good for the Church as he was should be shackled by an hysterical wife who was verging on insanity.

'Le Bois des Papillons' due to everyone's understandable dislike of it was not immediately inhabitable. It rather resembled Miss Haversham's wedding chamber in *Great Expectations*. It needed 'doing up' and whilst it was being 'done up' I was stuck with Laura and her idiotic terror of Robert's smile. How wicked it is not to realise when someone is really frightened literally out of their life!

Wearily I told my loyal secretary to let her in whenever she came to see me. With any luck by the time they had swept 'Le Bois des Papillons' clean of cobwebs and goats' dung we should be rid of her and the unwinning Miss Cook.

In the meantime I had to put up with her theories on Robert's murderous intentions. She was not afraid that he would attack her *physically*. But there were so many other more subtle ways of disposing of a person. There was poison, tampering with car engines, unexplained domestic accidents, inexplicable 'assaults' on the way home, electrical faults in the bathroom, or electric blankets, garden steps made slippery, banisters weakened so that hers would be compared with the mystery fall of poor Amy Robsart. There were rat poisons, tisanes – there were a thousand ways in which he could get rid of her.

In her dreams she saw him as a mediaeval cardinal with a score of hired assassins to hack her down. She had threatened his precious career and everything he did or said confirmed her suspicions.

She hardly dared sleep at night in case he tried to suffocate her. She lost weight and came near to a breakdown. Finally whilst toying with an unwanted breakfast she burst out hysterically, 'Robert, I'm leaving you.'

It was then that he made his remark about being relieved not to have to try and sleep with an intellectual wife. For this pleasure he was willing to make her quite a handsome allowance. He had private money and was not dependent on a clerical living. But there was to be one condition. His parishioners were to be informed that she had gone away on a lengthy holiday to restore her health. There was to be no mention of a separation. Laura told me bitterly, 'The worshipping congregation must never know that his wife had the audacity to leave him.'

Finally I saw both her and the unwinning Miss Cook off at the station. It was hard to decide which of them I was glad to see the back of most: the mournful Laura constantly whimpering that this proved her failure as a person, or her immensely tall and sullen friend.

Miss Cook had that unhappy habit of spitting in one's face when she spoke;

another of her unlovable characteristics was her language. Every other word had four letters.

When they were safely on their way my secretary and I did a little caper of joy round the office.

But the joy did not last very long. A stream of letters started to arrive from Laura and Miss Cook. There had apparently been a series of attempts by unknown intruders to break into 'Le Bois des Papillons'. The police had been informed and seemed surprised that anyone should chance their luck at finding the legendary resistance gold when the house was occupied. When it was empty they could understand these fruitless attempts. Personally I suspected that what really surprised them was that anyone should have the temerity to risk being spat in the eye by that foul-mouthed Amazon Miss Cook.

But Laura was convinced that the intruders were Robert's 'hired assassins' trying to do away with her under cover of seeking the mythical treasure. No one would connect the crime with Robert preaching sweetness and light in England. She thought it ominous that the break-ins should have increased since she had taken up residence.

My secretary and I groaned together but we wrote back to say that I thought it extremely unsuspicious. The fact that anyone had been eccentric enough to take the dilapidated 'Le Bois des Papillons' must have convinced those who still believed in the existence of the gold that it really was hidden in the house. They probably thought that Laura had only taken the place in order to conduct a day and night search, and so they were determined to forestall her.

It was my secretary who first suspected that I was falling in love with Laura. When I laughed she said that she had noticed a change in my attitude. In the place of 'that blessed woman and her absurd obsessions' it was 'that poor woman and what she must have gone through'. Naturally I went on scoffing at the idea but I did become aware that I was thinking of Laura in a different way. It started as straightforward pity in place of exasperation. Then I began thinking of her as a beauty taunted into making herself feel plain. It made me dwell on her beauty. I remembered her when I had first met her when she was soft-eyed with love for Robert, glowing and witty and gay. Then I realised that I had been a witness to the slow strangulation of her heart, the garrotting of her spirit, and that I had done nothing to help, in spite of all her pleas.

It was not until Robert smiled at me that I acknowledged to myself that I was in love with her. I had gone to suggest to him that he should allow her to move to an address unknown to him. Her bank and my own firm would have the address but until she calmed down I thought it would be wiser if she felt that Robert and his 'hired assassins' should not know her whereabouts.

He shook his head and smiled at me. I put the same construction on that smile as Laura had done. I saw what she meant. It looked dangerous. It was so completely unlike Robert. There was not a vestige of charm in it. He had obviously not practised it. He seemed an utterly different man and I hated him on the spot and forever.

My secretary told me not to be a fool and to curb my imagination. She said, rather bitterly I thought, 'What has now become "that poor persecuted woman" has infected you with her own neurosis. Robert's no villain. You've just been taken in by Laura.'

I promptly accused her of falling into the common groove of Robert-worship and we quarrelled for the first time in ten years of working together.

Then we had a reconciliation over our common dislike of Miss Cook. We read in the paper that a false store of gold coins said to have been buried by the French resistance workers in a house called 'Le Bois des Papillons' in the village of Vallon had been found by a Miss Ellen Cook. She had discovered it in the side of an old well which she had been trying to clear of mosquito larvae. But it had been proved to be a little joke on the part of the resistance workers against the Nazis who had occupied the house and tortured their leader. They had spread the rumour that their funds were hidden on the premises so that the Nazis should spend their time looking for it. When they found it they would have seen what Ellen Cook saw: an insulting collection of tin circles cut in the shape of coins with 'MERDE' written very carefully in the middle of them. My secretary and I laughed at the irony of our foul-mouthed Amazon coming across this little nest of swear words.

That must have been the last time that I ever laughed. At first I was relieved because I felt that this 'treasure trove' discovery must have convinced even Laura that her intruders had been genuine bullion enthusiasts and nothing to do with Robert or hired assassins. But two weeks after the 'haul' the severely lacerated body of Ellen Cook was found in the sludge at the bottom of the old well in which she had been putting oil to kill off the mosquito larvae. She had thirty-six knife wounds and her head had been cleaved into a neat half. It was a crime of monstrous hatred. Unfond as I was of Miss Cook I was utterly baffled to think who could possibly have borne her such a grudge. She knew hardly anyone in Vallon. My secretary suggested spitefully that I probably thought it was Robert taking his revenge because Ellen had been Laura's bodyguard. I confess that she managed to sow that seed in my mind.

The Vallon police were much calmer and more correct. They thought that someone had believed Ellen's find to be a trick to disguise the real whereabouts of the resistance funds and had tried to beat the information out of her.

But Laura could not be persuaded that one of Robert's 'hired assassins' had not mistaken Ellen for herself.

In spite of my secretary reminding me that I had once thought of Laura as 'nothing but a thorough nuisance with a deranged mind', I made arrangements to fly out to Vallon. Without fully realising it at the time, I had become obsessed with Laura and her cause. My secretary repeated, 'This woman has made you as potty as she is.'

I cannot explain my sudden change of heart over Laura. It's possibly better not to try. I know from my professional experiences that these extraordinary emotional somersaults are inexplicable.

On the journey to Vallon I tried to work out my own somersault. Perhaps it was because I felt that she was the only person who really needed me. Perhaps I had suddenly realised her incredible beauty, and perhaps because I had become so outraged at the crippling of such a brilliant mind by a man who was obviously her inferior. Also I had seen Robert's unbelievable smile, and saw what Laura meant.

Long before we reached the airport, I had decided to ask her to live with me until we could make Robert see that a divorce would be more dignified for him. It would only bring him more sympathy and adoration from doting parishioners. He would be knitted more mufflers and baked more cakes than any other parson in history. 'Best friend runs away with good shepherd's wife' would bring him the kind of favourable publicity he worked so hard to achieve. Then Laura and I could be married.

I found Laura in the psychiatric ward of a hospital outside Vallon. The doctor said that the shock of Ellen's death and her fears for her own life had made it impossible for her to remain at 'Le Bois des Papillons' even with police protection.

In his opinion she was by no means insane but her health both mentally and physically had been so undermined that she had to be regarded as seriously unstable and in no position to care for herself. Any mention of her husband made matters so much worse that severe medical methods had had to be employed such as padded cells, injections, and special relaxing baths.

The whole thing made me feel quite ill myself and I thought if Robert ever treated me again to that poisonous, condescending smile, I would smash it right off his face.

At first Laura refused to allow me to visit her. She thought I was a spy for Robert. Then I sent her in a little note: 'Laura, I love you. Peter.'

She saw me then. She was nearly as pale as her pillow case but she managed to laugh. 'I couldn't believe your note . . . I thought you must have gone as mad as me. Robert said no one could love me. He said it embarrassed men to have to pretend they weren't bored by me and that no one was more bored than you.'

I said, 'Laura, Robert is an egotistical swine and I hate every gut in his body. We'll get rid of him and we'll marry.'

Then before she could answer I noticed the woman in the next bed. She was doing something very strange with her left arm, circling it round her nose like an elephant's trunk. Laura saw me staring at her and whispered urgently, 'Don't upset her. The poor soul thinks she's a teapot.'

'Thinks she's a teapot!!'

Laura said, 'Shush!' She was in earnest but she was not far off the giggles. 'It's wicked to make fun of her. She's had some emotional catastrophe and she thinks her arm is her spout and keeps on asking me to pour her out!'

I went straight off to have a severe word with the doctor. I said, 'How dare you put Madame Vince next door to a teapot.'

The doctor smiled, 'Madame de Saille is quite harmless and she will be cured. She is already responding to treatment. Besides, it is good for Madame Vince to have to look after her, it takes her mind off her own troubles.'

Nevertheless I argued with him that for a woman in Laura's nervous state to be next to an obvious lunatic could only have fatal results. I insisted that she should be put in a private room. He was very much against this. He said that she needed constant attention and supervision. She would get that far better in a public ward than in a private room. In the ward there were always nurses whereas in a private room there were sometimes long intervals before anyone might find time to pay the patient a visit, and he was adamant that Laura was not yet fit enough to be left alone. When she had made sufficient improvement and he could feel more confident he would certainly transfer her to a private room.

But I knew better, of course. I was absolutely determined that she should be spared the horrors of teapots and people under the impression that they were the Queen of Prussia. The doctor gave in but made it perfectly clear that he would accept no responsibility and neither would his staff if Laura suffered a relapse.

She was moved to a private room.

Two days later she was missing. The only clue as to the reason for her disappearance was that her husband had arrived in Vallon and had sent her a bunch of flowers saying that he had heard that she had been ill and wished to see her. This threw her into such a panic that the nurse rushed off to prepare a calming injection. During this interval Laura had managed to escape out of the window. Pinned to her husband's bunch of flowers was a note:

'Dear Robert,
These will do for my grave. You had poor Ellen killed in mistake for me. But I'm going to save you any more errors of this kind.
Your once very, very loving wife,

Laura.'

A big police search was instantly organised. The doctor and staff of the hospital put the blame squarely on me. Had I not insisted on having her transferred to a private room she would never had been left unguarded, and this would never have happened.

Robert apparently was questioned for hours, and so was I.

Before he knew that she was missing Robert had written her a letter. The police took charge of it and I did not know the contents until the trial.

Laura never even knew that it had been sent. Her body was found at 'Le Bois des Papillons' in the bottom of the old well in which Ellen Cook's gold hunting murderer had flung her. Laura had cut her throat before tipping herself down the well. Her blood tinged the green sludge and the mosquito larvae so that it looked in patches as if someone had been pouring in bottles of burgundy.

Robert and I were not allowed to leave the town. We were 'free' – but observed from every corner. Robert came to my hotel to ask my help. He said, 'Look, Peter, the police are suspicious of me. I sent my poor Laura a letter. It really was written from my heart but they think that it was a well-timed cover-up. It was nothing of the sort. I was trying to explain things to her and get her to see me. Now, you know the truth, Peter. You and I alone know what Laura was like – all this ridiculous assassin nonsense – for God's sake come and speak up for me.'

It is absolutely true to say that I forgot what happened. I certainly went for him. I remember that. But I forgot exactly what I did. I can only remember his smile and without any doubt I smashed it off his face.

At my trial they read out his letter to Laura.

It said:

'My darling, and whatever you may think you are my darling. Please, please let the doctors and our good friend Peter Cowles get you over this fear that I am trying to kill you. I would rather kill myself. Your absence has made me realise what an abominable Christian I have been. In an odd way which I do not expect you to believe, my disgraceful behaviour was done for your sake. I felt that if I could impress my parishioners and make them like me it would impress you and make you like me. I have always felt so unworthy of you that it soured my whole nature.

If you had accused me of trying to murder your personality, your spirit or your soul, you would have been correct. I was frightened of you. I thought that your superior intellect would soon show me up for the cardboard prelate that I am, but quaintly enough I do love God and I should never have tried to shine at His cocktail parties in order to get my wife to admire me as much as my parishioners did. I doubt if He will forgive me for that! It is true that I tried to flatten you and make you frightened of me. I thought that that would keep you in lieu of love and respect. Please see me. My flowers are not poisoned. Get someone else to smell them! And if you will not see me please see our really great friend Peter Cowles. I really think that he will be the one to convince you that in spite of my appalling behaviour I really am devoted to you. Please put every faith in Peter Cowles. We have no greater friend. I promise to be a sincerely 'Good Shepherd' if you come back to me, but if you cannot forget everything and give me another chance I will give you your freedom and I strongly recommend you to put yourself in the hands of Peter Cowles. I think you would find much happiness with him.

Your loving and ever contrite husband,

Robert.'

Whilst I was listening to this letter at my trial I was thinking of Robert's 'smile' – the one that both Laura and I had mistrusted.

It was his genuine smile.

It showed the true Robert for once trying not to hide his insecurity and his guilt. It was the only smile that had not been practised in the mirror. His real self and his sincerity had broken through. He had been asking our help on those occasions but because it was lacking its usual sickening charm we had mistaken that piteous smile.

He never had the chance to prove whether he could have made a really 'Good Shepherd'. He died from the wounds I inflicted upon him.

That is why I am in prison for life.

THE CHAIR

by Roger Longrigg

'I selected, from the bill of fare, a cutlet,' replied Gregory Vardon to his friend's question. 'A lamb cutlet. Not without trepidation. I have known the chef to send up an underdone cutlet. It has occurred. But today's was excellent. And you, Charles?'

'My choice was comparable,' said Charles Corbishley, speaking with the gravity the subject demanded. 'Not at all dissimilar. My election, in a word, was a chump chop. With which I discussed a small carafe of the club claret.'

'A comfortable wine. Not distinguished but respectable.'

'Immature. But, at the price, what would you?'

Both men, who were very old, sighed in contemplation of the price of claret, which they frequently discussed, in this place, between themselves and with other members. Into the back morning-room of Blazon's Club the afternoon sun brought a wintry pretence of warmth. It gleamed on the coffee-urn, which dribbled on its table in the corner. It shamed the open fire, which nevertheless gave off a prodigious heat. It shone on Gregory Vardon's pink and well-scrubbed head; on Charles Corbishley's gold-rimmed bifocals it came and went, impertinently, as he wagged his ancient head.

'May I, Gregory,' said Charles, whose turn it was, 'summon a fellow and instruct him to bring you a glass of port wine?'

'I think that, of all things, a small glass of port is what I should most enjoy.'

'Good! Good!'

Charles was sitting at the end of the leather-covered sofa nearest to the wall by the fire. The bell was a yard away from him. He raised his rubber-tipped walking-stick and with it tried to stab the bell-push. He smote at the wall, leaving small circular marks on the wallpaper over a wide area surrounding the bell. He connected at last, and in triumph rang the bell for a long time.

A waiter appeared, a stunted Portuguese.

'A glass of vintage port, Gregory? Or shall we sustain ourselves more humbly with a beaker from the wood?'

Gregory appeared to reflect, to give the issue his full attention, to jump lightly to no ill-considered decision. 'A glass of the wood, I fancy,' he said at last.

Charles nodded with judicious approval. Had Gregory so far flown in the face of precedent (and invited Charles to spend so much more money) as to ask for vintage port, Charles would simply have disbelieved his own ears. They *offered* each other vintage port; the offer was not so much insincere as ritualistic.

'Be so good,' said Charles to the waiter, 'as to bring us two glasses of the wood port.'

Neither Charles nor Gregory talked, in any other place, in the orotund style they adopted in the public rooms of Blazon's. Gregory seldom *was* in any other place: but if shown a menu in a restaurant he would not have called it a bill of fare. Charles elsewhere drank, rather than discussed, carafes of wine. But in the club they were clubmen; they were clubmen with a vengeance; they went at it thoroughly. It was not exactly a game, nor a conscious parody: but it lent a certain spacious stateliness to lives of rigorous budgeting, to lonely existences on pensions: it was harmless: it was fun: if it was time-consuming this was, if anything, a positive advantage.

The waiter subscribed to the ritual dutifully but without enthusiasm. He brought two small glasses of cheap port on a silver tray, and accepted payment.

The whole transaction was thus brought to a successful conclusion. Charles settled back in his corner of the sofa with a deep and fulfilled sigh; Gregory back in his with a gentler sigh expressive of gratitude, admiration, and delighted anticipation of his port. Tomorrow he would sit in the corner nearer the wall. The rubber tip of his walking-stick would (ultimately) activate the bell-push. In stately, well-rehearsed phrases he would offer Charles a glass of vintage port and buy him a glass of wood port. They would make their port last until half past three. Then there was only an hour to kill until tea-time. Charles would spend the hour where he was, in one or other corner of the sofa. On his lap, fetched with unimaginable labour, would be an open copy of *Country Life*: but his head would be back, his jaw loosened, his eyelids lowered, his breathing slow, his digestion proceeding with gentle diligence to prepare his stomach for Earl Grey and crumpets. Gregory, for his part, would ascend the stairs to the library, step by exhausting step, stick in one hand and banister in the other. There, solitary, he would hobble to the Trollope shelf between the all-unneeded signs requiring silence. He would take down the second volume of *The Small House at Allington*, and manage a page or two, in his special chair by the fire, before his own head went back, his jaw descended, and he had his forty winks before tea.

Nothing could be more civilised, nothing more delightful. No disaster more unpleasant could be imagined than the serious dislocation of this routine.

Gregory sipped his port (spinning it out) bought in proper sequence by Charles Corbishley. He was disagreeably surprised to see, crossing the morning-room to the table where the magazines were spread, the burly tweed-clad person of a member called Martyn, a brash and pop-eyed barfly in his early 60s.

Gregory had disliked Martyn before the latter was a member of the club, before he knew his name, before even he heard the fellow's braying and penetrating voice. He remembered his first sight of Martyn, quite a recent encounter, not a dozen years ago. He was a guest. Someone had asked him to lunch. He was waiting for his host in the hall. He was waiting in an ostentatious way, standing with his legs apart in front of the hall fire, patronising the club with his presence, staring pop-eyed at members who were decently hanging up their coats or drinking seemly drinks; he was looking condescendingly at the prints of Bay Middleton and Stockwell; he had a carnation in his buttonhole; there were veins all over his nose; his ginger moustache was an offence. He looked an abrasive personality, an irritant, a heavyweight gadfly, a bumptious bounder.

Once or twice a year thereafter, for perhaps four years, the man reappeared at lunchtime, guest of the same host. He had, or acquired, friends in the club. He greeted them boisterously. They were not visibly enraged. They bought him drinks. Groups, which his voice dominated, had several drinks and came late in to luncheon. They could be heard talking about salmon-fishing, pheasant-shooting, politics, the stock-market. The man's host, after lunch, bought him vintage port or brandy. Gregory's dislike increased with each visit, every one of which he witnessed, since he was always in the club, since he had nowhere else to go. The man was everything Gregory had always hated and feared. He was the jeering red-kneed boy at Gregory's private school who discovered that Gregory's mother had published poems (privately printed at her own expense) and led the cruel beagle-pack of future proconsuls which hunted him all across the playing-fields. He was the loud, confident footballer, the physical man, the swot-hater, the Flashman, the know-all. In every phase of his gentle life Gregory had known and detested such men. This man was the essence of their awfulness. He more than irritated Gregory: he made him feel ill. At least he came to the club only twice a year; and at least, as a guest, he was not allowed into the back morning-room.

Then came a shock which spoiled Gregory's sleep and his digestion for weeks.

In the bar one evil April day, when he was ordering the small dry sherry with which he anticipated luncheon, he was introduced to Martyn.

The man who always gave Martyn lunch said: 'Ah, Gregory, well met.'

'Good morning,' said Gregory, who could nowadays remember few names.

'Let me buy you a drink.'

'No thank you.'

'I want you to meet Barry Martyn.'

'Oh yes?'

Gregory looked, with nervous politeness, in the direction of the other's outstretched arm. There, grinning like a hyena, guzzling a glass of champagne, with a carnation in his filthy buttonhole, was the man whose face Gregory hated.

'Change your mind about that drink.'

'No thank you.'

'You two ought to get together. Lot in common.'

Gregory looked at the speaker with horrified incredulity.

'Fishing,' said the idiot. 'Both mad about fishing.'

'Aha,' brayed Martyn. 'A brother of the angle. The lordly salmon or the wily trout?'

'Trout,' said Gregory, fighting down his rage and nausea.

'A dryfly purist, for a monkey,' shouted Martyn. His bulging *faux-bonhomme* eyes goggled at Gregory like those of lordly salmon or wily trout.

'Actually,' said Gregory, 'I . . .'

'Where do you fish?'

'I have not, for many years, owing to failing health and imperfect vision—'

'Where *did* you fish?'

'I was so very fortunate as to enjoy, for a number of seasons, the hospitality of—'

'I've got two miles of the Test. About the best there is, though I say it as shouldn't. I wouldn't swap a yard of it for Leckford or the Houghton water. Four and five pounders. You'll bear me out, Derek. Not much mayfly. Good sport with the medium olive, iron blue, BWO, little red sedge. I can give you a day any time you like. I mean it. Always delighted to let a keen chap have a go.'

'You accept,' said the monster's host.

But Gregory managed, after ten minutes of unpleasant labour, to persuade them that his refusal was final.

Worse followed.

Martyn's host, a spindly industrialist from Staffordshire, drew Gregory aside as he went in to lunch.

'Awfully pleased you got on so well with Barry Martyn,' he murmured. 'Felt sure you would. Very good fellow indeed, most generous, everybody likes him. I expect you've twigged?'

'No,' said Gregory. But a terrible premonition gripped his bowels.

'I've put him up for membership here. Rallying support. Want plenty of signatures. You'll sign, I trust.'

Gregory was rescued from an appalling predicament, but in an unpleasant way. He fell over. The tip of his stick skidded on the marble of the hall floor and he crumpled gently at the industrialist's feet. Martyn helped him up. He was shaken and humiliated but not hurt. He was assisted into a chair in the morning-room. He stayed there, omitting lunch, and drank one of his rare glasses of brandy. The economy of missing lunch more than defrayed the cost of the brandy.

A *member*. Constantly about. Braying, buying drinks, rendering hideous the quiet places where Gregory spent nearly all his waking and some of his sleeping hours.

Gregory went home, after an early and miserable dinner, to the bed-sitter in Kensington in which he slept and made his tea in the morning: but he did not sleep, or enjoy his tea, or enjoy his port after lunch the next day.

There was a long waiting-list. Martyn would not be a member for two years. Something could be done in that time. The committee could be alerted. With tact, a word in season, the opening of a few eyes . . . After a few weeks Gregory recovered his confidence and his digestion.

He mentioned the matter to Charles.

Charles said: 'I know the chap you mean. He served with a nephew of mine in the Bushytails. He is stated, credibly enough, to have worn the king's uniform, as it then was, with some distinction. I have accorded his candidature the small benefit of my support.'

'You have *signed*?'

45

'My signature is inscribed on the appropriate leaf of the book, and may there, by the curious or doubtful, be inspected.'

Charles, misled by a family connection, fed with lies, could not be made to see that Martyn's election must be prevented. Gregory tried elsewhere. 'Rather a merry bird,' said one member. 'Not an intellectual, but a merry enough egg.' 'Kind,' said another man. 'Good war,' said a third.

The months passed. On Martyn's page of the Candidates' Book the signatures grew thick as autumn leaves in Vallombrosa. Gregory knew some of the names and they were *perfectly respectable members*.

Martyn's visits in this period grew more frequent. He was the guest of other hosts. To Gregory it seemed that his laughter was louder, his eyes more protuberant, his nose redder, his carnation more ostentatious, with each jocose tuck-in. It seemed, moreover, that he was working some dreadful magic on existing members of the club. Men Gregory believed to be sober and well-conducted spent longer in the bar before lunch, and laughed more loudly over lunch; there was more calling from table to table; there was more chat in the morning-room; there was more widely-audible talk of salmon and pheasant, of by-elections and race-meetings.

Charles said he noticed no change. 'The conversations,' he said, 'to which you animadvert, are, I fancy, endemic to this and to similar institutions. Many of our Georgian and Regency predecessors had the same preoccupations, Gregory.'

Somewhat less that two years later, the list went up on the notice-board of candidates for the next election. Major Barrington Martyn was among them.

A week later the Election Committee met. Gregory sat, feeling suffocated in the morning-room, knowing what horrible errors were being transacted above him.

The following day, on the notice-board, appeared the list of duly elected new members: and the day after that Major Barrington Martyn came, ebulliently gleeful, to lunch for the first time as a member. Came into the back morning-room, as of right. Greeted, as of right, Charles and Gregory, drinking ritual port on their sofa. Goggled, swaggered, brayed, sent for brandy, smoked a cigar, dominated a group, and gave Gregory an attack of indigestion which ruined the rest of his day.

One comfort remained in a situation otherwise comfortless. The man worked. He came from an office and returned to it. Though rendered hideous at lunchtime, the club returned to normal seemliness soon after 2.15. Nor did Martyn come in every day. Twice a week was his average. On these nasty days Gregory adjusted his routine, which he was far too old to enjoy doing, but which was far the lesser of evils. He lunched early and went straight to the library. Charles Corbishley was huffy.

So for six years. An imperfect life, but bearable.

And then, at 2.45, crossing the morning-room, Martyn. Going to the magazines. Taking one. Sitting down with it. Lighting a cigar. Set for the afternoon. *No office?*

'No indeed,' said Charles Corbishley softly. 'Released from the treadmill.

Well-earned retirement with effect, I am assured, from last week. We shall henceforth see much more of the gallant and popular Major Martyn.'

They did, much more: saw and heard. Gregory, always quiet, became quieter. Always solitary, he became eremitic. He spent less and less time in the morning-rooms front and back, the hall, bar, coffee-room, strangers' room, and other thronged areas in which, like disease or explosive, Martyn was apt to erupt; he spent more and more time in the library. He blessed the library. It was asylum, heaven-haven, the last refuge of civilised man on earth, unassailably quiet, almost always marvellously empty. There were the shelves; there was his chair. The chair was perfect. It was by the fire and out of the draught. It was deep. Yet, by dint of the shape and position of the arms, it was easy to get out of. It was wonderfully comfortable for sleeping and (new diversion) for extended reading. In daylight his book was served by the large window behind; at night it was illuminated by a handsome table-lamp at his elbow. He could reach a bell-push with his stick.

He was safe from Martyn. No intellectual. Illiterate, in effect. The last man to frequent the library.

On Tuesday the 6th of November, nine months after Martyn's retirement, Gregory lunched later than usual. The sound of Martyn's voice, on the landing outside the card-room, had imprisoned him mouse-quiet in the library. Until the incubus withdrew he would wait. He waited for twenty-five minutes, so interminable were Martyn's vainglorious anecdotes. The laughter that greeted them was, must be, that of idiots or sycophants. The hateful noise receded at last. Gregory emerged. He ate some saddle of lamb: a somewhat expensive dish, but one of which Trollope had that morning put him in mind. At the far end of the dining-room Martyn, also alone, was lunching. He had a magazine on a rack in front of him and a bottle of wine beside him. Gregory shifted his position so that he did not have to look at Martyn eating his lunch.

Martyn got up and left the dining-room. Soon his voice would be braying among the lustres of the morning-room chandeliers.

Gregory paid for his lunch. He started slowly, slowly crossing the dining-room. A waiter held the door for him as he went out into the hall; the rubber tip of his stick squeaked on the marble. He felt stiff and weak but pretty fit. His life was narrow, but his life had always been narrow. He preferred a narrow life, a few certainties, a small well-trodden area, no dubious adventures, no explorations and no risks.

Gregory embarked on the stairs; stick firmly grasped in his right hand, banister in his left. Both feet on each step, left-right left-right. The stairs were no problem. He went up them better than Charles did, although Charles was two years younger. Charles had almost given up bridge because of getting upstairs to the card-room. What Gregory could not do, of course, was hurry. It was no deprivation. There was no hurry. Going upstairs was something to do. It occupied a few minutes. It helped fill the day. It brought tea-time closer.

Gregory went along the landing to the library. He opened the enormous door. He went in and straight to the ranks of Trollope. He took *Phineas Finn* from the shelf. He turned and started slowly towards his chair.

Martyn was sitting in his chair.

Gregory did not cry out, nor froth at the mouth, nor shed scalding tears. He kept his rage and disgust under firm Anglo-Saxon control. He stopped and stared. This was, itself, unusual and *outré* behaviour. It betrayed feeling as no member of a gentleman's club should, on the club premises, betray feeling. But Gregory was no superman. He could restrain himself from Latin or Levantine excesses, but he could not help stopping and staring.

Martyn glanced up. He waved affably to Gregory with his cigar. He said nothing. He could, it seemed, read the word 'Silence'. Perhaps he could read a few words more, as a book lay open on the arm of his chair. Of Gregory's chair.

Gregory stood as though paralysed for a long moment. Martyn glanced at him again, with indulgent surprise. He gestured with his cigar, friendly but dismissive, and returned to his pretence of reading. His gesture said that Gregory was welcome to any other chair in the library. Gregory did not want any other chair. He did not want to share the library with Martyn. He did not want his life in ruins.

His life, his new life. The one he had made, fashioned out of adversity, built on the crumbling fragments of what had gone before. Martyn had driven him out of the haunts of men into this booksy hermitage. So be it. Old as he was he had adjusted. He had become a reader, an all-day reader in a library chair instead of an hour-long napper in that same chair, contentedly absorbed by the writings of good men long dead. A new way of life. Not better than the old (glasses of port, a cautious camaraderie) nor worse, but different, and his own courageous creation.

Now this was ended. His refuge was razed. Like Reynard the Fox he found his last earth stopped.

He was distraught. What could he do? What did the future hold? He was an old, old man on a small pension, living with frugal simplicity in his Kensington bed-sitter, living, in a truer sense, here in his club. Old friends long dead, except those few in the club. Family long dead. Colleagues (few intimate) long dead. It was little enough he asked of the world. One chair. And that was gone.

If a different man had usurped his chair, what then? A man with a kind of right to it, a learned man, a man who belonged in the library, a don (there were dons in the club) or a High Court judge or a retired cabinet minister? Then perhaps, another adjustment. Hard at his age: possible. A different chair in the library. Hard, at his age. But he would have acknowledged the suitability, the other's right. Or he might have framed an appeal: not of a broken and tragic but of an old and cantankerous man, a character. It could have been so phrased that no don, judge, or minister of the crown would refuse. A distasteful course, but possible.

But in this case! In the face of this! A different chair? Unbearable. An appeal, an old man's plea? To Martyn, the red-nosed, the pop-eyed, the show-off, the sport, the bon viveur, the bully? Never, never, never.

Then what?

Gregory got out of the library somehow, his old legs trembling, his stick insecurely held. He got out onto the landing and leaned against the wall. Unstoppably, to his infinite shame, the tears began to roll down his cheeks. He groped blindly to the lavatory that served the jovial elders of the card-room. It was occupied. He turned and hobbled along the passage that led to the bedroom-floor stairs. An Irish housemaid passed him, coming down the stairs at a run, girlish but massive, a healthy cow of a housemaid. She looked at Gregory with alarm and concern. He sniffed and gestured angrily with his cane.

'Are you all right, sir?'

'Yes!'

She went away slowly along the passage, casting glances back over her meaty shoulder.

His tear-ducts at last ran dry. He dabbed at his cheeks. He went back on a bus to Kensington. No tea in the club for him today, no dinner there tonight. He knew he would weep again, thinking of his chair and of his life.

For two days he moped at home in helpless, babyish rage. He wept from time to time. Then the thought struck him (why so long delayed?) that Martyn had been visiting the library for the first and only time. Why should he ever revisit it? What could be there to divert him? He was a creature of crowds, bars, drinks, the sound of his own voice. The library, any library, would bore and puzzle him. He had tried it, avid for new sensations; he would not return.

Gregory ventured to the club. The hall porter greeted him warmly, concerned about his health. Elderly gentlemen who lived alone in digs and lodgings could be ill, unnoticed for days; could die and lie unnoticed for weeks. But Gregory was neat as always, walking no worse, unaltered, dry-eyed.

He went upstairs to the library. He opened the door, frightened. The fine old room was empty. His chair was empty. The cushions had been plumped out by a servant, the ashtrays had been emptied and polished, the fire banked up. All was well. Sanity and safety had returned.

Gregory found his book and settled down, feeling deeply happy and slightly foolish. What a fuss about nothing. He was getting senile. He must fight it.

He lunched. He ate boiled silverside and pease pudding, and drank a glass of still cider.

Martyn was nowhere to be seen. He was away, or ill, or had fallen drunkenly under a bus.

Gregory had a glass of port with Charles Corbishley. Neither could remember whose turn it was; Charles insisted it was his.

They went upstairs together. Charles was playing bridge. Gregory opened the door of the library.

Martyn was in his chair.

It was then, the moment that he saw him, that Gregory decided upon murder. It was a brainwave: a solution of immediate and inescapable rightness. It would solve the problem as nothing else would solve it. Gregory had nothing to lose, even if caught; he had his chair to gain.

Gregory went into the strangers' room, empty and elegant but comfortless. He sat in a high backed chair and brooded about method. It was an area in which he recognised, and regretted, his inexperience. His career – forty years of concern with ancient buildings, in a financial and administrative role – gave him no basis for current planning. His private life, almost wholly without episode, provided no useful precedent. Even his reading was unhelpful. Trollope? Mrs Gaskell? Thackeray? There were beasts like Martyn in them all, and in Surtees and the Brontës and George Eliot. There was violence in these books. People were clubbed to the ground in lonely places. But there were no methods spelled out by any of these authors for killing usurpers in club libraries.

The strangers' room had a writing table. There was a dip-pen with a relief nib, a dutifully filled if unused inkwell, a clean blotter, and a selection of club writing paper in a variety of sizes. Administrative habit held. Gregory drew a sheet from the rack, dipped the pen into the ink, and wrote in capital letters:

POSSIBLE METHODS.

His writing was small and legible; the vertical strokes wavered a little because he made them slowly and his hand trembled.

He began to list methods as they occurred to him, attempting, at this stage, no order:

> *Shooting*
> *Stabbing*
> *Strangulation*
> *Suffocation*
> *Poison (in beverage, in food, or by venomous reptile or insect)*
> *Blunt instrument or bludgeon*
> *Fall down stairs (assisted)*
> *Ejection from windows, defenestration*
> *Injection of air into blood-vessel*
> *Burning (immolation)*
> *Drowning*
> *Electrocution*
> *Crushing by avalanche, falling building or similar*
> *Explosion, as of bomb or grenade*
> *Gas*
> *Pushing under car, train*

He paused and sucked his pen, which tasted of boot polish and snuff. Ancient memories of the early cinema enabled him to add:

> *Tying to railway lines in path of oncoming train*
> *Circular saw*
> *Introduction into den of wild beasts*
> *Lashing to log above large waterfall*
> *Trampling by stampeding herd of maddened steers*

Other memories produced:

> *Slingshot or catapult (stone through temple)*
> *Death ray*

50

Contact with fatal disease (Red Death or similar)
Incarceration (cf. Amontillado), premature burial

Further thought contributed:

Starvation
Death by thirst (dehydration)
Driving to suicide (query: by hint of blackmail)
Inflation (compressed air)
Deflation (vacuum-pump)
Trampling by rogue elephants

Gregory was pleased with his list, which was a great deal longer than he had expected.

He examined each entry, critically, dispassionately, considering the problems, logistic and other, intrinsic to each.

To his dismay this examination disposed, at once, of nearly all his possible methods. He had no gun, poison, asp or scorpion, hypodermic needle, bomb, gas-shell, circular saw, menagerie, slingshot, ray-gun, bacilli of the Red Death, niche in cellar with available trowel and mortar, air-pump, or elephant. He saw no way of travelling to, let alone inducing Martyn to travel to, the edge of a lake or the brow of a waterfall. There was no feasible method of killing by starvation or thirst a man who belonged to Blazon's and had plenty of money. He had not the physical strength to eject Martyn, who might be expected to resist, from an upper window, to smash his skull with a club, or to tie him to the rails in the path of an oncoming train.

Possibilities, however, survived this winnowing. Stabbing. Electrocution. Tripping at the top of the stairs. Burning. And blackmail leading to suicide.

Gregory pondered each of these, chilly in the strangers' room, while tea-time came and went.

The force of administrative habit, from which long years of retirement had not released him, induced Gregory to place his possibles in alphabetical order:

Blackmail
Electrocution
Fire
Stabbing
Tripping (top of stairs)

After weeks of thought, intensive if not continuous, he decided to make his attempts in this order. If one failed he would proceed to the next; if one succeeded there would be no need to go on.

Blackmail. Gregory had left it in his list because it did not require, in a physical or mechanical sense, equipment he did not have, powers he could not summon. Gregory had heard that if you went up to no matter whom, approaching from behind, and whispered: 'All is known! Flee,' the archbishop himself would grab a suitcase and decamp, or (better) take a revolver from his cassock and shoot

51

himself. Gregory tried to picture the scene, casting himself in the role of victim. He pictured a stranger, or indeed a person known to him, whispering with urgent menace that all was discovered. What was discovered? What was there to discover? Nothing in Gregory's life. He had secrets – his false teeth, the occasional malfunction of his waterworks, his use of the dictionary when doing the crossword – but they were not, Gregory thought, what was meant. As to Martyn? He was, surely, too crass to have guilty secrets. He would rather trumpet his conquests (sexual), proclaim his fiddles (tax-evasive), make comic-heroic stories about his car accidents. His activities, his outrages, were of a public kind.

The conversation was lamentably predictable. 'All is discovered!' 'Yes, old boy, always has been.'

Four possibilities remained. Much reconnaissance was required. Gregory did the reconnaissance. He informed himself, in minutest detail, about Martyn's habits, his movements, the times he was here or there, the time he was alone in the library. It was agony to observe him in the chair, fat cigar to his fat lips, eyes fatly bulging over purple cheeks: but Gregory learned what he needed. The man's habits were regular. He was predictable. Things promised well for the four surviving possibilities.

Electrocution. The key was the table-lamp beside the chair. It was made of brass: a Doric column on a massive square base, the switch in the column three inches below the bulb. Gregory's knowledge of electricity was rudimentary, but he believed that, by de-earthing the plug and by re-routing the live wire to the brass, he could kill his enemy.

He was dissatisfied with his knowledge, and improved it. He spent some time with a courteous West Indian in a Kensington electrician's, enquiring (adroitly) after possible sources of *danger* in big brass table-lamps. He elicited wiring diagrams: wrong and right: how to be safe: how to kill.

He purchased a small screwdriver with a yellow insulated handle. He took screwdriver and diagrams to Blazon's. He waited his chance. What he required was an hour (an hour should suffice) during which Martyn was not in the library, but at the end of which he, and not some other, should come to the library: sit in the chair: require the table-lamp. A bright midday was useless. A dull sky, or a murky evening, would call the unsuspecting hand towards the brass. Many a promising occasion had to be passed up.

But the right occasion, after eleven weeks, arrived. The day was dark, heavy clouds moving sluggishly across the brown London sky. Martyn was in the club, not foul-hooking his fish or murdering tame pheasants. He had a guest for lunch, a pudgy financier, who would trundle in due course back to his extortions.

Between 1.30 and 2.30 Gregory could be sure of having the library to himself. All was planned. He would fix the lamp. Then he would lurk, innocently, feigning sleep, in a nearby chair. If by mischance some innocent should anticipate Martyn, make for the chair and lamp, Gregory could intervene and save him. It was unlikely. Martyn would come, cigar aglow, eyes abulge. Gregory would shrink back, so small and old as to be almost invisible. Pfft. A fault in the wiring. Gregory far elsewhere before Martyn was discovered, which might, indeed, be the following morning, when housemaids emptied ashtrays.

Gregory crept into the penumbrous library. He set to work on the plug. He knew what to do. Urgency lent deftness to his old fingers. The screws were hard to undo but he undid them. Crouching was hard on his knees but he compelled his knees to obedience. Plug done, earthless, its safety factor removed. He thrust it back into its socket. He addressed himself to the next, the crucial part. His screwdriver whirled. Flex snaked out at him. He consulted his diagrams. Wrong, right. The right now wrong, the wrong now right. With his left hand he grasped the brazen column of the lamp, with his right he groped among the bright-tipped wires which spiralled up its gut—

Bam. A great blow knocked the lamp out of his hands, knocked him into the chair (*the chair*), knocked him out.

Got a shock, they said. Lucky to be alive. Trying to mend the lamp, misguided old gentleman. Fancy him having a screwdriver.

His pulse was taken by a distinguished elderly physician (a member) who was dragged protesting from his Irish stew. All was well. Brandy was pressed to Gregory's lips. He drank the brandy. It ran like a fire down his gullet, reviving him wonderfully. He sat up, quite recovered.

Martyn, it appeared, had brought the brandy; his hand had held it to Gregory's bloodless old lips.

Many weeks passed before Gregory recovered strength and resolution to proceed. But his intention, during convalescence, never wavered.

Electricity, he concluded, had been beyond him. It was too technical, too modern. He had thought to understand but he had not understood. It took younger men. Better to rely on the natural, the elemental killers, the weapons of the cavemen and the ancient gods.

Fire.

The plan was simple but it took a great deal of careful and exhausting preparation. Gregory procured a gallon can. He caused it to be filled with petrol. He procured another. This was also filled. He tried to take both, in a suitcase, to Blazon's, but the suitcase was too heavy. He took one, wrapped in brown paper; he smuggled it, smiling with false brightness, past the hall-porter's box, and struggled with it up to the library. He hoped it would be taken for a bundle of books. He hid it on a floor-level shelf behind volumes of German pastoral literature. He imported the second gallon the same way, varying the wrapping in order to deceive. No one looked at him or at his shabby bundle.

Above the bookshelves, all round the library, stood urns of Attic character, gifts of a Victorian bishop. One of them, indecently decorated with paintings of Spartan athletes, stood above *the chair*.

The next phase took all that Gregory had of strength and resolution. He moved the library ladder all the length of the library. He climbed it, with one of his gallon cans. He hoisted the can from shelf to shelf, displacing books, until it rested by the urn on the top. With infinite difficulty he poured most of the petrol from the can into the urn. Some dribbled onto the books below, some onto Gregory. The place reeked of petrol. Time, and Martyn's cigars, would cure that.

Ten days later (he needed the rest) he added the second can. It was neither easier nor more difficult. He spilled less, but it seemed heavier. He was, to be sure, ten days older.

Gregory disinterred, that night, a spool of nylon from the elderly tangle of his fishing-gear. It was twenty-pound test; he had unlimited yards of it. It lived in his pocket for three weeks.

After three weeks opportunity again occurred. He put the ladder under the urn, and a loop of nylon about the urn. He let the nylon drop invisibly down the front of the bookshelf, trail invisibly across the floor, and finish in his hand, twenty feet away, in a small armchair in the semi-darkness.

Martyn came. He sat down. He lit his cigar. He opened his book. He never saw Gregory.

Gregory took up the slack of his nylon line. It rose from the floor and the bookcase; it was a visible silver thread, behind Martyn, between Gregory's hand and the death-laden urn.

Now! All worked to perfection. The thread tipped the urn. The urn upended over the chair. Flood of petrol, to be ignited by the cigar, to shroud Martyn in flames, to give him a noble, a Viking death which he did not deserve? No petrol. The urn tumbled, dry. Martyn sprang from his chair with a shout. He glanced at the urn, unbroken on the carpet beside him. He glanced up at the bookshelf. He shrugged and settled back to his book.

Gregory never moved.

An hour later Martyn went away. Gregory hobbled forward, to remove his telltale nylon and to examine the urn. The urn had a hole in the bottom. Not a new one, occasioned by its fall, but an old one, original, part of the design. The urn had, no doubt, been intended for plants.

Too elaborate, thought Gregory sadly. Too dependant on the treacherous and delusive gifts of Victorian bishops. He must be simpler, more basic, more primitive. He must rely upon a tool he could trust.

Stabbing.

He bought, in a Kensington ironmonger's, a kitchen knife, razor-sharp, needle-pointed, its blade a wicked eleven inches long.

Observation assured him that Martyn, in his gross way, unbuttoned his waistcoat when he sat in the library chair (*whose chair?*) to pretend to read his book. Penetration of tweed or worsted was therefore needless; only silk or poplin need be pierced. Great force was not needed, not with so sharp an instrument.

The placement was important. Gregory studied anatomical drawings in books in the public library. He required to hit the heart, avoid ribs. He practised, nightly for some weeks, on a dummy he constructed from a bolster, dressed in coat and waistcoat of his own. He drilled himself in the position he must adopt, given the position he knew Martyn adopted.

Nothing, nothing was this time left to chance.

Martyn came to the library. He sat down, waving to Gregory with his cigar, waving with the voiceless freemasonry of a fellow-user of the library.

Gregory went to the French section. He drew forth a book, long identified. He leafed through the pages. With a start of surprise, and a somewhat overplayed grunt of displeasure, he affected to discover that the pages were uncut. He went to a drawer in a writing-table. He took from the drawer a knife: not the heavy brass paper-cutter which lived there, but his Kensington kitchen knife. He began to cut the pages of the book. The light was bad where he stood. He hobbled, grumbling, to the window. He stood behind the chair.

Martyn glanced at him, sympathetic, preoccupied.

Trr, trr. The razor-sharp knife slit the pages of a forgotten French novel.

Gregory moved closer to the chair. Martyn's waistcoat was unbuttoned. His rib-cage was outlined, rib on rib, against the pink and white stripes of his shirt. Gregory examined his target. He picked his spot. It was an inch and a half to the left of a stripe in Martyn's Old Harrovian tie, an inch to the right of the buckle of his braces. Between ribs, straight to heart.

Gregory gulped. Could he do this? Plunge cold steel into the breast of an unsuspecting man? Yes! Martyn smelled of cigar-smoke and sandalwood hair-lotion. Gregory remembered Martyn; he remembered all the Martyns in his life; he looked at his chair. He could do it.

He kept up his camouflage, trr trr, cutting the pages, but looking at the triangle of pink and white shirt.

There was a sudden and shocking pain in his thumb. He looked down, aghast. Blood welled. He had cut himself. He cried out, unnerved by the redness and wetness of his blood. It was all over the book. His thumb hurt shockingly. He staggered, faint. An arm gripped him. He was lowered into a chair. His thumb was bound with a clean cotton handkerchief. Brandy was summoned and carried to his lips.

Martyn had caught him. Martyn had bandaged his thumb. Martyn had paid for the brandy.

A final possibility remained.

Tripping (top of stairs). Nylon again. Nylon had given satisfaction before; in the failure of attempt number two the fault had not been nylon's.

The stairs were broad, curved, and made of stone. There were posts each side at the top, between which a trip-wire could be stretched.

Thought convinced Gregory that he could not rig his trip-wire and leave it unattended, in the expectation of Martyn descending before anyone else descended. Someone was apt to come out of the card-room and go down the stairs. Not only would Gregory's ruse be discovered, and Martyn saved, but some bluff bridge-player would have his skull split and his back broken.

What Gregory had to do was to station himself at the top of the stairs, out of sight or innocently employed, holding one end of his nylon. At the approach of Martyn, but of no other, he would tighten. In the hurly-burly which would follow the death of Martyn, Gregory could, assuredly, detach his nylon. The method was so greatly simpler and surer than the others that it was, as now emerged, a pity that Gregory had not listed his ideas in reverse alphabetical order.

What had to be established was his own station. Undoubtedly the place was the card-room lavatory. No doubt of it. It chose itself. The nylon must be secured (with knots that, as a fisherman, Gregory had known and could relearn) to the further newel-post at the head of the stairs; it would lie, harmless and invisible, along the top step; it would loop round the nearer newel-post; at a slight angle it would cross the passage to the keyhole of the lavatory, and to Gregory's hand inside the lavatory door. When the door stood slightly ajar Gregory established that he could, through the crack, see the top of the stairs.

One further preparation remained.

Gregory obtained drawing-pins.

He went to the strangers' room. On a sheet of the largest club writing-paper he wrote OUT OF ORDER in ink, with the dip-pen. The letters wavered but were clearly legible. He blotted his work carefully. The message, in mirror-writing, glared from the blotting-paper. Gregory burned the blotting-paper in the fire in the strangers' room.

Some days later he lunched on a fillet of excellent haddock. He watched Martyn lunching alone. Martyn lunched heavily. Gregory joined Charles Corbishley for a glass of port. Charles paid for the port. Gregory then, for the first time in a dozen years, suggested a second glass of port. He astonished himself as much as he astonished Charles.

The port drunk, more quickly than usual, he went upstairs, also more quickly than usual. Excitement accelerated both his drinking and his ascent. He confirmed that Martyn was in the library, fatly occupying the chair. There were voices from the card-room. No one else was about. Gregory threaded the end of his nylon through the keyhole of the lavatory door. He led it across the passage, round the nearer newel-post, along the top of the stairs, and to the further newel-post. There he secured it with his relearned knot. He went back to the lavatory. He took his OUT OF ORDER notice from his pocket, and pinned it to the lavatory door with his drawing-pin.

He went into the lavatory, leaving the door ajar. He sat on the seat and watched.

After a very long time a bridge-player stumped from the card-room to the lavatory. He grunted with chagrin when he saw the notice. He stumped away to try elsewhere.

More time passed. It was very quiet. There was very little noise from the card-room, hardly more than a murmur, agricultural in quality, rather soothing than otherwise. The club was almost empty, before tea on a week-day. The sound of traffic hardly reached this central point of the solid old building.

Gregory faithfully gripped the plastic spool of his nylon. It seemed to him that he was transported backwards, seventy or more years in time, to the bows of a dinghy off the West Coast of Scotland: that he was fishing for mackerel with a hand-line; his cousin Maud was there in a tam-o'-shanter, and old Dougal the boatman . . .

'Good God, what are you doing there?'

'Fishing,' said Gregory thickly, emerging slowly from deep sleep, stupid and heavy-lidded from his second glass of port.

Martyn peered into the lavatory. He saw Gregory sitting, a little frail hunched figure, on the lavatory seat. He saw the spool in Gregory's hand, and the nylon line going from the spool through the keyhole.

Martyn said: 'What are you trying to catch?'

Then he began to laugh. His face purpled. Tears streamed down his cheeks. He tried to speak. The effort turned his laughter to coughing. He coughed helplessly, dangerously. His face went from scarlet to black. He staggered. He collapsed against the lavatory door, fighting, coughing, struggling for breath, a hand clutching his heart.

They said he died on his way to hospital. His heart failed owing to a paroxysm brought on by coughing, itself the result of mirth. He died of laughing.

'Scrutiny,' said Gregory solemnly, 'revealed the availability of ox-tail. Which I allowed myself to accompany with a dish of spinach. Now, my dear Charles, may I request a steward to carry us a glass of vintage port?'

'Wood-port, I thank you,' said Charles Corbishley.

'So be it.'

At half past three Gregory went up to the library. He read a page of *The Eustace Diamonds*, in his chair by the fire, before falling gently asleep until tea-time.

This story was originally published under the pseudonym of Ivor Drummond.

THE SECRET LOVER

by Peter Lovesey

'Pam.'

'Yes?'

'Will you see him this weekend?'

Pam Meredith drew a long breath and stifled the impulse to scream. She knew exactly what was coming. 'See who?'

'Your secret lover.'

She summoned a coy smile, said, 'Give over!' and everyone giggled.

For some reason, that last session of the working week regularly turned three efficient medical receptionists into overgrown schoolgirls. They were all over thirty, too. As soon as they arrived at the health centre on Saturday morning, they were into their routine. After flexing their imaginations with stories of what the doctors had been getting up to with the patients, they started on each other. Then it was never long before Pam's secret lover came up.

He was an inoffensive, harassed-looking man in his late thirties who had happened to walk into the centre one afternoon to ask for help. A piece of grit had lodged under his left eyelid. Not one of the doctors or the district nurse had been in the building at the time, so Pam had dealt with it herself. From her own experiences with contact lenses, she had a fair idea how to persuade the eye to eject a foreign body, and she had succeeded very quickly, without causing the patient any serious discomfort. He had thanked her and left in a rush, as if the episode had embarrassed him. Pam had thought no more about him until a fortnight later, when she came on duty and was told that a man had been asking for her personally and would be calling back at lunchtime. This, understandably, created some lively interest in Reception, particularly when he arrived at five minutes to one carrying a bunch of daffodils.

At thirty-three, Pam was the second youngest of the medical receptionists. She exercised, dieted and tinted her hair blonde and she was popular with many of the men who came in to collect their prescriptions, but she was not used to floral tributes. In her white overall she thought of herself as clinical and efficient. She had a pale, oval face with brown eyes and a small, neat mouth that she had been told projected refinement rather than sensuality. Lately, she had noticed some incipient wrinkles on her neck and taken to wearing polo-necked sweaters.

Under the amused and frankly envious observation of her colleagues, Pam had blushingly accepted the flowers, trying to explain that such a tribute was not necessary, charming as it was. However, when the giver followed it up by asking her to allow him to buy her a drink at the Green Dragon, she had found him difficult to refuse. She had stuttered something about being on duty after lunch, so he had suggested tomato juice or bitter lemon, and one of the other girls had given her an unseen nudge and planted her handbag in her hand.

That was the start of the long-running joke about Pam's secret lover.

Really the joke was on the others. They hadn't guessed it in their wildest fantasies, but things had developed to the extent that Pam now slept with him regularly.

Do not assume too much about the relationship. In the common understanding of the word, he was not her lover. Sleeping together and making love are not of necessity the same thing. The possibility was not excluded, yet it was not taken as the automatic consequence of sharing a bed, and that accorded well with Pam's innate refinement.

So it wasn't entirely as the girls in the health centre might have imagined it. Pam had learned over the first tomato juice in the Green Dragon that Cliff had a job in the cider industry which entailed calling on various producers in the West Midlands and South-West, and visiting Hereford for an overnight stay once a fortnight. He liked travelling, yet he admitted that the nights away from home had been instrumental in the failure of his marriage. He had not been unfaithful, but, as he altruistically put it, anyone who read the accounts of rapes and muggings in the papers couldn't really blame a wife who sought companionship elsewhere when her husband spent every other week away on business.

Responding to his candour, Pam had found herself admitting that she, too, was divorced. The nights, she agreed, were the worst. Even in the old cathedral city of Hereford, which had no reputation for violence, she avoided going out alone after dark and she often lay awake listening acutely in case someone was tampering with the locks downstairs.

That first lunchtime drink had led to another when Cliff was next in the city. The fortnight after, Pam had invited him to the house for a 'spot of supper', explaining that it was no trouble, because you could do much more interesting things cooking for two than alone. Cliff had heaped praise on her chicken *cordon bleu*, and after that the evening meal had become a fortnightly fixture. On the first occasion, he had quite properly returned to his hotel at the end of the evening, but the following time he had introduced Pam to the old-fashioned game of cribbage, and they had both got so engrossed that neither of them had noticed the time until it was well after midnight. By then, Pam felt so relaxed and safe with Cliff that it had seemed the most natural thing in the world to make up the spare bed for him and invite him to stay the night. There had been no suggestion on either side of a more intimate arrangement. That was what she liked about Cliff. He wasn't one of those predatory males. He was enough of a gentleman to suppress his natural physical instincts. And one night six weeks after in a thunderstorm, when she had tapped on his bedroom door and said she was feeling frightened, he had offered in the same gentlemanly spirit to come to her room until the storm abated. As it happened, Pam still slept in the king-size double bed she had got used to when she was married, so there was room for Cliff without any embarrassment about inadvertent touching. They had fallen asleep listening for the thunder. By then it was the season of summer storms so, next time he had come to the house, they had each agreed it was a sensible precaution to sleep together even when the sky was clear. You could never be certain when a storm might blow up during the night. And when the first chill nights of autumn arrived, neither of them liked the prospect of sleeping apart between cool sheets. Besides, as Cliff considerately mentioned, using one bed was less expensive on the laundry.

Speaking of laundry, Pam took to washing out his shirts, underclothes and pyjamas. She had bought him a special pair of bottle-green French pyjamas without buttons and with an elasticated waistband. They were waiting on his pillow, washed and ironed, each time he came. He was very appreciative. He never failed to arrive without a bottle of cider that they drank with the meal. Once or twice he mentioned that he would have taken her out to a restaurant if her cooking had not been so excellent that it would have shown up the cook. He particularly relished the cooked breakfast on a large oval plate that she supplied before he went on his way in the morning.

So Pam staunchly tolerated the teasing in the health centre, encouraged by the certainty that it was all fantasy on their part; she had been careful never to let them know that she had invited Cliff home. She was in a better frame of mind as she walked home that lunchtime. It was always a relief to get through Saturday morning.

As she turned the corner of her street, she saw a small car, a red Mini, outside her house, with someone sitting inside it. She wasn't expecting a visitor. She strolled towards her gate, noticing that it was a woman who made no move to get out, and whom she didn't recognise, so she passed the car and let herself indoors.

There was a letter on the floor, a greetings card by the look of it. She had quite forgotten that her birthday was on Sunday. Living alone, with no family to speak of, she tended to ignore such occasions. However, someone had evidently decided that this one should not go by unremarked. She didn't recognise the handwriting, and the postmark was too faint to read. She opened it and smiled. A print of a single daffodil, and inside, under the printed birthday greeting, the handwritten letter C.

The reason why she hadn't recognised Cliff's writing was that this was the first time she had seen it. He wasn't one for sending letters. And the postmark wouldn't have given Pam a clue, even if she had deciphered it, because she didn't know where he lived. He was vague or dismissive when it came to personal information, so she hadn't pressed him. He was entitled to his privacy. She couldn't help wondering sometimes, and her best guess was that since the failure of his marriage he had tended to neglect himself and his home and devoted himself to his job. He lived for the travelling, and, Pam was encouraged to believe, his fortnightly visit to Hereford.

Presently the doorbell chimed. Pam opened the door to the woman she had seen in the car, dark-haired, about her own age or a little older, good-looking, with one of those long, elegant faces with high cheekbones that you see in foreign films. She was wearing a dark blue suit and white blouse buttoned to the neck as if she were attending an interview for a job. Mainly, Pam was made aware of the woman's grey-green eyes that scrutinised her with an interest unusual in people who called casually at the door.

'Hello,' said Pam.

'Mrs Pamela Meredith?'

'Yes.'

The look became even more intense. 'We haven't met. You may not even know that I exist. I'm Tracey Gibbons.' She paused for a reaction.

Pam smiled faintly. 'You're right. I haven't heard your name before.'

Tracey Gibbons sighed and shook her head. 'I'm not surprised. I don't know what you're going to think of me, coming to your home like this, but it's reached the point when something has to be done. It's about your husband.'

Pam frowned. 'My husband?' She hadn't heard from David in six years.

'May I come in?'

'I suppose you'd better.'

As she showed the woman into her front room, Pam couldn't help wondering if this was a confidence trick. The woman's eyes blatantly surveyed the room, the furniture, the ornaments, everything.

Pam said sharply, 'I think you'd better come to the point, Miss Gibbons.'

'Mrs, actually. Not that it matters. I'm waiting for my divorce to come through.' Suddenly the woman sounded nervous and defensive. 'I'm not promiscuous. I want you to understand that, Mrs Meredith, whatever you may think of me. And I'm not deceitful, either, or I wouldn't be here. I want to get things straight between us. I've driven over from Worcester this morning to talk to you.'

Pam was beginning to fathom what this was about. Mrs Gibbons was having an affair with David, and for some obscure reason she felt obliged to confess it to his ex-wife. Clearly the poor woman was in a state of nerves, so it was kindest to let her say her piece before gently showing her the door.

'You probably wonder how I got your address,' Mrs Gibbons went on. 'He doesn't know I'm here, I promise you. It's only over the last few weeks that I began to suspect he had a wife. Certain things you notice, like his freshly ironed shirts. He left his suitcase open the last time he came, and I happened to see the birthday card he addressed to you. That's how I got your address.'

Pam's skin prickled. 'Which card?'

'The daffodil. I looked inside, I'm ashamed to admit. I had to know.'

Pam closed her eyes. The woman wasn't talking about David at all. It was Cliff, *her* Cliff. Her head was spinning. She thought she was going to faint. She said, 'I think I need some brandy.'

Mrs Gibbons nodded. 'I'll join you, if I may.'

When she handed over the glass, Pam said in a subdued voice, 'You *are* talking about a man named Cliff?'

'Of course.'

'He is not my husband.'

'What?' Mrs Gibbons stared at her in disbelief.

61

'He visits me sometimes.'

'And you wash his shirts?'

'Usually.'

'The bastard!' said Mrs Gibbons, her eyes brimming. 'The rotten, two-timing bastard! I knew there was someone else, but I thought it was his wife he was so secretive about. I persuaded myself he was unhappily married and I came here to plead with you to let him go. I could kill him!'

'How do you think I feel?' Pam blurted out. 'I didn't know there was anyone else in his life.'

'Does he keep a toothbrush and razor in your bathroom?'

'A face-flannel as well.'

'And I suppose you bought him some expensive aftershave?'

Pam confirmed it bitterly. In her outraged state, she needed to talk, and sharing the trouble seemed likely to dull the pain. She related how she and Cliff had met and how she had invited him home.

'And one thing led to another?' speculated Mrs Gibbons. 'When I think of what I was induced to do in the belief that I was the love of his life . . . ' She finished her brandy in a gulp.

Pam nodded. 'It was expensive, too.'

'Expensive?'

'Preparing three-course dinners and large cooked breakfasts.'

'I wasn't talking about cooking,' said Mrs Gibbons, giving Pam a penetrating look.

'Ah,' said Pam, with a slow dip of the head, in an attempt to convey that she understood exactly what Mrs Gibbons *was* talking about.

'Things I didn't get up to in ten years of marriage to a very athletic man,' Mrs Gibbons further confided, looking modestly away. 'But you know all about it. Casanova was a boy scout compared to Cliff. God, I feel so humiliated.'

'Would you like a spot more brandy, Mrs Gibbons?'

'Why don't you call me Tracey?' suggested Mrs Gibbons, holding out her glass. 'We're just his playthings, you and I. How many others are there, do you suppose?'

'Who knows?' said Pam, seizing on the appalling possibility and speaking her thoughts aloud. 'There are plenty of divorced women like you and me, living in relative comfort in what was once the marital home, pathetically grateful for any attention that comes our way. Let's face it: we're secondhand goods.'

After a sobering interval, Tracey Gibbons pushed her empty glass towards the brandy bottle again, and asked, 'What are we going to do about him?'

'Kick him out with his toothbrush and face-flannel, I suppose,' Pam answered inadequately.

'So that he finds other deluded women to prey on?' said Tracey. 'That's not the treatment for the kind of animal we're dealing with. Personally, I feel so angry and abused that I could kill him if I knew how to get away with it. Wouldn't you?'

Pam stared at her. 'Are you serious?'

'Totally. He's ruined my hopes and every atom of self-respect I had left. What was I to him? His bit in Worcester, his Monday night amusement.'

'And I was Tuesday night in Hereford,' Pam added bleakly, suddenly given a cruel and vivid understanding of the way she had been used. Sex was Monday, supper Tuesday. In her own way, she felt as violated as Tracey. An arrangement that had seemed to be considerate and beautiful was revealed as cynically expedient. The reason why he had never touched her was that he was always sated after his night of unbridled passion in Worcester. 'Tracey, if you know of a way to kill him,' she stated with the calm that comes when a crucial decision is made, 'I know how to get away with it.'

Tracey's eyes opened very wide.

Pam made black coffee and sandwiches and explained her plan. To describe it as a plan is perhaps misleading, because it had only leapt to mind as they were talking. She wasn't given to thinking much about murder. Yet as she spoke, she sensed excitedly that it could work. It was simple, tidy and within her capability.

The two women talked until late in the afternoon. For the plan to work, they had to devise a way of killing without mess. The body should not be marked by violence. They solemnly debated various methods of despatching a man. Whether the intention was serious or not, Pam found that just talking about it was a balm for the pain that Cliff had inflicted on her. She and Tracey sensibly agreed to take no action until they had each had time to adjust to the shock, but they were adamant that they would meet again.

On the following Monday evening, Pam received a phone call from Tracey. 'Have you thought any more about what we were discussing?'

'On and off, yes,' Pam answered guardedly.

'Well, I've been doing some research,' Tracey told her with the excitement obvious in her voice. 'I'd better not be too specific over the phone, but I know where to get some stuff that will do the job. Do you understand me?'

'I think so.'

'It's simple, quick and very effective, and the best thing about it is that I can get it at work.'

Pam recalled that Tracey had said she worked for a firm that manufactured agricultural fertilisers. She supposed she was talking about some chemical substance.

Poison.

'The thing is,' Tracey was saying, 'if I get some, are you willing to do your part? You said it would be no problem.'

'That's true, but—'

'By the weekend? He's due to visit me on Monday.'

The reminder of Cliff's Monday assignations in Worcester was like a stab of pain to Pam. 'By the weekend,' she confirmed emphatically. 'Come over about the same time on Saturday. I'll do my part, I promise you, Tracey.'

The part Pam had to play in the killing of Cliff was to obtain a blank death certificate from one of the doctors at the centre. She had often noticed how careless Dr Holt-Wagstaff was with his paperwork. He was the oldest of the five practitioners and his desk was always in disorder. She waited for her opportunity for most of the week. On Friday morning she had to go into his surgery to ask him to clarify his handwriting on a prescription form. The death certificate pad was there on the desk. At twelve-fifteen, when he went out on his rounds, and Pam was on duty with one other girl, she slipped back into the surgery. No one saw her.

Saturday was a testing morning for Pam. The time dragged and the teasing about her secret lover was difficult to take without snapping back at the others. She kept wondering whether Dr Holt-Wagstaff had noticed anything. She need not have worried. He left at noon, wishing everyone a pleasant weekend. At twelve-thirty, the girls locked up and left.

When Pam got home, Tracey was waiting on her doorstep. 'I came by train,' she explained. 'Didn't want to leave my car outside again. It's surprising how much people notice.'

'Sensible,' said Pam, with approval, as she opened the door. 'Now I want to hear about the stuff you've got. Is it really going to work?'

Tracey put her hand on Pam's arm. 'Darling, it's foolproof. Do you want to see it?' She opened her handbag and took out a small brown glass bottle. 'Pure nicotine. We use it at work.'

Pam held the bottle in her palm. 'Nicotine? Is it a poison?'

'Deadly.'

'There isn't much here.'

'The fatal dose is measured in milligrams, Pam. A few drops will do the trick.'

'How can we get him to take it?'

'I've thought of that.' Tracey smiled. 'You're going to like this. In a glass of his own buckshee cider. Nicotine goes yellow on exposure to light and air, and there's a bitter taste which the sweet cider will mask.'

'How does it work?'

'It acts as a massive stimulant. The vital organs simply can't withstand it. He'll die of cardiac arrest in a very short time. Did you get the death certificate?'

Pam placed the poison bottle on the kitchen table and opened one of her cookbooks. The certificate was inside.

'You're careful, too,' Tracey said with a conspiratorial smile. She delved into her handbag again. 'I brought a prescription from my doctor to copy the signature, as you suggested. What else do we have to fill in here? *Name of Deceased*. What shall we call him?'

'Anything but Cliff,' said Pam. 'How above Clive? Clive Jones.'

'All right. Clive Jones it is. *Date of death*. I'd better fill that in after the event. What shall we put as the cause of death? Cardiac failure?'

'No, that's likely to be a sudden death,' said Pam, thinking of post-mortems. 'Broncho-pneumonia is better.'

'Suits me,' said Tracey, writing it down. 'After he's dead, I take this to the Registry of Births, Marriages and Deaths in Worcester, and tell them that Clive Jones was my brother, is that right?'

'Yes, it's very straightforward. They'll want his date of birth and one or two other details that you can invent. Then they issue you with another certificate that you show to the undertaker. He takes over after that.'

'I ask for a cremation, of course. Will it cost much?'

'Don't worry,' said Pam. 'He can afford it.'

'Too true!' said Tracey. 'His wallet is always stuffed with notes.'

'He never has to spend much,' Pam pointed out. 'The way he runs his life, he gets everything he wants for nothing.'

'The bastard,' said Tracey with a shudder.

'You really mean to do it, don't you?'

Tracey stood up and look steadily at Pam with her grey-green eyes. 'On Monday evening when he comes to me. I'll phone you when it's done.'

Pam linked her arm in Tracey's. 'The first thing I'm going to do is burn those pyjamas.'

Tracey remarked, 'He never wore pyjamas with me.'

'Really?' Pam hesitated, her curiosity aroused. 'What exactly did he do with you? Are you able to talk about it?'

'I don't believe I could,' answered Tracey with eyes lowered.

'If I poured you a brandy? We *are* in this together now.'

'All right,' said Tracey with a sigh.

Sunday seemed like the longest day of Pam's life, but she finally got through it. On Monday she didn't go in to work. That evening, she waited nervously by the phone from six-thirty onwards.

The call came at a few minutes after seven. Pam snatched up the phone.

'Hello, darling.' *The voice was Cliff's.*

'Cliff?'

'Yes. Not like me to call you on a Monday, is it? The fact is, I happen to be in Worcester on my travels, and it occurred to me that I could get over to you in Hereford in half an hour if you're free this evening.'

'Has something happened?' asked Pam.

'No, my darling. Just a change of plans. I won't expect much of a meal.'

'That's good, because I haven't got one for you,' Pam candidly told him.

There was a moment's hesitation before he said, 'Are you all right, dear? You don't sound quite yourself.'

'Don't I?' said Pam flatly. 'Well, I've had a bit of a shock. My sister died here on Saturday. It wasn't entirely unexpected. Broncho-pneumonia. I've had to do everything myself. She's being cremated on Wednesday.'

'Your sister? Pam, darling, I'm terribly sorry. I didn't even know you had a sister.'

'Her name was Olive. Olive Jones,' said Pam, and she couldn't help smiling at her own resourcefulness. After she had poisoned Tracey with a drop of nicotine in her brandy, all it had wanted on the death certificate was a touch of the pen. 'We weren't close. I'm not too distressed. Yes, why don't you come over?'

'You're sure you want me?'

'Oh, I want you,' answered Pam. 'Yes, I definitely want you.'

When she had put down the phone, she didn't go to the fridge to see what food she had in there. She went upstairs to the bedroom and changed into a black lace *négligé*.

THE OLD MOB

by Desmond Lowden

Satchel Anderson got up at four that morning. He got his Merc out of the garage and drove off through the suburbs. By half-past four he'd reached the motorway, and by five was approaching the new spur where he was to meet the Geordie. Satchel parked on the hard shoulder and looked across at the floodlights of the twenty-four hour shift. He saw the timber claddings of the piles they were constructing, saw the thick wet cement they were pouring down inside. And then the gravel track he could reverse down, meaning he could get the body out of the boot without getting mud on his Merc.

He drove down to the site hut and got out. But it was then that the first thing went wrong. The Geordie wasn't there. Only his side-kick, the Irishman.

They went inside the hut. The Irishman, bent, cold in his bones and not yet forty-five. He wore a hand-stitched suit covered in white mud. And he had that squint of long eyelids, long upper lip, that came from smoking fags down to the stub.

'Noa, de Geordie, he boggered off,' he told Satchel. 'Boggered off two days back.'

'You're joking,' Satchel said.

'Noa, he went to de ski-ing.'

'Again?'

'Had dis call from him last noit. Cortina di Ampezzo. De *piste* is piss poor, he says, piss poor.' The man took a packet of Balkan Sobranies from his pocket. 'Me, oi doan't loik de ski-ing. Not de *apray*, de *avong*, or de *pondong* . . . Noa, oi cruises. Moastly oi cruises.'

'Get away,' Satchel said.

'Now, about dis consignment.' The Irishman put his hand out.

But Satchel shook his head. He knew all about Irishmen in hand-stitched suits, smoking Balkan Sobranies. Irishmen with their hands out. He went away to phone.

London told him to travel east, keep travelling east, and phone in every hour. 'Every *hour*?' Satchel asked. 'Listen, in three hours I'll hit the bleeding sea.'

That was all right, they told him. They wanted him there. What they were working on now was a burial at sea.

The coast bothered Satchel when he arrived. It was flat, grey, with not a dent, not a prick out at sea. The only pricks were on the marshy foreshore, bird-watching pricks maybe, with khaki anoraks and cameras. Satchel drove on, but later he came across more of them, standing in a car park by the road. And the cars behind them all had Press labels. Press, Jesus, that was all he needed with a stiff in the boot.

Satchel drove quicker, putting a lot of miles between himself and the car park. Until, that was, he had the shock that made him swerve off the road. Shock? Series of shocks. Warplanes, huge and spiky, came at him low, about ten feet off the deck. Each one a clap of thunder that flattened the marsh-reeds. Satchel, his hand shaking, switched on the radio, expecting to hear war was declared. But then he remembered East Anglia, and all that low-level flying. They were on his side.

He started the car again and came to low flat hills. His map told him he was nearing journey's end, the head of an estuary that wound up from the sea. Ten minutes later he got there. It was a small village. Most of it was mud. And what wasn't mud was little round stones made up into houses, a hotel, a shop, and a yacht chandler's. Stones also made up a wall that went up on the low hill and disappeared over the horizon. Satchel looked at it. He reckoned it had taken a hundred men a hundred years to build that wall.

He parked. In the hotel he found they served six different kinds of malt. In the shop he found paperbacks without any tits on the covers, and Eucryl tooth-powder. And going back outside, he saw something else that exactly fitted into the landscape. Down on the quay a detachment of the green welly brigade arrived in their Volvo. They stood in a line in their bright green wellingtons. They stared palely down at the mud, told Fiona to stop throwing stones. Then they pissed orf.

And Satchel should have been warned, but he wasn't. He followed instructions and went out on the marshes, driving carefully on a pot-holed track. Then a mast rose ahead of him, just as he'd been told it would, a massive mast, followed by massive spars, and a massive curving deck. It was one of those Thames barges with the wooden flipper things on the sides. And sitting waiting near the gang-plank was the man he'd come here to meet, Darcy.

As soon as he heard Darcy speak, the warning came back. That warning that was ten per cent green welly brigade, ten per cent Eucryl tooth-powder, and eighty per cent stone wall going up over the hill. Because Darcy, he knew in a flash, was no more no less than D'arcy, bl'eeding de'ath with a capital D'. He was as massive as his boat. His sweater, torn and fluffed, went up to a torn and fluffed face. And beneath his taut angry skin was bile that had bubbled since the Middle Ages.

And why, Satchel asked himself, why in God's name had three phone calls to London got him involved with this? The old mob? The real Mafia? The *real* wild boys?

But he knew the answer when Darcy crooked a finger and led him below. It was simple. They were saving money in London. Darcy was poor. He sat like some flaking figurehead against the huge barge timbers, and around him was poverty. There was the paraffin smell from the beat-up Aladdin stoves. There was the damp of the frayed straw-matting. There was junk furniture, and an old portable record-player with the ringmarks of glasses.

Darcy poured himself a tumbler of Scotch and gave Satchel none. 'Ship's captain,' he said then in a voice like a spadeful of gravel, 'used to be able to marry people, outside territorial waters. And bury them, of course. Legally allowed to dispose of troublesome stiffs. Had high hopes of founding the East Anglian Burial Service once. Considerable undercutting.'

Satchel nodded, trying to kick away a long black dog that was nosing at his crutch.

'Nowadays, different story, of course, I mean . . . *marriage?*' A bark of laughter. 'Always tell people they can surrender to uncontrollable urges on my ship. But the burial part . . . ' He sucked in his breath. ' . . . Only for a *vast* consideration.'

Vast, don't make me laugh, Satchel thought. He fingered the tight roll of twenties in his pocket, the Geordie's pay-packet, the two grand folding which he'd never handed over. It wasn't going to be anything like that here. Casually, Satchel dropped five hundred quid into the talk.

They sparred. Darcy sucking in his breath all the time, and shaking his head. Satchel upped it by fifties. But when he reached seven-fifty, the man started pouring him Scotches.

The sparring went on. The black dog went out, and a woman came in. She was lean and stooping. She had red hair, the kind that shone almost white. And she moved like a ghost, keeping behind Darcy all the time. Suddenly he turned. He shouted at her as soon as he saw her, and went on shouting. Satchel watched her. It was her eyes that bothered him. They shivered, like those old servant-discs used to shiver, in those big old houses when buttons were pressed. Because she was a servant, or Darcy treated her like one. She brought mugs of tea when they had tea-and-Scotch. Gentleman's Relish when they had sandwiches-and-Scotch. Brought them and said nothing.

Satchel got tired of sparring. He thought a moment, then he went up to eight-fifty. His last offer, he said.

'Call it a thou,' Darcy said. 'Extras come into it. I mean, I could say a few words, get out the old union jack.'

'Not for this one.' Satchel nodded in the direction of the bankside, the Merc. 'This one's not British.'

'Oh?' Darcy's eyes were sharp. 'Not your Arab. Your Arab's trouble.'

'No. Black.'

'Blackie, eh?'

'Well, it wasn't really us that handled it,' Satchel said apologetically. 'More like a sub-contract.'

'Blackie,' Darcy repeated. 'Natural sense of rhythm, the Blackie. What about funeral music? What if I played some jazz on my clarinet?' He got up then and went past the record-player, showing a clarinet on a stand.

'No.' Satchel spread out his hands. 'No music. Eight-fifty it is, or I go elsewhere.'

'Eight-fifty.' Darcy glanced across to where the woman was standing. 'All right. Game's on.'

The woman spoke, for the first time. 'Game's on, is it?' she asked, a hopeless shrug to her shoulders. 'Loonies, Nil. The Rest Of The World, Nil.'

Satchel didn't understand her. He went to the porthole that looked out on the bankside. And suddenly he stiffened. The black dog was at the boot of the Merc, up on the bumper, sniffing.

'Listen.' He turned. 'Listen, we could have trouble. I mean, it's mild, isn't it? The papers keep on about what a mild winter we're having . . . And that stiff, it should have been in concrete hours ago.'

'Good thinking,' Darcy said. He turned to the woman. 'Get it in the freezer.'

She moved away. Satchel offered to help her, but Darcy said, no, she was your yeoman stock. And she was. Through the porthole they watched her get out the long polythene bundle wound round with insulating tape. She got it up on her shoulder, and, swaying, brought it in over the gangplank.

They followed her, dark ahead of them through the tunnel of the ship. At one point there was a tight corner. A length of the insulating tape came unstuck, and a hand poked out.

Darcy looked at it. 'Thought you said he was black.'

'Well, more coffee-coloured,' Satchel said. 'More Gold Blend.'

The woman made no sound, showed no effort on her face as she rested the body finally by a long chest-freezer.

'Granny-size,' Darcy said darkly, and opened the lid.

He made room, shifting a forequarter of beef and a loin of lamb. Then the woman flipped the body in. Its hand came to rest, scooping up frozen peas.

'Could do with a cutlet,' Darcy said, rummaging around. 'Couple of good lean cutlets and some broccoli tips. How about you?'

Satchell pushed the hand back inside the polythene, restuck the tape. 'Don't fancy it myself,' he said.

Half-an-hour later Darcy pushed his empty plate to one side. Lamb-fat glistened on his chin. 'You know, my mother, God rest her soul, always used to make a cock-up of the French language,' he said. 'Lived in France half her life, yet every time she went to a butcher's shop she asked for *culottes d'agneau*. Lamb's knickers.'

'That so?' Satchel stared at him.

'Fact. Though maybe she knew about it. Certain amount of cunning in our family.' Darcy waved a fork in the air. 'Take her Georgian silver. At the end of her life she had no room for it. She knew we wanted it. She knew she didn't want us to have it. So she solved the whole problem with a stroke of genius. Sent the stuff over from France in the train. Two packing-cases, and she labelled them both Georgian silver.'

Satchel frowned. It wasn't the sort of story he liked to hear, it went against everything he stood for. Then his frown deepened. Suddenly he caught sight of his watch. Four o'clock, Jesus, how many Scotches to the bad was he?

He leaned forward. 'Listen,' he said, 'a couple of hours ago I gave you four hundred and twenty-five quid. The other half to come when you finish. Which I thought was going to be this evening.'

Darcy shook his head. 'Not a chance.'

'*Not?*'

'Tide's all wrong.'

'That right? When's High Tide then?'

'Oh nine thirty-four.'

And it was too quick. He was lying. Satchel looked across at the Scotch bottle, now nearing the end of its natural life.

'You're telling me it's tomorrow then?'

'Tomorrow as ever is.'

Satchel stood up, needing fresh air. 'Where do I go to get a slash?' he asked.

'Out there. First on the right.'

Starting away, Satchel suddenly heard a crash behind him. He turned. Darcy's food-plate lay smashed on the floor. The man had got up too quickly, was coming at Satchel now, reaching out for his pockets. 'Haven't got any Andrex, have you?'

'*What?*'

'Andrex. That tissue stuff. Jams up a ship's loo.' Darcy patted his pockets in turn. 'Surprising the number of people who try to smuggle Andrex in here.'

Satchel went off. He should have been warned, he told himself, should have been bleeding warned.

When he got back, the woman was there, picking up pieces of plate. Darcy had the record-player on, traditional jazz, and was playing along on his clarinet. And it wasn't that he was out of tune, wasn't even that it was all rasping breath and squeaks. It was that he was lurching around, his ears and neck red, and every time he lurched the record missed a groove.

He stopped, and swung round on the woman. 'Keep bloody still,' he shouted.

The woman froze where she was, hand halfway towards a piece of china. Darcy played on, lurched on. The record missed another groove.

Suddenly he went over and clouted her.

She didn't look up at him. 'Loonies, One. The Rest Of The World, Nil,' she said quietly.

He clouted her again.

'Loonies, Two. The Rest Of The World, Nil,' she said.

His arm went back once more.

Satchel looked at him. He looked on at the empty Scotch bottle. Jesus, he thought, the *energy* of the man. Then he left.

It was getting dark outside, and he was surprised by that. Even more surprised, as he drove back to the hotel in the village, to hear the sounds of drinking, the bar going in and out.

Satchel thought about it. There was only one kind of people could get a drink after hours, he knew. Only one kind of people could raise a large Scotch in a Temperance House in Llanelli. And then he saw them, the Press cars, parked by the hotel. The cars he'd seen earlier out on the marshes, just before the warplanes had come.

Going into the bar, it suddenly all came together. Because the word was, the shouted word, that it was Nato manoeuvres. The word was, that in the next war the West would last two days. That on the third day the only paper to file with would be *Pravda*.

And the word was, there were more manoeuvres tomorrow. Combined manoeuvres, at sea.

The barge-deck throbbed to the sound of the wheezy engine. Darcy spun the wheel and glowered out at the morning. He had his sailor hat on, the black dog was crouching beside him. It was his act, hungover, but still his act.

''Preciate your concern, m'dear feller, really do,' he said, unrolling a long tube of cardboard. 'But, see here. We go out in a straight line to the Territorial Limit thingy. And your war-johnnies fart around here. Always do. To the right. The right as you look at the map.'

Satchel had some idea it should be 'starboard', and 'chart', but he said nothing. They got out of the river without hitting anything. The marsh-reeds fell back behind them, and they wheezed out on a wide silver sea. Darcy got the woman to bring a bottle up on deck. He stoked up on his hangover, overtook it, then got attacks of Charles Laughton and Robert Newton, alternately.

They lasted until he looked at his watch, checked the chart, and cut the engine. The barge slowed up, and fell to slapping and rattling. Darcy moved into the centre of the deck. He looked at the woman and at Satchel. 'There,' he swung an arm round the empty horizon, 'miles and miles of bugger-all.'

Which was when the black tower, the size of four double-decker buses, followed by the black hull the length of two Inter-Cities, suddenly surfaced, close to their right.

'*Piss orf!*' Darcy shouted at the nuclear sub.

A huge metal voice came across from the black shape. 'You are in violation of restricted war-zone number six-four-three-stroke . . . '

Men appeared on the deck of the sub, ratings, with rifles.

'Loonies, Three. The Rest Of The World, Five,' the woman said to Darcy.

He swung round and got a large fat-barrelled pistol from a locker. Satchel went for him, but he wasn't at his best, not with the barrel of that pistol by his cheek. He ducked as it went off. A Verey light fizzed up into the air, stuck in the ratlines above, and rained red fire down on them. The dog howled.

Then there was a new sound. A metal launch had come from the sub. It bumped against the barge, and an officer and two ratings held it there. One rating came up over the side. He took the Verey pistol away from Darcy kindly, then hit him kindly, twice, on the face.

Darcy sat down.

The rating moved on to the woman. His voice was conversational. ''kin-ell,' he said ''kin-Icelandic, is he?'

The woman started to laugh. A slow, strange sound.

The rating came on. 'Not 'kin-Icelandic?' he asked Satchel.

'No. Not that.'

''kin-ecological then? 'kin-Greenpeace?'

'That's it,' Satchel said. 'Greenpeace.'

The rating offered him a Navy-issue fag. ''kin-save the whale,' he said. ''kin-know what you mean. 'kin-Jane Fonda, she's all tied up with your mob, isn't she?'

He lit Satchel's fag and went away to the bows of the barge. He took a line from the Navy launch and made it fast. Then they were towed, the sub keeping station behind them.

It went on for quite some time. Until there was the sound of a siren, and the tow-line slackened. The rating stubbed out his fag. ''kin-shame about Jane Fonda,' he said. 'Always reckoned she had such a good 'kin-body on her.'

He went back to the bows, untied the line, waved at Satchel, and disappeared over the side. The launch disappeared. The sub disappeared. The sea was suddenly flat and grey again, as if nothing had happened.

Darcy, two angry bruises on his face, crawled across the deck to the Scotch bottle.

Satchel kicked it away. 'No,' he said. 'No bleeding more of that. What we do now is wait ten minutes, then we get this stiff out of the freezer and chuck it over . . .'

Three strikes of combat-planes crashed over at mast-height. Satchel threw himself flat. The planes swung in towards the land. White smoke trails ziggered away from them. They did real damage to two hundred square yards of sand, then they swung away and disappeared.

Satchel picked himself up. But suddenly there was another sound, a drone, from out at sea. He turned. The horizon was full of square blocks, black square blocks, with huge bow-waves.

'Start the engine,' he shouted at Darcy. 'Will you just start that bleeding thing?'

But Darcy had got hold of the Scotch bottle again. He was drinking hard. And huffy.

'No,' he said.

'*No?*'

'Put it like this,' the man drank two fingers, then another two fingers, 'can *you* start it?'

Satchel turned towards the engine-hatch, the rusty pipes that were inside it, held together with wire.

''xactly,' Darcy said. He capped the Scotch bottle, hugged it to him. Then he turned. 'Things to settle here.'

He was looking at the woman. And she was crouching on the deck, frightened.

The drone from the sea was now a roar. The black boxes, maybe fifty of them in a line, swept past. Landing-craft, with rows of steel helmets inside them.

Darcy stood huge and mottled in the centre of the deck. 'She *laughed* when that war-johnny called me Icelandic,' he said.

'Oh, come on,' Satchel said. 'I mean. Jesus . . .'

But Darcy went to the woman, stood over her. 'I may have picked you up in some North London ghetto,' he shouted. 'But I've told you, I will not, repeat *not* put up with your Tulse Hill tendencies.'

He swung his arm back, clouted her. 'Loonies, *Four*. The Rest Of The World, Nine,' he screamed. 'Loonies, *Five*. The Rest Of The World, Five . . . '

Satchel turned away. He saw the landing-craft hit the beach. He saw the assault troops leap out into the surf. They did tricky things with hooks and nylon lines. They swarmed up the sand-cliff and captured the bus shelter at the top. Then they sat down.

' . . . Loonies, *Fourteen*. The Rest Of The World, Five. Loonies, *Fifteen* . . . '

Satchel went over and stopped it. The woman was clutching her left arm, it had bad bruises on it. Turning, Satchel found a bit of old canvas on a hatch-cover. He made her a sling, and she seemed more comfortable. But it wasn't her arm that bothered him, it was her eyes. There wasn't that flicker of yesterday, that nervousness. They just stared at Darcy with a slow burning hate.

Satchel walked towards him. 'Satisfied?' he asked.

Darcy shrugged.

'So what do we do now?'

'Now,' Darcy said. 'Now I have luncheon.'

'You're joking.'

'Twelve noon.' The man looked at his watch. 'I have a rump steak, I have mushrooms, and . . . ' he raised his voice for the woman's benefit, ' . . . and I have chips.'

'Chips?' she shouted back at him. 'I can't peel potatoes with one hand.'

'Course you can!' he bellowed. '*Course* you can peel potatoes with one bloody hand!'

She went below. More boats came up . . . but by now Satchel was expecting them, the Press boats, with their cameras at the ready. Darcy posed. And Satchel, crouching out of sight, let him. Jesus, he thought, in another second it'd be David bleeding Dimbleby. In another second it'd be Darcy leaning over the side, shouting, 'War-johnny called me Icelandic. Do I *look* Icelandic? And would you like to see the blackie in the freezer?'

The Press boats went away. Darcy drank Scotch, and gradually mellowed. 'Sorry about that little thingy with the good lady just now,' he said. 'Landlubbers don't know about these things. Different camps set up aboard ship, you see, always two different camps. Something to do with being out at sea. Strain, you know, the loneliness.' He pointed to the maybe two thousand people on the beach.

The rump steak, the mushrooms, and the chips arrived. Darcy ate them cross-legged on the hatch. He drank a little Scotch, played a little clarinet, drank a little more Scotch. Finally he sighed, and went over and started the rusty engine. 'Another day, another dollar,' he said.

And he earned his dollar. Two hours later, with a tiny *plop*, the polythene-wrapped bundle, chained to a forty-pound ballast weight, sank beneath the sea. Satchel paid over the second instalment of £425, and Darcy spun the wheel, heading for home.

There was mist, twilight over the marshes as they drew level with Satchel's parked Merc. Darcy got the woman to jump on to the bank with a line. She jumped, but then dropped the line, ran off among the reeds, and disappeared. The tide caught the long hull of the barge. It swung out across the estuary. The engine coughed and died.

Satchel expected Darcy to start shouting again. But he didn't. It was the last straw. 'M'dear feller,' he took Satchel's arm, 'don't ever, *ever* go to Tulse Hill.'

Darkness was on them by the time they'd unshipped the dinghy, by the time Darcy had rowed a line across to the mooring-post and back and started the winch. They edged in. Then Satchel looked up.

And saw the two flat-hats getting out of the police car on the bank.

'Nothing to worry about,' Darcy said. 'Dog licence, or some such lunacy. Always these damn creditors turning up. Usually I move on, and they just find these two holes in the bank. I change the ship's name, of course. Make a couple of subtle changes to the superstruct . . . '

But Satchel wasn't listening. Jesus, he thought, it'd better be those war-johnnies, sending someone round to complain.

But it wasn't. The flat-hats led the way below, to the freezer.

'Information laid, Sir,' the tall one said. 'Woman's voice.'

Satchel edged towards the door.

The flat-hat opened the freezer, removed a few plastic bags. And there, where the forequarter of beef should have been, was a dark hand, clutching frozen peas.

Satchel edged further away.

'Arabic gentleman, sir,' the flat-hat said.

'*Blast!*' from Darcy.

'Seems to be some signs of mutilation, sir,' the flat-hat said. 'This slice, cut out of the rump.'

Satchel's mouth dropped open.

'And some sort of note, sir. What's it say? "Loonies, Fifteen? The Rest Of The World, Ninety-Three?"'

Satchel ran.

THE LAST PLACE ON EARTH

by James McClure

The building breathed you in. You were wheeled down a ramp by the ambulance men, passing rockeries and lily ponds, and then across a patio of crazy-paving the colour of cornflakes. You peered over your toes, which gave twin peaks to the grey blanket covering you, and saw the huge glass doors marked clearly *IN*. The other set of doors did not have *OUT* on them.

You approached the *IN* doors. They remained closed. Then, with a loud and sudden sound, like a swimmer's gasp for air, they opened inwards, leaving you no time to think before the sky overhead vanished. You saw a pine ceiling, had a glimpse of a tropical fish tank, and the doors wheezed slowly shut again, clenching their jaws.

The visitor arrived at the wrong moment. His aunt had just had a suppository inserted. So he went through to the lounge of the hospice and sat down in front of the television set. The early evening news was on.

'Forty-three people are believed to have died today,' said the newscaster, as a film clip began, 'when a gas leak caused an explosion in this block of flats in South London.'

The dying, seated on either side of the visitor, shook their heads and tut-tutted and one said, 'Now, isn't that terrible? What is the world coming to?'

They had forgotten.

But one old man sat with his back to the television set, and toyed with his lighter, cigarette packet and a thick glass ashtray, while his urine dripped steadily down a tube into the clear plastic bag at his side. This old man looked angry and more interesting than the others.

So the visitor rose, wandered into the adjoining chapel, where magazines and paperbacks were kept beside the hymnals, and chose himself something that would serve as an excuse for changing seats. It was a May 1976 copy of *Country Life*.

'Evening,' said the visitor, as he sat down opposite the old man's wheelchair. 'You don't mind?'

The old man seemed to ignore him.

The visitor dipped the magazine each time he turned a page, sneaking quick glances across the low coffee table. He noted a middling mottled brow, dense brown hair protruding from each ear like mattress stuffing, full lips that were pale and striated, with gleams of scarlet in the cracks. He studied the weathered hands and their chipped fingernails, the ragged scar across the back of the right wrist such as barbed wire might make. He wondered where, in that heavy-limbed body, a dread thing was growing.

If one wanted to picture cancer cells, his aunt's doctor had said, then simply imagine a handful of thistle seeds tossed into a bed of poppies, and these thistles thrusting upwards, flourishing.

'What I mind,' said the old man, 'was not stopping.'

The visitor glanced up. 'Not stopping?' he said. 'Smoking, you mean?'

'Not stopping at home, more like!'

'You don't like it here?'

'Bah!'

'Oh, I don't know. When you compare it with—'

'I should've stopped outside and taken one more look.'

The visitor put down the magazine and leaned forward. 'I'm sorry,' he said, 'not quite with you.'

'The universe,' snapped the old man, pointing to the top of the coffee table. 'Right? And here, what they calls the solar system. Big ashtray's the sun, ciggie packet is this bleedin' planet, and that's me, a cheeky little blighter of a lighter, comin' in between! That's how we were, three score and more, with me shadow on the ground to prove it.'

The visitor nodded.

'Got bugger-all shadow now,' said the old man.

There was a soft bubbling from the tank of tropical fish over on the left. The visitor glanced that way, and then round the room. It was large and warm and very unhospitalish. The walls and ceiling were lined with pine in the Swedish manner, and the furnishings suggested the lounge of a comfortable if modest hotel. In one corner, there was a small alcove where hot and cold drinks were always available; in another, was the television set with its huge screen, and, to the right of it, hung a neat rack holding brochures that gave some idea of local scenic attractions, concerts, plays and exhibitions. Some stuffed toys, made under the guidance of the hospice's occupational therapist, lolled glassy-eyed on a wide shelf, sharing it with two boxes of Monopoly. Crocheted cushions abounded, so did big-leaved pot plants. The lighting was low, shadowless, and its sources invisible.

'Comfy enough,' said the old man, shrugging as he gave his own glance around. 'But still a bit of a disappointment – y'know, when it comes home to yer, this is the last place on earth.'

Then a grey-haired woman, wearing a chequered smock over drab street clothes, came up to the visitor and said, 'So sorry you wait, but your aunt she is ready for you now.'

The visitor's aunt waved a greeting at his reflection in the window as he entered the room behind her back. She had to lie on her right side most of the time, what with the oozing on her left.

'My sweet,' she said. 'Goodness, are those for me?'

He held out the bouquet in its flower-shop wrapping and wondered why her eyes darted aside before taking a second look.

'Oh, *carnations*,' she said. 'How lovely! So very, very red . . . '

'They come with Chloe's love, too, Aunt Judith.'

'See you give her mine, Richard, and tell her how pleased I am with them. Be a dear, won't you, and see if you can find that volunteer lady to have them popped in a vase right away.'

'The foreign one in the smock?'

His aunt nodded. 'Not *so* foreign,' she chided, knowing her nephew's prejudices of old. 'Mrs Daventry has been in England since only a few years after the war. Hasn't she the most marvellous, deep brown eyes?'

'She looks—' he began, then stopped himself.

You lay there and wanted to cry out, but the crab had you by the throat.

A new terror seemed impossible, after all you had gone through since the initial, mumbled diagnosis. That moment when a very young doctor, her lower lip trembling prettily, had pushed an X-ray plate into your hands and asked you, as a man of science, to take a look at it. One glance had been enough, and ahead of time your voice had failed. Not even a croak.

Yet there was indeed this new terror, far more terrible than any before, and what was worse, you didn't know the reason for it.

Or even what you had seen to make you so fearful.

'This is my nephew, Richard,' said the visitor's aunt, when Sister Braithwaite came in, as quietly as a nun. 'He brought me the carnations.'

'Gorgeous,' said Sister Braithwaite, sniffing them.

The visitor had to suppress a laugh. There was only one smell in that room, nothing else could compete with it, and nobody could possibly mistake it for the scent of carnations.

'And how is Mr Joliffe today?' said his aunt. 'I do miss our little chats together.'

Sister Braithwaite looked her very straight in the eye.

'Oh, dear, has he?' said his aunt. 'Then is there someone new in his room?'

'Yes, a professor.'

'Oh, really? Not from Oxford, by any chance? My late husband—'

'Leicester University, I believe,' said Sister Braithwaite, retreating to the doorway. 'Well, it's almost time for the drugs round.'

The visitor took this as his cue to look at his wristwatch. 'Half seven already! Chloe will—'

'Off you go, my sweet,' said his aunt. 'We've had a lovely natter, but I must confess I'm feeling a little tired now.' And she looked at him most accusingly.

'Mrs Daventry has told the voluntary help organiser that she wants to resign,' Staff Nurse Pam Clement remarked to Sister Braithwaite in the day wing, to which they had retreated for a quick cigarette apiece. 'I overheard her ringing her at home only about five minutes ago.'

'That's a bit out of the blue!' said Sister Braithwaite, undoing her silver belt buckle. 'Seemed as happy as a lark at tea time – and of all the volunteers, she's the only one I'd really miss around here.'

Staff Nurse Clement nodded. 'Not a trace of bloody do-gooder in her.'

'Empathy. I know sweet FA about Mrs Daventry, but one thing sticks out a mile: that woman's seen a *lot* of suffering in her time.'

'Making it stranger she should want to chuck it all of a sudden.'

'But don't we all? I'm forever writing out my resignation!'

The two women laughed, and shared the match flame.

'I'll try and have a word with her,' Sister Braithwaite said. 'Perhaps she could do with the support of our stress group. I don't see why it should be restricted to trained staff.'

'God,' sighed Staff Nurse Clement, running a hand over her freckled face. 'I can guess what the talk's going to be about at the next one.'

'Paraplegic, carcinoma larynx, spinal secondaries, no next of kin, eyes that bore holes in you, terrified out of his wits . . .?'

'Uhuh, Prof Thingy.'

'But it shouldn't be for long. Have you seen the whopping morphine dosage he's on?'

You swallowed your morphine and dreamed great swirling, chaotic dreams with moments of shrill clarity.

Faces.

Thousands of faces, each with an open mouth.

If there were screams, you did not hear them.

One face keeps returning, spinning by, smiling.

Then a huge empty beach and a great stillness, except down at the sea's edge, where a crab has its claws deep in the neck of a thrashing eagle.

That one face.

You awake, and it's looking at you.

But not quite.

The next night, the visitor called at eight to see his aunt again, but first detoured into the lounge. 'And how did today go?' he asked the old man in the wheelchair.

'Boring,' said the old man. 'No flowers?'

'Chocolates. "Boring" in what way?'

'Dead boring,' said the old man, and cackled at the visitor's expression. 'You remind us,' he added, 'of that smarmy doctor what comes round, sort of rubbing his hands like he was soapin' 'em, and says to me, "Well, William and how are we today?" So I says, "I'm dyin' to get out of here, doc!" You should've seen the face on *him* by the time I was finished.'

The visitor laughed. 'You're a character,' he said.

'No, I'm not, I'm a dying man, son. And different to you, I know what I'm going to die of, no scope for the old imagination.'

'And that's what bores you?'

'Aye, a bit.' The old man nodded at the group around the television set. 'With most of them, it's quite a relief, really, this knowin'. Frightens yer, gets yer dander up, can ruin yer religion if you're that way inclined, but it's still a weight off your mind – y'know, being certain it won't be no car crash, all trapped screamin' in the wreckage, or Flight Bing-bong to sunny Spain goin' smack into a mountain. Personally, I'd high hopes of another kind.'

The visitor noticed a flare of yesterday's anger return, twisting the striated lips slightly. 'And what were these hopes?' he asked.

'Same as yours, son! Goin' hammer and tongs till the old ticker can't take any more, but the lass with her legs around yer keeps cheerin' you on!'

Beginning to colour, the visitor gave a crooked smile. 'For a moment there, I thought you could read minds,' he said.

'Not just the chocolates.'

'Sorry . . . ?'

'You've also,' said the old man, with a gleam in his rheumy eye, 'brung along a bit o' paper for the old lady to sign . . . '

The visitor stared at him, turned about and walked away, his cheeks burning.

'I spoke to Mrs Daventry this morning,' said the voluntary help organiser, telephoning from home, 'and I think she must just have become over-tired the other day. She tells me she's carrying on as a volunteer as per usual.'

'Are you sure that's all it was?' said Sister Braithwaite, watching Mrs Daventry pass her desk in the corridor.

'I can't imagine any other reason, Sister.'

'Fine. And by the way, one of your volunteer drivers left a day patient stranded here this afternoon.'

'*Not* that wretched vicar's wife again! Was the patient Mr Gibb?'

You knew what the new terror was. For weeks, you had been preparing to die a particular natural death, and as *unnatural* as that had seemed, it was at least something a man could adjust to. Nobody had a right to so many years, only to live out his allotted span, and this was what, with the help of the hospice, you had expected to do. Yet now you knew you couldn't count on even that any longer.

Your dreams told you so.

'Professor,' a nurse was saying, leaning over so you could look up at her. 'See? I've brought your morphine.'

You shut your mouth tightly.

'You're being very silly, you know! We have got to control the pain. You don't want more pain, do you?'

You nodded.

'You *don't* want your morphine?'

You nodded again.

The ward sister came and gave you your morphine, not by mouth but with an injection. She threw the syringe away. The pain subsided and the dreams began. There was no way of stopping them.

★　　　★　　　★

'What has the house to do with my being in here?' demanded Aunt Judith.

The visitor hastily changed the subject: 'Oh, by the way, how is your new neighbour getting on?'

'The professor?' she said, brightening.

'That's right. Has he been across to see you, like Mr Joliffe?'

'Heavens, no. Quite immobile, Madge tells me, and unable to speak as part of his condition. What's fascinating is, he's apparently spent his life in medical research trying to find a cure for you-know-what.'

The visitor felt strongly that his aunt should face up to the word. 'You mean cancer?'

She helped herself to another chocolate.

'Yes, ironic,' said the visitor. 'Must make things a lot worse, too, if you're a medic and know all the options, symptoms, et cetera, what can be done for you and what can't. I know I'd be happier being left in the dark.'

'I won't be left in the dark,' said his aunt, with a sudden show of strong feeling. 'I was very cross last night when that little nurse tried to put the lights off before I—'

'Hello, my duck!' said a broad, homely woman, wheeling in the drinks trolley. 'Cocoa, two sugars, in a beaker? Or is it your night for a drop of something a bit stronger?' And she winked like a barmaid.

'Madge, you really are naughty!' said Aunt Judith, delighted. 'Whatever will my nephew think I get up to in here?'

Something wasn't right. Sister Braithwaite had experienced this sense of unease once before as a young VSO nurse in a mission hospital in Africa, and the next morning a one-eyed orderly and two orphans were reported missing – he'd stolen the babes to sell for witchdoctor's medicine, the black auxiliaries had said.

'A penny for them, Sue,' whispered Staff Nurse Clement, pausing at the desk in the corridor.

'Sorry?' said Sister Braithwaite, brusquely.

'Be like that . . . ' said Staff Nurse Clement with a shrug, walking off.

Annoyed with herself for her rudeness and for giving way to a ridiculous mood she couldn't define, Sister Braithwaite rose and moved with a brisk step, hoping to make amends by seeing to one of the external tumours herself. Pam Clement had admitted in the stress group to finding them particularly distressing.

An unexpected smell coming from the staff changing room made her pause and look in. Staff Nurse Wong was dabbing at a mark on her overcoat with cotton wool soaked in a dry-cleaning fluid.

'Ah, so that's it!' said Sister Braithwaite.

'Sister? My bike chain came off and I ended up with grease everywhere. I noticed this bottle of—'

'Have you managed to fix the bike? If not, ring Security and Max—'

'It's fine now, thank you, Sister.'

81

Sister Braithwaite remained in the doorway, wishing she could avoid the stereotype but seeing Theresa Wong as inscrutable. That lovely, heart-shaped face, with its neat-as-a-button nose and cherry-pink mouth, never gave one any idea of what was going on in her head. And she politely declined every invitation to join the stress group.

'I noticed when I came on tonight,' said Sister Braithwaite, 'that your Kardexes on the professor were – well, a bit skimpy. Those notes are there to help us pick up the threads, Staff.'

'So sorry, Sister.'

'Why were they like that? Do you have difficulty with that patient?'

'He's—'

'Yes? Go on, dear . . .'

'He is unusual, Sister,' said Staff Nurse Wong, very evenly and inscrutably.

Again, Sister Braithwaite was aware of her sense of unease.

You dreamed of wards and of operating theatres, of great pain and suffering.

You felt nothing.

The crab, in the head-dress of eagle feathers, sat on its rock.

The visitor made for the exit, thinking how like a spaceship the inside of the hospice could appear at times. It had the same sort of passages in the ward area, the hum of hidden machinery, a small kitchen like a galley, tiny storerooms with everything from bed sheets to ginger ale, neatly stowed, and outside its windows, all eternity.

He glanced into a room and saw the old man there, moving his hand back and forth in front of the bulb in his reading light. The old man looked round.

'Er, popped by to say good night,' said the visitor.

'Thought you was Mrs Daventry.'

'Yes, the volunteer lady.'

'Smasher, she is,' said the old man. 'Funny habits, mind.'

The visitor stepped into the room. 'Such as?' he said, intrigued.

'Writes phone numbers on herself.'

Disappointed, the visitor said with a grudging laugh, 'But I do that sometimes!' And he mimed a quick scribble on the back of his left hand.

'That's never where she puts it,' said the old man. 'Good night.'

'The remarkable thing, Sister,' said Dr Murphy-Jones, the consultant, the next evening, 'is that the professor seems to have rallied, to be fighting tooth and nail to stay alive.'

She sighed. 'It often amazes me, the will to live.'

'Yet, when I saw him on admission, he appeared totally resigned. Has he had a visitor, someone who has—'

'No visitors, not one. The professor hasn't any kith and kin either, as you know.'

'And he hasn't been making any use of his pad to write on?'

'Hasn't touched it. We literally haven't had a word out of him.'

'Odd, very odd. And a bit of an embarrassment, between ourselves. I thought we'd have that bed free by the weekend.'

'His quality of life isn't . . . '

'Quite. Perhaps we could increase the dosage a fraction.'

You were so cold. Drenched in your sweat and shivering. As cold as a naked man left out in the snow on a stretcher.

You remembered the letter. 'I am very curious about the experiments with animal heat. Personally I believe these experiments may bring the best and most sustained results.'

You remembered the letter because you could feel the heat.

Seeping into you.

The visitor brought his wife, Chloe, his other aunt, and a distant cousin. They had been told by the hospice that a sudden relapse had occurred.

Sister Braithwaite, the one who moved like a nun and had peppermint on her breath, met them outside the lounge. 'It could be tonight,' she said. 'If anyone would like a bed, we do have a guest room – and more beds can be put up in the chapel.'

They nodded their thanks.

'Then if you'll come along with me,' said Sister Braithwaite.

The old man was watching them from in front of the tropical fish tank. He raised his scarred hand in greeting, and the visitor smiled. God knows why, but it was good to see him.

As the visitor reached his aunt's room, he glanced across into the room almost opposite it. A gaunt, bone-coloured man was shivering in his sleep and making movements that were shocking.

'It's going to be one of those nights, Pam,' said Sister Braithwaite, too much canteen food distending her again, making her silver buckle bite.

Staff Nurse Clement snorted. 'Christ, don't tell me! Mrs Grosvenor, the new admission, lung, has started deliriums.'

'I'd better get Dr Murphy-Jones down.'

'He'll have to be here sooner or later, so you might as well.'

'I've not had a moment since coming on to go through the Kardex properly – any special problems?'

'No, not really,' replied Staff Nurse Clement. 'That dozy OT has gone and upset old William. Thought Tess Wong's notes on the professor were a bit weird.'

'Yes, I talked to her about that last night.'

'Oh?'

'They were skimped.'

'No, *weird* weird, Sue.'

'In what way?'

'I've never – well, I don't know what to think.'

*   *   *

Aunt Judith, although greatly weakened, had adopted an imperious manner. With a limp wave of her hand, she dismissed the attention being paid her by close members of her family and demanded that Madge fetch Mrs Daventry.

'I've got a feeling she's probably off home by now, my duck,' said Madge. 'But I'll go and look in the changing room, see if we can catch her.'

Mrs Daventry came in, dressed in her street clothes and carrying her handbag. She nodded pleasantly, then went and took Aunt Judith's hand. Nothing was said, but the face of the dying woman became tranquil and she smiled. The visitor found Mrs Daventry a chair.

Then he studied her, covertly. The woman was probably in her mid-fifties, slightly-built, a little bowed in the legs like someone once poorly nourished, and had raven black hair that set off her pale, high-cheeked face. Her brown eyes, it was true, were remarkable; large and luminous, as deep as wells. Wells filled with tears, he added as an afterthought, before scorning such mawkish sentiment.

But he couldn't see where she wrote telephone numbers on herself, no matter how hard he looked.

Sister Braithwaite sat at her desk in the corridor and stared at the notes made on the professor by Staff Nurse Wong.

The notes were indeed far more comprehensive than those of the previous day. They gave a very good idea of how the professor had spent the last eight hours, both as a person and as an organism under attack. They said, in short that he'd displayed signs of great agitation, but was physically no worse.

What Pam Clement had called the 'weird' part had been placed in brackets at the end:

(Observation: On looking in on the patient at 4.20 p.m., I found him asleep on his right side, facing the door, and shivering. I felt his arm but it was not cold. I still took his temperature but it was normal. I noticed an indentation in his bed on the far side. The coverlet had been crushed and creased from the level of his shoulders to his feet. I smoothed out his coverlet and left.)

You were freezing.

You had been taken from the water with a rectal temperature of 86 degrees Fahrenheit.

You were on a wide bed.

Between two naked women.

And the crab was writing in the sand.

It wrote: 'Once the test persons regained consciousness, they never lost it again, quickly grasping their situation and nestling close to the naked bodies of the women. The rise of body temperature then proceeded at approximately the same speed as with test persons swathed in blankets.'

You read and approved what had been written, but pointed out certain exceptions to the rule.

'An exception,' scrawled the crab with its pincer, 'was formed by four test persons who practised sexual intercourse between eighty-six and eighty-nine point five degrees. In these persons, after coitus, a very swift temperature rise ensued, comparable to that achieved by means of a hot-water bath.'

Ja, ja, you agreed, yet there was another exception more extraordinary than that, Dr Rascher – whereupon, a thousand fighter pilots, downed in the icy North Sea in special suits designed by you, applauded.

'Chloe, this is the old gentleman I've told you about,' said the visitor. 'Mr William – er, I'm sorry, I'm not sure I know your last name.'

'Atkins, son – same as Tommy, and no better off than 'e was at the Somme!'

'Pleased to meet you, Mr Atkins,' said the visitor's wife, pale behind the cosmetics on a plain, hard face. 'May I sit down?'

'Fancy plonking yourself in me lap, luv?'

But she declined with an awkward laugh, taking the seat opposite his wheelchair. 'I had to get out of there for a while,' she said, fanning herself with a copy of *Woman's Own.* 'It's so . . . well, depressing.'

'I see the others what come with you have hopped it already,' said the old man. 'Wasn't it that what the taxi came for?'

The visitor nodded. 'Even worse for them, the same generation,' he explained. 'Can I get you both a drink of some sort from the corner? Coffee, perhaps? Tea?'

'No, I'll see to that, Richard,' said Chloe. 'You'd better get back to poor Aunt Judith.'

'Mrs Daventry's with her, so I don't see—'

'Off you go, Richard,' she said softly in that special tone of hers.

He went. His aunt was alone.

'Mrs Daventry has gone to tell Sister I've asked her to spend the night,' said Aunt Judith. 'She's a widow, you see, so it won't make any difference.'

Close to wakening, your dreams changed.

You were in a snow-filled ditch with a dead horse and greasy black smoke was rising in the sky behind the barbed wire. It was the first time you had ever felt such cold. You were freezing.

Then fleeing.

Killing.

You had another man's clothes, another man's name.

Soon, if you were careful, only you would know the difference.

And you were careful, you were welcomed in, given another man's life to begin. Leicester University. Unbelievable.

Yet always fleeing.

Never far enough.

On second thoughts, Sister Braithwaite decided to ask Mrs Daventry if she really had the strength to make a night of it, having already spent much of the day in the hospice.

So she left her desk and hurried after her, seeing Mrs Daventry stop outside the professor's room, hesitate, and then go in. When she reached the room itself, Mrs Daventry was standing at the foot of the bed, rubbing her arm, and the professor was gazing at her, his eyes huge in their sunken sockets.

'So we're awake again?' said Sister Braithwaite, walking in. 'I suppose you've met Mrs Daventry before?'

To her surprise, he shook his head violently.

'Yes, wide awake,' said Mrs Daventry. 'It is what I noticed.'

'You've more than enough on your plate across the way,' said Sister Braithwaite. 'Are you sure that family isn't imposing on you too much? I'd pack anybody else off home, you know that!'

'No, I have the strength, Sister. If you will excuse me . . . '

Sister Braithwaite remarked to the patient when they were alone, 'She's a saint that woman – I never thought I'd live to say that of anyone.'

The professor turned his head away and stared out of his window at the night, so dark and empty out there.

'I'll close your curtains,' said Sister Braithwaite.

The visitor glanced up and was shaken to see the expression on his wife's face. 'Good God, Chloe,' he whispered, 'whatever's happened—?'

'Richard, take me home this instant.'

'But Aunt Ju—'

'Damn and blast Aunt Judith!' she hissed, her face very white. 'Get – me – out – of – here.'

So he scrambled to his feet in a fluster, to be calmed by Mrs Daventry laying a hand on his arm.

'You can return later,' Mrs Daventry said, 'or maybe not, as circumstances they are permitting. Your aunt will altogether be safe in my keeping.'

'Thank you,' he said, 'thank you very much.' And wanted to hug her, his emotions were in such a turmoil.

Chloe dug her long nails into his hand as he led her away up the short passage, to the right and then to the left, heading towards the lounge and the exit.

'No!' said Chloe, stopping. 'I won't go *near* there, not near that horrible old man again!'

'But I don't know another way out, so be sensible! And what do you mean by—'

'Richard!'

He turned and hurried her in the opposite direction, still very confused. Then, passing two empty wheelchairs beside some other equipment, a sudden insight made him laugh. A cruel laugh, but what the hell, Chloe's cold blood had been a bitter disappointment to him.

*   *   *

You were awake and the crab had you by the throat and still the dreaming went on. But it wasn't dreaming, it was remembering.

That final, fascinating exception being, Dr Rascher, as you yourself wrote and I endorsed, one woman was able to warm a frozen man faster than two women. Your report read: 'I attribute this to the fact that in warming by means of one woman personal inhibitions are avoided and the woman clings more closely to the chilled person. Here, too, return of full consciousness was notably rapid.'

'There,' said the ward sister, 'all nice and clean again, and time for your medicine, professor.'

You shook your head.

The prick of a needle.

Bzzzzzzzt – bzzzzzzzt – bzzzzzzzt . . .

Once a patient pressed that button, that heavy droning device buzzed and buzzed until someone had hurried in to switch if off and enquire what the matter was. Sometimes the matter was all too self-evident.

Sister Braithwaite, hastening in one direction, heard the sound stop and then begin again. This meant a second patient needed attention, so she spun on her heel and set off to see who this could be. She passed a doorway and saw Mrs Daventry sitting quietly, holding the old woman's hand.

No more than a quick glimpse, it left an odd impression: Mrs Daventry's face had seemed set very hard and those luminous eyes were as cold as ice. Some trick of the lighting.

The crab had made a quill of one of the eagle feathers. It started pricking out numbers. Blue numbers. Sets of numbers.

Then scurried across the beach, digging and scattering the pebbles to expose experimental bone grafts and gas gangrene wounds, all fascinating. In the rock pools, poison bullets grew in clusters, ready for testing, and here a sea anemone was swallowing a lethal dose of typhus. Down at the bright arc of sparkling surf, gypsies were being made to see how long they could live on salt water.

'Crab!' you cried. 'Crab, I never noticed you at Ravensbrück!'

Bzzzzzzzt – bzzzzzzzt – bzzzzzzzt . . .

There it was, going again!

'I'm dying for a quick puff,' muttered Staff Nurse Clement.

'Not tonight, Josephine,' Sister Braithwaite muttered back, pushing the dressings trolley. 'How is Mrs Daventry faring over on the other side?'

'I've not had a moment.'

'She'll ring if she needs us.'

'Where *is* Dr Murphy-bloody-Jones?'

'Hush, Staff! That's no way to speak of God.'

'It is, when you're left to do his dirty work for him!'

★   ★   ★

Now the ravens were circling and the crab was lying low.

A winter landscape, with the snow outside striking a white light up through the barred windows and brightening the whole room, making it a bridal suite. On the bed, fresh from the snow, with a rectal temperature of 86 degrees Fahrenheit, a brutish young Pole. Pressed against him, a skinny female with black shining hair, naked and shivering, too. He warmed slowly. There was time to see the female was of poor background, a sufferer from rickets. There was time to study her face, and find in it evidence of the sub-human. There was even time to memorise its every line and hollow, if need be.

There was no need, but it must have happened.

'My God!' Dr Rascher exploded with a laugh. 'The animal thinks he's woken up in Heaven! Just look . . . '

Everyone was looking, smirking. The Pole, mumbling, had clutched the female to him, and now wept as he suckled at her flat breast, his loins already slowly heaving.

'Temperature reading?' said Dr Rascher.

You glanced at the dial, calling out: 'Eighty-eight and rising!'

'*And* rising . . . ' echoed Dr Rascher, giggling.

The brute rolled over on to the female. She whispered softly, kissed his ear and opened her legs, welcoming him.

Dr Rascher gaped. 'What is this?' he said. 'Even here, she can enjoy it?'

'I think,' said the cameraman, 'she is sorry for him, that's all. She knows he gets his benzine injection when this is over.'

'Degenerate!' snapped Dr Rascher, then giggled again. 'These Poles . . . ! See this rabbit is kept for me, she excites certain possibilities.'

'Ninety degrees!' you reported.

'Yes, she must be kept and fed well,' declared Rascher. 'In nineteen forty-six, I propose beginning a series of experiments which . . . '

He talked on, but you were no longer listening. You were watching. As the Pole bucked harder and harder, moving to his climax, the female submitted herself totally to him, throwing back her arms and grasping the bedposts. Her limbs were thin but beautiful, marred only by her concentration-camp number, tattooed in blue on the left inner arm.

Then they cried out together.

'What was that?' asked Sister Braithwaite, pausing with the flame an inch from her cigarette.

'Didn't hear a sound,' said Staff Nurse Clement.

Sister Braithwaite was trembling like on that night in Africa. 'It was—' she began, then swallowed. 'Look, I can't explain, I just think we'd better get back.'

They left the day wing and went first to the six-bed ward, found everyone asleep and started checking on the one-bed side wards.

'Funny smell down this way,' said Staff Nurse Clement.

'Oh, that's Staff Wong and her blessed greasy coat.'

'Pardon?'

'You're right, that was two days—'

'Oops!' said Staff Nurse Clement, coming to a sudden halt in a doorway. 'Guess who's . . . ' And she tiptoed in. 'Yes, he has – the professor's gone,' she said, reaching out to close an eyelid. 'A bit sudden.'

'And look at the way he's arched back, Pam! That really isn't natural.'

'What isn't natural? asked Dr Murphy-Jones, wandering in amiably. 'I say, quite a spasm. I hope you're not suggesting foul play, are you, Sister? This is surely the last place on—'

'No, no, it's simply I—'

'Excellent! You've someone you'd like me to take a look at!'

'Yer-yes, please,' said Sister Braithwaite, trying to get a grip on herself. 'If you'll just come this way, doctor.'

As she turned out into the corridor, she caught a glimpse of Mrs Daventry holding the old woman's hand, which was clenched tightly now. The light was playing another of its tricks, for when Mrs Daventry glanced round to give a quick, gentle smile, she looked absolutely beautiful, a young girl.

Both Dr Sigmund Rascher's own fate and his reports to Heinrich Himmler, the letter writer, are dealt with in detail in The Rise and Fall of the Third Reich *by William L. Shirer.*

A LIGHT ON THE ROAD TO WOODSTOCK

by Ellis Peters

The King's court was in no hurry to return to England, that late autumn of 1120, even though the fighting, somewhat desultory in these last stages, was long over, and the enforced peace sealed by a royal marriage. King Henry had brought to a successful conclusion his sixteen years of patient, cunning, relentless plotting, fighting and manipulating, and could now sit back in high content, master not only of England but of Normandy, too. What the Conqueror had misguidedly dealt out in two separate parcels to his two elder sons, his youngest son had now put together again and clamped into one. Not without a hand in removing from the light of day, some said, both of his brothers, one of whom had been shoveled into a hasty grave under the tower at Winchester, while the other was now a prisoner in Devizes, and unlikely ever to be seen again by the outer world.

The court could well afford to linger to enjoy victory, while Henry trimmed into neatness the last loose edges still to be made secure. But his fleet was already preparing at Barfleur for the voyage back to England, and he would be home before the month ended. Meantime, many of his barons and knights who had fought his battles were withdrawing their contingents and making for home, among them one Roger Mauduit, who had a young and handsome wife waiting for him, certain legal business on his mind, and twenty-five men to ship back to England, most of them to be paid off on landing.

There were one or two among the miscellaneous riff-raff he had recruited here in Normandy on his lord's behalf whom it might be worth keeping on in his own service, along with the few men of his household, at least until he was safely home. The vagabond clerk turned soldier, let him be unfrocked priest or what he might, was an excellent copyist and a sound Latin scholar, and could put legal documents in their best and most presentable form, in good time for the King's court at Woodstock. And the Welsh man-at-arms, blunt and insubordinate as he was, was also experienced and accomplished in arms, a man of his word, once given, and utterly reliable in whatever situation on land or sea, for in both elements he had long practice behind him. Roger was well aware that he was not greatly loved, and had little faith in either the valour or the loyalty of his own men. But this Welshman from Gwynedd, by way of Antioch and Jerusalem and only God knew where else, had imbibed the code of arms and wore it as a second nature. With or without love, such service as he pledged, that he would provide.

Roger put it to them both as his men were embarking at Barfleur, in the middle of a deceptively placid November, and upon a calm sea.

'I would have you two accompany me to my manor of Sutton Mauduit by Northampton, when we disembark, and stay in my pay until a certain lawsuit I have against the abbey of Shrewsbury is resolved. The King intends to come to Woodstock when he arrives in England, and will be there to preside over my case on the twenty-third day of this month. Will you remain in my service until that day?'

The Welshman said that he would, until that day or until the case was resolved. He said it indifferently, as one who has no business of any importance anywhere in the world to pull him in another direction. As well Northampton as anywhere else. As well Woodstock. And after Woodstock? Why anywhere in particular? There was no identifiable light beckoning him anywhere, along any road. The world was wide, fair and full of savour, but without signposts.

Alard, the tatterdemalion clerk, hesitated, scratched his thick thatch of grizzled red hair, and finally also said yes, but as if some vague regret drew him in another direction. It meant pay for some days more, he could not afford to say no.

'I would have gone with him with better heart,' he said later, when they were leaning on the rail together, watching the low blue line of the English shore rise out of a placid sea, 'if he had been taking a more westerly road.'

'Why that?' asked Cadfael ap Meilyr ap Dafydd. 'Have you kin in the west?'

'I had once. I have not now.'

'Dead?'

'I am the one who died.' Alard heaved lean shoulders in a helpless shrug, and grinned. 'Fifty-seven brothers I had, and now I'm brotherless. I begin to miss my kin, now I'm past forty. I never valued them when I was young.' He slanted a rueful glance at his companion and shook his head. 'I was a monk of Evesham, an *oblatus*, given to God by my father when I was five years old. When I was fifteen I could no longer abide to live my life in one place, and I ran. Stability is one of the vows we take – to be content in one stay, and go abroad only when ordered. That was not for me, not then. My sort they call *vagus* – frivolous minds that must wander. Well, I've wandered far enough, God knows, in my time. I begin to fear I can never stand still again.'

The Welshman drew his cloak about him against the chill of the wind. 'Are you hankering for a return?'

'Even you seamen must drop anchor somewhere at last,' said Alard. 'They'd have my hide if I went back, that I know. But there's this about penance, it pays all debts, and leaves the record clear. They'd find a place for me, once I'd paid. But I don't know . . . I don't know . . . The *vagus* is still in me. I'm torn two ways.'

'After twenty-five years,' said Cadfael, 'a month or two more for quiet thinking can do no harm. Copy his papers for him and take your ease until his business is settled.'

They were much of an age, though the renegade monk looked the elder by ten years, and much knocked about by the world he had coveted from within the cloister. It had never paid him well in goods or gear, for he went threadbare and thin, but in wisdom he might have got his fair wages. A little soldiering, a little clerking, some horse-tending, any labour that came to hand, until he could turn his hand to almost anything a hale man can do. He had seen, he said, Italy as far south as Rome, served once for a time under the Count of Flanders, crossed the mountains into Spain, never abiding anywhere for long. His feet still served him, but his mind grew weary of the road.

'And you?' he said, eyeing his companion, whom he had known now for a year in this last campaign. 'You're something of a *vagus* yourself, by your own account. All those years crusading and battling corsairs in the midland sea, and still you have not enough of it, but must cross the sea again to get buffeted about Normandy. Had you no better business of your own, once you got back to England, but you must enlist again in this muddled mêlée of a war? No woman to take your mind off fighting?'

'What of yourself? Free of the cloister, free of the vows!'

'Somehow,' said Alard, himself puzzled, 'I never saw it so. A woman here and there, yes, when the heat was on me, and there was a woman by and willing, but marriage and wiving . . . it never seemed to me I had the right.'

The Welshman braced his feet on the gently swaying deck and watched the distant shore draw nearer. A broad-set, sturdy, muscular man in his healthy prime, brown-haired and brown-skinned from eastern suns and outdoor living, well-provided in leather coat and good cloth, and well-armed with sword and dagger. A comely enough face, strongly featured, with the bold bones of his race – there had been women, in his time, who had found him handsome.

'I had a girl,' he said meditatively, 'years back, before ever I went crusading. But I left her when I took the Cross, left her for three years and stayed away seventeen. The truth is, in the east I forgot her, and in the west she, thanks be to God, had forgotten me. I did enquire, when I got back. She'd made a better bargain, and married a decent, solid man who had nothing of the *vagus* in him. A guildsman and counsellor of the town of Shrewsbury, no less. So I shed the load from my conscience and went back to what I knew, soldiering. With no regrets,' he said simply. 'It was all over and done, years since. I doubt if I should have known her again, or she me.' There had been other women's faces in the years between, still vivid in his memory, while hers had faded into mist.

'And what will you do,' asked Alard, 'now the King's got everything he wanted, married his son to Anjou and Maine, and made an end of fighting? Go back to the east? There's never any want of squabbles there to keep a man busy.'

'No,' said Cadfael, eyes fixed on the shore that began to show the solidity of land and the undulations of cliff and down. For that, too, was over and done, years since, and not as well done as once he had hoped. This desultory campaigning in Normandy was little more than a postscriptum, an after-thought, a means of filling in the interim between what was past and what was to come, and as yet unrevealed. All he knew of it was that it must be something new and momentous, a door opening into another room. 'It seems we have both a few days' grace, you and I, to find out where we are going. We'd best make good use of the time.'

There was stir enough before night to keep them from wondering beyond the next moment, or troubling their minds about what was past or what was to come. Their ship put into the roads with a steady and favourable wind, and made course into Southampton before the light faded, and there was work for Alard checking the gear as it was unloaded, and for Cadfael disembarking the horses. A night's sleep in lodgings and stables in the town, and they would be on their way with the dawn.

'So the King's due in Woodstock,' said Alard, rustling sleepily in his straw in a warm loft over the horses, 'in time to sit in judgement on the twenty-third of the month. He makes his forest lodges the hub of his kingdom, there's more statecraft talked at Woodstock, so they say, than ever at Westminster. And he keeps his beasts there – lions and leopards – even camels. Did you ever see camels, Cadfael? There in the east?'

'Saw them and rode them. Common as horses there, hard-working and serviceable, but uncomfortable riding, and foul-tempered. Thank God it's horses we'll be mounting in the morning.' And after a long silence, on the edge of sleep, he asked curiously into the straw-scented darkness: 'If ever you do go back, what is it you want of Evesham?'

'Do I know?' responded Alard drowsily, and followed that with a sudden sharpening sigh, again fully awake. 'The silence, it might be . . . or the stillness. To have no more running to do . . . to have arrived, and have no more need to run. The appetite changes. Now I think it would be a beautiful thing to be still.'

The manor which was the head of Roger Mauduit's scattered and substantial honour lay somewhat south-east of Northampton, comfortably under the lee of the long ridge of wooded hills where the King had a chase, and spreading its extensive fields over the rich lowland between. The house was of stone, and ample, over a deep undercroft, and with a low tower providing two small chambers at the eastern end, and the array of sturdy byres, barns and stables that lined the containing walls was impressive. Someone had proved a good steward while the lord was away about King Henry's business.

The furnishings of the hall were no less eloquent of good management, and the men and maids of the household went about their work with a brisk wariness that showed they went in some awe of whoever presided over their labours. It needed only a single day of watching the Lady Eadwina in action to show who ruled the roost here. Roger Mauduit had married a wife not only handsome, but also efficient and masterful. She had had her own way here for three years, and by all the signs had enjoyed her dominance. She might, even, be none too glad to resign her charge now, however glad she might be to have her lord home again.

She was a tall, graceful woman, ten years younger than Roger, with an abundance of fair hair, and large blue eyes that went discreetly half-veiled by absurdly long lashes most of the time, but flashed a bright and steely challenge when she opened them fully. Her smile was likewise discreet and almost constant, concealing rather than revealing whatever went on in her mind; and though her welcome to her returning lord left nothing to be desired, but lavished on him every possible tribute of ceremony and affection from the moment his horse entered at the gate, Cadfael could not but wonder whether she was not, at the same time taking stock of every man he brought in with him, and every article of gear or harness or weaponry in their equipment, as one taking jealous inventory of his goods and resolved to make sure nothing was lacking.

She had her little son by the hand, a boy of about seven years old, and the child had the same fair colouring, the same contained and almost supercilious smile, and was as spruce and fine as his mother.

The lady received Alard with a sweeping glance that deprecated his tatterdemalion appearance and doubted his morality, but nevertheless was willing to accept and make use of his abilities. The clerk who kept the manor roll and the accounts was efficient enough, but had no Latin, and could not write a good court hand. Alard was whisked away to a small table set in the angle of the great hearth, and kept hard at work copying certain charters and letters, and preparing them for presentation.

'This suit of his is against the abbey of Shrewsbury,' said Alard, freed of his labours after supper in hall. 'I recall you said that girl of yours had married a merchant in that town. Shrewsbury is a Benedictine house, like mine of Evesham.' His, he called it still, after so many years of abandoning it; or his again, after time had brushed away whatever division there had ever been. 'You must know it, if you come from there.'

'I was born in Trefriw, in Gwynedd,' said Cadfael, 'but I took service early with an English wool-merchant, and came to Shrewsbury with his household. Fourteen, I was then – in Wales fourteen is manhood, and as I was a good lad with the short bow, and took kindly to the sword, I suppose I was worth my keep. The best of my following years were spent in Shrewsbury, I know it like my own palm, abbey and all. My master sent me there a year and more, to get my letters. But I quit that service when he died. I'd pledged nothing to the son, and he was a poor shadow of his father. That was when I took the Cross. So did many like me, all afire. I won't say what followed was all ash, but it burned very low at times.'

'It's Mauduit who holds this disputed land,' said Alard, 'and the abbey that sues to recover it, and the thing's been going on four years without a settlement, ever since the old man here died. From what I know of the Benedictines, I'd rate their honesty above our Roger's, I tell you straight. And yet his charters seem to be genuine, as far as I can tell.'

'Where is this land they're fighting over?' asked Cadfael.

'It's a manor by the name of Rotesley, near Stretton, demesne, village, advowson of the church and all. It seems when the great earl was just dead and his abbey still building, Roger's father gave Rotesley to the abbey. No dispute about that, the charter's there to show it. But the abbey granted it back to him as tenant for life, to live out his latter years there undisturbed, Roger being then married and installed here at Sutton. That's where the dispute starts. The abbey claims it was clearly agreed the tenancy ended with the old man's death, that he himself understood it so, and intended it should be restored to the abbey as soon as he was out of it. While Roger says there was no such agreement to restore it unconditionally, but the tenancy was granted to the Mauduits, and ought to be hereditary. And so far he's hung on to it tooth and claw. After several hearings they remitted it to the King himself. And that's why you and I, my friend, will be off with his lordship to Woodstock the day after tomorrow.'

'And how do you rate his chances of success? He seems none too sure himself,' said Cadfael, 'to judge by his short temper and nail-biting this last day or so.'

'Why, the charter could have been worded better. It says simply that the village is granted back in tenancy during the old man's lifetime, but fails to say anything about what shall happen afterwards, whatever may have been intended. From what I hear, they were on very good terms, Abbot Fulchered and the old lord, agreements between them on other matters in the manor book are worded as between men who trusted each other. The witnesses are all of them dead, as Abbot Fulchered is dead. It's one Godefrid now. But for all I know the abbey may hold letters that have passed between the two, and a letter is witness of intent, no less than a formal charter. All in good time we shall see.'

The nobility still sat at the high table, in no haste to retire, Roger brooding over his wine, of which he had already drunk his fair share and more. Cadfael eyed them with interest, seen thus in a family setting. The boy had gone to his bed, hauled away by an elderly nurse, but the Lady Eadwina sat in close attendance at her lord's left hand, and kept his cup well filled, smiling her faint, demure smile. On her left sat a very fine young squire of about twenty-five years, deferential and discreet, with a smile somehow the male reflection of her own. The source of both was secret, the spring of their pleasure or amusement, or whatever caused them so to smile, remained private and slightly unnerving, like the carved stone smiles of certain very old statues Cadfael had seen in Greece, long ago. For all his mild, amiable and ornamental appearance, combed and curled and courtly, he was a big, well-set-up young fellow, with a set to his smooth jaw. Cadfael studied him with interest, for he was plainly privileged here.

'Goscelin,' said Alard by way of explanation, following his friend's glance. 'Her right-hand man while Roger was away.'

Her left-hand man now, by the look of it, thought Cadfael. For her left hand and Goscelin's right were private under the table, while she spoke winningly into her husband's ear; and if those two hands were not paddling palms at this moment Cadfael was very much deceived. Above and below the drapings of the board were two different worlds. 'I wonder,' he said thoughtfully, 'what she's breathing into Roger's ear now.'

What the lady was breathing into her husband's ear was, in fact: 'You fret over nothing, my lord. What does it matter how strong his proofs, if he never reaches Woodstock in time to present them? You know the law: if one party fails to appear, judgement is given for the other. The assize judges may allow more than one default if they please, but do you think King Henry will? Whoever fails of keeping tryst with him will be felled on the spot. And you know the road by which Prior Heribert must come.' Her voice was a silken purr in his ear. 'And have you not a hunting-lodge in the forest north of Woodstock, through which that road passes?'

Roger's hand had stiffened round the stem of his wine cup. He was not so drunk but he was listening intently.

'Shrewsbury to Woodstock will be a two- or three-day journey to such a rider. All you need do is have a watcher on the road north of you, to give warning. The woods are thick enough, masterless men have been known to haunt there. Even if he comes by daylight, your part need never be known. Hide him but a few days, it will be long enough. Then turn him loose by night, and who's ever to know what footpads held and robbed him? You need not even touch his parchments – robbers would count them worthless. Take what common thieves would take, and theirs will be the blame.'

Roger opened his tight-shut mouth to say in a doubtful growl: 'He'll not be travelling alone.'

'Hah! Two or three abbey servants – they'll run like hares. You need not trouble yourself over them. Three stout, silent men of your own will be more than enough.'

He brooded, and began to think so, too, and to review in his mind the men of his household, seeking the right hands for such work. Not the Welshman and the clerk, the strangers here; their part was to be the honest onlookers, in case there should ever be questions asked.

They left Sutton Mauduit on the twentieth day of November, which seemed unnecessarily early, though as Roger had decreed that they should settle in his hunting-lodge in the forest close by Woodstock, which meant conveying stores with them to make the house habitable and provision it for a party for, presumably, a stay of three nights at least, it was perhaps a wise precaution. Roger was taking no chances in his suit, he said; he meant to be established on the ground in good time, and have all his proofs in order.

'But so he has,' said Alard, pricked in his professional pride, 'for I've gone over everything with him, and the case, if open in default of specific instructions, is plain enough and will stand up. What the abbey can muster, who knows? They say the abbot is not well, which is why his prior comes in his place. My work is done.'

He had the faraway look in his eye, as the party rode out and faced westward, of one either penned and longing to be where he could but see, or loose and weary and being drawn home. Either a *vagus* escaping outward, or a penitent flying back in haste before the doors should close against him. There must indeed be something desirable and lovely to cause a man to look towards it with that look on his face.

Three men-at-arms and two grooms accompanied Roger, in addition to

Alard and Cadfael, whose term of service would end with the session in court, after which they might go where they would, Cadfael horsed, since he owned his own mount, Alard afoot, since the pony he rode belonged to Roger. It came as something of a surprise to Cadfael that the squire Goscelin should also saddle up and ride with the party, very debonair and well-armed with sword and dagger.

'I marvel,' said Cadfael drily, 'that the lady doesn't need him at home for her own protection, while her lord's absent.'

The Lady Eadwina, however, bade farewell to the whole party with the greatest serenity, and to her husband with demonstrative affection, putting forward her little son to be embraced and kissed. Perhaps, thought Cadfael, relenting, I do her wrong, simply because I feel chilled by that smile of hers. For all I know she may be the truest wife living.

They set out early, and before Buckingham made a halt at the small and penurious priory of Bradwell, where Roger elected to spend the night, keeping his three men-at-arms with him, while Goscelin with the rest of the party rode on to the hunting-lodge to make all ready for their lord's reception the following day. It was growing dark by the time they arrived, and the bustle of kindling fire and torches, and unloading the bed-linen and stores from the sumpter ponies went on into the night. The lodge was small, stockaded, well-furnished with stabling and mews, and in thick woodland, a place comfortable enough once they had a roaring fire on the hearth and food on the table.

'The road the prior of Shrewsbury will be coming by,' said Alard, warming himself by the fire after supper, 'passes through Evesham. As like as not they'll stay the last night there.' With every mile west Cadfael had seen him straining forward with mounting eagerness. 'The road cannot be far away from us here, it passes through this forest.'

'It must be nearly thirty miles to Evesham,' said Cadfael. 'A long day's riding for a clerical party. It will be night by the time they ride past into Woodstock. If you're set on going, stay at least to get your pay, for you'll need it before the thirty miles is done.'

They went to their slumber in the warmth of the hall without a word more said. But he would go, Alard, whether he himself knew it yet or not. Cadfael knew it. His friend was a tired horse with the scent of the stable in his nostrils; nothing would stop him now until he reached it.

It was well into the middle of the day when Roger and his escort arrived, and they approached not directly as the advance party had done, but from the woods to the north, as though they had been indulging in a little hunting or hawking by the way, except that they had neither hawk nor hound with them. A fine, clear, cool day for riding, there was no reason in the world why they should not go roundabout for the pure pleasure of it – and indeed, they seemed to come in high content! – but that Roger's mind had been so preoccupied and so anxious concerning his lawsuit that distractions seemed unlikely. Cadfael was given to thinking about unlikely developments, which from old campaigns he knew to prove significant in most cases. Goscelin, who was out at the gate to welcome them in, was apparently oblivious to the direction from which they came. That way lay Alard's highway to his rest. But what meaning ought it to have for Roger Mauduit?

The table was lavish that night, and lord and squire drank well and ate well, and gave no sign of any care, though they might, Cadfael thought, watching them from his lower place, seem a little tight and knife-edged. Well, the King's court could account for that. Shrewsbury's prior was drawing steadily nearer, with whatever weapons he had for the battle. But it seemed rather an exultant tension than an anxious one. Was Roger counting his chickens already?

The morning of the twenty-second of November dawned, and the noon passed, and with every moment Alard's restlessness and abstraction grew, until with evening it possessed him utterly, and he could no longer resist. He presented himself before Roger after supper, when his mood might be mellow from good food and wine.

'My lord, with the morrow my service to you is completed. You need me no longer, and with your goodwill I would set forth now for where I am going. I go afoot and need provision for the road. If you have been content with my work, pay me what is due, and let me go.'

It seemed that Roger had been startled out of some equally absorbing preoccupation of his own, and was in haste to return to it, for he made no demur, but paid at once. To do him justice, he had never been a grudging paymaster. He drove as hard a bargain as he could at the outset, but once the agreement was made, he kept it.

'Go when you please,' he said. 'Fill your bag from the kitchen for the journey when you leave. You did good work, I give you that.'

And he returned to whatever it was that so engrossed his thoughts, and Alard went to collect the proffered largesse and his own meagre possessions.

'I am going,' he said, meeting Cadfael in the hall doorway. 'I must go.' There was no more doubt in voice or face. 'They will take me back, though in the lowest place. From that there's no falling. The blessed Benedict wrote in the Rule that even to the third time of straying a man may be received again if he promise full amendment.'

It was a dark night, without moon or stars but in fleeting moments when the wind ripped apart the cloud covering to let through a brief gleam of moonlight. The weather had grown gusty and wild in the last two days, the King's fleet must have had a rough crossing from Barfleur.

'You'd do better,' urged Cadfael, 'to wait for morning, and go by daylight. Here's a safe bed, and the King's peace, however well enforced, hardly covers every mile of the King's highroads.'

But Alard would not wait. The yearning was on him too strongly, and a penniless vagabond who had ventured all the roads of Christendom by day or night was hardly likely to flinch from the last thirty miles of his wanderings.

'Then I'll go with you as far as the road, and see you on your way,' said Cadfael.

There was a mile or so of track through thick forest between them and the highroad that bore away west-north-west on the upland journey to Evesham. The ribbon of open highway, hemmed on both sides by trees, was hardly less dark than the forest itself. King Henry had fenced in his private park at Woodstock to house his wild beasts, but maintained also his hunting chase here, many miles in extent. At the road they parted, and Cadfael stood to watch his friend march steadily away towards the west, eyes fixed ahead, upon his penance and his absolution, a tired man with a rest assured.

Cadfael turned back towards the lodge as soon as the receding shadow had melted into the night. He was in no haste to go in, for the night, though blustery, was not cold, and he was in no mind to seek the company of others of the party now that one best known to him was gone, and gone in so mysteriously rapt a fashion. He walked on among the trees, turning his back on his bed for a while.

The constant thrashing of branches in the wind all but drowned the scuffling and shouting that suddenly broke out behind him, at some distance among the trees, until a horse's shrill whinny brought him about with a jerk, and set him running through the underbrush towards the spot where confused voices yelled alarm and broken bushes thrashed. The clamour seemed some little way off, and he was startled as he shouldered his way headlong though a thicket to collide heavily with two entangled bodies, send them spinning apart, and himself fall a-sprawl upon one of them in the flattened grass. The man under him uttered a scared and angry cry, and the voice was Roger's. The other man had made no sound at all, but slid away very rapidly and lightly to vanish among the trees, a tall shadow swallowed in shadows.

Cadfael drew off in haste, reaching an arm to hoist the winded man. 'My lord, are you hurt? What, in God's name, is to do here?' The sleeve he clutched slid warm and wet under his hand. 'You're injured! Hold fast, let's see what harm's done before you move . . . '

Then there was the voice of Goscelin, for once loud and vehement in alarm, shouting for his lord and crashing headlong through bush and brake to fall on his knees beside Roger, lamenting and raging.

'My lord, my lord, what happened here? What rogues were those, loose in the woods? Dared they waylay travellers so close to the King's highway? You're hurt – here's blood . . . '

Roger got his breath back and sat up, feeling at his left arm below the shoulder, and wincing. 'A scratch. My arm . . . God curse him, whoever he may be, the fellow struck for my heart. Man, if you had not come charging like a bull, I might have been dead. You hurled me off the point of his dagger. Thank God, there's no great harm, but I bleed . . . Help me back home!'

'That a man may not walk by night in his own woods,' fumed Goscelin, hoisting his lord carefully to his feet, 'without being set upon by outlaws! Help here, you, Cadfael, take his other arm . . . Footpads so close to Woodstock! Tomorrow we must turn out the watch to comb these tracks and hunt them out of cover, before they kill . . . '

'Get me withindoors,' snapped Roger, 'and have this coat and shirt off me, and let's staunch this bleeding. I'm alive, that's the main!'

They helped him back between them, through the more open ways towards the lodge. It dawned on Cadfael, as they went, that the clamour of furtive battle had ceased completely, even the wind had abated, and somewhere on the road, distantly, he caught the rhythm of galloping hooves, very fast and light, as of a riderless horse in panic flight.

The gash in Roger Mauduit's left arm, just below the shoulder, was long but not deep, and grew shallower as it descended. The stroke that marked him thus could well have been meant for his heart. Cadfael's hurtling impact, at the very moment the attack was launched, had been the means of averting murder. The shadow that had melted into the night had no form, nothing about it rendered it human or recognisable. He had heard an outcry and run towards it, a projectile to strike attacked and attacker apart; questioned, that was all he could say.

For which, said Roger, bandaged and resting and warmed with mulled wine, he was heartily thankful. And indeed, Roger was behaving with remarkable fortitude and calm for a man who had just escaped death. By the time he had demonstrated to his dismayed grooms and men-at-arms that he was alive and not much the worse, appointed the hour when they should set out for Woodstock in the morning, and been helped to his bed by Goscelin, there was even a suggestion of complacency about him, as though a gash in the arm was a small price to pay for the successful retention of a valuable property and the defeat of his clerical opponents.

In the court of the palace of Woodstock the King's chamberlains, clerks and judges were fluttering about in a curiously distracted manner, or so it seemed to Cadfael, standing apart among the commoners to observe their antics. They gathered in small groups, conversing in low voices and with anxious faces, broke apart to regroup with others of their kind, hurried in and out among the litigants, avoiding or brushing off all questions, exchanged documents, hurried to the door to peer out, as if looking for some late arrival. And there was indeed one litigant who had not kept to his time, for there was no sign of a Benedictine prior among those assembled, nor had anyone appeared to explain or justify his absence. And Roger Mauduit, in spite of his stiff and painful arm, continued to relax, with ever-increasing assurance, into shining complacency.

The appointed hour was already some minutes past when four agitated fellows, two of them Benedictine brothers, made a hasty entrance, and accosted the presiding clerk.

'Sir,' bleated the leader, loud in nervous dismay, 'we here are come from the abbey of Shrewsbury, escort to our prior, who was on his way to plead a case at law here. Sir, you must hold him excused, for it is not his blame nor ours that he cannot appear. In the forest some two miles north, as we rode hither last night in the dark, we were attacked by a band of lawless robbers, and they have seized our prior and dragged him away . . .'

The spokesman's voice had risen shrilly in his agitation, he had the attention of every man in the hall by this time. Certainly he had Cadfael's. Masterless men some two miles out of Woodstock, plying their trade last night, could only be the same who had happened upon Roger Mauduit and all but been the death of him. Any such gang, so close to the court, was astonishing enough, there could hardly be two. The clerk was outraged at the very idea.

'Seized and captured him? And you four were with him? Can this be true? How many were they who attacked you?'

'We could not tell for certain. Three at least – but they were lying in ambush, we had no chance to stand them off. They pulled him from his horse and were off into the trees with him. They knew the woods, and we did not. Sir, we did go after them, but they beat us off.'

It was evident they had done their best, for two of them showed bruised and scratched, and all were soiled and torn as to their clothing.

'We have hunted through the night, but found no trace, only we caught his horse a mile down the highway as we came hither. So we plead here that our prior's absence be not seen as a default, for indeed he would have been here in the town last night if all had gone as it should.'

'Hush, wait!' said the clerk peremptorily.

All heads had turned towards the door of the hall, where a great flurry of officials had suddenly surged into view, cleaving through the press with fixed and ominous haste, to take the centre of the floor below the King's empty dais. A chamberlain, elderly and authoritative, struck the floor loudly with his staff and commanded silence. And at sight of his face silence fell like a stone.

'My lords, gentlemen, all who have pleas here this day, and all others present, you are bidden to disperse, for there will be no hearings today. All suits that should be heard here must be postponed three days, and will be heard by his Grace's judges. His Grace the King cannot appear.'

This time the silence fell again like a heavy curtain, muffling even thought or conjecture.

'The court is in mourning from this hour. We have received news of desolating import. His Grace with the greater part of his fleet made the crossing to England safely, as is known, but the *Blanche Nef*, in which his Grace's son and heir, Prince William, with all his companions and many other noble souls were embarked, put to sea late, and was caught in gales before ever clearing Barfleur. The ship is lost, split upon a rock, foundered with all hands, not a soul is come safe to land. Go hence quietly, and pray for the souls of the flower of this realm.'

So that was the end of one man's year of triumph, an empty achievement, a ruinous victory, Normandy won, his enemies routed, and now everything swept aside, broken apart upon an obstinate rock, washed away in a malicious sea. His only lawful son, recently married in splendour, now denied even a coffin and a grave, for if ever they found those royal bodies it would be by the relenting grace of God, for the sea seldom put its winnings ashore by Barfleur. Even some of his unlawful sons, of whom there were many, gone down with their royal brother, no one left but the one legal daughter to inherit a barren empire.

Cadfael walked alone in a corner of the King's park and considered the foolishness of mortal vainglory, that was paid for with such a bitter price. But also he thought of the affairs of little men, to whom even a luckless King owed justice. For somewhere there was still to be sought the lost prior of Shrewsbury, carried off by masterless men in the forest, a litigant who might still be lost three days hence, when his suit came up again for hearing, unless someone in the meantime knew where to look for him.

He was in little doubt now. A lawless gang at liberty so close to a royal palace was in any case unlikely enough, and Cadfael was liable to brood on the unlikely. But that there should be two – no, that was impossible. And if one only, then that same one whose ambush he had overheard at some distance, yet close enough, too close for comfort, to Roger Mauduit's hunting-lodge.

Probably the unhappy brothers from Shrewsbury were off beating the wilds of the forest afresh. Cadfael knew better where to look. No doubt Roger was biting his nails in some anxiety over the delay, but he had no reason to suppose that three days would release the captive to appear against him, nor was he paying much attention to what his Welsh man-at-arms was doing with his time.

Cadfael took his horse and rode back without haste towards the hunting-lodge. He left in the early dusk, as soon as the evening meal was over in Mauduit's lodging. No one was paying any heed to him by that time of day. All Roger had to do was hold his tongue and keep his wits about him for three days, and the disputed manor would still be adjudged to him. Everything was beautifully in hand, after all.

Two of the men-at-arms and one groom had been left behind at the hunting-lodge. Cadfael doubted if the man they guarded was to be found in the house itself, for unless he was blindfolded he would be able to gather far too much knowledge of his surroundings, and the fable of the masterless men would be tossed into the rubbish-heap. No, he would be held in darkness, or dim light at best, even during the day, in straw or the rush flooring of a common hut, fed adequately but plainly and roughly, as wild men might keep a prisoner they were too cautious to kill, or too superstitious, until they turned him loose in some remote place, stripped of everything he had of value. On the other hand, he must be somewhere securely inside the boundary fence, otherwise there would be too high a risk of his being found. Between the gate and the house there were trees enough to obscure the large holding of a man of consequence. Somewhere among the stables and barns, or the now empty kennels, there he must be held.

Cadfael tethered his horse in cover well aside from the lodge and found himself a perch in a tall oak tree, from which vantage point he could see over the fence into the courtyard.

He was in luck. The three within fed themselves at leisure before they fed their prisoner, preferring to wait for dark. By the time the groom emerged from the hall with a pitcher and a bowl in his hands, Cadfael had his night eyes. They were quite easy about their charge, expecting no interference from any man. The groom vanished momentarily between the trees within the enclosure, but appeared again at one of the low buildings tucked under the fence, set down his pitcher for a moment while he hoisted clear a heavy wooden bar that held the door fast shut, and vanished within. The door thudded to after him, as though he had slammed it shut with his back braced against it, taking no chances even with an elderly monastic. In a few minutes he emerged again empty-handed, hauled the bar into place again, and returned, whistling, to the hall and the enjoyment of Mauduit's ale.

Not the stables nor the kennels, but a small stout hay store built on short wooden piles raised from the ground. At least the prior would have fairly snug lying.

Cadfael let the last of the light fade before he made a move. The wooden wall was stout and high, but more than one of the old trees outside leaned a branch over it, and it was no great labour to climb without and drop into the deep grass within. He made first for the gate, and quietly unbarred the narrow wicket set into it. Faint threads of torchlight filtered through the chinks in the hall shutters, but nothing else stirred. Cadfael laid hold of the heavy bar of the storehouse door, and eased it silently out of its socket, opening the door by cautious inches, and whispering through the chink: 'Father . . . ?'

There was a sharp rustling of hay within, but no immediate reply.

'Father Prior, is it you? Softly . . . Are you bound?'

A hesitant and slightly timorous voice said, 'No.' And in a moment, with better assurance: 'My son, you are not one of these sinful men?'

'Sinful man I am, but not of their company. Hush, quietly now! I have a horse close by. I came from Woodstock to find you. Reach me your hand, Father, and come forth.'

A hand came wavering out of the hay-scented darkness to clutch convulsively at Cadfael's hand. The pale patch of a tonsured crown gleamed faintly, and a small, rounded figure crept forth and stepped into the thick grass. He had the wit to waste no breath then on questions, but stood docile and silent while Cadfael re-barred the door on emptiness and, taking him by the hand, led him softly along the fence to the unfastened wicket in the great gate. Only when the door was closed as softly behind them did he heave a great, thankful sigh.

They were out, it was done, and no one would be likely to learn of the escape until morning. Cadfael led the way to where he had left his horse tethered. The forest lay serene and quiet about them.

'You ride, Father, and I'll walk with you. It's no more than two miles into Woodstock. We're safe enough now.'

Bewildered and confused by so sudden a reversal, the prior confided and obeyed like a child. Not until they were out on the silent highroad did he say sadly, 'I have failed of my mission. Son, may God bless you for this kindness which is beyond my understanding. For how did you know of me, and how could you divine where to find me? I understand nothing of what has been happening to me. And I am not a very brave man . . . But my failure is no fault of yours, and my blessing I owe you without stint.'

'You have not failed, Father,' said Cadfael simply. 'The suit is still unheard, and will be for three days more. All your companions are safe in Woodstock, except that they fret and search for you. And if you know where they will be lodging, I would recommend that you join them now, by night, and stay well out of sight until the day the case is heard. For if this trap was designed to keep you from appearing in the King's court, some further attempt might yet be made. Have you your evidences safe? They did not take them?'

'Brother Orderic, my clerk, was carrying the documents, but he could not conduct the case in court. I only am accredited to represent my abbot. But, my son, how is it that the case still goes unheard? The King keeps strict day and time, it's well known. How comes it that God and you have saved me from disgrace and loss?'

'Father, for all too bitter reason the King could not be present.'

Cadfael told him the whole of it, how half the young chivalry of England had been wiped out in one blow, and the King left without an heir. Prior Heribert, shocked and dismayed, fell to praying in a grieving whisper for both dead and living, and Cadfael walked beside the horse in silence, for what more was there to be said? Except that King Henry, even in this shattering hour, willed that his justice should still prevail, and that was virtue in any monarch. Only when they came into the sleeping town did Cadfael again interrupt the prior's fervent prayers with a strange question.

'Father, was any man of your escort carrying steel? A dagger, or any such weapon?'

'No, no, God forbid!' said the prior, shocked. 'We have no use for arms. We trust in God's peace, and after it in the King's'

'So I thought,' said Cadfael, nodding. 'It is another discipline, for another venture.'

By the change in Mauduit's countenance Cadfael knew the hour of the following day when the news reached him that his prisoner was flown. All the rest of that day he went about with nerves at stretch and ears pricked for any sensational rumours being bandied around the town, and eyes roving anxiously in dread of the sight of Prior Heribert in court or street, braced to pour out his complaint to the King's officers. But as the hours passed and still there was no sign, he began to be a little eased in his mind, and to hope still for a miraculous deliverance. The Benedictine brothers were seen here and there, mute and sombre-faced; surely they could have had no word of their superior. There was nothing to be done but set his teeth, keep his countenance, wait and hope.

The second day passed, and the third day came, and Mauduit's hopes had soared again, for still there was no word. He made his appearance before the King's judge confidently, his charters in hand. The abbey was the suitor. If all went well, Roger would not even have to state his case, for the plea would fail of itself when the pleader failed to appear.

It came as a shattering shock when a sudden stir at the door, prompt to the hour appointed, blew into the hall a small, round, unimpressive person in the Benedictine habit, hugging to him an armful of vellum rolls, and followed by his black-gowned brothers in close attendance. Cadfael, too, was observing him with interest, for it was the first time he had seen him clearly. A modest man of comfortable figure and amiable countenance, rosy and mild. Not so old as that night journey had suggested, perhaps forty-five, with a shining innocence about him. But to Roger Mauduit it might have been a fire-breathing dragon entering the hall.

And who would have expected, from that gentle, even deprecating presence, the clarity and expertise with which that small man deployed his original charter, punctiliously identical to Roger's according to the account Alard had given, and omitting any specific mention of what should follow Arnulf Mauduit's death – how scrupulously he pointed out the omission and the arguments to which it might give rise, and followed it up with two letters written by that same Arnulf Mauduit to Abbot Fulchered, referring in plain terms to the obligatory return of the manor and village after his death, and pledging his son's loyal observance of the obligation.

It might have been want of proofs that caused Roger to make so poor a job of refuting the evidence, or it might have been craven conscience. Whatever the cause, judgement was given for the abbey.

Cadfael presented himself before the lord he was leaving barely an hour after the verdict was given.

'My lord, your suit is concluded, and my service with it. I have done what I pledged, here I part from you.'

Roger sat sunk in gloom and rage, and lifted upon him a glare that should have felled him, but failed of its impact.

'I misdoubt me,' said Roger, smouldering, 'how you have observed your loyalty to me. Who else could know . . . ' He bit his tongue in time, for as long as it remained unsaid no accusation had been made, and no rebuttal was needed. He would have liked to ask: How *did* you know? But he thought better of it. 'Go, then, if you have nothing more to say.'

'As to that,' said Cadfael meaningly, 'nothing more need be said. It's over.' And that was recognisable as a promise, but with uneasy implications, for plainly on some other matter he still had a thing to say.

'My lord, give some thought to this, for I was until now in your service, and wish you no harm. Of those four who attended Prior Heribert on his way here, not one carried arms. There was neither sword nor dagger nor knife of any kind among the five of them.'

He saw the significance of that go home, slowly but with bitter force. The masterless men had been nothing but a children's tale, but until now Roger had thought, as he had been meant to think, that that dagger-stroke in the forest had been a bold attempt by an abbey servant to defend his prior. He blinked and swallowed and stared, and began to sweat, beholding a perilous gulf into which he had all but stumbled.

'There were none there who bore arms,' said Cadfael, 'but your own.'

A double-edged ambush that had been, to have him out in the forest by night, all unsuspecting. And there were as many miles between Woodstock and Sutton Mauduit returning as coming, and there would be other nights as dark on the way.

'Who?' asked Roger in a grating whisper. 'Which of them? Give him a name!'

'No,' said Cadfael simply. 'Do your own divining. I am no longer in your service, I have said all I mean to say.'

Roger's face had turned grey. He was hearing again the plan unfolded so seductively in his ear. 'You cannot leave me so! If you know so much, for God's sake return with me, see me safely home, at least. You I could trust!'

'No,' said Cadfael again. 'You are warned, now guard yourself.'

It was fair, he considered; it was enough. He turned and went away without another word. He went, just as he was, to Vespers in the parish church, for no better reason – or so he thought then – than that the dimness within the open doorway beckoned him as he turned his back on a duty completed, inviting him to quietness and thought, and the bell was just sounding. The little prior was there, ardent in thanksgiving, one more creature who had fumbled his way to the completion of a task, and the turning of a leaf in the book of his life.

Cadfael watched out the office, and stood mute and still for some time after priest and worshippers had departed. The silence after their going was deeper than the ocean and more secure than the earth. Cadfael breathed and consumed it like new bread. It was the light touch of a small hand on the hilt of his sword that startled him out of that profound isolation. He looked down to see a little acolyte, no higher than his elbow, regarding him gravely from great round eyes of blinding blue, intent and challenging, as solemn as ever was angelic messenger.

'Sir,' said the child in stern treble reproof, tapping the hilt with an infant finger, 'should not all weapons of war be laid aside here?'

'Sir,' said Cadfael hardly less gravely, though he was smiling, 'you may very well be right.' And slowly he unbuckled the sword from his belt, and went and laid it down, flatlings, on the lowest step under the altar. It looked strangely appropriate and at peace there. The hilt, after all, was a cross.

Prior Heribert was at a frugal supper with his happy brothers in the parish priest's house when Cadfael asked audience with him. The little man came out graciously to welcome a stranger, and knew him for an acquaintance at least, and now at a breath certainly a friend.

'You, my son! And surely it was you at Vespers? I felt that I should know the shape of you. You are the most welcome of guests here, and if there is anything I and mine can do to repay you for what you did for us, you need but name it.'

'Father,' said Cadfael, briskly Welsh in his asking, 'do you ride for home tomorrow?'

'Surely, my son, we leave after Prime. Abbot Godefrid will be waiting to hear how we have fared.'

'Then, Father, here am I at the turning of my life, free of one master's service, and finished with arms. Take me with you!'

THE BOUDICCA KILLING

by *Anthony Price*

A foolish boy throws a stone at his brother on the mountainside, and starts an avalanche – that is how it begins. Not by accident, but not by deliberate intent either.

A syndicate of City financiers complains that it has been cheated over certain military and civilian contracts in Britain.

The complaint is unofficial (which it has to be, for no actual law has been broken), but the complainants are determined to make trouble for the man who has beaten them at their own game. So they maintain piously that, just as their lost investment in the new province was originally undertaken for patriotic rather than commercial reasons, now their sole concern is for the welfare of the state, that first and highest duty of every citizen.

Thus is the stone cast, and the avalanche set in motion.

At first, however, it is no more than a shiver on the loose scree of the hillside. For if the syndicate has indirectly sustained a great loss over its British investment, many others have also lost their money – and directly – as a result of the terrible insurrection in that unhappy province.

Two colonies of veterans have been destroyed; vast quantities of military stores and private goods have gone up in smoke during the sack of Londinium; many thousands of persons, both citizens and freemen, not to mention valuable slaves, have been massacred – in effect, both debtors and their property; and many other debtors among the native aristocracy are now proscribed rebels, whose wealth (such as remains of it) is the legitimate booty of the armed forces, which not even Caesar himself may safely appropriate.

Yet once in motion, an avalanche may not be hindered – and a fiscal investigation is inexorable.

This is not because the fiscal inspectors set any store whatsoever by the syndicate's patriotism; nor are they usually very interested, all things being equal, in the particular identity of contract-holders, provided such men pay their taxes.

Yet they are also by nature intensely suspicious men, and Gnaeus Alfrenius Cotta is a new name in their files.

Gn. Alfrenius Cotta, recently in a modest way of business in Ostia, but now a major financial power in the City.

Gn. Alfrenius Cotta, who has made a fortune out of Britain, where everyone else had lost money.

Gn. Alfrenius Cotta, who (so it transpires) knows how the dice will fall before they have been thrown.

I: *In the City*

The Colonel of *Arcani* goes to that office between the Capitoline and the Palatine where such briefings are held, under orders to proceed without delay to that Province.

There are present three senior fiscal clerks, together with the Sub-prefect of the Imperial Courier Service, and a freedman from the Palace (whom the Colonel instantly identifies as one of Caesar's principal secretaries-of-state).

One of the clerks speaks first.

He sketches the course of the late British insurrection; which the Colonel understands better than any fiscal clerk, not only because such things are his business but also because he has served in Britain, which (he surmises) is why he is now under orders for the island, and not Hierosolyma (where there is also trouble, as usual).

The clerk concludes: 'Colonel, it amounts to this: after the despatches of the late Decianus Catus, Procurator of the Province, we received the first true account of the situation from the noble Governor, Gaius Suetonius Paulinus.'

That is good, thinks the Colonel. Caesar's justice has made Decianus 'the late' and Suetonius 'the noble' – which is as things should be.

'By that time the *colonia* at Camulodunum has been destroyed—'

'And one whole battlegroup of the Ninth Legion, says the second clerk, the one with rabbit's teeth. 'Three regular cohorts of the line – *obliterated*!'

He makes it sound like an entry on the wrong side of one of his ledgers. Which for him no doubt it is, thinks the Colonel bitterly. The best footsloggers in the world are . . . expensive – to a clerk.

'They were ambushed on the march, in wooded country,' adds Rabbit's-teeth. 'It's a situation the legions have never learned to handle. Varus couldn't – and they still can't.'

So Rabbit's-teeth is an amateur tactician. And the nearest thing Rabbit's-teeth has seen to 'wooded country' is the Garden of Lucullus.

The Sub-prefect, who has served in Germany, has the grace to look uncomfortable; the Colonel, who has served in Britain and knows that hell is a dank, dripping, trackless undergrowth without end, merely smiles politely and asks to see the Governor's despatch.

It is short, and to the point.

And, although it is from the noble Governor himself, who one week later won the greatest victory of the reign, over a British horde outnumbering his army ten-to-one, it smells unmistakably of Roman defeat, disaster and death.

Decianus Catus, Procurator of Britain, has fled the Province. The Twentieth Legion has disobeyed orders, failing to march to the Governor's aid, and the Second is too far away; the Ninth (what is left of it) is closely besieged in its camp. Consequently, the Governor must abandon Londinium and Verulamium, which are now indefensible, and retire to his field army in the north-west – one tired Legion with its auxiliary regiments.

If Queen Boudicca and her savages catch him on the road, or if she ambushes his army (shades of Rabbit's-teeth!) before he can conduct that army to his chosen battle-ground, or if she waits ten days until his supplies are exhausted, then Rome in Britain is finished. That must be faced, and plans laid accordingly by Caesar.

Alternatively, within seven days, if the Gods favour Rome, the Governor will have the honour of laying a great victory at the feet of Caesar.

So . . . the Governor writes of victory, but expects defeat, like a gambler throwing against a Venus. It is a dead man's despatch, with expectation overshadowing hope.

'Is that clear, Colonel?' says the first clerk.

The room is cooler now. In his youth the Colonel has seen (as the clerks and the freedmen have not seen, though the Sub-prefect may have seen) what the savages do to their prisoners. And, remembering a grove on the high chalk downs, he recalls particularly how ingenious the British women were in impaling a young officer of the Batavians, who was his special friend, who was still alive when—

No! That is not a proper memory for a Colonel of the *Arcani*.

The Colonel nods.

'Very well.' The first clerk accepts the nod. 'When the syndicate heard the contents of that despatch, which they did within an hour of its receipt—'

Now the Colonel understands more: one of Caesar's chief ministers is in the syndicate.

'—they commenced to offer their contracts on the open market in the City. And their provincial debts.'

'At a reduced rate?' asks the Colonel, deliberately insulting.

'Not initially . . . You must remember, Colonel, that Decianus Catus had made light of the rising in *his* despatches. Rather, he emphasised the number of slaves taken during the Governor's campaign in the north-west – and the gold mines of the new territories . . . The syndicate made it sound as though they were putting new shares on the market, with new areas for capital development.'

The Colonel nods again, dutifully. High finance isn't so very different from betting on the races: the biggest wins are always to be made on outsiders.

But this race has to be different – and the Sub-prefect is looking decidedly uncomfortable.

'Someone talked?'

Even the first clerk looks uncomfortable. Imperial couriers who talk only talk once – or twice, the second time being when they admit that they talked. Which is positively the last time that they ever talk.

'And then the market fell – and Cotta started to buy?' The Colonel is beginning to enjoy himself, and to like Gn. Alfrenius Cotta, who has evidently beaten the official odds.

'Not immediately . . . The market was nervous – Decianus Catus has a bad name—'

'Nobody bought.' It is the third clerk who speaks, a goat-faced man who has been silent hitherto. 'British investments have never been attractive. The slaves are unsatisfactory, and the cost of mineral extraction is high unless it's under local control. And the loan repayments from the local aristocracies have been unreliable. We should never had invaded the island.'

Rabbit's-teeth nods to that. 'So the syndicate dropped its prices. And then the details of that despatch leaked out—'

'The bottom dropped out of the market,' says Goat-face. 'On the second day – in the afternoon.'

'And then Cotta bought?'

'No,' says Goat-face. 'Then he started to *borrow*.'

'To – borrow?'

'Yes, Colonel. You see – you must understand – this man Cotta is . . . was . . . nothing special, financially speaking . . . Mostly import-export, Massilia-Ostia. Plus a few contracts the bigger groups had missed – only four in Britain—'

'His agent there is his nephew, his sister's son,' supplements Rabbit's-teeth eagerly. 'The youth has – *had* – a minor post on the staff of the Procurator, Decianus Catus—'

'The *late* Decianus Catus,' murmurs Goat-face. 'But . . . the point is, he had no cash on hand. He had to borrow in order to buy.'

'More than borrow,' amends Rabbit's-teeth. 'He called in all his debts – he mortgaged all his property . . . And then he took out second mortgages. He sold his villa at Praenestina—'

'At a loss,' says the first clerk.

'At a loss. And then he mortgaged his sister's property,' says Rabbit's-teeth. 'And *then* he borrowed on the open market!'

Goat-face gestures abruptly. 'He went beyond all reason and prudence – he borrowed on risk-cargoes in transit, even. And he has a reputation in Ostia for good sense – sharp, but sensible—'

'Which helped his credit in Ostia.' Rabbit's-teeth nods.

'He even borrowed from the syndicate—' Goat-face smiles. 'Short-term, high interest – they took him for a stupid provincial, and he took *them*—'

'But he didn't buy openly,' says Rabbit's-teeth. 'It was all through nominees – more provincials.'

'He bought everything they had, including that palace we're building for the client-king in the south,' says Goat-face. 'By the eighth day – all signed, sealed and delivered. Plus a dozen other contracts from . . . other groups.'

The Prince's ministers had sold out too, naturally.

'He owns half the Province now,' says Rabbit's-teeth. 'If he had a son he'd have to call the child "Britannicus".'

'But he has no son. Only that nephew, whom he exiled to Britain because they mistrusted each other,' murmurs the first clerk. 'Tiberius Alfrenius Martinus . . . Britannicus . . .'

It adds up to one conclusion, and one only. They have been at pains to make that clear.

'So – he knew,' says the Colonel.

'He knew,' Goat-face nods. '*And he knew before we did.*'

It is Goat-face who is the senior clerk, the Colonel decides. It irritates him that he did not guess that more quickly.

But now he does not wish to compound that error.

The despatch he has seen was not the latest despatch, there has to be another—
Queen Boudicca dead, her Army destroyed, the Province saved!

The noble Governor, Gaius Suetonius Paulinus, would have sent that despatch no less quickly than its predecessor. It would have taken maybe a day or two longer, travelling from the battlefield, but it would have taken the same route, under the same absolute priority of the imperial Governor's seal – courier, and fast galley, and courier; relay after relay, the best men on the fastest horses, along the imperial highways. Ever since the Varus disaster, fifty years before, when there had been disgraceful scenes of panic in the City, bad news had always been brought to Caesar first, before being released to the Senate; and even good news, travelling on its own fair wind, is supposed to reach the Palatine Hill first.

But if that has been compromised then the Sub-prefect should be looking more unhappy . . .

Which he is not. (And Caesar's freedman hasn't spoken a word either, yet; but then his job is to listen and report back, no more, of course.)

So the Colonel says nothing. And for a moment or two no one else wishes to speak, either.

'And that is the sum of our problem,' says Goat-face finally. (Naturally, it must be Goat-face.) 'He knew – but he could not have known.'

Rabbit's-teeth surreptitiously signs himself against evil.

The first clerk speaks: 'It is the time factor, Colonel . . . No one in his right mind would have risked what Alfrenius Cotta did, unless he was certain. Because he pledged himself, and his freedom, and his life . . . and his family—'

'Three times over,' cuts in Rabbit's-teeth, actuarially.

'But he is in his right mind,' says Goat-face. 'Yet he started raising money *before* Boudicca was defeated. And he began buying *before* the victory despatch had crossed the Narrow Sea to Gaul—'

'Which leaves us with only two explanations,' says Rabbit's-teeth. 'First . . . sorcery – of the worst kind!'

'Um . . . present knowledge of a future event, that is,' says the first clerk. 'The supernatural.'

'Of which there have been cases – well-authenticated cases—' Rabbit's-teeth is cut off by a look from Goat-face.

'Well-authenticated cases . . . *after* the event.' Goat-face looks at the Colonel dispassionately. 'But there has *never* been a case where the immortal Gods have helped a small businessman to make a large fortune while Caesar himself is sacrificing on the Altar of Victory in the hope of a sign from heaven.'

Rabbit's-teeth is crestfallen. Caesar's freedman begins to look interested.

Goat-face continues to observe the Colonel. 'The noble Governor's despatch foreshadowed a great defeat. But someone else evidently knew better – and what is more, he knew better enough to convince Gnaeus Alfrenius Cotta, who is certainly nobody's fool, that he knew better, Colonel.'

No one rejects this reasoning.

'Now . . . I think I know *who*, Colonel . . . since there is only one person who could have known.'

The Colonel begins to understand what is required of him.

'What I need to know is *how*—'

The imbecile innocence of the Sub-prefect's expression confirms the understanding: his service has not failed twice.

'—and I want to know quickly.' Goat-face's voice is like marble. 'So . . . this day you will leave the City, carrying Caesar's formal congratulations to the noble Governor, Gaius Suetonius Paulinus—'

II: *In the Province*

Britain is different from Germany in the early autumn. In a few weeks it will be bare, and every gutter will be choked with fallen leaves, but now it is a riot of red and yellow and gold, where Germany is an eternal dark green.

These are the colours which the Colonel remembers, when the world was young and he was a junior staff officer of auxiliaries.

But now it is different in a different way, with the fresh scars of hastily dug ditches and the raw wood of new palisades around every halt on the road to Londinium; and the town itself a burnt-out horror smelling of damp ash and rotting flesh, in which he sleeps under canvas for one night only, thankful to obey the letter of his orders to the last syllable.

Except that what follows, as he moves on towards the noble Governor's field headquarters, is worse, even allowing for the satisfaction of the crowded prison camps in which the women and children are held (there are no male adult prisoners in the forward areas; the Gallic irregular cavalry are spearheading the mopping-up operations, and they are head-hunters by both inclination and religion, and they are earning their bounty-money; so . . . satisfaction and yet death and devastation are always depressing, even when justly imposed on the guilty – and these natives are undeniably guilty).

But tonight he is dining with the Governor himself, as befits his Praetorian rank and his status as Caesar's honoured messenger, carrying greetings from the Roman Senate and People.

(What the Governor does not know is that his is a political mission: Caesar has no use for governors who win victories which take the imagination of the Roman Senate and People, such men must be cut down to smaller size – Goat-face has made that abundantly clear in private, with the freedman's nod.

(And that makes his task both distasteful and difficult; distasteful, because he admires the noble Governor's brilliant victory over odds; and difficult . . .

(Difficult, because there is not one shred of evidence so far that the noble Governor has conspired with Tiberius Alfrenius Martinus – and Gnaeus Alfrenius Cotta – to execute a gigantic fraud on Caesar and the City . . .

(Difficult, because the dates check out – the noble Governor was still fighting when Gn. Alfrenius Cotta was borrowing . . .

(Difficult, because when the noble Governor abandoned Londinium nobody, but *nobody*, knew which way Boudicca was marching; indeed, if anything, the consensus was that she would destroy the Governor and his army first, and the town afterwards, for which very sensible reason ten thousand Roman settlers and friendly tribesmen remained there, hoping for the best, and died there very unpleasantly when she stormed the decaying ramparts before chasing the Governor . . .

(*So* difficult that the Colonel is almost of a mind to agree with Rabbit's-teeth on the matter of sorcery . . .

(Almost, but not quite. For Tiberius Alfrenius Martinus, nephew to Gnaeus Alfrenius Cotta and formerly a tax accountant with the late, unlamented Procurator, Decianus Catus, is now the trusted military secretary of the noble Governor. And that, in the circumstances of the Procurator's behaviour, is a very curious promotion, which makes no sense at all . . .

(And which, therefore, requires investigation.)

So . . . now the Colonel is dining with the noble Governor, and the last of the food has been removed, and the small talk, though it is apparently continuing, is in fact over—

'Wasn't that young Alfrenius Martinus I saw taking notes at your briefing this afternoon, my lord?' enquires the Colonel conversationally.

'My secretary?' The noble Governor is mellowed by the wine and the day's gratifying head-count. 'You know him?'

'I know his uncle slightly – one of the coming men in the City . . . But I thought young Martinus was on Catus's staff?'

The Governor frowns momentarily, and then smiles in quick succession, no doubt thinking first of his former procurator, whose crass stupidity caused the insurrection, and then of the fate of both procurator and insurrectionists.

'Yes, so he was. But . . . '

The Colonel listens as the Governor, wine-mellowed, talks—

It had been just after the news had been confirmed that the Twentieth Legion hadn't marched: what had already become a serious tribal uprising was something far worse now – it had a Varus-disaster premonition about it now.

The Governor was desperately tired, quite drained by bad news; and, what was worse, he knew he was beginning to despair. Also, the last of the galleys was waiting to slip its moorings, and he had a despatch (which he now believed would be the last of his career) to send aboard, but he had no one to take it down in writing for him.

'Who?' he snapped at the Guards sergeant.

'Alfrenius Martinus – Tiberius Alfrenius Martinus, my lord.'

He didn't want to see anyone, and the name meant nothing to him. But he knew that fear was infectious, and he must not let it spread from him.

'Very well – I'll see him.'

He turned away, waiting until the sergeant had made himself scarce.

Tiberius what-was-his-name was youngish and short and rather fat, and he wore an ill-fitting uniform, and the smell of the infection was already on him. 'Yes?'

Martinus saluted self-consciously and badly, and began to explain what he was, rather than who. Which was a mistake, because at the mention of the Procurator's name the Governor cut him off brutally.

'You are too late. Your master has run for it – and I'm damned if I'm giving you a place on the despatches galley. Get out!' It was a measure of the Governor's weariness that this death sentence gave him no special satisfaction.

But Martinus stood firm. 'I wasn't too late. I chose to stay, sir.'

'Oh?' The words registered only partially. 'Then that was very foolish of you.'

Martinus swayed, as though embarrassed. 'My . . . my father was a soldier. A-and his father – my grandfather – was a soldier.' He blinked. 'It would have been . . . dishonourable.'

The Governor discovered that he could still be surprised. The fellow was sweating with fright, and he was also ridiculous. But he was nevertheless volunteering to die with his betters – a bloody tax-man – and *that* wasn't ridiculous.

'I know I'm no soldier' – Martinus blinked again – 'but they said . . . in the Officers' Mess . . . that your secretary had run away. So I thought—' He stopped suddenly, and seemed to take his fear, if not his courage, in both hands. 'They said, if the army is to have a chance, then Boudicca must attack Londinium first. But they don't think she will . . . But I think there's a way, sir . . . '

The Governor nodded, speechlessly. It would be stupid, whatever it was, it would be stupid. But he mustn't laugh, because this man's 'honour' was like a flower on a dunghill – and his fear was something they possessed in common. So he mustn't laugh.

'Sir – if Boudicca believes that the Procurator is still here in the town . . . They say he had her flogged under her own roof – if she thought he was still here—'

The Governor felt a pang of disappointment. In spite of himself, in spite of instinct and appearances, he had hoped for a miracle.

'Martinus . . . ' He edited out the sharpness. 'Martinus, this city – this town – is full of spies. He's gone, the bastard – and they saw him go, Martinus.'

'Yes, sir.' Martinus nodded. 'But not all of them – and the ones who didn't will want to report that he's still here. If we give them something to report – if we give them rumours even . . . We could say the galley grounded in the estuary, and you'd had him brought back – and we could put guards on his house . . . Just a rumour, sir – that might be enough to decide her . . . Just the outside chance of taking him *alive*—'

Plainly ridiculous. Boudicca knew well enough that Catus had run away, and even if she didn't then the obvious military logic of attacking the army first was the only thing that made sense.

And yet—

'Just the chance, sir.' Martinus bared his teeth. 'If she could lay her hands on him . . .'

Yet there was something about this little fellow which lent force to his words. Suddenly the Governor caught the undertone of anger beneath the fear.

So that was it, then: if Tiberius Something Martinus had Decianus Catus in his hands now, the bastard would die as slowly as if he'd fallen to Boudicca, Queen of the Iceni!

It had never occurred to him to take such elemental passions into the reckoning, to be weighed against the better strategy. Yet if the image of Decianus Catus impaled living on a sharpened stake could fire a snivelling tax-man, how much more might a well-placed rumour distort Boudicca's judgement?

He was clutching at straws. But they were all he had.

He was also staring poor little Martinus out of countenance.

But he felt better—

'I have a despatch to send. Can you take dictation?'

'Sir?' Martinus stiffened. 'Yes, sir!'

'After that . . . we'll see what we can do with your rumours.' Absurdly, the Governor felt much better. The thought of Martinus drawing his rusty sword against a great hairy Briton might be laughable, but he had seven thousand heavy infantry up the road from this doomed town – Roman infantry, the true Rome – who knew how to use their swords. And Martinus could meanwhile draw his pen to good effect to settle Decianus Catus, whatever the outcome.

The little man was trying to speak again.

'Yes?'

'I was wondering, sir . . . Might I send a private letter – two private letters – with your despatch?' He fumbled beneath the armour. 'I have them here, sir.'

'What?' The Governor found he had accepted the letters.

'To my mother, sir. I – I am her only son . . . And – and to my uncle, sir. She is a widow.'

The Governor read the two letters, and as he read them the last of his tiredness and fear fell away from him.

This – *this* – was also the true Rome, here in this unprepossessing little pen-pusher, as surely as in his unbeatable footsloggers.

And these were words he would never forget.

'Very well – send them.' He returned the letters. 'But now–'

Now they were going to beat that damned woman Boudicca.

And that, says the noble Governor, was what they did.

III: *In the Forward Headquarters*

The Colonel is still following the noble Governor into the newly pacified – totally devastated – territory of the Iceni two days later (with that damned woman only a dark memory now), and it is raining. (And that is another thing the Colonel recalls from '96 – the rain.) Off the log corduroys of the camp the lines are already halfway to quagmires.

115

But the tent of Tiberius Alfrenius Martinus, with its charcoal brazier and its plank floor, is snug and warm – as befits that of the Governor's chief secretary, whom the Governor has been pleased to honour with the rank of acting-colonel for the duration of the emergency.

The chief secretary/acting-colonel is busy drafting tomorrow's operational orders when the Colonel enters the tent.

(The chief secretary/acting-colonel is also still in uniform too, which seems to support the camp joke – that he is so proud of his armour that he sleeps in it. But then it is better-fitting now, the Colonel notes.)

He looks up at his visitor, clearly a little irritated at this interruption of his work. He is a world away – a great victory away, and the Governor's favour away, and a private fortune away – from the frightened tax-man of former days.

So shock tactics are called for: the Colonel tosses his Imperial warrant on to the table, with its seal of life and death uppermost.

To the slave at Martinus's shoulder he says: 'Get out.'

The slave has never seen that seal, and perhaps Martinus hasn't either. But he has heard of it.

'Leave us,' he orders his slave. Then: 'Can I help you, Colonel?'

'You can. And you will.' The Colonel looks round for a seat. There is a stool piled with papers – quartermaster's reports, muster rolls, casualty lists and head-count tallies. He tips them on to the floor and sits down opposite Martinus.

'I don't know how you did it, Tiberius Alfrenius Martinus. But I know you did it somehow.'

Martinus says nothing.

'And I know that you are a liar.'

Still nothing.

'A considerable liar. Not an only son, for example. And your father was a tally-clerk. And his father was also a tally-clerk. For a start – a considerable liar, Tiberius Alfrenius Martinus.'

Martinus smiles . . . as if to say that these are minor matters now.

'Very well!' The stool is uncomfortable. 'Then I'll tell you a story, Tiberius Alfrenius Martinus . . .

'There was once a tax official – a *junior* tax official – who was sent to the south coast of Britain, to Noviomagus, to collect the Procurator's share of the palace contractors' bribes. But when he got back to Londinium – not without difficulty – he found that a revolt had broken out—'

Martinus stirs suddenly, as though he wants to speak.

'No! Don't spoil my story!' The Colonel cuts him off. 'This *very junior* tax official also finds that his master, the Procurator, has already run away. And there is only one galley left . . . and when he tries to bribe his way aboard – with the Noviomagus gold – he is turned away with a sharp sword. Because the last galley is reserved for the Governor's last despatch . . . and no one – no one else – and least of all a damned tax official – is going aboard, at any price.

'So *he* – our minor cog in the broken wheel of Decianus Catus – *he* then goes in despair to the Governor's headquarters, to see if his gold will buy safety there.

'But it won't. Because gold has lost its value in Londinium. It won't buy a berth on the last galley. And all the roads are cut now, anyway. And the Governor himself is about to abandon the town and march to almost certain defeat, if Boudicca keeps her head and does the right thing. And then the town will fall.

'So when he offers his gold to the officers they just laugh at him – and offer him a breast-plate two sizes too big and a nasty sharp sword – No! Don't deny it, Tiberius Alfrenius Martinus – I've talked to them, and I know what happened!'

The stool is quite excruciating, really.

'But now it becomes interesting, because we come to what I don't know . . . Because you went to the Governor, and you suggested to him how he might lure Boudicca to Londinium while he chose his battlefield – very good!

'And you sent two letters by his courier – two Roman letters to warm the heart of a Roman general on the eve of battle—

' "*Mother – I write to you on the eve of battle. I hope to serve with honour, fighting beside my General and Governor, the noble Gaius Suetonius Paulinus. Know that I shall not disgrace Father's memory, and that, should I fall, my last thought but one will be of you, and my last of Rome, the Great Mother of us all.*

Your loving and dutiful son,

Tiberius"

' "*Uncle – I write to you on the eve of the battle. The odds are against us. If I should fall, I charge you by the glorious memory of my father, your brother, who also gave his life for Rome, to comfort and sustain my dear mother.*

Your dutiful nephew,

Tiberius"

'—letters engraved on that general's heart,' continues the Colonel, gazing on Martinus not without admiration.

'But what is engraved on my heart is . . . that you are a most ingenious and absolute liar, Tiberius Alfrenius Martinus – and I want to know *what was in the letters you actually sent*, not in those which you showed to the Governor.'

He leans forward and taps the seal on the warrant to emphasise this request. But now there is a cast of obstinacy in Martinus's expression: on the strength of his acting-rank, and the Governor's favour, and his new wealth, he is still inclined to cover his dice with his cup and bet on them.

'Pardon me, Colonel – I know of no letters – a few small . . . inaccuracies, perhaps – slips of the tongue made in a moment of enthusiasm, no more. But the Governor will forgive them, Colonel. And I know that I have committed no crime' – his eyes flick for an instant to the seal – 'no crime whatsoever, Colonel.'

No crime. And he has the Governor nicely calculated: the noble Gaius Suetonius Paulinus will never admit being taken for a fool by this man, it will be against the dignity of his great victory.

Martinus knows that. He strokes his breast-plate as if to emphasise his knowledge. Nothing can be proved, and the past will bury the past. He is guilty, but safe.

'So, Colonel—?' The pudgy little hand continues to massage the gilded bronze, which no gentleman would wear at such an hour – certainly no officer—

· In that moment the Colonel sees his way, towards which that hand has pointed.

Under his bronze, Martinus must be frightened, because everyone is frightened by that seal.

Under that bronze is a man who knows his law and his rights as a citizen. But not his miliary law, for a guess—

And under that bronze is a snob, a parvenu and a social climber – as might be expected of a junior tax official—

So . . . the stick and the carrot.

'No crime?' The Colonel pretends to be comfortable. 'It is our belief, as the facts indicate, that you entered into direct communication with the woman Boudicca, without your commander's knowledge or consent . . . whereby you obtained details of her plans, on which you acted—'

'No—'

'*And*, under military law in the field, and in uniform – and with your rank – on my authority alone I can have you flogged and crucified, Tiberius Alfrenius Martinus. Which will get you conveniently out of the Governor's way—'

'*No*—'

The stick has landed squarely on those white buttocks. The man doesn't know his military law – but he has seen what the scourge and the cross-tree can do to a man.

'*But* . . . Caesar is merciful.' Now for the carrot: the Colonel balances himself carefully. 'And he is also grateful—'

Martinus's battle line is bending: surprise has joined fear in the frontal assault.

'Grateful. For it was *you* who put backbone into the noble Governor, Tiberius Alfrenius Martinus – it was you who saved Britain with your treason!'

One last reinforcement is needed. The Colonel calls it up.

'Your uncle is a crude person – rich now, but still crude. Your family's influence requires proper representation in the City . . . In the equestrian order at once . . . and, in due time, in the Senate itself.' By a miracle the words do not choke their speaker. 'All we need to know, before your equestrian sponsors are nominated, is . . . exactly how you knew what Boudicca was going to do, sir.'

The line is shattered. Dreams of gentility are too much for it.

'But . . . that is to say . . . I didn't actually *know* . . . '

It is a moment to hold one's breath. And to smile, as one colonel to another, encouragingly.

'You are right – I came back, and *he* had gone—' There is the flare of anger which the Governor saw. 'He had gone, and they laughed at me. I could have crucified him—'

So the Governor had been right, too!

'And I could have crucified my uncle with him – for sending me to this filthy place!'

But the Governor had also been quite wrong too, evidently.

'Then . . . one of the officers said . . . he said I needn't worry. Because in a few days' time we'd all be heroes – or we'd all be dead . . . if we were lucky . . . He said the Governor needed a secretary, and if he took me on at least it would be quick – win or lose – when *she* caught up with us. *Aut Caesar, aut nihil* – one way or the other—'

'So I wrote the letters – the real ones—'

' "*Mother – Do exactly what I order, no more and no less. In two days' time take the enclosed letter to my uncle, Alfrenius Cotta, together with all the monies I have remitted to you to hold for me. Tell him you have just received the letter and instruction from a stranger. Do not tell him of the delay. Do not fail me. Destroy this letter at once.*

Your loving son,

Tiberius."

' "*Uncle – In haste. The Army has won a great victory. Londinium and the two veterans' colonies have been destroyed, but the rest of the Province is substantially undamaged. I am acting as the Governor's secretary and will delay his victory despatch for six days. I send this letter in advance by a secure messenger. My mother brings it to you with my savings to invest in Britain at your discretion. Act quickly to make us rich.*

Your dutiful nephew,

Tiberius." '

The Colonel looks at Martinus incredulously. 'You didn't know?'

Martinus spreads his hands. 'Nobody knew, Colonel. But they all said – all the officers said – that these savages only have one big battle in them. We couldn't get away . . . so they'd either wipe us out completely, like Varus. Or we'd smash them to pieces—'

'*But you didn't know, man*—'

'I knew it would be one way or the other. And if I was wrong, then I bloody well wouldn't be there to admit it. But if I was right – I'd be rich, Colonel.'

'So you gave him your money?'

Martinus smiles. 'I had to make him believe me – and if there's one thing my dear uncle believes, it's money. So I bought his belief with my savings, Colonel – it was an investment, you might say.'

'But you could have ruined him—?'

'Yes. And that was also part of the investment.' Another, colder memory freezes the smile. 'He would have been ruined – and I would have been dead—'

Martinus pauses for a moment to listen to the incessant sound of the rain on the canvas above him.

'—Dead. But also avenged on him for condemning me to death on this frightful island, Colonel.'

Beyond the downpour there is the distant noise of the Gallic irregulars celebrating drunkenly over the day's trophies.

Martinus brightens. 'But I was right. And now we're both rich . . . And being right and rich isn't yet a crime in the City – is it, Colonel?'

THE IRONY OF HATE

by Ruth Rendell

I murdered Brenda Goring for what I suppose is the most unusual of motives. She came between me and my wife. By that I don't mean to say that there was anything abnormal in their relationship. They were merely close friends, though 'merely' is hardly the word to use in connection with a relationship which alienates and excludes a once-loved husband. I murdered her to get my wife to myself once more, but instead I have parted us perhaps for ever, and I await with dread, with impotent panic, with the most awful helplessness I have ever known, the coming trial.

By setting down the facts – and the irony, the awful irony that runs through them like a sharp glittering thread – I may come to see things more clearly. I may find some way to convince those inexorable powers that be of how it really was; to make Defending Counsel believe me and not raise his eyebrows and shake his head; to ensure, at any rate, that if Laura and I must be separated she will know as she sees me taken from the court to my long imprisonment, that the truth is known and justice done.

Alone here with nothing else to do, with nothing to wait for but that trial, I could write reams about the character, the appearance, the neuroses, of Brenda Goring. I could write the great hate novel of all time. In this context, though, much of it would be irrelevant, and I shall be as brief as I can.

Some character in Shakespeare says of a woman, 'Would I had never seen her!' And the reply is: 'Then you would have left unseen a very wonderful piece of work.' Well, would indeed I had never seen Brenda. As for her being a wonderful piece of work, I suppose I would agree with that too. Once she had had a husband. To be rid of her for ever, no doubt, he paid her enormous alimony and had settled on her a lump sum with which she bought the cottage up the lane from our house. On our village she made the impact one would expect of such a newcomer. Wonderful she was, an amazing refreshment to all those retired couples and cautious weekenders, with her clothes, her long blonde hair, her sports car, her talents and her jet-set past. For a while, that is. Until she got too much for them to take.

From the first she fastened on to Laura. Understandable in a way, since my wife was the only woman in the locality who was of comparable age, who lived there all the time and who had no job. But surely – or so I thought at first – she would never have singled out Laura if she had had a wider choice. To me my wife is lovely, all I could ever want, the only woman I have ever really cared for, but I know that to others she appears shy, colourless, a simple and quiet little housewife. What, then, had she to offer to that extrovert, that bright bejewelled butterfly? She gave me the beginning of the answer herself.

121

'Haven't you noticed the way people are starting to shun her darling? The Goldsmiths didn't ask her to their party last week and Mary Williamson refuses to have her on the fête committee.'

'I can't say I'm surprised,' I said. 'The way she talks and the things she talks about.'

'You mean her love affairs and all that sort of thing? But, darling, she's lived in the sort of society where that's quite normal. It's natural for her to talk like that, it's just that she's open and honest.'

'She's not living in that sort of society now,' I said, 'and she'll have to adapt if she wants to be accepted. Did you notice Isabel Goldsmith's face when Brenda told that story about going off for a weekend with some chap she'd picked up in a bar? I tried to stop her going on about all the men her husband named in his divorce action, but I couldn't. And then she's always saying, "When I was living with so-and-so" and "That was the time of my affair with what's-his-name". Elderly people find that a bit upsetting, you know.'

'Well, we're not elderly,' said Laura, 'and I hope we can be a bit more broad-minded. You do like her, don't you?'

I was always very gentle with my wife. The daughter of clever domineering parents who belittled her, she grew up with an ineradicable sense of her own inferiority. She is a born victim, an inviter of bullying, and therefore I have tried never to bully her, never even to cross her. So all I said was that Brenda was all right and that I was glad, since I was out all day, that she had found a friend and companion of her own age.

And if Brenda had befriended and companioned her only during the day, I daresay I shouldn't have objected. I should have got used to the knowledge that Laura was listening, day in and day out, to stories of a world she had never known, to hearing illicit sex and duplicity glorified, and I should have been safe in the conviction that she was incorruptible. But I had to put up with Brenda myself in the evenings when I got home from my long commuting. There she would be, lounging on our sofa, in her silk trousers or long skirt and high boots, chain-smoking. Or she would arrive with a bottle of wine just as we had sat down to dinner and involve us in one of those favourite debates of hers on the lines of 'Is marriage a dying institution?' or 'Are parents necessary?' And to illustrate some specious point of hers she would come out with some personal experience of the kind that had so upset our elderly friends.

Of course I was not obliged to stay with them. Ours is quite a big house, and I could go off into the dining room or the room Laura called my study. But all I wanted was what I had once had, to be alone in the evenings with my wife. And it was even worse when we were summoned to coffee or drinks with Brenda, there in her lavishly furnished, over-ornate cottage to be shown the latest thing she had made – she was always embroidering and weaving and potting and messing about with water colours – and shown too the gifts she had received at some time or another from Mark and Larry and Paul and all the dozens of other men there had been in her life. When I refused to go Laura would become nervous and depressed, then pathetically elated if, after a couple of blissful

Brenda-less evenings, I suggested for the sake of pleasing her that I supposed we might as well drop in on old Brenda.

What sustained me was the certainty that sooner or later any woman so apparently popular with the opposite sex would find herself a boy friend and have less or no time for my wife. I couldn't understand why this hadn't happened already and I said so to Laura.

'She does see her men friends when she goes up to London,' said my wife.

'She never has any of them down here,' I said, and that evening when Brenda was treating us to a highly coloured account of some painter she knew called Laszlo who was terribly attractive and who adored her, I said I'd like to meet him and why didn't she invite him down for the weekend?

Brenda flashed her long green-painted fingernails about and gave Laura a conspiratorial woman-to-woman look. 'And what would all the old fuddy-duddies have to say about that, I wonder?'

'Surely you can rise above all that sort of thing, Brenda,' I said.

'Of course I can. Give them something to talk about. I'm quite well aware it's only sour grapes. I'd have Laszlo here like a shot, only he wouldn't come. He hates the country, he'd be bored stiff.'

Apparently Richard and Jonathan and Stephen also hated the country or would be bored or couldn't spare the time. It was much better for Brenda to go up and see them in town, and I noticed that after my probing about Laszlo, Brenda seemed to go to London more often and that the tales of her escapades after these visits became more and more sensational. I think I am quite a perceptive man and soon there began to form in my mind an idea so fantastic that for a while I refused to admit it even to myself. But I put it to the test. Instead of just listening to Brenda and throwing in the occasional rather sour rejoinder, I started asking her questions. I took her up on names and dates. 'I thought you said you met Mark in America?' I would say, or 'But surely you didn't have that holiday with Richard until after your divorce?' I tied her up in knots without her realising it, and the idea began to seem not so fantastic after all. The final test came at Christmas.

I had noticed that Brenda was a very different woman when she was alone with me than when Laura was with us. If, for example, Laura was out in the kitchen making coffee or, as sometimes happened at the weekends, Brenda dropped in when Laura was out, she was rather cool and shy with me. Gone then were the flamboyant gestures and the provocative remarks, and Brenda would chat about village matters as mundanely as Isabel Goldsmith. Not quite the behaviour one would expect from a self-styled Messalina alone with a young and reasonably personable man. It struck me then that in the days when Brenda had been invited to village parties, and now when she still met neighbours at our parties, she never once attempted a flirtation. Were all the men too old for her to bother with? Was a slim, handsome man of going on fifty too ancient to be considered fair game for a woman who would never see thirty again? Of course they were all married, but so were her Paul and her Stephen, and, if she were to be believed, she had had no compunction about taking them away from their wives.

123

If she were to be believed. That was the crux of it. Not one of them wanted to spend Christmas with her. No London lover invited her to a party or offered to take her away. She would be with us, of course, for Christmas lunch, for the whole of the day, and at our Boxing Day gathering of friends and relatives. I had hung a bunch of mistletoe in our hall, and on Christmas morning I admitted her to the house myself, Laura being busy in the kitchen.

'Merry Christmas,' I said. 'Give us a kiss, Brenda,' and I took her in my arms under that mistletoe and kissed her on the mouth. She stiffened. I swear a shudder ran through her. She was as awkward, as apprehensive, as repelled as a sheltered twelve-year-old. And then I knew. Married she may have been – and it was not hard now to guess the cause of her divorce – but she had never had a lover or enjoyed an embrace or even been alone with a man longer than she could help. She was frigid. A good-looking, vivacious, healthy girl, she nevertheless had that particular disability. She was as cold as a nun. But because she couldn't bear the humiliation of admitting it, she had created for herself a fantasy life, a fantasy past, in which she queened it as a fantasy nymphomaniac.

At first I thought it a huge joke and I couldn't wait to tell Laura. But I wasn't alone with her till two in the morning and then she was asleep when I came to bed. I didn't sleep much. My elation dwindled as I realised I hadn't any real proof and that if I told Laura what I'd been up to, probing and questioning and testing, she would only be bitterly hurt and resentful. How could I tell her I'd kissed her best friend and got an icy response? That, in her absence, I'd tried flirting with her best friend and been repulsed? And then, as I thought about it, I understood what I really had discovered, that Brenda hated men, that no man would ever come and take her away or marry her and live here with her and absorb all her time. For ever she would stay here alone, living a stone's throw from us, in and out of our house daily, she and Laura growing old together.

I could have moved house, of course. I could have taken Laura away. From her friends? From the house and the countryside she loved? And what guarantee would I have had that Brenda wouldn't have moved too to be near us still? For I knew now what Brenda saw in my wife, a gullible innocent, a trusting everlastingly credulous audience whose own inexperience kept her from seeing the holes and discrepancies in those farragos of nonsense and whose pathetic determination to be worldly prevented her from showing distaste. As the dawn came and I looked with love and sorrow at Laura sleeping beside me, I knew what I must do, the only thing I could do. At the season of peace and goodwill, I decided to kill Brenda Goring for my own and Laura's good and peace.

Easier decided than done. I was buoyed up and strengthened by knowing that in everyone's eyes I would have no motive. Our neighbours thought us wonderfully charitable and tolerant to put up with Brenda at all. I resolved to be positively nice to her instead of just negatively easy-going, and as the New Year came in I took to dropping in on Brenda on my way back from the post or the village shop, and if I got home from work to find Laura alone I asked where

Brenda was and suggested we should phone her at once and ask her to dinner or for a drink. This pleased Laura enormously.

'I always felt you didn't really like Brenda, darling,' she said, 'and it made me feel rather guilty. It's marvellous that you're beginning to see how nice she really is.'

What I was actually beginning to see was how I could kill her and get away with it, for something happened which seemed to deliver her into my hands. On the outskirts of the village, in an isolated cottage, lived an elderly unmarried woman called Peggy Daley, and during the last week of January the cottage was broken into and Peggy stabbed to death with her own kitchen knife. The work of some psychopath, the police seemed to believe, for nothing had been stolen or damaged. When it appeared likely that they weren't going to find the killer, I began thinking of how I could kill Brenda in the same way so that the killing could look like the work of the same perpetrator. Just as I was working this out Laura went down with a 'flu bug she caught from Mary Williamson.

Brenda, of course, came in to nurse her, cooked my dinner for me and cleaned the house. Because everyone believed that Peggy Daley's murderer was still stalking the village, I walked Brenda home at night, even though her cottage was only a few yards up the lane or narrow path that skirted the end of our garden. It was pitch dark there as we had all strenuously opposed the installation of street lighting, and it brought me an ironical amusement to notice how Brenda flinched and recoiled when on these occasions I made her take my arm. I always made a point of going into the house with her and putting all the lights on. When Laura began to get better and all she wanted in the evenings was to sleep I sometimes went earlier to Brenda's, had a nightcap with her, and once, on leaving, I gave her a comradely kiss on the doorstep to show any observing neighbour what friends we were and how much I appreciated all Brenda's kindness to my sick wife.

Then I got the 'flu myself. At first this seemed to upset my plans, for I couldn't afford to delay too long. Already people were beginning to be less apprehensive about our marauding murderer and were getting back to their old habits of leaving their back doors unlocked. But then I saw how I could turn my illness to my advantage. On the Monday, when I had been confined to bed for three days and that ministering angel Brenda was fussing about me nearly as much as my own wife was, Laura remarked that she wouldn't go across to the Goldsmiths that evening as she had promised because it seemed wrong to leave me. Instead, if I was better by then, she would go on the Wednesday, her purpose being to help Isabel cut out a dress. Brenda, of course, might have offered to stay with me instead, and I think Laura was a little surprised that she didn't. I knew the reason and had a little quiet laugh to myself about it. It was one thing for Brenda to flaunt about, regaling us with stories of all the men she had nursed in the past, quite another to find herself alone with a not very sick man in that man's bedroom.

So I had to be sick enough to provide myself with an alibi but not sick enough to keep Laura at home. On the Wednesday morning I was feeling a good deal

better. Dr Lawson looked in on his way back from his rounds in the afternoon
and pronounced, after a thorough examination, that I still had phlegm on my
chest. While he was in the bathroom washing his hands and doing something
with his stethoscope, I held the thermometer he had stuck in my mouth against
the radiator at the back of the bed. This worked better than I had hoped,
worked, in fact, almost too well. The mercury went up to a hundred and three,
and I played up to it by saying in a feeble voice that I felt dizzy and kept
alternating between the sweats and the shivers.

'Keep him in bed,' Dr Lawson said, 'and give him plenty of warm drinks. I
doubt if he could get up if he tried.'

I said rather shamefacedly that I had tried and I couldn't and that my legs felt
like jelly. Immediately Laura said she wouldn't go out that night, and I blessed
Lawson when he told her not to be silly. All I needed was rest and to be allowed
to sleep. After a good deal of fussing and self-reproach and promises not to be
gone more than two hours at the most, she finally went off at seven.

As soon as the car had departed, I got up. Brenda's house could be seen from
my bedroom window, and I saw that she had lights on but no porch light. The
night was dark, moonless and starless. I put trousers and a sweater on over my
pyjamas and made my way downstairs.

By the time I was halfway down I knew that I needn't have pretended to be ill
or bothered with the thermometer ploy. I *was* ill. I was shivering and swaying,
great waves of dizziness kept coming over me, and I had to hang on to the
banisters for support. That wasn't the only thing that had gone wrong. I had
intended, when the deed was done and I was back home again, to cut up my coat
and gloves with Laura's electric scissors and burn the pieces on our living room
fire. But I couldn't find the scissors and I realised Laura must have taken them
with her to her dressmaking session. Worse than that, there was no fire alight.
Our central heating was very efficient and we only had an open fire for the
pleasure and cosiness of it, but Laura hadn't troubled to light one while I was
upstairs ill. At that moment I nearly gave up. But it was then or never. I would
never again have such circumstances and such an alibi. Either kill her now, I
thought, or live in an odious *ménage à trois* for the rest of my life.

We kept the raincoats and gloves we used for gardening in a cupboard in the
kitchen by the back door. Laura had left only the hall light on, and I didn't think
it would be wise to switch on any more. In the semi-darkness I fumbled about in
the cupboard for my raincoat, found it and put it on. It seemed tight on me, my
body was so stiff and sweaty, but I managed to button it up, and then I put on the
gloves. I took with me one of our kitchen knives and let myself out by the back
door. It wasn't a frosty night, but raw and cold and damp.

I went down the garden, up the lane and into the garden of Brenda's cottage. I
had to feel my way round the side of the house, for there was no light there at all.
But the kitchen light was on and the back door unlocked. I tapped and let myself
in without waiting to be asked. Brenda, in full evening rig, glittery sweater, gilt
necklace, long skirt, was cooking her solitary supper. And then, for the first
time ever, when it didn't matter any more, when it was too late, I felt pity for

her. There she was, a handsome, rich, gifted woman with the reputation of a seductress, but in reality as destitute of people who really cared for her as poor old Peggy Daley had been; there she was, dressed for a party, heating up tinned spaghetti in a cottage kitchen at the back of beyond.

She turned round, looking apprehensive, but only, I think, because she was always afraid when we were alone that I would try to make love to her.

'What are you doing out of bed?' she said, and then, 'Why are you wearing those clothes?'

I didn't answer her. I stabbed her in the chest again and again. She made no sound but a little choking moan and she crumpled up on the floor. Although I had known how it would be, had hoped for it, the shock was so great and I had already been feeling so swimmy and strange, that all I wanted was to throw myself down too and close my eyes and sleep. That was impossible. I turned off the cooker. I checked that there was no blood on my trousers and my shoes, though of course there was plenty on the raincoat, and then I staggered out, switching off the light behind me.

I don't know how I found my way back, it was so dark and by then I was light-headed and my heart was drumming. I just had the presence of mind to strip off the raincoat and the gloves and push them into our garden incinerator. In the morning I would have to get up enough strength to burn them before Brenda's body was found. The knife I washed and put back in the drawer.

Laura came back about five minutes after I had got myself to bed. She had been gone less than half an hour. I turned over and managed to raise myself up to ask her why she was back so soon. It seemed to me that she had a strange distraught look about her.

'What's the matter?' I mumbled. 'Were you worried about me?'

'No,' she said, 'no,' but she didn't come up close to me or put her hand on my forehead. 'It was – Isabel Goldsmith told me something – I was upset – I . . . It's no use talking about it now, you're too ill.' She said in a sharper tone than I had ever heard her use, 'Can I get you anything?'

'I just want to sleep,' I said.

'I shall sleep in the spare room. Good night.'

That was reasonable enough, but we had never slept apart before during the whole of our marriage, and she could hardly have been afraid of catching the 'flu, having only just got over it herself. But I was in no state to worry about that, and I fell into the troubled nightmare-ridden sleep of fever. I remember one of those dreams. It was of Laura finding Brenda's body herself, a not unlikely eventuality.

However, she didn't find it. Brenda's cleaner did. I knew what must have happened because I saw the police car arrive from my window. An hour or so later Laura came in to tell me the news which she had got from Jack Williamson.

'It must have been the same man who killed Peggy,' she said.

I felt better already. Things were going well. 'My poor darling,' I said, 'you must feel terrible, you were such close friends.'

She said nothing. She straightened my bedclothes and left the room. I knew I should have to get up and burn the contents of the incinerator, but I couldn't get up. I put my feet out and reached for the floor, but it was as if the floor came up to meet me and threw me back again. I wasn't over-worried. The police would think what Laura thought, what everyone must think.

That afternoon they came, a chief inspector and a sergeant. Laura brought them up to our bedroom and they talked to us together. The chief inspector said he understood we were close friends of the dead woman, wanted to know when we had last seen her and what we had been doing on the previous evening. Then he asked if we had any idea at all as to who had killed her.

'That maniac who murdered the other woman, of course,' said Laura.

'I can see you don't read the papers,' he said.

Usually we did. It was my habit to read a morning paper in the office and to bring an evening paper home with me. But I had been at home ill. It turned out that a man had been arrested on the previous morning for the murder of Peggy Daley. The shock made me flinch and I'm sure I turned pale. But the policemen didn't seem to notice. They thanked us for our co-operation, apologised for disturbing a sick man, and left. When they had gone I asked Laura what Isabel had said to upset her the night before. She came up to me and put her arms round me.

'It doesn't matter now,' she said. 'Poor Brenda's dead and it was a horrible way to die, but – well, I must be very wicked – but I'm not sorry. Don't look at me like that, darling. I love you and I know you love me, and we must forget her and be as we used to be. You know what I mean.'

I didn't, but I was glad whatever it was had blown over. I had enough on my plate without a coldness between me and my wife. Even though Laura was beside me that night, I hardly slept for worrying about the stuff in that incinerator. In the morning I put up the best show I could of being much better. I dressed and announced, in spite of Laura's expostulations, that I was going into the garden. The police were there already, searching all our gardens, actually digging up Brenda's.

They left me alone that day and the next, but they came in once and interviewed Laura on her own. I asked her what they had said, but she passed it off quite lightly. I supposed she didn't think I was well enough to be told they had been enquiring about my movements and my attitude towards Brenda.

'Just a lot of routine questions, darling,' she said, but I was sure she was afraid for me, and a barrier of her fear for me and mine for myself came up between us. It seems incredible but that Sunday we hardly spoke to each other and when we did Brenda's name wasn't mentioned. In the evening we sat in silence my arm round Laura, her head on my shoulder, waiting, waiting . . .

The morning brought the police with a search warrant. They asked Laura to go into the living room and me to wait in the study. I knew then that it was only a matter of time. They would find the knife, and of course they would find Brenda's blood on it. I had been feeling so ill when I cleaned it that now I could no longer remember whether I had scrubbed it or simply rinsed it under the tap.

After a long while the chief inspector came in alone.

'You told us you were a close friend of Miss Goring's.'

'I was friendly with her,' I said, trying to keep my voice steady. 'She was my wife's friend.'

He took no notice of this. 'You didn't tell us you were on intimate terms with her, that you were, in point of fact, having a sexual relationship with her.'

Nothing he could have said would have astounded me more.

'That's absolute rubbish!'

'Is it? We have it on sound authority.'

'What authority?' I said. 'Or is that the sort of thing you're not allowed to say?'

'I see no harm in telling you,' he said easily. 'Miss Goring herself informed two women friends of hers in London of the fact. She told one of your neighbours she met at a party in your house. You were seen to spend evenings alone with Miss Goring while your wife was ill, and we have a witness who saw you kissing her good night.'

Now I knew what it was that Isabel Goldsmith had told Laura which had so distressed her. The irony of it, the irony . . . Why hadn't I, knowing Brenda's reputation and knowing Brenda's fantasies, suspected what construction would be put on my assumed friendship with her? Here was motive, the lack of which I had relied on as my last resort. Men do kill their mistresses, from jealousy, from frustration, from fear of discovery.

But surely I could turn Brenda's fantasies to my own use?

'She had dozens of men friends, lovers, whatever you like to call them. Any of them could have killed her.'

'On the contrary,' said the chief inspector, 'apart from her ex-husband who is in Australia, we have been able to discover no man in her life but yourself.'

I cried out desperately, 'I didn't kill her! I swear I didn't.'

He looked surprised. 'Oh, we know that.' For the first time he called me sir. 'We know that, sir. No one is accusing you of anything. We have Dr Lawson's word for it that you were physically incapable of leaving your bed that night, and the raincoat and gloves we found in your incinerator are not your property.'

Fumbling in the dark, swaying, the sleeves of the raincoat too short, the shoulders too tight . . . 'Why are you wearing those clothes?' she had asked before I stabbed her.

'I want you to try and keep calm, sir,' he said very gently. But I have never been calm since. I have confessed again and again, I have written statements, I have expostulated, raved, gone over with them every detail of what I did that night, I have wept. Then I said nothing. I could only stare at him. 'I came in here to you, sir,' he said, 'simply to confirm a fact of which we were already certain, and to ask you if you would care to accompany your wife to the police station where she will be charged with the murder of Miss Brenda Goring.'

TOWER OF SILENCE

by Maurice Richardson

I'm fond of my club. There is something deliciously reassuring in its leathery eunuchoid cosiness and all-male meals. Yes, I know waitresses have taken over; but ours are the right type, respectable old nannies, not those menopausal Medusas wafting scent over your game pie.

Of course it has its defects. One of them is a convention of mateyness that makes it difficult to escape bores; but it's extremely comfortable and has a good library. I only wish I could spend more time in it but as a budding psychiatrist, registrar at a large suburban mental hospital, I'm lucky to get half a day a fortnight.

This day I was cosseting myself. I'd just shaken off an attack of 'flu and felt I deserved a treat. I lunched alone, an invalid's lunch of foie gras, chicken fricassee, and claret. Then I retired with a large glass of tawny port and coffee to the red leather sofa in the bow window of the smoking room which is the most euphoric sofa I know.

There are several doctors among the members. We've quite a medical tradition. I was once told this was the only club in London where you could find two venerealogists giving the under-porter a free consultation on the billiard table. And we include a sprinkling of psychiatrists, among them two analysts who started as Freudian and Jungian enemies and have now become bosom chums in some nebulous doctrinal half-way house, and are rumoured to exchange patients every leap year. All of us refrain from talking shop, all of us with one exception. And now, as I opened my eyes from my postprandial coma, I found him sitting beside me: the one and only Dr Gilhooley, the Ancient of Days, or as some call him the Ancient Mariner. He's certainly the oldest member, but it's incorrect to call him the Club Bore because he can be extremely interesting. However he likes to take his time over it, and unless I've got an afternoon off I prefer not to be the one of three that he stoppeth.

He is a small well-proportioned man of the type whose heart doesn't have to do too much work. His face has wizened into a faintly reptilian cast but his hazel eyes still shine and his movements have a lizard-like agility. He always wears comfortable looking, well-cut flannel suits and soft silk shirts with flapping collars.

'I was hoping you would wake,' he said. 'I wanted to congratulate you on your DPM.'

The Diploma of Psychological Medicine is a compulsory hurdle in the career of the budding psychiatrist. It was cute of him to know that I'd passed it.

'I hope,' he said, with an old man's cackle which was meant to signal a joke, 'that you haven't overstrained your cerebral cortex. You remember Batty Tuke's hypothesis?'

'I'm afraid I don't,' I said. 'I think he was a bit before my time.'

'He was indeed. Sir J Batty Tuke. That was his real name. He was a big noise in Edwardian psychiatry. He held that over-exertion of the brain was a frequent cause of insanity. One of his ideas was – whisper it – that many a young doctor never recovered from passing his examinations.'

I ordered two more glasses of port. Dr Gilhooley approved of tawny as less onerous on arteries and alimentary canal than vintage, and I sat back at ease, ready for more curiosities of Edwardian psychiatry. But with the liability of old age his mood changed abruptly. He was off on a detailed description, not far short of total recall, of the film of *Murder on the Orient Express*.

'Now tell me,' he said, 'would you say that a situation, in which a dozen people conspire together to murder one individual in such a way that suspicion cannot fall on any one of them, is likely to be found in real life?'

I said I thought it must be very rare, though I supposed you might find it in a closed institution like a prison or a ship or a barracks.

'But not, you would think, in a mental hospital?'

'Good heavens no. At least I should hope not.'

'And yet such a murder was committed in Wendover which, if I mistake not, is where you are at present a registrar.'

'Is that really true? It must have been a very long time ago.'

'It was. Considerably before you were born. Would you like to hear the story? Of course if one were telling it to a lay audience one would set the scene. For you that's not necessary . . .'

Wendover is one of those huge mental hospitals, like Hanwell and Friern which were built in the middle of the last century. It's a Betjemanic architect's nightmare in greyish yellow brick. Only in the last fifteen years or so has it become decongested and even partly modernised. It still leaves an enormous amount to be desired but compared to what it was I daresay it's a demi-paradise.

Dr Gilhooley took a large swig of port and licked his lips which I noticed were bluish and faintly mottled like some rare orchid. 'I will now proceed with this atrocious history,' he said. 'The period is about the turn of the century. The hospital looked much the same then as it does now. But there was one feature you will not have seen because it has been pulled down. That was the tower, which commanded a view of the entire hospital grounds. It was a watch tower. In those days nearly all patients were certified and the authorities were obsessed with escapes. Bear this tower in mind . . . I hardly know how to convey to you the difference between mental hospitals then and now. Let me see, when did you qualify?'

'Seven years ago.'

'In that case you've never experienced a male refractory ward in the days before the chlorpromazine revolution. There were fights and tussles the whole day long. Patients in states of acute catatonic excitement would be confined to the padded rooms. Hypomanics would pester and incite the others until trouble started . . .'

131

'Of course,' I said, 'only a small proportion of patients were excitable at the same time.'

'True enough. But the role of the staff, both doctors and nurses, was largely custodial. Bless my soul, why when I was a young man the male nurses wore dark blue uniforms and peaked caps like prison warders. And a lot of them ate their dinners off newspapers. Not that they were any the worse for that. Some of the unlettered types made good nurses. They had a kind of natural animal sympathy.'

I said I wondered what they would have thought of a really modern mental hospital run on therapeutic community lines with daily group meetings of doctors, patients and nurses.

'They'd have had a fit,' Dr Gilhooley said.

'Mind you,' I said, 'even in our enlightened days you sometimes get a lot of opposition. When ward community methods were first introduced there was often bitterness among the staff. They felt insecure, not so much afraid, if you follow me, but anxious lest their authority was going to be taken away from them.'

Dr Gilhooley pressed his lips together. 'Do you know what a bear-pit is?' he said. 'I don't mean what the Elizabethans had instead of television. A bear-pit in old fashioned mental hospital parlance was a field about a hundred yards square surrounded by high wooden palings. There might be a few trees growing in it and there would certainly be some seats. Every fine afternoon some two hundred of the more severely ill male patients would be turned loose in the bear-pit for their daily exercise. You might see a young man writing on a tree with a stick, like Orlando in *As You Like It* only he would be chasing his writing round the trunk. There would be catatonics standing about in odd stereotyped positions. Some would be stalking round and round at a furious pace. Nobody spoke to anybody. Nurses in uniform sat on the seats. Bear-pits were not uncommon until right up to the last war. That gives you some idea of conditions. Of course there was a lot of variation between hospitals. But they were hopelessly understaffed. You hear a lot about that today, but when Wendover held two thousand six hundred patients there was one Medical Superintendent and four medical officers. The Superintendent was a law unto himself. If he was slack, and the atmosphere flaccid, the MOs might degenerate. In one or two hospitals I've known they did nothing but drink and play snooker all round the clock.'

'Booze and billiards,' I said. 'The occupational diseases of primitive psychiatry. But aren't you laying it on a bit thick, Dr Gilhooley?'

'No, my dear boy, I promise you I'm not. There were foci of enlightenment here and there. But as I say everything depended on the Superintendents. These had their eccentricities. There was one I served under who was mad about cricket and believed it had special therapeutic virtues. When he advertised for an MO he used to put, "Only keen cricketers need apply. Slow bowler preferred." Then there was dear old Chesney who was Superintendent at Coverdale. He was crazy about hydrotherapy. The continuous bath. It used to be very popular at one time especially for manic-depressives. If you look up "Baths" in the standard English Dictionary of Psychological Medicine for eighteen ninety-two you'll find sixteen different varieties. That's as true as I'm sitting here. Of course, facilities were extremely limited so Chesney had a gigantic shallow tank constructed . . .'

I looked at my watch. Nearly time for strong tea and anchovy toast. Dr Gilhooley was delighted at having a captive audience for so long. He snapped his fingers with pleasure. Still fully wound up, he unreeled a string of bizarre anecdotes. At a mental hospital in the Channel Islands there had been a schizophrenic, a man of no education, who, if you handed him a fossil, would give you a most vivid description of the landscape of its period. The Superintendent used to show him off to visitors. At another hospital a Scandinavian sailor had passed at one single evacuation a pound and three quarters of pebbles. In nineteen thirty-one Dr Alexander Cannon, a medical officer on the staff of Colney Hatch had been requested to resign his appointment because he had written a book called *The Invisible Influence* in which he claimed to have levitated, together with eighteen pieces of luggage, across a chasm in Tibet . . . 'But I am digressing,' Gilhooley said. 'Senility, of course. Now I was going to tell you a horrible story, wasn't I? What was it about?'

'It happened at Wendover in the old days. Something to do with a tower.'

'Of course. Of course. Well, now, it all began with the reign of a new Superintendent. Wantage, the old Superintendent who retired had been one of the passive custodial type. "Let's have a quiet peaceful hospital," he used to say. There was always a strong smell of paraldehyde in his wards. He was bone lazy. He was a member of the Garrick and used to play bridge there a lot. It got so that when they wanted him to attend to hospital business they would telephone the club and say: "Urgent message for Dr Wantage. Patient's escaped." When he got back, breathless, to Wendover they'd greet him with: "It's all right, doctor. Patient's been recovered. But while you're here would you mind signing these forms?"

'Well, the new Superintendent, Dr Makins, was the exact opposite of old Wantage, burning with reformist zeal. And of course all his reforms meant more work for the staff. He insisted that terminal schizophrenics, who had been left to vegetate, should be taken for walks by two nurses every day. He stalked through the hospital regrading patients, unlocking locked wards. In no time he had the staff loathing his guts.'

'What about the medical staff?' I asked.

'They had to toe the line, of course. They didn't like it, but there was nothing they could do about it. Anyway they weren't so far gone in sloth that they couldn't respond to Makins's therapeutic enthusiasms. All might have been well if it hadn't been for the tragedy, which I'm just coming to.'

Dr Gilhooley broke off to offer me a fat Turkish cigarette from an elderly but still posh-looking leather case. He followed up with a history of cigarette-smoking in England from the Crimean War onwards, with special reference to the virtues of Macedonian as opposed to Virginian tobaccos. I steered him back to Wendover by tapping the glass of my watch.

'You are eager for the denouement, what I believe is known as the pay-off. Very well. I shan't keep you waiting any longer. Now among the patients Dr Makins had upgraded was a man named Beavis. When Makins first examined him he was in the Refractory Ward. He'd been diagnosed as manic-depressive, manic phase with distinct paranoid tendencies. This, as you know, is not an uncommom combination, and it can lead to very uncertain and aggressive behaviour. Beavis was a middle-aged man of some intelligence and education. He made a favourable impression on Makins, was quiet and orderly and free from any signs of delusions. He complained that he was being kept strictly confined to the ward and not allowed to go out or occupy himself in any way. Makins asked him if he had any particular occupation in mind and he said: "Yes, carpentry." Makins discussed his case with the Medical Officer in charge of the male side, and the Ward Charge, who were both in attendance. He told them in his opinion Beavis had recovered from his manic attack and should be upgraded with a view to possible discharge in a matter of weeks. The Ward Charge begged to differ. He said Beavis was a very tricky patient, given to sudden fits of violence when you least expected them. "I warn you, Doctor Makins, sir," he said respectfully, "he's very deceptive. He'll be good as gold for days at a time and then without any warning he'll turn nasty. And of course when the moon's at the full there's no holding him."

'Makins wasn't standing for this. "Don't give me that superstitious rubbish, my man," he snapped. "It's not surprising if a patient of his intelligence gets irritable when he's kept cooped up like this. I'm regrading him to Ward Three as from today until further notice. See that he's taken over there before dinner time."

'So Beavis was upgraded to Ward Three, and there was more muttering among the male nurses. I always say that if you take your hospital nursing staff by and large you'll find a small proportion of saints, a more or less average collection of people who'll be both nice and nasty, and a small proportion of bullies. Among the average bunch there may be not a few who'll swing one way or the other, nice or nasty, all according to the general tone of the place. And that comes from the top.'

Dr Gilhooley darted me one of his bright lacertilian glances to make sure I was listening and poured us out two cupfuls of dark brown tea strong enough to induce an attack of anxiety neurosis. 'Of course,' he said, 'it must be admitted that Makins was not a tactful man. Reformers seldom are. He was a congenital fusspot and he had a genius for putting people's backs up. But he is not to be blamed for what happened. No he is not to be blamed. For a little while all went well. Beavis's equilibrium remained undisturbed. He worked long hours in the carpenter's shop, making a model of a Roman galley, and gave no trouble in the ward. And then the precipitating factor arrived on the scene. You may say that with psychotics there is always a precipitating factor ready to hand. That may or may not be so. It doesn't alter the fact that this was a piece of damned bad luck. In the course of his reforms Dr Makins, as well as regrading patients, had been shifting some of the nurses around, for he thought, rightly no doubt in some cases, that several of them had been too long in the same ward. The changes were made after a confabulation between Makins and the Head Male Attendant, Tunstall. This official, equivalent to the Matron on the Women's side, was a very powerful figure in the hospital hierarchy of those days. He was allowed the dignity of wearing a swallow tail coat at hospital functions. Tunstall was very jealous of his own personal authority, and opposed to any libertarian reforms on principle; but being a Pecksniffian hypocrite, as well as a man of considerable natural organising ability, he'd managed to keep up a suitable façade of co-operation in front of the new Superintendent. Now one nurse who had been moved from the Refractory Ward was a certain Birkbeck, a youngish man from the north. A bit of a rough diamond. Like not a few male nurses he'd been a soldier. He was genial on the surface and popular with his colleagues but he was inclined to be rather a bully. And between him and Beavis there was a long standing feud. Beavis had sneered at him and touched him on the raw with that intuitive feeling for the weak spot which paranoid manics possess. There had been one rough house between them and the Ward Charge had accepted Birkbeck's version. And now Birkbeck was moved to Ward Three and the first patient he saw was Beavis.

'You might think that the appearance of his deadly enemy would depress Beavis, like a prisoner who's been recaptured; and that at first was what it seemed to do; but only at first. You can imagine the tension that was generated between these two: the intelligent educated imaginative patient and the ignorant loutish male nurse. It was like a thunderstorm piling up in stages. One stage was when Birkbeck persuaded Oakes, the Ward Charge in Three, that Beavis should be searched every time he came back from his carpentry.'

'Not,' I said, 'an altogether unreasonable suggestion, surely?'

'Possibly not. But the searching, I understand, was carried out by Birkbeck with the maximum of indignity. Beavis retaliated by compiling a notebook which he called 'Crimes of the Male Nurse Henry Birkbeck'. It was found afterwards in his locker. The final stage was reached when a mischievous patient told Beavis that Birkbeck, and the Ward Charge, and the Head Male Attendant, and the Medical Officer responsible for the Ward were all petitioning the Superintendent to have Beavis sent back to the Refractory Ward.

'That afternoon the storm burst. Beavis comes in from the carpenter's shop and stands meekly in front of Birkbeck waiting to be searched. Birkbeck bends forward a little as he runs his hands over him. Beavis whips out a small chisel which he's been hiding up the sleeve of his overalls and drives it into Birkbeck's neck, slap into the carotid. Blood spouts. Birkbeck collapses and is dead in a matter of seconds.

'Staff come running. Beavis is taken to the Refractory Ward and locked up alone in a full padded room nearest the entrance to the ward. So that's your first murder for you.'

'No mystery there,' I said.

'No indeed. And not much about the next either. Well, as you may imagine the shock was felt right through the hospital. Beavis, of course, as a certified patient, was outside the law. However, there were demands for a detailed investigation from several quarters: the Commissioners, the local police and coroner's office, the Asylum Workers Federation, and not least from the Superintendent himself. He didn't exactly improve matters by calling meetings of the male nursing staff, in relays, and telling them that they mustn't imagine that what had happened was going to make the slightest difference to his policy of reform. It was very late that night before everyone settled down to sleep, and there was a big run on the chloral. And next morning what do you think they found? Surely you can guess?'

'Oh come, now,' I said. 'Even if I could, which I can't, I wouldn't want to spoil your pleasure in telling me.'

Dr Gilhooley rubbed his aged mottled hands. 'Next morning,' he croaked dramatically, 'on the concrete flooring at the foot of the tower, they found the body of Beavis. His skull was fractured. There were no marks of violence upon him. Now what do you make of that?'

'I suppose,' I said sportingly, trying to keep up the mystery, 'it could have been suicide.'

'Suicide my stethoscope! It was murder, carried out with the precision of a military operation. Motive? Partly vengeance but mainly a demonstration to intimidate the Superintendent, a warning to him to drop his reforms. Tunstall, the Head Male Attendant, was the organising genius behind it all. The killing of Birkbeck brought to a head the trouble that had been brewing between him and the Superintendent. Tunstall called a meeting of twelve of the male nurses whom he thought were most incensed. There was some stump oratory on the lines of: "Our colleague has been foully murdered with deliberate malice aforethought by one who, though he is a certified patient, knew full well what he did, and all because of the new and perilous system of licence and misrule which has been imposed upon us. If we do not take action now, and drastic action at that, our lives will no longer be safe." And so on and so forth. They then put it to the vote and solemnly announced that Beavis was guilty of murder . . .

'They stole quietly along to the Refractory Ward where Beavis was asleep. They put a strait-jacket on him, and told him he had been tried in his absence and found guilty of the wilful murder of Birkbeck. They were taking the law into their own hands and were going to execute just sentence upon him. Then they gagged him and carried him out of the ward and up the steps of the tower. They removed the strait-jacket and the gag and slung him over.'

'But what about the MO on night duty?'

'They hadn't forgotten him. They'd laced his cocoa. They'd thought of everything, even to removing any traces of the gag.'

'But wasn't there a frightful row? You don't mean to say they got away with it?'

'There was hell to pay. But there was absolutely no evidence to show that Beavis hadn't chucked himself off the top of the tower. They'd been very careful how they'd handled him and they'd planted on him a master key which opened all locks in the hospital, making sure it had his fingerprints on it and no one else's. The suggested explanation was that Beavis had somehow managed to pinch a key from the Head Male Attendant's office. It could neither be proved nor disproved. So the Coroner's jury brought in an open verdict. The Superintendent swore they were a lot of murdering blackguards. The men threatened an action for slander. The atmosphere got so strained that the authorities transferred the Superintendent and appointed a new one.

'Tell me,' I said, 'were you yourself on the staff at the time? Surely not?'

'Indeed I was not,' said Gilhooley. 'That would make me a centenarian. I was told the story when I first joined the hospital staff as a very junior MO just qualified. I was told it over cocoa on night duty by an elderly ward charge who had been a young nurse at the time. He took no part in it himself, but he heard all about it . . . Well, there you are. It's not a very nice story but we're not a very nice species.'

I heaved a deep sententious sigh. 'Ah well,' I said. 'In the great global therapeutic community of the future which is our only salvation . . . .'

Dr Gilhooley interrupted me sharply. 'Good gracious! Is that your idea of the millennium? It's not mine . . .'

'What is?' I asked.

'A nice snug club and a captive audience.'

DEATH IN THE LONG GRASS

by Geoffrey Rose

Think of me if ever you go down to Redemption City. Especially if you go down at night, as I did, when you can hardly tell the fireflies from the stars and can't lay your hand on the horizon.

I'd been put ashore that afternoon. It was an unscheduled stop. When I showed the Captain my little bit of paper he had to comply, but he didn't much like me or my little bit of paper. We hung about until they'd raised an immigration official from somewhere – the grave, by the look of him – and then formalities were hurried through in the Captain's cabin, where a breeze fluttered the green curtains. It was tea-time when I left. The string quartet were playing hit tunes of 1910 while the old women who'd occupied the best armchairs immediately after lunch plied deft fingers among the cakes. They may not have known which century they were living in, but they never made a mistake about feeding-time. They'd heard I was to be put ashore, and regarded me with furtive contempt or sympathy as if I'd not paid my fare. The sympathetic gave me messages for nephews and grandsons who had 'done very well' somewhere in the mysterious interior, or told me of uncles who'd been killed there by pygmies. They spoke of that continent as one better seen from off-shore than penetrated. I didn't disbelieve them, but my little bit of paper was binding on me as well as on those I showed it to. So I was set on the quay of a small town – I never knew its name – and the liner made full steam away, glad to see the last of me. I may have been a briefly lingering puzzle to the old women as they resumed the novels and knitting which must amuse them through the long hours until dinner.

I was left alone on the quay. The immigration official saw no reason to keep me company. I stood waiting for the motor-car which was to meet me. The air was full of rose-gold light. It coloured the mountains and the sea. The naïve might have thought it meant something good was going to happen, but I knew all that would happen was that in a few minutes darkness would fall. The illuminations, then darkness. And if you ask what the illuminations are for, what they celebrate, you're told they celebrate only themselves. And by the time you know that, they're over. So I wasn't expecting anything good. The appearance of my transport fairly soon and no trouble in the meantime would be good enough for me. Men were sitting outside the several cafés, talking intensely but quietly, gesturing often, greeting friends among those who promenaded the quay. Some wore jackets draped on their shoulders, cape fashion. Some walked with arms linked or about each other's neck. There was much embracing and hand-holding when friends met. No women to be seen. Presumably they were penned in the shuttered houses, kept for work and pleasure, while affection was a thing among men. I didn't mind that. What I did mind was that although courtesy kept their eyes averted from a stranger, all were aware of me, their consciousness transfixing me as if each had turned and thrown a knife. I've seen plenty of open violence. I can cope with that. I mean you can take your choice, join the fight or run away. But in those languid southern towns there's a covert violence which keeps you shifting from one foot to the other. So I was glad to see the motor-car.

It was dark by that time. I didn't tell the driver he was late. It would have meant nothing to him. Late and Early have as little meaning down there as Right and Wrong. Things just happen. He drove fast and recklessly. I shut my eyes so I shouldn't see when our road was only a few feet wide between mountain face and abyss. Dangers I'm not paid for upset me. 'On important business, Boss?' asked the driver. Obviously he reckoned anybody who had a liner stop there must be important.

'It's important to me,' I said.

'You come to kill somebody?'

'D'you have much death here?'

'No more than anywhere else. But sooner sometimes.' He grinned and took both hands from the wheel to light a cigarette, as if demonstrating his point. I shut my eyes again. We didn't say anything else. There didn't seem anything else to say. At intervals I opened my eyes and saw the fireflies and the stars spelling bright words I didn't know. At last I saw a new brightness – the lights of a city below us. That's a language I know too well.

We stopped at an hotel and the driver carried my bag through the revolving door. The entrance hall was used as a lounge too. Men sat drinking there. They were better dressed than the men at the quay but had the same air of latent hostility. Otherwise it was an entrance hall like a hundred others – marble floor, probably imitation, big fan spinning near the ceiling, palms in pots, those deadly fronds that strangle the life out of you from Bournemouth to Paraguay. Some of the drinkers appeared to know my driver. They called to him in Spanish and he answered. One, a tall man with an eagle face, approached us. He too wore his jacket like a cape, and had altogether the manner of an operatic brigand – a self-conscious swagger, a pointless bravado. He stopped about a yard from me, arms akimbo, head flung back, and said something in a challenging tone. I asked the driver to translate.

'I tell them you are interested in death. He says death is in the long grass.'

'What does that mean? Is it a local saying?'

The stranger spoke again, very rapidly.

'What now?'

'He says he doesn't want to die in the long grass.'

'Tell him that so far as I'm concerned he doesn't have to.' He appeared to go on saying it, repeating the same words over and over with growing excitement, until two of his companions drew him back to his chair.

'He was a great patriot,' said the driver. 'But he had a bad time in the Revolution, and it left him not quite right.' I looked again at the flightless eagle, thinking him an ill omen for his country and for my mission in it, and continued to the reception desk.

The next morning had no room for gloomy thoughts. The city glittered, an architecture of air and light. In the street, far below my balcony, water–carts were working. Flowers which lined and divided the street caught drops of spray and sparkled like flowers in Paradise.

My first business was with the Chief of Police. I wasn't pleased to recognise him as the brigand of the hotel foyer, the man who was so particular about where he would die. I'd assumed he'd been on the wrong side of the Revolution, but come to think of it those who had weren't likely to be seen much in public. Obviously he'd been given his post as a reward. I don't care for policemen whose minds are affected. I don't care for policemen who sit drinking with the town lay–abouts. I don't care for foreigners who speak English with a more educated accent than I do. And least of all do I care for a man whose eyes are as blank and anonymous when he takes off his dark glasses as they were before.

'Why didn't you speak English last night?' I asked as he motioned me to a chair.

'It doesn't do to advertise all one's accomplishments.' He read my little bit of paper with a great show of courtesy. The courtesy was in inverse ratio to the help, I reckoned. The ship's Captain had scowled because he must do what I asked. This fellow smiled because he wasn't going to do anything. 'I am at your service,' he said. 'But you must understand our difficulties. In your country the law was made a long time ago. Here it is still on the anvil, and the strongest party wields the hammer.' He enjoyed listening to himself so much that my listening too would have seemed an intrusion. I looked round the room and wondered whether I should be offered a drink, preferably with ice. The blacksmith metaphors went on. Perhaps that was how he had started life. You find some funny ups and downs in those revolutionary countries. I became aware that he'd stopped talking. 'So the long and short of it,' I said, giving him a chance to repeat anything important.

'The long and short of it,' he replied, handing my papers back across the desk, 'is that you have come to the wrong country. You want to extradite a man who has killed somebody and stolen a million of money. Death is so common here and money so scarce that neither crime appears real to the third party.'

'Who's the third party?'

His smile faded. The third party must have got into the act while I wasn't listening.

'The people. Not the law enforcers nor the law breakers, but that third party who determine the effective strength of law. In England the public respect law, so your work is easy. We have no more criminals than you, but our people despise law, sympathising rather with the man on the run than the man with the warrant.'

'I'd already sensed that,' I said, remembering the loungers on the quay. 'But I'm surprised you call it a poor country. This town looks prosperous enough.'

'We have no money of our own. Foreign governments finance us, pay us to hate each other and sometimes to kill each other. So you see we cannot take seriously the charges against this man.' He tapped the extradition order, which I hadn't yet picked up. 'We shall be very polite, but we shall not really care. What will you drink?'

While he poured it I wondered when his mental unbalance would appear. No sign of it so far. Perhaps it needed a little alcohol, as a cliff-top house which looks safe seen from landward will collapse at the next lick of sea.

'D'you have many English here?'

'All nationalities come here, English among them. I don't know why.' He seemed to include my visit in the riddle.

'My superiors believe this man will come into a city – one, because he'll think himself safer in a crowd, and two, because it's his proper climate.'

'Yes.' I couldn't tell whether he meant, Yes that's sound reasoning, or Yes that's the kind of thing one's superiors do think. 'Foreign visitors must surrender their passports and the people with whom they stay must submit details to us. At least that's the regulation. Reputable hotel-keepers observe it. No visitor corresponding with the description and picture you sent us has been reported. But your man might use a false passport. Also there are other hotels which let rooms by the hour, if you understand me.'

'Disorderly houses, we call them.'

'Disorderly houses. That is exquisite. I must remember. A man with plenty of money might stay in such a place and never be asked for his passport. We will make a tour. It will amuse you. And you might find your man.'

'But you doubt it?'

'You have known me long enough to know that I doubt most things.'

'Where would you hide if you were on the run?'

He had risen, and now paused in the act of taking his jacket from the back of his chair. 'I? You are not looking for me.'

'But where would you?'

'I would not come into the city. I would stay outside, in the long grass.'

'Where death is.'

'What?'

'You said last night that death is in the long grass.'

'So it is.' He stood silent a minute before continuing, 'But if I were on the run I would go there. Death is a game two can play, and out there the best man doesn't always win. Let us begin our tour.'

We drove through the city in a big white motor-car, siren wailing. 'Is that necessary?' I asked.

'No, but we must assert ourselves.'

The assertion made no difference. Nobody hurried out of our way, or even turned to look at us. He appeared amused by this universal contempt.

'If my man is in one of these places he'll be up and away when he hears that thing blaring.'

'Don't worry. If the customers jumped up at every police siren they would never do what they come to do.'

We entered an older part of the town – narrower streets, wrought-iron

141

balconies, coats-of-arms over doors, these elegances partly hidden by washing hung to dry. Beyond a gateway empty of gates I glimpsed a courtyard with a well and a grand flight of stairs leading nowhere, broken in mid-air. We stopped outside one of the houses. 'Business is good,' said my companion, pointing to window boxes full of geraniums. He broke off a cluster and put it in my button-hole, saying, 'We must look a little festive or we shall frighten them.'

A man was sitting at a desk inside, like the receptionist at a pretentious hairdresser's. His rings, watch, tie-pin and a bit of chain round his wrist all glittered in the sunlight. Don't ask me what the chain was. Maybe he'd broken loose from a golden prison. I'm not sure that his hair didn't sparkle too. He and the Police Chief smiled at each other as if they shared a good joke. The Chief said to me, 'This man speaks only Spanish. You will forgive my speaking it a moment?'

'Why not? You spoke it to me last night.' As he grew more suave I grew more brusque. I wondered how we should finish if we spent long together. While they talked I stood at an open window. It overlooked a courtyard where a fountain was playing. The soft lisping of the voices behind me mingled with the tinkle of the water in its white marble basin. Probably that fountain had been playing three or four hundred years, and there was something both sad and comforting in the thought that it would be playing all the mornings of my life while I sweated in noisy streets far away, never to see it again.

'He does not think your man is here, but we will look.' I turned from the window reluctantly and followed him upstairs. I've never seen a house less disorderly. Instead there was the earnest concentration of a chess tournament. We looked into room after room. Some were shuttered, some explosive with the collision of sunlight and white walls. Some were noisy, some so quiet I could hear the tinkling of my fountain. Sometimes the occupants were aware of us, sometimes not. Over them all the Chief waved a forgiving hand. 'So much flesh so early in the morning!' he murmured, shutting yet another door. Sometimes a woman spoke or beckoned us, and he laughed, but nothing else broke the monotony and I soon lost interest. I knew my man wasn't there. I'd told them in London he wouldn't be. He was somewhere in the green areas of the map, in the forests where an army could hide. 'You seem preoccupied,' said the Chief. 'It's not very interesting, I'm afraid.' He sounded like the apologetic proprietor of a third-rate circus. We left that house and visited others, identical except that none of them had a fountain. Coming out of the last I said, 'D'you ever wish you were back in the long grass again?' 'Señor,' he said. I looked round to see who Señor was. Apparently it was me, and the prelude to an unusually solemn pronounce-ment, for he stopped and faced me.

'Señor, there is a day for the long grass and a day to get out of it. Some of my friends lost count of the days. They lie out there for ever.' I knew then that he had changed sides. I knew then that he ought to have died with his friends, and that in some degree he had. But that was his problem. I had my own. We parted there. He put the car and driver at my disposal so I could look at the outlying country, and he walked back to headquarters.

*   *   *

The driver wasn't sounding our siren now. Perhaps it only went with the Chief. Perhaps, like me, he preferred quiet. The city is compact, and we were soon out of it on the mountain road. I've said there's a lot of forest. There's a lot of everything, forest and mountain and river and the plain – pampa, they call it – where the long grass grows. Everything except town. That's in a minority, and might vanish altogether, you feel, if the landscape pushed a bit harder. I could see the lot spread out below me like a map as we climbed. I didn't mind keeping my eyes open with this driver. He was a cautious lad, hugging the mountain and taking it slow. Somewhere down there my man was hiding. Maybe if I shouted he would put his head out. Like a line in a play I'd seen, something about 'Holler your name to the reverberating hills'. (Don't think I go to the theatre for pleasure. I was there on duty.) Up we went, into the sky. The driver stopped when we could go no higher and waved at the view as if I ought to get out and admire, so I did. It was worth looking at. It shimmered in the heat haze rising from it, and was silent with a silence so solid you could touch it. Far away I saw a line of white where the waters of the ocean broke on the shore. At that distance you got no sense of movement. And the man I wanted had all this. We drove on, dropping now toward the tree tops. Steam rose from them where the sun was evaporating the night dews, and the heat came up at you like hot hands. Now we could hear the shrieks of birds and the gibbering of animals. What had seemed perfect silence was in fact composed of a thousand noises, just as that apparently motionless whiteness on the shore was the effect of an endlessly repeated movement. Nothing was what it seemed, and that's an uncomfortable climate for my work. I fingered my revolver in its shoulder holster. We reckoned our man was armed and likely to resist arrest. So would I if I had a murder against me, a country for my playground and a million to spend on toys.

'Inca,' said the driver, pointing. It's the name of the Indians who ruled there until the Spaniards thumped them in fifteen hundred and something. I looked round, expecting to see one, but there was nobody. 'Inca,' he repeated, still pointing, and then I saw ruins among the trees. I waved him on. I wasn't a tourist. We passed a luxury coach, full of people, going the opposite way. 'Inca,' he said again.

Later we arrived at a village. It confirmed the Police Chief's account of poverty. The people standing about had an appearance half Indian half Spanish. The two strains had not enhanced but rather neutralised each other. They'd forgotten how to be Indians without learning how to be Europeans, and stood in the sunlight with apathetic eyes. A few women were making basketwork or weaving cloth. I'd seen such things highly priced in London shops, and I wondered what fraction of that price was received here. There was no news of my man. The driver inquired, on his Chief's instructions, I suppose, and signified the empty result with gestures and head shaking. We drove out of the village, and some way beyond it I got my first view of the famous long grass. Acres of that feathery stuff you see in old ladies' gardens. But out there, growing densely, shoulder-high and rippling more like a sea than the real one, it's a different thing. I began to understand the Chief's obsession with it. I couldn't see its farther limits. Two or three horsemen moved in the middle distance. Only the horses' heads were visible. I should have liked to drive on, following my hunch, but my movements are watched more closely than the criminal's. I signalled the driver to turn back.

In the city the blue and green blinds of siesta were lowered. I found the Chief sitting on the raised terrace of a café. At the other tables men slept sternly, as if they had weighed the arguments for sleep and wakefulness before deciding, but he stared straight in front of him. Perhaps he was afraid that if he shut his eyes death might catch him unawares.

'While you have been seeking clues,' he said, 'I have let them come to me.'

'Don't mystify me. I'm growing old.' I beckoned a waiter. At first I thought he disliked me personally, but watching him serve others I saw he simply disliked people.

'There is a ruined temple in the forest,' continued the Chief.

'I think I saw it.'

'There are several, but you may have seen this one. It is a tourist attraction. For years it had an unofficial custodian, an old half-breed with a smattering of languages and a way with visitors. Today I hear he is dead.' So? Did he want a contribution to the wreath? 'Also I hear he has a successor. A white man.'

'That would be a crazy hiding-place.'

'If it seems so crazy that nobody looks, it would be a wise one.'

'Pull him in, then.'

'I may be wrong, and one mustn't advertise mistakes. Every afternoon in summer an excursion goes to the ruins. We have missed today's. I hoped you would be back sooner. But tomorrow we will join the excursion, mingle with the excursionists and take a look at the new custodian.' Having said this he began to drink in earnest, and I got no more sense out of him that afternoon. I suppose it was polite of him to have waited.

All that evening I wondered why he was being so helpful. I wondered alone, having turned down his invitation to join him. Let him topple over the cliff in his usual company. Being alone is my luxury, and it's perfect abroad. At home there's always somebody treading on the edges. After dinner I decided to reconnoitre the temple. A tourist isn't remarkable in ruins by moonlight. I slung a camera round my neck and said 'Inca' to a taxi driver. We were soon there, and, as I'd hoped, I wasn't the only visitor. It was an uncomfortable place. Terraces rising one above another. And pyramids. Not smooth sided like the Egyptian, but with steps cut in them, for the purpose of them had been at the top. They weren't built to a point, but stopped short in a small platform, and that had been the altar where human hearts were torn out for sacrifice. Anybody who took the job of caretaker here needed watching. I walked round, warily. The place oppressed me, as if it were balanced on my head. The moon was big. Shadows solid as masonry lay across my path. I kept well clear of those pyramids. A lump of stone let go from the top would have a respectable momentum by the time it reached bottom, which I'd rather not be there to measure. No sign of the new caretaker. Maybe like others of that profession he only took care not to be seen. Maybe he didn't live on the premises. I hadn't hoped to find him tonight. I wanted to familiarise myself with the lay-out of the place so I should know its short-cuts and emergency exits tomorrow. That done, I returned to my hotel and slept.

Next morning the Chief seemed no worse for his drinking, though it was hard for me to judge what might be better and worse with him. At least he was coherent. 'Today is the day!' he announced on seeing me.

'You're sure it's my man at the temple?'

'No, but anyway it will be amusing.'

I remembered he'd said the same about our tour of the Houses, so I didn't fix my hopes too high. 'It's kind of you to take a hand yourself,' I said. 'Specially after saying you wouldn't.'

'At this time of year I find the streets constricting. I shall enjoy an escape.'

'Shan't we be a bit too near the long grass for you?'

He smiled, like an adult smiling at a child's view of something. Perhaps for him the long grass wasn't a place any more, but a state of mind.

'I saw the beginning of it yesterday,' I persisted, trying to force his explanation. 'It looked like a sea. There were three horsemen. You felt they would sink deeper and deeper until they drowned.'

'You should be careful,' he said.

We played cards until excursion time. Business seemed slack. Or perhaps they didn't bother him with routine. We didn't talk any more. Only the click of cards on the desk. Just before two we settled our debts and walked to the excursion depot, accompanied at a distance by several of his men. The other passengers were holidaymakers who didn't look at us twice, but I noticed a stiffening in the driver's attitude, and his observance of speed limits was exemplary. The Chief sat beside me, staring at something out of sight as usual. I heard without listening the guide's commentary on what we passed and on the treat ahead. At the temple we were free to follow the guide or please ourselves. The other police went with the crowd, but the Chief held me back a moment. 'I should like you to have my gun,' he said.

'There's nothing wrong with mine.'

'To please me.'

I accepted. I didn't intend using a gun if I could help it.

'And may I have yours?' he said.

An old South American custom? I examined the revolver he'd lent me. I hadn't lost by the swop. We hurried to catch up with the crowd, not wanting to attract attention. The temple looked different in sunlight, like a room where you've had bad dreams. But you know the dreams are only hiding. They might be hiding in my companion's head. I mean a remembrance of blood-thirsty gods must linger, a remembrance of ancestors ready to spill and shed blood for them.

145

'D'you think he's had a tip-off?' I asked.

'I am confident he hasn't.'

Everybody else's confidence worried me. In London they were confident he would hide in a town, simply because they'd pledged themselves to catch him quick and there was only a handful of towns against a lifetime of wilderness. I was the only one who wasn't confident, and on top of making me feel unsociable that meant I should get the blame when everybody else's confidence proved wrong. Still we mooched round with the tourists. Still no sign of our suspect. The weaker of the party began to straggle, and the Chief took the chance to send out scouts. When they reported he said, 'The man is here but keeping out of sight. We must wait until the coach leaves.'

When the coach had gone the ruins were strangely silent. Shadows of late afternoon lay on them, and soon the bad dreams would emerge. I was conscious of being among natives, who might respond unpleasantly to the influence of the place. I wanted my man alive.

'Let's start before it's dark,' I said. 'Where is he?'

'We will drive him this way so you can make the arrest.'

'Does everybody understand there's to be no shooting if it can possibly be avoided?'

'Of course.'

I was left alone in what I suppose had been a street. It felt more like an arena now. I waited, watching sunset colour the stone. If they didn't hurry we should lose him in the dark. Even now recognition would be impossible until I was near enough to make an easy target. The low sun would be behind him, too. I waited. They were taking their time. The air had cooled and the colour was nearly gone when two shots splintered the silence.

'He's coming your way,' shouted the Chief. 'And he's shooting.'

A figure appeared on the top terrace, silhouetted against the last of the light. I saw the gun in his hand and saw him raise it.

'You'll only make it worse for yourself,' I called, dropping flat. He stood a moment. The light was too poor for me to risk a shot. Then he retreated over the skyline. I ran up the terraces. When I reached the top the sun's last glimmer had sunk right down to the horizon and my man had vanished. After a while I found the Chief.

'He came back your way,' I said. 'How did he get past you?'

'We drove him your way. Why didn't you shoot?'

'The light was too bad. I couldn't be sure of only laming him.'

'I fired, but he was zig-zagging up the terraces.'

'Between us we made a pretty poor show,' I muttered angrily. He was angry, too. Angrier, maybe. He recalled his men. I hoped to see a prisoner among them, but they brought only their sullen selves and stood staring at us as if wondering what the excitement was about. A search of the ruins found nothing. 'At least we're on the right track,' said the Chief. 'A man with a gun who shoots when challenged is likely to be the man you want.'

'Did he answer?'

'No. But I spoke English and obviously he understood.'

'Did you recognise him from his photograph?'

'The light was poor. So was the photograph.'

'He can't have gone far. Let's get after him.'

'He can't have gone far, but nor can we without transport or lights. I will call up more men and at dawn we will search again. He can't go far before then and he shall not escape a second time. But next time you must not be afraid of shooting.'

We spent the night in that village I'd seen the day before. Its apathetic people received us without surprise or welcome. The Chief and I shared a hut which its owners vacated for us after giving us food. Having eaten, I wrapped myself in a blanket. There was nothing else to do. I slept badly. Something in our evening's misadventure troubled me. I couldn't see it clearly. I couldn't see how my man had escaped unless the Chief had let him, nor why the Chief was so angry with me. Maybe he was a coward. Maybe he'd funked the arrest. Maybe he was angry with himself, and was simply passing it on to me. But he seemed too smooth a character for that. Waking and dozing I puzzled over it. Every time I woke I saw him smoking at the window. At dawn he shook me. They'd brought us cups of a foul brew they called coffee, and horses were ready outside. I'd never ridden before, bar falling off a cart horse when I was three, and these were bareback, so you can imagine the picture I made. But even that didn't raise a smile among the villagers. We set off, the Chief riding beside me and keeping a hand on my reins. He had mustered many more men for today's hunt and we made a formidable posse. Still I wondered why, after his first show of indifference, he was taking so active a part in my business, and how he'd overcome his dread of the long grass – for that was obviously where we were heading. Perhaps he'd had orders.

We took the same road I'd been driven along yesterday. There was the pampa rippling in front of us. The sun was still low, and hit you full in the eyes across the top of it. We plunged in, the horses immediately up to their necks like those I'd seen. The men unslung the rifles from their shoulders. I glanced at my companion's face. There was no sign of emotion, but his habitual dark glasses and a borrowed sombrero didn't leave much room. Borrowing hats had been a good idea. Already the sun was fierce. When it got on top of us it would hammer any uncovered man into the ground and leave him there. Until reaching the pampa we'd ridden in a group, but entering it the men spread out, on instinct or command, into a single rank of which the Chief and I were the centre. And so we advanced, the intervals between riders increasing until the line was as extended as it could be without any man losing sight of his immediate neighbours. Behind this line walked several villagers holding dogs on long leashes. These brutes showed none of their masters' apathy. Only the Chief and I rode together. I couldn't see either end of our line. Nor could I see any limit to the plain on either side, but I guessed those limits lay even farther than the farthest riders. All I could see was the man on the left of me, the Chief, the man on his right and the grass going on for ever. All I could hear was the grass giving way to the horses' legs as they advanced at a steady pace and the panting of the dogs. Nobody spoke. The Chief sat his horse badly, slouched, yet he scarcely needed the reins to govern it, often letting them go and using only his legs. As ever, his eyes were fixed on something out of sight. The men riding beside us scanned the ground with a regular glance from side to side, like the sweep of a scythe. The whole operation reminded me of harvesting. I pictured the fugitive running before us, silly with terror, to seek the diminishing cover that remained, as I'd seen small animals run. Supposing he was in the pampa, as the Chief believed. I couldn't make out his reasons for believing it. The trouble with a foreigner speaking English is that you can never be sure he means what he says. Like a parrot. The sun was rising fast and its heat was a fist in your face.

'What's beyond this plain?' I asked.

'The river.'

'Can he cross it? Going so slowly we may not catch him this side.'

'He'll never reach it. A horse can walk comfortably through the grass. Not so a man, who must force not only his legs but his whole body through. He'll be exhausted long before the river.'

I felt almost sorry for him. Was what he'd done worth all this? His crime wasn't clear to me. I knew there was a precise killing and an approximate million in it, but whether he'd done the murder to get the money or to keep it or to conceal it I never knew. I even tried not to think of him by name. That only makes it worse, as giving a name to your chickens makes it harder to wring their necks.

At midday we dismounted to rest. The horses lay down to escape the sun and we followed their example. The villagers had brought provisions for us. I ate some kind of fruit mess, which tasted better than it looked, and drank water. Lying in the grass I felt like a kid again. It reminded me of lying on my face in a meadow pretending the grass was a jungle. I could see none of our party except the Chief. He wasn't talking. He wasn't drinking, either, though he carried a flask of wine. I lay with my hat pulled over my eyes, inhaling the smell of horses and grass, wondering about the man in front. Our disappearance must have seemed a miracle to him. But he would know better. No lunch break for him, poor devil. I fell asleep then. I was woken by the Chief shaking me, and couldn't remember at first where I was or what I had to get up for.

Consequently we were later mounting than the rest and moved off a bit behind them. The Chief did nothing to mend this gap, so we were thrown into a kind of isolation, if not intimacy, where I felt bound to break silence.

'Does this remind you of the old days?' I asked.

Slowly he turned his head, as if it had a long way to go, and long he stared at me, as if he'd never seen me before. Then he said, 'Where is yesterday?' I didn't know where it was. I was making conversation, not opening a metaphysical conference. 'It is here,' he continued, tapping his forehead. 'Not there,' sweeping a dismissive hand across the landscape. 'And where is tomorrow?' I kept my mouth tight shut. 'Here too,' tapping again. 'And where are yesterday and tomorrow when the brain stops?' I was sorry I'd mentioned it.

The regular movement of the horses and the monotony of the scene were hypnotic. A lot of time slipped by without my noticing, until I saw the sky getting that old familiar flush. This would be the fourth sunset I'd seen in that country and I didn't want to see many more.

'His stamina's better than you expected,' I said. 'It'll be dark soon.'

'We shall catch him this side of the river,' he repeated. 'I have an instinct for these things.'

'How far's the river?'

'We shall catch him before dark. That is when a fugitive loses hope.'

'I should have thought it was when he gained it.'

'It's not pursuit that exhausts a man. It's anxiety. Pursuit stops and starts, but anxiety is incessant. Sooner or later comes a night when you can't bear the prospect of the sun rising again on uncertainty. So you stand and wait for them.'

Was that how it had been with him? During my trance we'd lagged farther behind the line and even the villagers with their dogs had got in front of us. It seemed a daft position for the commander – his men beyond call and his rear unguarded. I kept looking over my shoulder. If my man had somehow slipped through the line, we two stragglers might present an irresistible target. Specially if he had a silencer. These backward glances strengthened my fancy that the pampa was a sea. Now we were far out on it. I could see no perimeter, no firm ground. In the nearly invisible distance was what might be a mountain range but might equally be a bank of clouds. My companion said a river lay not far in front, but for all evidence of it the grass might go on for ever, to the edge of the world.

He stopped and put a hand on my arm. The air had begun to turn opaque and I shivered at its sudden chill. 'He is near,' he whispered. 'I sense it.'

'How did he give them the slip?' I asked, nodding at the distant sombreros.

'They are townsmen,' he replied scornfully.

'Let's fire a shot to turn them back.'

'No. This one is artful. We must not alarm him. Dismount – but quietly.' I slipped off to stand beside him. 'Stay here with the horses,' he said, 'and I will find him.'

'He's my man.'

'But this is not your country. You have my gun still? Then don't be afraid to use it.'

'Don't be eager to use mine,' I said, detaining him.

'I shall do only what is necessary.' He looked at me a moment, then evaporated into the grass. That's how I can best describe the swiftness and silence of his action. A flash of old fieldcraft, justifying his contempt for townsmen. I stood between the horses for cover and kept a watch all round. The radius of vision was short now. No sound but the fidgeting of the horses. If the Chief was moving, it was with the same deadly soundlessness I'd admired. The other man must have equal cunning, though recalling his dossier I couldn't imagine where he'd learnt it. I couldn't tell where either of them was. One each side of me perhaps. I hoped they wouldn't hit the referee.

'He's coming towards you,' called the Chief. 'Be careful.' The advice seemed superfluous. I drew my gun, pushed off the safety catch and slowly turned. I had a good few hundredweight of horsemeat to shield me, but bits remained exposed. Like my head. Then I saw a movement – a slight movement of the grass just as I was turning away from it in my slow spin. It was checked immediately. I called him by name then. 'Give up,' I said. 'There's a troop of trigger-happy cowboys in front. We're both off our home ground here. Come out with your hands high and we can be on a plane for England tonight.'

He fired. It annoyed me that he should be vicious enough to shoot and silly enough to miss.

'Do that again and I'll fire,' I said.

He did it again, hitting my shoulder, and I kept my promise. He fell forward out of the grass. It was the Chief, and he was dead.

I knew the answer to the riddle. I opened his gun – my gun – to confirm it. Only two shots left. Two fired at the temple last night, two fired now. The man I was looking for had fired none, because he'd never been there to fire any. Only the Chief, tired of running away from death. The comrades he'd betrayed were dead or in prison, but they must have relatives. Endless ramifications of revenge. Tired of looking over his shoulder, he had appointed me his executioner.

The shooting had attracted his men, who returned through the dusk like a slow cortège.

Why hadn't he done it himself? Later I heard rumours of a wife behind shutters somewhere. The pension, maybe? Perhaps there was a suicide clause. Perhaps giving me his gun had been the nearest he could get.

The man I wanted was caught in Birmingham.

FAMILY BUTCHER

by George Sims

Pasterne is arguably the prettiest village in the Hambleden valley. Skirmett, Frieth, Fingest and Ibstone all have their attractions as does Hambleden itself, and Turville is surmounted by a delightful windmill perched on a hill-top, a rarity indeed in the Chilterns, but Pasterne most conforms to a picture-postcard village. There is the large green, immaculately trimmed, known as Pasterne Pound, with carefully preserved oak stocks, and a dozen brick and flint cottages grouped round the green just as if some Edwardian water colourist had placed them there for a painting. The village pond is a fine example too, kept fresh by a spring, with white ducks and mallards, and occasionally a nesting pair of swans. Postcards on sale in the village stores-cum-Post Office sell well in the summer months, particularly those featuring the pond and the rather eccentrically placed Norman church which appears to have turned its back on Pasterne due to its being the sole relic of an even earlier settlement. But people in picture-postcard villages live lives much the same as the rest of us.

Another popular view of the village shows a northern aspect of the Pound with Daniel Patchin's butcher shop centrally placed, together with his Pound Cottage and the copse which hides Lord Benningworth's Manor House. Patchin's shop was originally an Elizabethan cottage that has been a good deal refurbished over the centuries, but the exterior, apart from the small shop window, must appear much as it did originally with its massive black oak beams and the plaster walls that are freshly white-washed each year. The name Daniel Patchin is in large white italic letters on the black façade, together with the trade description Family Butcher in smaller capitals.

Patchin's ancient establishment and the Post Office Stores are the only village shops: both are attractive and 'quaint', looking rather like the toy shops favoured by children of less sophisticated epochs. And Patchin's shop too is a model one for he is fanatical about personal cleanliness and hygiene: he wears a fresh apron twice a day, and the wash-basin at the rear of the shop is much used but kept spotless as are the display area and the large bench where Patchin works, 'looking more like a surgeon than a butcher', as Lord Benningworth once described him to some friends. Patchin's shop window always has a sparse display: a brace of pheasants, which he may well have shot himself, a hare, a local chicken or two, and one specimen of the prime meat he has for sale. Inside the shop there is a similarly small amount of meat on show: very likely just a side of Scotch beef hanging up with a Welsh shoulder of lamb. Under the impeccable refrigerated display counter there will be some of the famous Patchin sausages. Anything else that is required Daniel Patchin will have to fetch from the large cold room which takes up most of the rear portion of the shop.

151

The same shop when run by Daniel's father Gabriel was well known throughout the Chilterns in the 1930s, as was Reuben Patchin's before that: Daniel Patchin has an equally enviable reputation. Though the population of the village is not large enough to support such a thriving business, and Lord Benningworth who owns most of the village and the surrounding land is against more houses being built locally, callers come regularly from High Wycombe, Henley and Marlow for their meat. The Patchin sausages are still made exactly as detailed in Reuben's 1912 recipe with generous amounts of pork, herbs, spices and freshly ground black pepper; they bear no resemblance at all to the products churned out in factories, and they attract customers from as far away as Slough and Oxford.

Daniel Patchin, a quiet, sometimes taciturn man, is widely respected. He seems to live for his work and is busy throughout a long day for five and a half days each week. Wednesday is early closing and that afternoon he devotes to either fishing or shooting according to the season. When he returned from the Korean war Daniel Patchin came to an amicable unwritten agreement with Lord Benningworth that on Sundays he would act as an unpaid forester for the estate, keeping Benningworth's copses and woodland in good order, felling all diseased treees and clearing undergrowth, in return for which service he was allowed to keep all the timber he wanted. Every Sunday is devoted to this occupation and Patchin has a wood-yard at the back of his cottage where villagers can purchase logs and firewood.

The Patchin family has lived in Pasterne for centuries but the Benningworth connection with the locality is even more ancient: Lord Benningworth can trace his ancestry back in this country to a Baron Will de Benningworth in 1220, and there are stone effigies of another Benningworth Knight and his Lady installed in the church in 1290. The churchyard also houses many Patchin graves, but the earliest is dated 1695 with the epitaph:

> *Good people all as you*
> *Pas by looke round*
> *See how Corpes' do lye*
> *For as you are som time Ware We*
> *And as we are so must you be*

Occasionally in an evening Daniel Patchin may stroll round the churchyard, eyeing the graves, particularly those of his own family. He likes those epitaphs which hint of un-Christian attitudes for he has a cynical, mordant sense of humour; he is not a church-goer. During his army service in Korea he found out that human life there was as cheap as that of turkeys at Christmas and he adopted a stoic's attitude to life and death. Serving as an infantryman he was awarded the Military Medal for his bravery in hand-to-hand fighting and won the nick-name 'Pig-sticker' from his comrades for his skill with the bayonet.

Daniel Patchin leads a very quiet life, devoted to work and country pursuits including gardening in the evenings. Lord Benningworth will sometimes stroll to the edge of his copse with a friend to point out Patchin's garden with its fine rose-beds and lines of potatoes, peas and beans as straight as guardsmen on parade. Patchin's wife Angela is ten years younger than him and before the marriage was known as a pretty, jolly and slightly flighty girl in Skirmett where she was brought up in a large farming family. The Patchins have no children as Angela proved to be barren, and over the ten years of marriage she has taken on the Patchin family's traits of seriousness and quiet outward mildness. She is a natural blonde with very fair, clear skin who blushes easily: any compliment from Benningworth's son and heir before he left to work in America would always make her change colour. She works behind the till in a cubicle-like office in the shop on Patchin's busiest days, always on Friday and Saturday, and occasionally on Thursday. Patchin employs a boy who makes himself generally useful on Friday evenings and Saturday mornings, otherwise he does all the work himself. He is a stocky man with massive muscles, enormously strong. Behind the shop there is a large shed which was used for all the slaughtering for the business up till about twenty years ago, and that is where Patchin despatches local poultry and scores of turkeys and geese at Christmas.

It was on a glorious late May afternoon that Daniel Patchin first became suspicious of his wife. It was a Monday and at lunch she had said that she would go for a walk in the afternoon. Returning at five she looked in at the shop to ask if he would like a cup of tea. He nodded and asked if she had enjoyed the walk. She hesitated and he looked up from the mincing machine to see that she had blushed and was nervously fiddling with the buttons on her blouse as if to make sure they were all fastened. It would be difficult to imagine a more observant man than Daniel Patchin: his whole life both at work and during his time away from the shop had sharpened his perceptions. He had made a life-time study of his customers and of nature; it was his sole inactive hobby. The slightest change in a pensioner's expression, even the movement of an eye, was enough to tell Patchin that he was proffering a too expensive piece of meat; the faintest ripple at the end of a roach 'swim' caught his notice as did the sound of a twig snapping. When she did not reply about the obvious pleasures of a country walk on a perfect May afternoon, Patchin covered his wife's loss for words with a quick comment about an old woman who always called in for broth bones on a Monday.

When Angela left the shop Patchin gave her back an intense look, noticing that she had changed completely from the clothes she had worn at lunch. When she returned with the tray of tea, she had covered her pretty white blouse with an old brown cardigan. She was still nervous, restless, very slightly ill at ease. Patchin knew that she was a hopeless liar but did not ask any more questions. There was a fresh smell of lemon soap and Patchin knew she had washed her face, probably plunging it repeatedly into cold water to get rid of the faint, pink flush. Again he covered her silence with talk of how he might go down to the river that evening. The season for coarse-fishing did not start till mid-June but it was something he occasionally did out of season, inspecting favourite angling haunts to see how they had been affected by the high level of the Thames in winter.

153

During the next few weeks he added to his short list of pastimes the one of observing his wife: nothing that she did escaped him, even the merest hint of exasperation or frustration was filed away silently in his head – but nothing unusual ever attracted a comment from him.

It would not have required special ability as an observer to note Angela Patchin's revived interest in her clothes; even on Monday mornings when she did her weekly wash and on Wednesdays when she usually cleaned Pound Cottage from top to bottom she stopped wearing her old navy skirt and blossomed out in a new green one worn with a pretty apron, or jeans. She went to the Marks and Spencer store in Reading ostensibly to buy a summer frock but returned with several packages.

One Monday afternoon when Angela had gone for another walk Patchin closed the shop for a quarter of an hour and thoroughly inspected her chest of drawers. He took meticulous care in moving and replacing the various things; he found several new items of underwear including a particularly skimpy pair of knickers and a brassière designed to thrust size thirty-six breasts up and outwards as if proffering them to some lusty lad in a Restoration play. But which lusty lad? – that was the question that teased Daniel Patchin's brain, taking his attention away from his work so that he tended for the first time in his life to become a little absent-minded and not quite the usual model of efficiency. It was immediately noted by the villagers – 'Seems more human somehow', was the general verdict though expressed in different ways.

For a while Patchin speculated as to whether Lord Benningworth's son had returned to Pasterne and was again flattering Angela: if so it seemed a more serious matter than before, now apparently extending to her amply filled blouse. But an inquiry, casually phrased, to the Benningworths' housekeeper informed Patchin that the heir to the estate was still working happily in New York and did not plan to return home before Christmas.

Patchin's reaction to Angela's unusual behaviour varied considerably. At times he became quite fascinated by his secret observation in a detached way, as he had once studied an elusive old pike in a pool near Hambleden Mill: for weeks throughout one autumn he had tried various baits to entice the wily monster until he realised that the pike could be stirred into action only by a fish with fresh blood on it; so Patchin had served up a dace, liberally doused in blood, and the pike had succumbed. At other times Patchin experienced a feeling of cold fury that someone was stealing his wife from him – he was quite certain that it was happening. Once he woke with a horrid start in the middle of the night convinced that the telephone had rung just once, and then lay awake consumed with feelings of jealousy and twisted lust – he did not fall asleep till just before the alarm bell rang at six.

Perhaps Angela's changed attitude to sex was the most obvious give-away. Before the Monday afternoon walks and the new clothes she seemed to have regarded it as a rather boring routine matter to be managed as quickly as possible before turning away to sleep. Now she never turned away and was always ready for sex, keener than he could ever remember her being. Her kisses were open-mouthed and lingering, her embraces passionate and urgent – as he brooded on this he realised that 'urgent' was the key word – that was it, she was urging him on to more effort so that he resembled, when her eyes were closed, her other, very passionate lover. Even after an orgasm she was unsatisfied, longing for something else. It would be impossible to describe the various feelings Patchin experienced as his wife became ever more knowing in bed, with wanton behaviour and explicit movements trying to get him to obtain the results she enjoyed elsewhere. One night she wanted him to make love in a new position and as she determinedly pushed him into place he could see the grim joke of it so clearly that he nearly laughed. Nothing could make it more plain that Angela had a very virile, enthusiastic lover, much more skilled at the amatory arts than he would ever be; a lover who liked first to be inflamed by skimpy knickers and a 'display' brassière, and then performed perfectly.

It was not until a Friday in the middle of June that Patchin was able to indentify his cuckold enemy. He disturbed Angela while she was making a phone call when he entered Pound Cottage that lunch time a few minutes earlier than usual. As he opened the door the telephone was slammed down and Angela ran upstairs to cover her confusion. That afternoon Ray Johnson, the youngest postman in the area, called in at the shop ostensibly for a pound of sausages and some bacon. Johnson grinned over at Angela in the little office, calling out: 'Afternoon Mrs Patchin.' Angela did not reply but just nodded, flushing very slightly. Apart from that tell-tale flush there was something subtle about the way Johnson addressed her, with just an inflection of the 'Mrs Patchin', as though the formal mode of address was something of a joke between the pair. Daniel Patchin took his time in the cold storage room to give them a chance for a few words. The moment he opened the door Ray Johnson stopped talking and grinned foolishly as though he had forgotten what he was going to say.

Idiot, Patchin thought, you young idiot, but passed over the momentary awkwardness for Johnson by commenting on the sausages: 'Cook's specials this lot. Part of a batch I made up for the Manor. The old man likes just an extra pinch of pepper.'

Having once seen his wife with Johnson there was no longer any doubt in Patchin's mind, for it seemed to him as if there was some invisible but subtly tangible connection between them, an unspoken intimacy born of their long afternoons together, probably in Calcot Wood where there were some idyllic glades. As he did up the bacon and sausages and the embarrassed couple said nothing Patchin could visualise them on a green sward in a patch of dappled sunlight – the flimsy knickers being removed together with the trick brassière – and then Angela's urgent movements as the mutual madness began. Patchin felt as though his obsessive thoughts might show on his usually phlegmatic face so he cleared his throat loudly and shook his head, saying, 'Sorry. Throat's a bit sore. Hope it's not a summer cold.'

Ray Johnson gave Patchin an unusually serious, not altogether friendly look as he replied, 'Yes. Let's hope not.' The look negated the banal response and Patchin thought: Liar. It would please you if I came down with pneumonia. For the first time it struck him that the feeling of jealousy might not all be on one side. Probably Johnson was also jealous, of the nights when Patchin slept with Angela; possibly Johnson was coming to hate him as he had hated the unknown lover.

Later that afternoon, when Angela had gone back to the cottage to make some tea, Daniel Patchin stood at the open door of the shop staring at the pond where a pair of Canada geese had alighted and were being harried and made unwelcome by the aggressive though small coots which dashed in and out of the reeds, making proprietorial noises. And indeed Patchin did not miss anything that happened on the pond, noting how the mallards vanished and the white ducks kept out of the noisy quarrel like only faintly interested spectators. But Patchin's mind was elsewhere, brooding on his predicament: it was the first time since the Korean war that Patchin felt he was faced with a problem he did not know how to handle. Ray Johnson was a tall slight lad with curly black hair and a mouth that always seemed to be open, either grinning or laughing to show very white teeth. Johnson was easily the most popular of the local postmen; he was extremely cheerful, full of banter and old jokes. Patchin had always found that slightly irritating – but now the trifling feeling of irritation was replaced by the strong one of implacable enmity. Patchin had no intention of confronting Angela with his suspicions or of trying to surprise the lovers in the act, even though he thought it could be arranged one Monday afternoon in Calcot Wood. For all he knew Angela might then decide to leave him – he did not know how heavily their reasonably prosperous and comfortable life together weighed against the hours of passion spent with Lothario Johnson. No, the only answer was to get rid of him as the coots would undoubtedly rid themselves of the intruding Canada geese.

After the break for tea Patchin got down to work again. Friday evening was one of his busiest times as dozens of joints had to be prepared for the weekend – he had some particularly choosy customers who liked to have their meat prepared in the finicky French manner and he was quite willing to cater to their tastes. A great deal of beef had been ordered for that weekend and his young assistant was not up to preparing it, being capable of carrying out only the humblest jobs. Patchin set the boy to mincing pork and then began butchering two sides of beef, attacking the carcase with relish.

Once supper was finished he could hardly wait to get Angela to bed: knowing that she was the young man's mistress had the strange, unexpected effect of doubling his lust for her. And she semed equally ready for sex, falling back on the bed and raising her knees, smiling at him in a new way, a smile that contained a hint of amusement at his fumbling efforts to please her. This time it was his turn to be left feeling unsatisfied and empty even though he took her twice, as if possessing her half a dozen times would not be enough to assuage his restless yearning.

From mid-June Daniel Patchin spent most of his Sundays in Calcot Wood – it was by far the largest area of woodland owned by Lord Benningworth. One Sunday he decided to devote to searching for clues as to the lovers' meeting-place and did come on a bed of crushed ferns with a strange sensation that left him feeling slightly sick. From the improvised bed he made his way down to a deserted cottage in the remotest part of the wood, a spot that never seemed to be reached by the sun as it stood in the shadow of Calcot Hill. It had been a game-keeper's cottage up to 1939 but the pre-war Benningworth regime of having a game-keeper had been dropped and the remote, unattractive cottage was let, when Patchin was a youth, to a strange old man called Ted Ames, then left to rot. Lord Benningworth was a true conservative in that he was against change of any kind, even that of having a wreck of a building knocked down. The old widower Ames had eventually gone off his head and been taken away to a mental hospital in 1948, where he died. Since then the cottage had been stripped of its gutters and drain-pipes; most of the roof was still sound but rain had dripped in through a few missing tiles and some of the rafters were rotten, covered in mould: even on the warmest summer day the old cotttage smelt of dank decay. There was fungus on the kitchen walls and weeds were gradually invading the ground floor rooms, sprouting up from the cracks in the brick floors.

Daniel Patchin stood absolutely still for a long while staring at the ruined building which some villagers claimed was haunted by Ted Ames. Patchin did not believe in ghosts, spirits, Heaven or Hell: he believed that the Universe was incomprehensible and absolutely indifferent to mankind. Suddenly he said aloud: 'What a waste. Pity not to make some use of the old place.' The second sentence, spoken in a particularly mild voice, ended on a faintly questioning note and for the first time he moved his head as though he were talking to someone and waiting for a comment on his suggestion. Then he gave the idea engendered by his memory of a certain feature of the ancient fireplace in Ames's kitchen a mirthless smile and turned on his heel.

Throughout Calcot Wood there were piles of logs that Patchin built till he was ready to remove a truckload. There was also a hut where he kept a chain-saw, tins of petrol, axes and bags of wood chips and sawdust. He looked around to make sure that there was no one about, and began to carry sacks of sawdust and chippings over to the cottage; he felt a great satisfaction in commencing work on his plan.

On succeeding Sundays Daniel Patchin spent a good deal of time in transport-ing dry branches and brushwood; he also used his van to move cans of paraffin, half-empty tins of paint, plastic bags that had contained dripping, sacks of fat, soiled rags and other rubbish. These he carefully planted throughout the cottage, gradually turning it into a massive bonfire.

While the preparations in Calcot Wood were proceeding satisfactorily Patchin made a study of Ray Johnson's working life. By casual questions to the village Postmistress, who delighted in gossip, he wormed out the routine of Johnson and other postmen in the area. One of his discoveries was that Johnson often had either Monday or Wednesday afternoon off, and this was confirmed for him on the first Wednesday in July when Angela took a surprising interest in his fishing plans for that afternoon. Usually she was bored by angling so he answered these questions with concealed, wry humour. Then, prompted by a whim, he took more time than usual in his preparation for the weekly expedition to the Thames. His fishing equipment was the simplest that could be devised – he despised the 'London crowd' who invaded the river at weekends weighed down with paraphernalia. He had an all-purpose rod, a few hooks and floats and one reel carried in an army haversack. As he pretended to fuss over these things, and to take an unusually long time in making the flour paste for bait, he could see that Angela was very much on edge, nervous and yet pleasurably excited at the same time. She had not mentioned going out so he suspected that there might be a plan for Johnson to visit Pound Cottage while he was away: 'While the cat's away the mice will play,' he said over and over in his mind as he rolled the ball of dough between his strong, dry fingers.

When he at last set off in the van he was again ironically amused that Angela came out to wave goodbye as though to be certain of his departure. Patchin spent an hour on the river-bank but was not in the mood for fishing. The reeds were haunted by colourful dragon-flies and there was a brief darting visit from a kingfisher – sights that usually pleased him, but on this occasion he was hardly aware of anything about him, feeling rather like a ghost returned to haunt the scene of past pleasures.

Patchin drove back from the Thames with not much heart for what lay immediately ahead, but he now felt it was essential to make quite sure of the situation. In Pasterne he parked his van by the pond and appeared to stare down into its clear water for a while. Such behaviour on his part would not excite comment for he had been known to catch stickle-backs and frogs there to use as bait when angling for pike.

After some minutes of staring with unseeing eyes Patchin ambled back to his closed shop, then walked through it into the garden that led up to Pound Cottage. He trod noiselessly over the lawn and entered the side door very quietly. Within a minute his suspicions were dramatically confirmed: through the board ceiling that separated the living-room from the bedroom he heard the squeaking springs of his double bed, squeaking so loudly that it seemed as if the springs were protesting at the extraordinary behaviour of the adulterous couple. Then there began a peculiar rhythmical grunting noise and his wife called out something incomprehensible in a strange voice.

Patchin retreated noiselessly, got back into his car and returned to Hambleden Mill. He fished stolidly for three hours with a dour expression on his face – an expression that some North Korean soldiers had probably glimpsed before he killed them with his bayonet. Usually he returned small fish to the river but on that afternoon he just ripped them off the hook and threw them on the bank.

Returning home again at about his usual time, Patchin found his wife in an excellent mood. Fornication seemed to be good for her health as she appeared blooming. A delicious supper had been prepared for him and Angela had popped over to the village stores to buy a bottle of the dry cider he favoured. She looked quite fetching with her flushed cheeks, her curly blonde hair freshly washed, and the two top buttons of a new pink blouse left undone, but Patchin could not respond at all; momentarily he found it difficult to keep up the pretence of not knowing about her affair and felt as though an expression of suspicion and cold contempt must appear on his face. When he went to wash he stared in the mirror and was surprised to find the usual phlegmatic expression reflected.

After supper Angela wanted to stroll around in the garden. It was something Patchin normally enjoyed, seeing the results of all his hard work, for in July the garden looked at its best with the rose-beds 'a picture' as Angela said, and usually it was very satisfactory to inspect the neat rows of vegetables. Instead he experienced a most unusual mood of emptiness and frustration – everything seemed hollow and meaningless.

While his wife bent down to smell a rose Daniel Patchin stared up at the clear evening sky. He knew his enjoyment of life was temporarily lost, and that it would not return until he was rid of the man who threatened his marriage. Angela came and stood by him, took his hand and placed it on her firm round breast, an action that would have been quite out of character a few months before; but her new sensuality did not move him at all, and when they went to bed making love to her was like a ritual, quite spoilt by his memory of the protesting bed-springs.

Patchin decided to try to put his plan of murder into effect on the second Wednesday in July. Angela went for a walk again on the Monday of that week, so according to his understanding of the postman's routine it seemed probable that Ray Johnson would be working on the Wednesday afternoon. If so he would then be driving down the narrow lane that skirted Calcot Wood to clear a remote, little-used post-box at about 3 p.m.

On the Wednesday Patchin felt quite calm and confident that everything would go as he devised. He set off from Pound Cottage promptly at 2 p.m. after an excellent lunch of roast loin of pork with the first new potatoes from the garden and a large helping of broad beans. His haversack had been got ready on the previous evening: it now contained some other things as well as fishing tackle – rubber gloves, matches, a ball of extremely tough cord, sticking plasters and a foot-long piece of iron pipe.

Parking his van just off the lane by the wood in a cunningly chosen spot where it would not be seen, Patchin took his haversack and walked quickly through the wood to Ames's cottage. He experienced pleasurable excitement in doing so and in inspecting the fire he had laid in the kitchen grate. It consisted of three fire-lighters, paper spills and wood chippings, a few sticks and numerous small pieces of coal. It had been constructed with the care that a chaffinch gives to making its nest, and he estimated that it would burn intensely for an hour or two. 'Quite long enough to roast a joint,' he said in an expressionless voice as he got up from his crouching position in front of the grate.

After inspecting the trails of wood chippings soaked in paraffin which he had laid throughout the cottage like long fuses to explosive charges, he glanced round the wildly overgrown plot that had once been a garden. Rank grass a foot high contended with massive clumps of nettles, giant docks and cow parsley.

159

He did not think that it would be possible to trace foot-prints on such a terrain, but also he did not expect his enterprise to be risk-free. There were bound to be risks in a life governed by mere chance.

It was 2.45 p.m. when he walked back through the wood to the narrow, twisting lane. He wore the rubber gloves with his left hand in his old fishing-jacket pocket and the other plunged into the haversack that hung from his right shoulder. He positioned himself in the lane so that he would be on the driver's side of the van when it approached him. The oppressive mood which had dogged him for so many weeks lifted and he whistled as he waited – a rather tuneless version of *As time goes by* which he repeated over and over again.

At 3 p.m. precisely he heard a motor engine in the lane and got ready to wave the van down if it was driven by Johnson. For the first time that afternoon excitement seized him, with a thumping of his heart and a sudden tremor of fear such as he had always experienced before hand-to-hand fighting in Korea. He had once said to another soldier there: 'Everyone's afraid at times. Anyone who says he isn't is either a liar or a fool.'

As the Post Office van came round the corner Patchin waved it down, first tentatively then more vigorously as he spotted Johnson's head of black curly hair. Johnson stopped the van, rolled its window further down and called out, 'What's up?'

Patchin walked slowly across to the van, limping very slightly and holding himself as though he was in pain. 'Sorry, sorry,' he said. 'Bit of trouble.' He came close to the van door and stood silent, with his eyes half-closed and swaying slightly as though he was going to faint.

With a puzzled expression in which there was just the faintest hint of suspicion Johnson opened the van door and began to get out – his height made doing so a rather awkward business. Patchin took out the iron pipe and hit Johnson on the head, a measured blow by someone who had considerable experience in stunning animals. Johnson lurched forward and then fell in a heap, just like a poleaxed bullock. Patchin bundled him back into the van, got into the driving seat and drove off down the lane, whistling the same tune again. After a hundred yards he turned off on to a track which led in the direction of the gamekeeper's cottage. Before leaving the red van he pressed Johnson's fingers on the steering-wheel, then bundled the body up and carried it on his shoulder as easily as he managed a side of beef.

He also paused in the decaying doorway to impress Johnson's fingerprints on two empty paraffin cans, and carried him through to the kitchen. The tall man was still inert, but as Patchin dropped his burden on to the cement floor Johnson's eyelids flickered. Patchin sat him up like a ventriloquist's dummy and then knocked him out with a blow to the jaw that would have floored most boxers.

Patchin put sticky plasters over Johnson's large mouth, then worked on the unconscious man with the skill he always showed in preparing joints. He put his legs neatly together and bound them tightly from above the knee to the ankles, using the same binding technique he used in repairing his fishing rod, pulling the

160

cord so tight that the legs became immobile; he left a loop by the ankles. He repeated the process with the limp arms. Then came the part that gave him most satisfaction: lifting the two loops on to the hooks that had once supported a turn-spit in front of the fire. Immediately Johnson was suspended like an animal carcase ready to be roasted. Patchin lit the fire in the grate and left the cottage.

Before taking off his rubber gloves Patchin picked up the empty paraffin cans and left them near the old garden gate which was half hanging off its hinges, then strode off to the place where he had hidden his own van. The time was 3.30 and everything had gone exactly as he had hoped. There was always blind chance of course – for instance the remote possibility that another pair of lovers might be trespassing in the woods and see him striding along so purposefully, but there was nothing he could do about it.

Driving to the Thames, Patchin mentally examined his plan again and formulated one or two more things to be done. As soon as he had parked the van near Hambleden Mill he assembled his rod and line right down to putting on the bait, a thing he never did till he was actually on the river bank, so that anyone seeing him might think he had already been fishing and was trying another spot. Then, carrying the assembled rod, he walked along the gravel path and over the complicated series of weirs which cross the Thames at Hambleden Mill. As he approached the lock he watched to see whether the keeper there might be in sight and was relieved to be able to cross unseen.

Patchin threw his piece of iron pipe into the river before spending an hour angling: he fished like a young boy, close in to the bank where there were more bites to be had but the fish were always small. He caught a tiny roach and three gudgeon but was quite satisfied with them, leaving the last gudgeon on the hook as he walked back to the lock. Good fortune was still with him for the lock-keeper was now at work opening the gates for a motor cruiser. The keeper, who knew Patchin well, called out, 'Any luck Dan?'

'Not much. Just tiddlers,' Patchin called out, shaking his rod so that the suspended gudgeon twisted about at the end of the line. 'Think I'll use them to try for a pike in the pool by the mill. See you.'

'Yes, see you. Will you keep me a nice small chicken for the weekend?'

'Yes. Right.' Patchin walked off just fractionally quicker than he did nor-mally. With excitement working in him at the prospect of revisiting Ames's cottage it was not easy to appear just as usual. For once he was grateful that he had a rather expressionless face.

His mind on other things, he mechanically dismantled the fishing rod and line as quickly as he could. 'Yes, all going to plan,' he said aloud though there was no one within a hundred yards of him.

Driving back to the lane once more he experienced a suprising feeling of let-down and anti-climax. It was true that it had all gone without a hitch as far as he could tell, but somehow it seemed a bit too easy. There would have been more satisfaction if he could have allowed the tall but puny Johnson a chance to fight, some ludicrous attempt at self-defence which he would have brushed away derisively, as easily as a tom-cat deals with a rat.

161

Once in Calcot Wood again Patchin's nose twitched. There was a faint aroma like that of roast pork which had greeted him at lunch time at Pound Cottage. It grew stronger at every step he took. Desultory grey fumes struggled up from the ancient chimney. The smell was very strong in the hall and unpleasantly so in the kitchen which reeked of cooking odours and where a blackened, twisted carcase was still roasting and dripping fat into a dying fire.

Despite the smell Patchin stayed there looking at the object which bore no resemblance to the once garrulous postman. Patchin's hatred of the man had quite disappeared now that there was no longer any need for it – he was not gloating over his victim, but musing on the quintessential evanescence of man. How easily was man humbled, how soon was he changed into rotting meat! It had been just the same in Korea: one minute his friend 'Dusty' Seddon had been telling a dirty joke, the next moment lying mute with most of his face blown off.

Pausing in the hall, Patchin set light to a pile of paraffin-soaked sawdust and then lit the trails of wood-chips and retreated to the sagging front door, throwing the box of matches behind him.

The fire had taken a firm grip on the cottage before Patchin had even left the garden: he could hear it raging and roaring unseen until a sheet of flame sprang up at one of the diamond-leaded windows. For the second time that day Patchin experienced a slight attack of nerves; momentarily his right hand shook and for a few minutes he seemed to be walking on lifeless legs, having to make an extraordinary amount of effort just to propel himself along.

Seated in his van Patchin took out a large handkerchief and wiped his forehead which was sweating profusely, and allowed himself a few minutes rest before driving off in his customary careful manner. Was there something he had overlooked – perhaps a trifling slip which might lead the police to his door in a few days' time? As he navigated a series of lanes and minor roads that would put him once again on the main road from Hambleden to Pasterne, his mind was exercised by the nagging suspicion that he might have made one vital mistake.

Calm gradually returned as he drove slowly along, and he began to think of the possible effect of the fire on the Benningworth estate. The large garden of rank grass and weeds should act as a barrier between the fire and Calcot Wood, but even if it did spread then Lord Benningworth owed him a favour for all the hard work he had put in there as amateur forester for twenty-five years. A sudden thought made Patchin smile. The Benningworth family motto, *Esse quam videri*, 'To be rather than to seem to be', was well known in the locality; it was a pity that Ray Johnson had not known that Daniel Patchin also had a motto: 'What I have I hold.'

When Patchin arrived in Pasterne he felt completely normal. His pleasant life had been momentarily threatened with an upheaval but that was now all over. The village looked particularly lovely in the late afternoon sunlight. The white ducks were sedulously paddling to and fro as though they were paid to do so, and swifts were skimming over the clear pond's mirror-like surface, occasionally dipping down to it, hunting midges. The Postmistress's black and white cat moved carefully over the neatly clipped grass as if it might be stalking a newt and sat down at the edge of the pond. 'Pretty as a picture,' Patchin said.

Walking along to Pound Cottage Daniel Patchin thought of what he should say when he saw Angela. It was essential to appear absolutely as normal so that when she heard of the perplexing tragedy in Calcot Wood nothing about his behaviour should prompt suspicion in her mind. Then he understood Angela's difficulty in appearing quite normal or saying anything about that walk she had taken on the glorious May afternoon because phrases that he went over in his mind seemed artificial and suspicious. 'Nice afternoon, but I didn't catch anything' – false. 'I enjoyed it, but not good fishing weather' – unnatural.

But Patchin need not have worried, for as soon as he opened the side door he heard the squeak of protesting bed-springs and Angela calling out in a voice that sounded false and unnatural.

THE BELVEDERE

by Jean Stubbs

The memory of cousin Fanny troubles me so greatly that I wake crying in the night. There is a candle burning against the dark, and Nanny sleeps in an adjoining room with her door open so that she can come to me quickly. Mamma must have her sleep, they say, but she sits with me during the day and sews rows of lace onto the baby's clothes and tells me fairy-tales. They shaved my head when the fever began and I wear a little linen cap bordered by a frill. Mamma says my hair will grow again, and when I am better she will send me to Aunt Dith who lives by the sea. But just yet I am not strong enough to travel, and hardly strong enough to support a nightmare I can in no way convey to them. They changed my room so that I should not see the belvedere at the end of the garden, but it shimmers pale and terrible in my dreams. Cousin Fanny stands at the foot of my bed and smiles and smiles. Sometimes she begins to glide towards me with her arms outstretched: a phantom walking in its phantom sleep. And then I scream myself back to a reality hardly less fearful than the things that haunt me.

Our house in Blackheath was large enough for a dozen children, standing in its own garden, and we thought ourselves a fortunate family. Papa worked in the City and wore a black silk top-hat and a black frock-coat. But in the evenings he donned a plum-coloured velvet jacket and an embroidered cap with a silk tassel. Mamma stayed at home, arranging the life of everyone and the proper state of everything from attic to basement. She discussed the day's menus with Cook and our lessons with the governess, and the flowers and vegetables with the gardener. And in the afternoons, unless she was resting on the sofa, she visited or received ladies like herself.

We should indeed have been nine children, but four of us had died in infancy and lay at rest in the churchyard under two weeping cherubs and a stone urn. We visited their grave every Sunday after morning service to contemplate the bliss that was our sorrow, and to garland them with flowers. And on the anniversary of each death we spent the day quietly at home, and remembered them in our evening prayers. Mamma told us they had gone to a better place and it was wrong to grieve. Yet she wore black for a year after their decease, and the boys had crêpe bands sewn on their left sleeves, and all the joys of heaven could not stop her mourning them.

After baby Rachel died of diphtheria Papa took Mamma to Italy for her health, and she returned full of delightful and impractical fancies. At least, Papa said they were impractical, and when the orange trees refused to grow – proving him right – he advised her to mark the Italian tour with a more tangible and durable memento. She had loved the churches built delicately upon hills, through whose campanile one glimpsed the blue skies and feathers of cloud, and she mentioned this in her pretty, beseeching manner during breakfast.

'I cannot build you a church, my love,' said Papa, smiling, 'that is too great an undertaking. But we shall build a belvedere at the end of the garden if you wish, and fashion it after the Italian style.'

Mamma clasped her hands and cried that she would treasure that above all things.

'And what *is* a belvedere, James?' Papa asked, seeing that he was not attending to the conversation and improving his knowledge. 'Define it, if you please.'

James, concealing a pet white mouse in the pocket of his Norfolk jacket, replied that he thought a belvedere was a very *little* church.

'Your thought is an erroneous one, James,' said Papa, taking his gold watch from his waistcoat pocket. 'If you do not know something you should always say so, and ask permission to look up the word in the dictionary. I believe I have five minutes to spare. Bring me the dictionary.'

'This is exceeding kind of Papa,' said Mamma automatically. 'For he is a very important man with a great deal to do, and every minute is precious to him.'

James mumbled his thanks, stumbled out of his chair, concealed the mouse in a drawer on his way to the study (from which it would later leap onto a shrieking housemaid) and returned with a heavy volume in very small print. He stood pink and upright but one could tell he was no lexicographer, and I could see Mamma praying that he would not drop the book or wrinkle the pages. And with Papa's watch ticking away in his right hand like an accuser, and Papa's eyes fixed first on it and then on him, James made a clumsy job of finding the right place.

'A belvedere is a raised turret,' he said at last, and Mamma breathed out, 'from which one views the scenery. It is formed from the Italian *bel*, meaning *beautiful*, and the verb *vedere*, meaning *to see*.'

'Very well, James. Remember that definition. A word remembered is a word gained, and an extensive vocabulary is the mark of a cultivated person.'

Then he put back his watch, folded *The Times* in three and went off to that mysterious temple in the City, from which flowed the means to keep a wife and five children, a staff of eight and an establishment whose conservatory alone was a matter of envy to all who saw it.

Richard and Edward were being trained for life at a public school, so that left James and me to the tuition of our governess, and baby Frederick was scarcely in breeches. Mamma lay on the sofa after breakfast, and though I should not have dared mention it I guessed why. It meant a great many nods and winks between the women servants, frequent injunctions not to make a noise and disturb poor Mamma, and in due time a new baby in the nursery. I have never understood why Mamma was ill for months, since babies are found in an instant lying under currant bushes or flown in by a stork or produced like a conjuror's rabbit from Dr Fogg's bag. But that was an adult mystery which one seemed destined never to unravel.

I think I may say, without excessive pride, that before cousin Fanny came I used to be a good child. I had long learned, in my ten years, that to please Mamma I must be pretty and loving, and to gratify Papa modest and docile. I could not please my three elder brothers except by staying out of their way, but I kissed and petted little Frederick – who was not old enough to dislike girls, and indeed preferred me to anyone. But I was never a clever child, and though Nanny said, 'Better to be good than clever,' I noticed that goodness was treated as a dull quality whatever anyone said. None of the servants made a favourite of me as Cook made of James (in spite of his mice), or Nanny of her first-born Richard (now a stalwart fifteen and naughty at Marlborough), or Nora, the housemaid, of Edward (who coaxed macaroons from her in the holidays). And everyone loved Frederick though goodness could hardly be reckoned as his forte. Perhaps I was something of a favourite with Papa whom I longed to charm as Mamma did. She would laugh and glance sideways at him, and lift her hands gracefully to her crown of black hair to touch it into perfection. My hair had long since been abandoned, except for a torment of curl-papers before parties, and hung down my back: brown and neat and without distinction. Neither were music and needlework my accomplishments as they were hers. I produced samplers in a misery of pricked fingers and sorry tears, and they had to be washed and ironed before presentation in the parlour. Whereas Mamma's *petit point* graced chairs and stools and fire-screens. I had not struck half a dozen wrong notes on the piano before the penny on the back of each hand fell down, proving that I did not even arch them properly let alone play accurately. But Mamma could play and sing like an angel. I used to creep down and sit on the stairs when she had a Musical Evening, hoping she would sing a song called *Somewhere a Voice is Calling*. Now I am afraid of it, because it seems to beckon to the realm where cousin Fanny lies; and I pray that I, at least, might live for ever so that I do not have to join her there. And then I remember that I, above all others, am least fitted to pray to God – Who Sees and Knows All Things. So I drift into a limbo of sleep, and watch the belvedere stand in ghostly beauty, and watch cousin Fanny walk in ghostly horror.

The belvedere came first. Papa, who is as Miss Wilder our governess says 'a most cultivated gentleman', designed the turret from numerous Italian models. So that, though it belonged to no particular school or style, it appeared to be the essence of every belvedere created. Mamma sat smiling and sewing with an air about her that I envied and could not fathom. Now, from the depths of my separateness, I know it was the air of the well-beloved. In my envy I tried to attract Papa's attention and made him spill a bottle of Indian ink on the parlour carpet, which I suppose was my just desert – only I should not have been envious had I been well-beloved too. He was exceedingly angry.

My papa's taste was impeccable, as Mamma always said, but I felt considerably disappointed by the size of the belvedere. I had imagined a tower twenty feet high and it was not above ten: very slender and beautiful in a pale stone, with its narrow steps leading to a view that perhaps the Italians would not have pronounced perfect, but nevertheless extremely pleasant. From the garden side it held no awe, but ours was sloping ground so that a drop, calculated to inspire a delightful terror, lay on the other side. Mamma and Papa might gaze when and as they liked, and the two elder boys were cautioned to be careful, but James and I were only allowed to ascend in the company of a responsible adult. Little Frederick was not permitted at all, and spent his days attempting to reach the forbidden area and scale what must have appeared a veritable Babel. Visitors exclaimed over its splendour and originality, though Papa's business friends chaffed him for such a display of useless loveliness.

'You must be a warm man to put up a piece of feminine foolery!' said Mr Bullock, and Papa laughed and said it was a present to Mamma.

I asked him what 'warm' meant, and he told me that it was a slang word, on no account to be used by any of us, which suggested that he had a great deal of money. I was proud to think that my papa could be important enough to spend as he pleased.

The belvedere came first, and cousin Fanny came second. We had not heard of Mamma's sister Eleanor before the envelope arrived bordered in black. And her explanation was so worded as to confuse me further.

'We have not spoken of Eleanor, your aunt Eleanor, for many years. What she did is of no matter now, but between herself and her Maker. Suffice it to say that she sinned, she suffered, and by the grace of God is now in heaven. She has left behind her one child, a daughter of thirteen whom she calls Fanny – I suppose she was christened Frances after my dear mother . . .'

'If she was christened at all,' said Papa.

'Why should she not be christened?' I asked. 'Is not every child christened? I thought it must be the law, Papa.'

'Your dear papa was joking. He merely refers to the fact that Aunt Eleanor and Frances lived for many years abroad where things are very different from here. Most certainly the child was christened, Mr Brook.'

She never addressed my papa as 'Mr Brook' except on very formal occasions, and I felt he had erred.

'My sister begs me to look after the child,' said Mamma hurriedly, but his momentary indiscretion had given her strength. She moved closer to him so that I should not hear, and said something about money in trust.

'Money of what complexion?' Papa said sternly.

I crawled under the table and sat there, hidden by the chenille cloth with its tawny silk tassels.

'The letter has been written by a nun, my dear Charles. My sister would hardly deceive *her*. Perhaps the – perhaps her – Mr Marechale settled something on the child quite legitimately. We cannot punish the daughter for the mother's transgressions. No one claims her. She is at present being cared for in the convent where my sister died.'

'Popish nonsense. I'll have no rag, tag and bobtail in my house.'

For the first time since I had known her Mamma set up her will against Papa's. A child was involved. A child of mature years, certainly, of obscure background and strange origins. But one of those blessed creatures who are admitted to the

Gates of Heaven, being innocent of heart and mind.

'My sister had a sound Protestant upbringing, Mr Brook. In France, as you know even better than myself . . .' A marital sop. '. . . the national religion is that of the Roman Church. The nuns possibly took her in out of kindness because she had neither friends nor relatives. We are all equal in the sight of God. The child cannot be blamed.'

In the end Papa agreed that Fanny should live with us for a few months, with the proviso that she should also be sent to a suitable boarding school if she showed signs of contaminating us. She had not been in the house a fortnight before she established herself as another favourite.

'Eleanor was always the family beauty,' said Mamma fondly, 'and Fanny is the image of her mother.'

Her beauty was undoubted, even in that transitory stage between childhood and womanhood where awkwardness reigns. Her hair curled black and glossy down her back, she held herself like a queen, her manners were faultless, her gratitude immense without being embarrassing. Mamma had Miss Briggs, the dressmaker, in the house for a month sewing new clothes.

'Since these – though most elegant, my dear Fanny – are a little unsuitable for your years.'

Fanny agreed humbly, anxious not to offend, but asked if she might keep her French wardrobe in memory of her own mamma. Since no other solution occurred to my own mother (one can hardly pass finery on to the poor and deserving) she allowed this. Indeed, as I hung jealously and uncertainly about the fringes of this new relationship, I discovered that Fanny was allowed a great deal, and by the means of seeming to give in to authority. It was an attitude I had been neither clever enough nor ruthless enough to adopt myself, and I hated her for her strategies.

Somewhere in that past which will never, I imagine, come to light, Fanny had learned how to deceive. She was a mistress of deception: subtle, plausible and intuitive. She had found that people could be manipulated through their own weaknesses, and she sought out those weaknesses with a frightening degree of perception. My family were revealed to me for what they were not, and they will never seem the same again. It is not only Fanny's ghost and the pale belvedere which haunt me now. It is the awakening to something even more terrible: the knowledge that the people who comfort and care for me are strangers, victims even frailer than myself. I wake, not safe and whole with my feet on that daisy-field of innocence, but shrieking on the edge of a long drop. And those who seek to save me tread the same precipice and do not know it for what it is. Where Fanny is now I cannot tell, but we shall never be safe from her, being no better. She deceived others, but we deceive ourselves.

Take Nanny, who arrived in our happy household to nurse Richard: a rosy-faced wholesome girl from Clapham. Fifteen years here taught her nothing more than the homely threats and axioms she employed when she came. They have robbed her of her freshness, perhaps of marriage to some honest man who might have made her contented. When she used to warn us that the bogey-man came for disobedient children, or promise us that to eat our crusts would make our hair curl, we believed her. The facts that no bogey ever appeared, even when we were naughtiest, that my poor hair never altered from its straight and stubborn fall, seemed due only to one's good fortune or personal sinfulness. I know her now to be both powerless and untruthful because Fanny found her out, and found her out for a purpose.

The new baby, another boy, was at first fretful, then quiet, and then listless. The doctor prescribed a month at the sea.

'How *I* should like a month at the sea,' said Fanny wistfully.

'If wishes were horses, then beggars would ride!' Nanny replied sharply, because rumours of Fanny's background had been hot gossip among the servants and she regarded Fanny as being less than her self and more fortunate.

'I feel that the sea air would benefit me,' said Fanny gently. 'Dear Nanny, may I hold baby for a few minutes?'

'No, Miss. He'll be better presently. He wants his Nanny, don't you, my lamb? Go you downstairs, Miss, and take Miss Helen with you. Children should be seen and not heard.'

Fanny gave her a peculiar look, but took my hand and led me into the parlour, where I presently heard her treading softly round the subject of the seaside. But it appeared that Papa's expenses were heavy enough, and the cost of Mamma, Nanny and the baby were all he was prepared to afford. Not that Fanny asked him outright, merely tried out the ground.

She made her first night excursion shortly afterwards. I woke to see her gliding from our bedroom into the nursery next door, where little William was crying persistently. My curiosity was too strong to permit me to remain, and I followed her, much as Adam must have followed Eve in that first bite of the forbidden fruit. My fault was a secondary one, it was to taste equally bitter.

William's cries ceased and on that instant Fanny pushed open the door. I crept in after her and saw a frozen tableau, a moment of time captured and delineated. Nanny, her hair plaited, her usual severity softened by a dressing-jacket, stood mouth open with the baby in her arms. A little bottle was on the table beside her.

'I *thought* you were giving him laudanum,' said Fanny, soft and triumphant, and her fingers closed on the bottle.

'Put that down at once, Miss!' said Nanny, low and fierce. 'You've got a nasty mind from those foreign parts. That's good wholesome drops, that is. The doctor left them for Master William.'

Coolly, Fanny unstoppered the bottle and smelled it.

'Laudanum,' she said, and smiled.

Nanny stowed the baby in his bassinette and made a snatch for the evidence. I had never seen her before, except as a pillar of authority, and her terror sickened me. Fanny held the bottle high.

'If you come any nearer,' she said quietly, 'I shall smash the bottle and fetch Mrs Brook to smell it.'

There was a long and dreadful silence. Then Nanny began, in a voice I had not heard, to coax her to give it up.

169

'Come, Miss,' she said, placating. 'You're a good clever young lady. You know as well as me that it isn't good for Master William to cry so. Give it to me like a kind young lady.'

Fanny said softly, 'I need a month at the seaside, Nanny. I have been deeply disturbed since my mamma's death. I walk in my sleep.'

I saw cunning come into Nanny's round red face and little black eyes.

'Do you, Miss?'

'I might have been walking in my sleep tonight,' said Fanny gently. 'And you know that sleep-walkers see nothing. Only they should not be wakened and frightened. They need rest. You know that, Nanny.'

'Yes, Miss,' said Nanny, and she trembled so much that she was forced to sit down. But she never took her eyes from Fanny's face. They were sending each other instructions in the silence.

'I had a brother that walked in his sleep,' said Nanny, after a pause. '*He* needed a rest and a change, but we were a poor family. And your mamma's death upset you, I don't doubt, Miss. Poor young lamb,' she added automatically.

Fanny held the bottle out, smiling.

'You must tell Mrs Brook that you found me sleep-walking,' she said.

'Yes, Miss. I shall, Miss. Perhaps you should come with us, to take your mind off your trouble. Mrs Brook will see the sense of that, I'm sure.'

She took the proffered bottle and her manner changed instantly.

'And now get you back to bed,' she said. 'I'll have no wicked liars in *my* nursery. I've been fifteen years in this household and never a word of complaint from anybody. If I tell Mrs Brook anything it will be that you're a bad influence. Don't think we don't know about *you*, Miss, belowstairs. I'll make it hot for you with the master, too. *He* had his doubts, but the mistress won't say no to an act of charity. And don't think as you're the only clever one round here. I can play a few tricks equal to any of yours! Off with you!'

Fanny's smile never faltered.

Very evenly, she said, 'I know you drink, too, though you *are* clever about it. I have a bottle of gin to show my aunt.'

Nanny's hand went to her mouth, confronted by a personal bogey.

'Did you think I should be so stupid as to take your word?' said Fanny wondering. 'Now you do exactly as you are told. And goodnight to you.'

She turned serenely away and found me behind the door, watching.

'Here endeth the first lesson,' she said, unperturbed.

'Miss Helen,' Nanny whispered. 'You don't believe a word she says, I know. You've always been a *good* girl. You'll not let her make trouble between me and your dear mamma, will you?'

I was terrified to find myself a witness, and even more afraid when Fanny put her arms about me.

'Dear cousin Helen,' she said persuasively, 'we all have our faults. You have seen Nanny's and mine tonight. Do you want to see your own?' And she shook me gently, playfully. 'Tell me,' she said, 'what will you say to your mamma tomorrow?'

As though I had been taught I said, 'You have been walking in your sleep and need a rest and change, Fanny.'

'Now we are truly sisters. Closer than sisters usually are, since we *know* each other.'

'But are you going to let Nanny give William laudanum?' I asked.

'That is Nanny's business. Nanny knows best.'

I showed the first and last spark of courage.

'*I* could tell Mamma,' I said.

Fanny laughed.

'Mamma would not find anything if you did. And I know nothing. I was walking in my sleep.'

These two, then, understood each other and had wiped the incident from their minds. I stood on the outside of a drama which I was to watch over and over again: a fearful little play in which the victim acquiesced and Fanny forgot to accuse. I had thought our family a model of domestic perfection, and myself a model of unobtrusive goodness. Fanny showed me what we truly were, and the revelation was terrible.

Our governess, Miss Wilder, became her next victim. No one knew her age, except perhaps Mamma, but she was elderly and certainly unmarriageable: the sixth and insignificant daughter of a poor parson, who had picked up sufficient knowledge to be entrusted with a girl's education. It was she who kindly washed and ironed my samplers before they could be shown. She who placed the pennies on the back of my hands so that I should arch them properly over the keyboard. She who made me sit upright for an hour, with a ruler tied to my spine, to learn deportment. She who struggled to lodge the names and dates of kings, French irregular verbs, the art of sketching and a few simple mathematical essentials, into my muddled head. James's curriculum was slightly different but he showed no more signs of brilliance than I did, and she welcomed Fanny, who from the first was quick, obedient and adaptable.

Our life at home was restricted, our outings infrequent and educational, and only Miss Wilder could be entrusted with the choice and guardianship of these excursions into the world. Fanny, accustomed to a broader canvas, intended to use the governess as a passport by gaining her approbation, undermining her confidence, and at last showing her who was mistress of the situation. She began by using her superior knowledge of the French language.

Miss Wilder had learned the tongue painstakingly, never venturing farther than the bounds prescribed, and she was flustered by Fanny's fluency and ease of idiom. Her early estimate, that this would be a pupil in whom she could feel pride and show off as an ornament to her teaching, survived a number of quiet impertinencies. But the day that Fanny had instructed us first in her choice of epithets, and then applied them to the bewildered governess, sent us into covert grins and then open laughter.

Miss Wilder, sensing rebellion, asked Fanny sharply to remember her manners.

'I owe my knowledge of your native tongue merely to *industry*, my dear

Fanny. I cannot compete with you in *argot!*'

Unshaken, Fanny begged her pardon, but I felt Miss Wilder had been unwise to indulge in that little slap. Fanny had made her less important in our eyes, certainly, and hurt her self-esteem, but the governess was not Nanny and not so easily routed. Fanny discovered that Miss Wilder was devoted to her family, and encouraged her to recount their many excellencies, drawing her out and leading her on until the simple woman betrayed herself.

'My papa was, and is still, a particularly fine classical scholar. Indeed, it was he who taught me Latin, though Greek – I fear – was always beyond me. Why, I have seen my papa sit at his desk, in the brief time that his duties allowed him, and translate passages from William Shakespeare into both languages. It was he who first gave me an insight into Greek and Roman history. Ah! How can Richard and Edward call them *dry*? They were people, even as ourselves, though in widely different times and circumstances. I can remember the winter afternoon when he related the tale of the Trojan Wars and they came alive to me. I saw the plumes nodding on those stern helms, the dust at the chariot wheels, the devotion of brave Menelaus forgiving his erring Helen – how fortunate you are, dear Helen, to be the possessor of that lovely name! – and Troy burning.'

She was alive now. Plain and poor and absurd, and alive. I looked at her amazed, and Fanny looked at her with calculation.

'But, Miss Wilder,' she said, with a soft urgency, 'you have inherited your papa's own gift – that of making history seem here and now. Do, I beg of you, tell us something more.'

'Helen should be mastering her French verbs,' said Miss Wilder, recalled to the cold rice pudding of duty. 'I know that you may amuse yourself by reading the plays of Racine, but Helen has much to learn.'

'And learn she shall! Dear Miss Wilder, I shall help her when we are together, and so relieve you of a dull task. Do not be distressed, Helen dear, that I call it dull. Miss Wilder has your interests at heart, but when one knows a language through and through it is hard to turn back to the beginning. And if I help Helen – and you shall judge the results for yourself, Miss Wilder, you shall see I am no idle boaster – will you not, just for half an hour or so, instruct us in a wider, subject?'

'There is no need . . . indeed, I am not sure it is *proper*,' said poor Miss Wilder, 'to instruct you in classical history. If you were boys that would be different – though their instruction should come later when they are at school. It is sufficient that you know your *own* history. That is all I am supposed to impart.'

'Not *proper*?' cried Fanny, astonished. 'Not proper, when your own papa – who should best know how a young lady may be educated – thought fit to instruct *you*, dear Miss Wilder?'

She had her there, and the governess hesitated.

'Dear Helen, would you not rather have two lessons than one?' Fanny persisted. 'Would you not rather work at your French with me, in our own time, and have the inestimable value of Miss Wilder's insight into classical history in the schoolroom?'

I was long since lost in the thicket of her intentions, and promised that I would work hard if only the magic of the Trojan Wars was unfolded. Fanny kept my word for me and added a private torment of her own: waking me at all times of the night and forcing me to chant irregular verbs until I begged for sleep. She was wonderfully clever in that way, keeping her promises, keeping her counsel, leaving no loophole in her schemes, no place where an accusing finger might point.

And Miss Wilder, flattered by her interest and attention, made history come alive. Even I, though Hector and Achilles and Paris and Helen and Menelaus might pillage and fight and betray four Troys for all I cared, even I was captured. I look back in a double pity for the governess: a pity for what became of her and for what she had not become. Trapped in that undistinguished body, cramped in that rigorous background, was a great romantic. Her vocabulary broadened under the impact of old wars and passions and encompassed them with love. Flames leaped and crackled, the horse loomed wooden and impelling upon the shore, the body of Hector rode its sorry way through the dust, fierce plumes nodded on bronze helmets, and Helen was once more beautiful.

Fanny waited until they were a part of our daily life before she crushed them and Miss Wilder.

'I wonder what our dear Queen would think of such things?' she observed.

Miss Wilder paused, at a loss between Troy and respectable Windsor.

'Is it not strange,' Fanny continued, in her most speculative voice, 'that a Christian gentleman such as your dear papa, Miss Wilder, should set such store by pagan violence?'

Miss Wilder said stoutly that one must take a broad view, but she had been made uncertain.

'Well, I am very sorry, Fanny, if you regret asking me. I did mention – when you were so insistent – that I wondered if such history was proper for a young lady,' said Miss Wilder stiffly.

'But you are in charge of *us*. We are not in charge of *you*, dear Miss Wilder,' said Fanny, appearing puzzled by a vast discrepancy. 'If you had truly thought it improper you would surely not have told us at all.'

She sighed to herself, brooding.

'You have made so many improvements in my education, dear Miss Wilder. Encouraging me to read the plays of Racine, extending my knowledge in so many spheres. And I have worked hard. You said yourself I was a great credit to you. It would be such a pity if my aunt and uncle felt it necessary to send me to a boarding school for young ladies. And, of course, with Helen old enough to be my companion, she would go too. And I had so hoped that we three should be together for a few more years – which would bring little Frederick into your excellent charge, and perhaps other dear children too in good time.'

I sat very small and tight and sick in my chair. Miss Wilder sat small and upright in hers, amid the smoking ruins of Troy. And I prayed, for I knew she was a good woman, that she could conquer Fanny.

I had reckoned, in my innocence that I now see as ignorance, without

173

domestic economy. Out of her salary Miss Wilder sent home money to support an ailing mother and an aged father. If she could hold on to her position for even another five years she might merit a little pension. But with a hint of improperness attached to her references, with the improbable chance of finding another place at her age, with the near-impossibility of achieving a position half so comfortable, she was defeated. Still, she waged one more campaign: a very brief one.

'Do I understand that you intend to complain to your uncle and aunt?' she asked, very dignified.

'Oh no, dear Miss Wilder. I was but drawing a picture of two different societies, and wondering if you might be good enough to take me and James and dear Helen to such places as would continue to broaden our minds? Do you not find the present education of young ladies a little narrow? In your charge we should discover more than any boarding school could offer.' She cast up her eyes. 'Paintings, sculptures, manuscripts. All the spiritual wealth of London would be ours.'

I think that the governess, like the rest of us, could draw a veil between what she knew to be true and what she preferred to believe. Pinched by her circumstances, Miss Wilder chose to forget the threat (which, of course, Fanny then forgot as well) and regard this plea as a genuine desire for self-improvement. Fanny had other plans, and an ally in James who had always found the governess dull and myself duller. Together they pressed their advantage, lengthening the time allowed in the new museums, losing themselves by walking away while she explained some educational point to me, asking questions she could not – or did not wish – to answer. And everything was done so subtly, with Fanny as leader (for James was simply a brash twelve-year-old boy who would soon go to Marlborough and thought it all a tremendous lark) that Miss Wilder could never put her finger on what was wrong. Her reprimands were met with an immediate and solemn apology, her suggestions ignored, her authority flouted. And lest she attempt to curtail our expeditions Fanny had tutored James in conversations which he had with Papa. So that Papa praised the governess for bringing him out and was ready for him to be brought out still further.

It was a dark November afternoon, with a hint of fog, when Fanny asked Miss Wilder to give us a little discourse on Renaissance paintings and drew us aside as she launched upon a long praise of Raphael's Madonna.

'I have got some money from Miss Wilder's purse,' she said, flushed with triumph, 'and James and I are going to see London on top of a bus. Will you come with us? We can slip out when she reaches the next room.'

'That's *stealing*! James, that's *stealing*!' I whispered.

He was shaken, but only for a moment. Fanny was masterly in argument.

'Certainly it is not stealing. The money is not Miss Wilder's. It is your papa's and he meant it for us. Think of all the sights we shall see. Buckingham Palace and St Paul's Cathedral. The Tower and Lambeth Palace. And there will be enough for us to have a cup of coffee at a stall and a penny slab of Nelson cake afterwards.'

I could see it all. The knifeboard buses were splendid contraptions, with rooftop seats and a legion of advertisements on their sides and back: Horlick's Malted Milk, Zebra Grate Polish, Pears Soap, Coleman's Mustard, Heinz 57 Varieties, Sanitas Non-Poisonous and Fragrant Disinfectant. The winding stair to the top was an adventure in itself. And then to take a seat which set all London before one's eyes; and to look down on the driver, wrapped against the cold and flicking his two great horses to a jolting trot; was nothing short of perfection.

'But what shall we tell Papa?' I asked, sorely tempted.

'We shall say we were lost. I shall ask a policeman to direct us when we have done with sight-seeing. And, of course, I shall apologise to Miss Wilder and make sure she is not blamed.'

'Are you children attending to me?' cried Miss Wilder, aware of the whispers and no doubt fearing they were directed at her.

'Yes, indeed, Miss Wilder,' said Fanny promptly. 'Helen was inquiring of me whether Raphael used the same model for all his madonnas. For are not the faces very like?' As the governess hesitated and consulted her catalogue Fanny whispered, 'Are you coming with us, Helen?'

I shook my head and she pinched my arm.

'Stay here then, Miss! And hold your tongue!' And she nodded so meaning-fully in warning that I should not have dared do otherwise.

When we reached the next room they had gone. But even Fanny could not cajole, blackmail or bully the weather, and a London pea-souper brought her plans into disrepute.

It was eleven o'clock at night when a policeman brought James and Fanny home. James seemed genuinely afraid, but she merely worried lest she was unable to talk her way out of the escapade. She had also miscalculated a Puritan conscience, for Miss Wilder, seeking the safety of her soul rather than her position, had confessed all. I saw simple goodness and honesty made into a weapon of defeat, for in her anxiety the governess had painted a picture of herself which showed her as a monster of depravity: unfitted to instruct or care for tender minds and bodies. She was upstairs, packing her trunk and weeping fit to put out all the flames of Troy, when the policeman knocked at our imperial front door.

Had I, who knew far more than Miss Wilder, attempted to set matters right? Had I exposed cousin Fanny as a liar, a spy and a thief? The fears that really gnaw one's courage are nameless ones, and I feared my cousin more than the eye of God. My feeble props of truth would be kicked contemptuously away, my accusations proved unfounded, myself branded as an envious mischief-maker, if I faced Fanny. So I said nothing, and was praised for being a good child who stayed close to my governess, and she praised me too – dropping a tear on my head, and begging me to persevere with my music and needlework. And Fanny, once the situation cleared and she was confined to her room for two days with a scolding and no puddings, knew my sin of omission and played upon it. And there again all my beliefs were shattered, for James threw off the escapade with ease, showing no sorrow once his punishment was over, merely saying, 'Poor old Wilder' with a lack of respect that relegated her to the shadows for ever. It was I who *cared* – for all my weaknesses – who took the burden of her dismissal upon myself. The other two, uncaring, were freed from remorse.

Lest she be thought wicked and hard-hearted, Fanny took upon herself to walk in her sleep and be found weeping silently in corners. So that my parents forgave her, and wooed her back to her normal self.

'Do not, on any account, waken poor Fanny suddenly, if you should find her walking again!' my mamma urged. 'It is highly injurious to the mind. You may recollect that we had to take her to the sea for a month when she first came, on that account.'

I recollected more than my mamma would ever know, for poor William lay on my conscience still, though he was now a fine and sturdy little child, beginning to walk.

Forbidden pleasures were Fanny's driving force, and for a long time the belvedere had attracted her, but because of the long fall on the other side we children never found the opportunity to mount it without an adult companion. There she would stand, demurely away from the edge, and admire the view with a peculiar glint in her eyes. So far its position had confounded her, for my papa built it not only for its view but for its location. The belvedere was under observation from the back of the house at all times. My mamma's escritoire faced it from the window, the servants faced it from the kitchen, the gardener and the gardener's boy were given strict instructions to see it untenanted except on specified occasions. So only at night could it beckon, pale and tall and beautiful, from the end of the lawn, and only at night did Fanny attempt it at last. She did not intend to enjoy it alone, and chose her companion carefully. James would regard it as another lark, which did not interest her. She needed someone with her who did not want to go, who was afraid of heights and disobedience, who could suffer as an accomplice and a victim in one. She chose me.

I woke to find her dressed in one of her French gowns: a delicious affair of pleats and bows and swathed green taffeta, tucked up at the back to show four formal frills below. Her little heeled *glacé* kid boots were buttoned. The art of a French milliner had created the be-ribboned and be-flowered hat. Tormeline drops hung from her small pierced lobes. She looked far older than her fourteen years.

'Some time,' said Fanny softly, 'you must try my clothes on. Though we must take care your mamma does not see you.'

The future threat hung over my head, as though the present threat were not enough.

'Put on your wrapper,' Fanny ordered. 'We are going to climb the belvedere. And if you so much as creak a stair, Miss, I shall see you are blamed for it!'

Trembling, I followed her obediently: a lost soul, losing itself further. I had long since ceased to pray to God, since apparently He did not hear.

The night was a diamond of moonlight and frost, and the tower rose still and pure at the end of the garden. Ahead of me stalked Fanny, aware of her fashionable dress even though she had but one slave to observe it. We mounted the stone steps and the chill struck through my slippers, but Fanny's boots clicked nimbly up and she drew a deep breath of fulfilment as we reached the top. She meant to enjoy herself to the utmost and to annihilate me.

'Do you believe in God, dear Helen?' she asked idly, running her fingers along the parapet.

I said I did, though I was no longer sure. I knew that the Devil existed and was abroad, but his heavenly opponent seemed to have suffered a decline.

'And do you believe that good will prevail?' she asked.

I mumbled an assent and she laughed.

'Then you have learned nothing,' she said. 'Do you believe that you are a good child, Helen?'

I said, on the edge of tears, that I feared I was not. She smiled at me, amused and confident and beautiful.

'You are even more wicked than you know,' she said. 'For you are like all these good people, you see what you want to see and act only if it serves. You could have gone to your mamma, with Nanny's laudanum, and though Nanny would have lost her position she would not have left without harming me – and you could have told your mamma how I behaved. You did not speak for Miss Wilder, nor tell your papa that the money in her purse was not lost but stolen – and by me. You have stood by a hundred times, dear Helen, and watched me do what you would call wrong. And you will watch a thousand times, and still say nothing.

'For you are not good, you are weak. You are not obedient, you are a coward. You do not love the truth, you are a hypocrite. And however hard you pray it will make no difference, for you are not honest.'

I cried, through my tears, 'God forgives sinners. He does. He does. I shall tell my papa and my mamma everything.'

'You had better be careful,' she said quietly, 'for you are not clever, and they might think you had lost your mind. You are easily influenced, dear Helen, and things prey upon you. I shall be with you, night and day. I shall tell your mamma that someone should be with you. Someone who loves you as a sister and will watch over you. Night and day, until you go mad. Don't make a noise or I shall rouse the house and say I found you sleep-walking in the garden!'

I pressed both hands over my mouth and the tears ran from my fingers.

'And now,' said Fanny briskly, 'I am going to walk the parapet. And then *you* are going to walk it. Do not tell me otherwise. I can make you. You know that.'

'But if I fall?' I whispered. 'What if I should fall?'

She looked at me, dark and beautiful, and said, 'Then you would go to Hell.'

She had taught me deception over the last year. I was not clever enough to reach ahead of her to forestall what she might do, but the past was rich with examples of what she had done. As I watched her, arms outstretched for balance, little boots pointed delicately, face absorbed in the sweet terror of daring, I formed a deception of my own and rehearsed it in my mind.

'I heard Fanny walking in her sleep, Mamma. Poor poor Fanny. Her dreams must have transported her to those happy days she spent with her own mamma. For when I opened my door – softly, so that I should not startle her, for you have ever told me that sudden awakening injures the brain – there was poor dear Fanny dressed in her fine clothes. I followed her at a distance – like a *mouse*, Mamma, truly – to see she came to no harm.

'Oh, Mamma, Mamma, she walked through the house and into the garden – I did not think she would have dared, for was she not always obedient, and fearful of heights? Mamma, she began to mount the belvedere!

'Should I leave her, unconscious as she was, and rouse you? Should I follow her as rapidly and silently as I could, and fetch her down again? I did not know. Even as I hesitated she climbed upon the parapet! And then, Mamma, I could not *help* it, I cried, "*Fanny!*"'

I had become her mind, and to savour the full extent of my iniquity I said, 'Fanny?' very softly, so that she should know what I meant to do. And in that moment of becoming her I knew the headiness of supreme power. She turned and saw what was written in my face. Her own reflected mortal terror. So she was human after all, and could be overthrown. Her fear was luxury to me. I screamed '*Fanny!*' as though I would warn her – and pushed. Her shriek matched my own while she fell.

I have even told them, again and again, what really happened, but they hush and cradle me, and Dr Fogg shakes his head and says that the shock has temporarily disturbed my mind. For they know we were the best of friends, walking always with our arms about each other, smiling. And they know that Fanny is safe in heaven with her mamma, and that in time I shall be glad for her eternal bliss.

So she lies with the other children beneath the weeping cherubs and their urn, and when I am better I shall visit the grave after morning service each Sunday. And once a year we shall remember the anniversary of her untimely and unlucky death, and mention her in our evening prayers. And her memory will remain with us until we join her.

Now and for a long time hence I shall see the belvedere rise in my dreams, and Fanny will smile upon me from the foot of my bed, and no one will ever be the same again. She has taught me that nothing is what it seems, that the innocent may be judged guilty, that God turns His face away from the penniless and the helpless, that the betrayed may suffer more than the betrayer. I wonder whether her suggestions are true or false. *Does* my mamma tell lies about her household accounts so that she may have more money for dress? *Does* my papa visit another lady near the city? *Was* Richard almost expelled for gambling at Marlborough? *Did* Edward crouch at the housemaid's door to watch her undress, and *did* Nora see him and merely call him a saucy wretch? *Could* James have stolen those grapes from the greenhouse and let the gardener's boy be whipped for it? All these, and many more thoughts trouble me. And when I turn to Him who is without spot or stain, and beg His Mercy, there is no help to be found there either. I see Him point an accusing finger and pronounce that judgement which will live with me all my days.

'Thou shalt not kill.'

THE FLAW

by Julian Symons

1

'Drink your coffee.'

Celia sat feet up on the sofa reading a fashion magazine, the coffee cup on the table beside her. 'What's that?'

'I said drink your coffee. You know you like it to be piping hot.'

She contemplated the coffee, stirred it with a spoon, then put the spoon back in the saucer. 'I'm not sure it's hot enough now.'

'I poured it only a couple of minutes ago.'

'Yes, but still. I don't know that I feel like coffee tonight. But I do want a brandy.' She swung her legs off the sofa and went across to the drinks tray. 'A celebratory brandy. Can I pour one for you?'

'What are we celebrating?'

'Me, Giles, not you. I'm celebrating. But you want me to drink my coffee, don't you? All right.' She went swiftly back, lifted the coffee cup, drank the contents in two gulps and made a face. 'Not very hot. Now may I have my brandy?'

'Of course. Let me pour it for you.'

'Oh no, I'll do it myself. After all, you poured the coffee.' She smiled sweetly.

'What do you mean?'

'Just that we've both had coffee. And you poured it. But I gave it to you on the tray, remember?'

Sir Giles got up, put a hand to his throat. 'What are you trying to say?'

'Only that if I turned the tray round you'll have got my cup and I shall have got yours. But it wouldn't matter. Or would it?'

He made for the door and turned the handle, but it did not open. 'It's locked. What have you done with the key?'

'I can't imagine.' As he lumbered towards her, swaying a little, she easily evaded him. 'You think I'm a fool, Giles, don't you? I'm not, that's your mistake. So this is a celebration.'

'Celia.' His hand was at his throat again. He choked, collapsed on to the carpet and lay still.

Celia looked at him thoughtfully, finished her brandy, prodded him with her foot and said, 'Now, what to do about the body?'

The curtain came down. The first act of *Villain* was over.

2

'I enjoyed it enormously,' Duncan George said. 'Is it all right if I smoke?'

'Of course.' Oliver Glass was busy at the dressing-table, removing the make-up that had turned him into Sir Giles. In the glass he saw Dunc packing his pipe and lighting it. Good old Dunc, he thought, reliable dull old Dunc, his reactions are always predictable. 'Pour yourself a drink.'

'Not coffee, I hope.' Oliver's laugh was perfunctory. 'I thought the play was really clever. All those twists and turns in the plot. And you enjoy being the chief actor as well as the writer, don't you, it gives you an extra kick?'

'My dear fellow, you're a psychologist as well as a crime writer yourself, you should know. But after all, who can interpret one's own writing better than oneself? The play – well, between these four walls, it's a collection of tricks. The supreme trick is to make the audience accept it, to deceive them not once or twice but half a dozen times, to make them leave the theatre gasping at the cleverness of it all. And if that's to be done, Sir Giles has to be played on just the right note, so that we're never quite certain whether he's fooling everybody else or being fooled himself, never quite sure whether he's the villain or the hero. And who knows that better than the author? So if he happens to be an actor too, he must be perfect for the part.'

'Excellent special pleading. I'll tell you one thing, though. When the curtain comes down at the end of the first act, nobody really believes you're dead. Oliver Glass is the star, and if you're dead they've been cheated. So they're just waiting for you to come out of that cupboard.'

'But think of the tension that's building while they wait. Ready, Dunc.'

He clapped the other on the shoulder, and they walked out into the London night. Oliver Glass was a slim, elegant man in his fifties, successful both as actor and dramatist, so successful that he could afford to laugh at the critic who said that he had perfected the art of over-acting, and the other critic who remarked that after seeing an Oliver Glass play he was always reminded of the line that said life is mostly froth and bubble. Whether Oliver did laugh was another matter, for he disliked any adverse view of his abilities. He had a flat in the heart of the West End, a small house in Sussex, and a beautiful wife named Elizabeth who was fifteen years his junior.

Duncan George looked insignificant by his side. He was short and square, a practising psychiatrist who also wrote crime stories, and he had known Oliver for some years. He was typified for Oliver by the abbreviation of his first name, *Dunc*. He was exactly the kind of person Oliver could imagine dunking a doughnut into a cup of coffee, or doing something equally vulgar. With all that, however, Duncan was a good fellow. Oliver tolerated him as a companion.

They made their way through the West End to a street off Leicester Square where the Criminologists' Club met once a quarter, to eat a late supper followed by a talk on a subject of criminal interest. The members were all writers about real or fictitious crime, and on this evening Oliver Glass was to speak to them on 'The Romance of Crime', with Duncan George as his chairman. When he rose and looked around, with that gracious look in which there was just a touch of contempt, the buzz of conversation ceased.

181

'Gentlemen,' he began, 'criminologists – fellow crime writers – perhaps fellow criminals, I have come tonight to plead for romance in the world of crime, for the locked room murder, the impossible theft, the crime committed by the invisible man. I have come to plead that you should bring wit and style and complexity to your writings about crime, that you should remember Stevenson's view that life is a bazaar of dangerous and smiling chances, and the remark of Thomas Griffiths Wainewright when he confessed to poisoning his pretty sister-in-law: "It was a terrible thing to do, but she had thick ankles." I beseech you not to forget those thick ankles as a motive, and to abandon the dreary books some of you write concerned with examining the psychology of two equally dull people to decide which destroyed the other, or looking at bits of intestines under a microscope to determine whether a tedious husband killed his boring wife. Your sights should be set instead on the Perfect Crime . . .'

Oliver Glass spoke, as always, without notes, fluently and with style, admiring the fluency and stylishness as the words issued from his mouth. Afterwards he was challenged by some members, Duncan George among them, about the conjectural Perfect Crime. Wasn't it out of date? Not at all, Oliver said, Sir Giles in *Villain* attempted it.

'Yes, but as you remarked yourself, *Villain's* a mass of clever tricks,' Dunc said. 'Sir Giles wants to kill Celia as a kind of trick, just to prove that he can get away with it. Or at least, we think he does. Then you play all sorts of variations on the idea, is the poison really a sleeping draught, does she know about it, that kind of thing. Splendid to watch, but nobody would actually try it. In every perfect murder, so called, there is actually a flaw.' There was a chorus of agreement, by which Oliver found himself a little irritated.

'How do you know that? The Perfect Crime is one in which the criminal never puts himself within reach of the law. Perhaps, even, no crime is known to have taken place, although that is a little short of perfection. But how do we know, gentlemen, what variations on the Perfect Crime any of us may be planning, may even have carried out? "The desires of the heart are as crooked as corkscrews," as the poet says, and I'm sure Dunc can bear that out from his psychiatric experience.'

'Any of us is capable of violence under certain circumstances, if that's what you mean. But to set out to commit a Perfect Crime without a motive is the mark of a psychopath.'

'I didn't say without motive. A good motive for one man may be trivial to another.'

'Tell us when you're going to commit the Perfect Crime, and we'll see if we can solve it,' somebody said. There was a murmur of laughter.

Upon this note he left, and strolled home to Everley Court, passing the drunks on the pavements, the blacks and yellows and all conditions of foreigners, who jostled each other or stood gaping outside the sex cinemas. He made a slight detour to pass by the theatre, and saw with a customary glow of pleasure the poster: *Oliver Glass in* Villain. *The Mystery Play by Oliver Glass.* Was he really planning the Perfect Crime? There can be no doubt, he said to himself, that the idea is in your mind. And the elements are there, Elizabeth and deliciously unpredictable Evelyn, and above all the indispensable Eustace. But is it more than a whim? Do I really dislike Elizabeth enough? The answer to that, of course, was that it was not a question of hatred but of playing a game, the game of Oliver Glass versus Society, even Oliver Glass versus the World.

And so home. And to Elizabeth.

A nod to Tyler, the night porter at the block of flats. Up in the lift to the third floor. Key in the door.

From the entrance hall the apartment stretched left and right. To the left Elizabeth's bedroom and bathroom. Almost directly in front of him the living-room, further to the right dining-room and kitchen, at the extreme right Oliver's bedroom and bathroom. He went into the living-room, switched on the light. On the mantelpiece there was a note in Elizabeth's scrawl: *O. Please come to see me if back before 2 a.m. E.*

For two years now they had communicated largely by means of such notes. It had begun – how had it begun? – because she was so infuriatingly talkative when he wanted to concentrate. 'I am an artist,' he had said. 'The artist needs isolation, if the fruits of genius are to ripen on the bough of inspiration.' The time had been when Elizabeth listened open-eyed to such words, but those days had gone. For a long while now she had made comments suggesting that his qualities as actor and writer fell short of genius, or had pointed out that last night he had happily stayed late at a party. She did not understand the artistic temperament. Her nagging criticism had become, quite simply, a bore.

There was, he admitted as he turned the note in his fingers, something else. There were the girls needed by the artist as part of his inspiration, the human clay turned by him into something better. Elizabeth had never understood about them, and in particular had failed to understand when she had returned to find one of them with him on the living-room carpet. She had spoken of divorce, but he knew the words to be idle. Elizabeth had extravagant tastes, and divorce would hardly allow her to indulge them. So the notes developed. They lived separate lives, with occasional evenings when she acted as hostess, or came in and chatted amiably enough to friends. For the most part the arrangement suited him rather well, although just at present his absorption with Evelyn was such . . .

He went in to see Elizabeth.

She was sitting on a small sofa, reading. Although he valued youth above all things he conceded, as he looked appraisingly at her, that she was still attractive. Her figure was slim (no children, he could not have endured the messy noisy things), legs elegant, dainty feet. She had kept her figure, as – he confirmed, looking at himself in the glass – he had kept his. How curious that he no longer found her desirable.

'Oliver.' He turned. 'Stop looking at yourself.'

'Was I doing that?'

'You know you were. Stop acting.'

'But I am an actor.'

'Acting off stage, I mean. You don't know anybody exists outside yourself.'

'There is a respectable philosophical theory maintaining that very proposition. I have invented you, you have invented me. A charming idea.'

'A very silly idea. Oliver, why don't you divorce me?'

'Have you given me cause?'

'You know how easily it can be arranged.'

He answered with a weary, a world-weary sigh. She exclaimed angrily and he gave her a look of pure dislike, so that she exclaimed again.

'You *do* dislike me, don't you? A touch of genuine feeling. So why not?' She went over to her dressing-table, sat down, took out a pot of cream.

He placed a hand on his heart. 'I was—'

'I know. You were born a Catholic. But when did you last go to church?'

'Very well. Say simply that I don't care to divorce you. It would be too vulgar.'

'You've got a new girl. I can always tell.'

'Is there anything more tedious than feminine intuition?'

'Let me tell you something. This time I shall have you followed. And *I* shall divorce *you*. What do you think of that?'

'Very little.' And indeed, who would pay her charge account at Harrods, provide the jewellery she loved, above all where would she get the money she gambled away at casinos and race meetings? She had made similar threats before, and he knew them to be empty ones.

'You want me as a kind of butterfly you've stuck with a pin, nothing more.'

She was at work with the cream. She used one cream on her face, another on her neck, a third on her legs. Then she covered her face with a black mask, which was supposed to increase the effectiveness of the cream. She often kept this mask on all night.

There had been a time when he found it exciting to make love to a woman whose face was not visible, but in her case that time had gone long ago. What was she saying now?

'Nothing gets through to you, does it? You have a sort of armour of conceit. But you have the right name, do you know that? *Glass* – if one could see through you there would be nothing, absolutely nothing there. Oliver Glass, *you don't exist*.'

Very well, he thought, very well, I am an invisible man. I accept the challenge. Elizabeth, you have signed your death warrant.

3

The idea, then, was settled. Plans had to be made. But they were still uncertain, moving around in what he knew to be his marvellously ingenious mind, when he went to visit Evelyn after lunch on the following day. Evelyn was in her early twenties, young enough – oh yes, he acknowledged it – to be his daughter, young enough also to be pleased by the company of a famous actor. But beyond that, Evelyn fascinated him by her unpredictability. She was a photographer's model much in demand, and he did not doubt that she had other lovers. There were times when she said that she was too busy to see him, or simply that she wanted to be alone, and he accepted these refusals as part of the excitement of the chase. There was a perversity about Evelyn, an abandonment to the whim of the moment, that reached out to something in his own nature. He felt sometimes that there was no suggestion so outrageous that she would refuse to consider it. She had once opened the door of her flat naked, and asked him to strip and accompany her down to the street.

Her flat was off Baker Street, and when he rang the bell there was no reply. At the third ring he felt annoyance. He had telephoned in advance, as always, and she had said she would be there. He pushed the door in a tentative way, and it swung open. In the hall he called her name. There was no reply.

The flat was not large. He went into the living-room, which was untidy as usual, glanced into the small kitchen, then went into the bedroom with its unmade bed. What had happened to her, where was she? He entered the bathroom, and recoiled from what he saw.

Evelyn lay face down, half in and half out of the bath. One arm hung over the side of the bath, the other trailed in the water. Her head rested on the side of the bath as though her neck was broken.

He went across to her, touched the arm outside the bath. It was warm. He bent down to feel the pulse. As he did so the arm moved, the body turned, and Evelyn was laughing at him.

'You frightened me. You bitch.' But he was excited, not angry.

'The author of *Villain* should be used to tricks.' She got out, handed him a towel. 'Dry me.'

Their lovemaking afterwards had the frantic, paroxysmic quality that he had found in few women. It was as though he were bringing her back from the dead. A thought struck him. 'Have you done that with anybody else?'

'Does it matter?'

'Perhaps not. I should still like to know.'

'Nobody else.'

'It was as though you were another person.'

'Good. I'd like to be a different person every time.'

He was following his own train of thought. 'My wife puts on a black mask after creaming her face at night. That should be exciting, but it isn't.'

Evelyn was insatiably curious about the details of sex, and he had told her a good deal about Elizabeth.

'I'm good for you,' she said now. 'You get a kick each time, don't you?'

'Yes. And you?'

She considered this. She had a similar figure to Elizabeth's but her features were very different, the nose snub instead of aquiline, the eyes blue and wide apart. 'In a way. Being who you are gives me a kick.'

'Is that all?'

'What do you mean?'

'Don't you like me?'

'It's wet to ask things like that. I never thought you were wet.' She looked at him directly with her large, slightly vacant blue eyes. 'If you want to know, I get a kick out of you because you're acting all the time. It's the acting you like, not the act. And then I get a kick out of you being an old man.'

He was so angry that he slapped her face. She said calmly, 'Yes, I like that too.'

By the time that night's performance was over his plan was made.

4

In the next two weeks Tyler, the night porter at Everley Court, was approached three times by a tall, bulky man wearing horn-rimmed spectacles. The man asked for Mrs Glass, and seemed upset to learn on every occasion that she was out. Once he handed a note to Tyler and then took it back, saying it wouldn't do to leave a letter lying around. Twice he left messages, to say that Charles had called and wanted to talk to Mrs Glass. On his third visit the man smelled of drink, and his manner was belligerent. 'You tell her I must talk to her,' he said in an accent that Tyler could not place, except that the man definitely came from somewhere up north.

'Yes, sir. And the name is—'

'Charles. She'll know.'

Tyler coughed. 'Begging your pardon, sir, but wouldn't it be better to telephone?'

The man glared at him. 'Do you think I haven't tried? You tell her to get in touch. If she doesn't I won't answer for the consequences.'

'Charles?' Elizabeth said when Tyler rather hesitantly told her this. 'I know two or three people named Charles, but this doesn't seem to fit any of them. What sort of age?'

'Perhaps about forty, Mrs Glass. Smartly dressed. A gentleman. Comes from the north, maybe Scotland, if that's any help.'

'No doubt it should be, but it isn't.'

'He seemed—' Tyler hesitated. 'Very concerned.'

On the following day Oliver left a note for her. '*E. Man rang while you were out, wouldn't leave message. O.*' She questioned him about the call.

'He wouldn't say what he wanted. Just rang off when I said you weren't here.'

'It must be the same man.' She explained about him. 'Tyler said he had a northern accent, probably Scottish.'

'What Scots do you know named Charles?'

'Charles Rothsey, but I haven't seen him for years. I wish he'd ring when I'm here.'

A couple of evenings later the wish was granted, although she did not speak to the man. Oliver had asked her to give a little supper party after the show for three members of the cast, and because two of them were women Duncan was invited to even up the numbers. Elizabeth was serving the cold salmon when the telephone rang in the living-room. Oliver went to answer it. He came back almost at once, looking thoughtful. When Elizabeth said it had been a quick call, he looked sharply at her. 'It was your friend Charles. He rang off. Just announced himself, then rang off when he heard my voice.'

'Who's Charles?' one of the women asked. 'He sounds interesting.'

'You'd better ask Elizabeth.'

She told the story of the man who had called, and it caused general amusement. Only Oliver remained serious. When the guests were going he asked Duncan to stay behind.

'I just wanted your opinion, Dunc. This man has called three times and now he's telephoning. What sort of man would do this kind of thing, and what can we do about it?'

'What sort of man? Hard to say.' Duncan took out his pipe, filled and lit it with maddening deliberation. 'Could be a practical joker, harmless enough. Or it could be somebody – well, not so harmless. But I don't see that you can do much about it. Obscene and threatening phone calls are ten a penny, as the police will tell you. Of course if he does show up again Elizabeth could see him, but I'd recommend having somebody else here.'

This was, Oliver considered, adequate preparation of the ground. It had been established that Elizabeth was being pursued by a character named Charles. There was no doubt about Charles's existence. He obviously existed independently of Oliver Glass, since Tyler had seen him and Oliver himself had spoken to him on the telephone. If Elizabeth was killed, the mysterious Charles would be the first suspect.

Charles had been created as somebody separate from Oliver by that simplicity which is the essence of all fine art. Oliver, like Sir Giles in *Villain,* was a master of disguise. He had in particular the ability possessed by the great Vidocq, of varying his height by twelve inches or more. Charles had been devised from a variety of props like cheek pads, body cushions and false eyebrows, plus the indispensable platform heels. He would make one more appearance, and then vanish from the scene. He would never have to meet anybody who knew Oliver well, something which he slightly regretted. And Charles on the telephone had been an actor whom Oliver had asked to ring during the evening. Oliver had merely said he couldn't talk now but would call him tomorrow, and then put down the receiver.

In the next few days he noticed with amusement tinged with annoyance that Elizabeth had fulfilled her threat of putting a private enquiry agent on his track. He spotted the man hailing a taxi just after he had got one himself, and then getting out a few yards behind him when he stopped outside Evelyn's flat. Later he pointed out the man to Evelyn, standing in a door-way opposite. She giggled, and suggested that they should ask him up.

'I believe you would,' he said admiringly. 'Is there anything you wouldn't do?'

'If I felt like it, nothing.' She was high on some drug or other. 'What about you?'

'A lot of things.'

'*Careful* old Oliver.' What would she say if she knew what he was planning? He was tempted to say something but resisted, although so far as he could tell nothing would shock her. She suddenly threw up the window, leaned out and gave a piercing whistle. When the man looked up she beckoned. He turned his head and then began to walk away. Oliver was angry, but what was the use of saying anything? It was her recklessness that fascinated him.

His annoyance was reflected in a note left for Elizabeth. '*E. This kind of spying is degrading. O.*' He found a reply that night when he came back from the theatre. '*O. Your conduct is degrading. Your present fancy is public property. E.*'

5

That Oliver Glass had charm was acknowledged even by those not susceptible to it. In the days after the call from Charles he exerted this charm upon Elizabeth. She went out a good deal in the afternoons, where or with whom he really didn't care, and this gave him the chance to leave little notes. One of them ran: '*E. You simply MUST be waiting here for me after the theatre. I have a small surprise for you. O,*' and another: '*E. Would supper at Wheeler's amuse you this evening? Remembrance of things past . . . O.*' On the first occasion he gave her a pretty ruby ring set with pearls, and the reference in the second note was to the fact that they had often eaten at Wheeler's in the early months after marriage. On these evenings he set out to dazzle and amuse her as he had done in the past, and she responded. Perhaps the response was unwilling, but that no doubt was because of Evelyn. He noticed, however, that the man following him was no longer to be seen, and at their Wheeler's supper mentioned this to her.

'I know who she is. I know you've always been like that. Perhaps I have to accept it.' Her eyes flashed. 'Although if I want to get divorce evidence it won't be difficult.'

'An artist needs more than one woman,' Oliver said. 'But you must not think that I can do without you. I need you. You are a fixed point in a shifting world.'

'What nonsense I do talk,' he said to himself indulgently. The truth was that contact with her nowadays was distasteful to him. By the side of Evelyn she was insipid. A great actor, however, can play any part, and this one would not be maintained for long.

Only one faintly disconcerting thing happened in this, as he thought of it, second honeymoon period. He came back to the flat unexpectedly early one afternoon, and heard Elizabeth's voice on the telephone. She replaced the receiver as he entered the room. Her face was flushed. When he asked who she had been speaking to, she said, 'Charles.'

'Charles?' For a moment he could not think who she was talking about. Then he stared at her. Nobody knew better than he that she could not have been speaking to Charles, but of course he could not say that.

'What did he say?'

'Beastly things. I put down the receiver.'

Why was she lying? How absurd, how deliciously absurd, if she had a lover. Or was it possible that somebody at the supper party was playing a practical joke? He brushed aside such conjectures because they did not matter now. Nothing could interfere with the enactment of the supreme drama of his life.

6

Celia's intention in *Villain* was to explain Sir Giles's absence by saying that he had gone away on a trip, something he did from time to time. Hence the remark about disposition of the body at the end of Act One. Just after the beginning of the second act the body was revealed by Celia to her lover shoved into a cupboard, a shape hidden in a sack. A few minutes later the cupboard was opened again, and the shape was seen by the audience, although not by Celia, to move slightly. Then, after twenty-five minutes of the second act, there was a brief blackout on stage. When the lights went up Sir Giles emerged from the cupboard, not dead but drugged.

To be enclosed within a sack for that length of time is no pleasure, and in any ordinary theatrical company the body in the sack would have been that of the understudy, with the leading man changing over only a couple of minutes before he was due to emerge from the cupboard. But Oliver believed in what he called the theatre of the actual. In another play he had insisted that the voice of an actress shut up for some time in a trunk must be real and not a recording, so that the actress herself had to be in the trunk. In *Villain* he maintained that the experience of being actually in the sack was emotionally valuable, so that he always stayed in it for the whole length of time it was in the cupboard.

The body in the sack was to provide Oliver with an unbreakable alibi. The interval after Act One lasted fifteen minutes, so that he had nearly forty minutes free. Everley Court was seven minutes' walk from the theatre, and he did not expect to need much more than twenty minutes all told. The body in the sack would be seen to twitch by hundreds of people, and who could be in it but Oliver?

In fact Useful Eustace would be the sack's occupant. Eustace was a dummy used by stage magicians who wanted to achieve very much the effect at which Oliver aimed, of persuading an audience that there was a human being inside a container. He was made of plastic, and inflated to the size of a small man. You then switched on a mechanism which made Eustace kick out arms and legs in a galvanic manner. A battery-operated timer in his back could be set to operate at intervals ranging from thirty seconds to five minutes. When deflated, Eustace folded up neatly, into a size no larger than a plastic mackintosh.

Eustace was the perfect accomplice, Useful Eustace indeed. Oliver had tried him out half a dozen times inside a sack of similar size, and he looked most convincing.

On the afternoon of The Day he rested. Elizabeth was out, but said that she would be back before seven. His carefully worded note was left on her mantelpiece. '*E. I want you at the flat ALL this evening. A truly sensational surprise for you. All the evening, mind, not just after the show. O.*' Her curiosity would not, he felt sure, be able to resist such a note.

During Act One he admired, with the detachment of the artist, his own performance. He was cynical, ironic, dramatic – in a word, superb. When it was over he went unobtrusively to his dressing room. He had no fear of visitors, for he was known to detest any interruption during the interval.

And now came what in advance he felt to be the only ticklish part of the operation. The cupboard with the sack in it opened on to the back of the stage. The danger of carrying out an inflated Eustace from dressing-room to stage was too great – he must be inflated on site, as it were, and it was possible although unlikely that a wandering stage hand might see him at work. The Perfect Crime does not depend upon chance or upon the taking of risks, and if the worst happened, if he was seen obviously inflating a dummy, the project must be abandoned for the present time. But fortune favours the creative artist, or did so on this occasion. Inflation of Eustace by pump took only a few moments as he knelt by the cupboard, and nobody came near. The timer had been set for movement every thirty seconds. He put Eustace into the sack, waited to see him twitch, closed the cupboard's false back, and strolled away.

He left the theatre by an unobtrusive exit used by those who wanted to avoid the autograph hunters outside the stage door, and walked along head down until he reached the nearest Underground station, one of the few in London equipped with lockers and lavatories. Unhurriedly he took Charles's clothes and shoes from the locker, went into a lavatory, changed, put his acting clothes back in the locker. Spectacles and revolver were in his jacket pocket. He had bought the revolver years ago, when he had been playing a part in which he was supposed to be an expert shot. By practice in a shooting range he had in fact become a quite reasonable one.

As he left the station he looked at his watch. Six minutes. Very good.

Charles put on a pair of grey gloves from another jacket pocket. Three minutes brought him to Everley Court. He walked straight across to the lift, something he could not do without being observed by Tyler. The man came over, and in Charles's husky voice, with its distinctive accent, he said: 'Going up to Mrs Glass. Expecting me.'

'I'll ring, sir. It's Mr Charles, isn't it?'

'No need. I said, she's expecting me.'

Perfectly, admirably calm. But in the lift he felt, quite suddenly, that he would be unable to do it. To allow Elizabeth to divorce him and then to marry or live with Evelyn until they tired of each other, wouldn't that after all be the sensible, obvious thing? But to be *sensible*, to be *obvious*, were such things worthy of Oliver Glass? Wasn't the whole point that by this death, which in a practical sense was needless, he would show the character of a great artist and a great actor, a truly superior man?

The lift stopped. He got out. The door confronted him. Put key in lock, turn. Enter.

The flat was in darkness, no light in the hall. No sound. 'Elizabeth,' he called, in a voice that did not seem his own. He had difficulty in not turning and leaving the flat.

He opened the door of the living-room. This also was in darkness. Was

Elizabeth not there after all, had she ignored his note or failed to return? He felt a wave of relief at the thought, but still there was the bedroom. He must look in the bedroom.

The door was open, a glimmer of light showed within. He did not remember taking the revolver from his pocket, but it was in his gloved hand.

He took two steps into the room. Her dimmed bedside light was switched on. She lay on the bed naked, the black mask over her face. He called out something and she sat up, stretched out arms to him. His reaction was one of disgust and horror. He was not conscious of squeezing the trigger, but the revolver in his hand spoke three times.

She did not call out but gave a kind of gasp. A patch of darkness showed between her breasts. She sank back on the bed.

With the action taken, certainty returned to him. Everything he did now was efficient, exact. He got into the lift, took it down to the basement and walked out through the garage down there, meeting nobody. Tyler would be able to say when Mr Charles had arrived, but not when he left.

Back to the Underground lavatory, clothes changed, Charles's clothing and revolver returned to locker for later disposal, locker key put in handkerchief pocket of jacket. Return to the theatre, head down to avoid recognition. A quick glance at his watch as he opened the back door and moved silently up the stairs. Nearly thirty minutes had passed.

He knelt at the back of the cupboard and listened to a few lines of dialogue. The moment at which the body was due to give its twitch had gone, and Eustace proved his lasting twitching capacity by giving another shudder, of course not seen by the audience because the cupboard door was closed. Eustace had served his purpose. Oliver withdrew him from the sack and switched him off. With slight pressure to get out the air he was quickly reduced and folded into a bundle. Oliver slipped the bundle inside his trousers, and secured it with a safety pin. The slight bulge might have been apparent on close examination, but who would carry out such an examination upon stage?

Beautiful, he thought, as he wriggled into the sack for the few minutes before he had to appear on stage. Oliver Glass, I congratulate you in the name of Thomas de Quincey and Thomas Griffiths Wainewright. You have committed the Perfect Crime.

7

The euphoria lasted through the curtain calls and his customary few casual words with the audience, in which he congratulated them on being able to appreciate an intelligent mystery. It lasted – oh, how he was savouring the only real achievement of his life – while he leisurely removed Sir Giles's make-up, said goodnight, and left the theatre still with Eustace pinned to him. He made one further visit to the Underground, as a result of which Eustace joined Charles's clothes in the locker. The key back in the handkerchief pocket.

As he was walking back to Everley Court, however, he realised with a shock that something had been forgotten. The note! The note which said positively that he would be at the flat during the interval, a note which if the police saw it would certainly lead to uncomfortable questions, perhaps even to a search, and discovery of the locker key. The note was somewhere in the flat, perhaps in Elizabeth's bag. It must be destroyed before he rang the police.

He nodded to Tyler, took the lift up. Key in door again. The door open. Then he stopped.

Light gleamed under the living-room door.

Impossible, he thought, impossible. I know that I did not switch on the light when I opened that door. But then who could be inside the room? He took two steps forward, turned the handle, and when the door was open sprang back with a cry.

'Why, Oliver. What's the matter?' Elizabeth said. She sat on the sofa. Duncan stood beside her.

He pulled at his collar, feeling as though he was about to choke, then tried to ask a question but could not utter words.

'Come and see,' Duncan said. He approached and took Oliver by the arm. Oliver shook his head, resisted, but in the end let himself be led to the bedroom. The body still lay there, the patch of red between the breasts.

'You even told her about Elizabeth's bedtime habits,' Dunc said. 'She must have thought you'd have some fun.' He lifted the black mask. Evelyn looked up at him.

Back in the living-room he poured himself brandy and said to Elizabeth, 'You knew?'

'Of course. *Would supper at Wheeler's amuse you this evening?* Do you think I didn't know you were acting as you always are, making some crazy plan. Though I could never have believed it – it was Dunc who guessed how crazy it was.'

He looked from one of them to the other. 'You're lovers?' Duncan nodded. 'My dreary wife and my dull old friend Dunc – a perfect pair.'

Duncan took out his pipe, looked at it, put it back in his pocket. 'Liz had kept me in touch with what was going on, naturally. It seemed that you must be going to do something or other tonight. So Liz spent the evening with me.'

'Why was Evelyn here?' His mind moved frantically from one point to another to see where he had gone wrong.

'We knew about her from having you watched, and all that nonsense about Charles made me think that Elizabeth must be in some sort of danger. So it seemed a good idea to send your note to Evelyn, so that she could be here to greet you. We put the flat key in the envelope.'

. 'The initials were the same.'

'Just so,' Dunc said placidly.

'You planned for me to kill her.'

'I wouldn't say that. Of course if you happened to mistake her for Liz – but we couldn't guess that she'd put on Liz's mask. We just wanted to warn you that playing games is dangerous.'

'You can't prove anything.'

'Oh, I think so,' Dunc said sagely. 'I don't know how you managed to get away from the theatre, some sort of dummy in the sack I suppose? No doubt the police will soon find out. But the important thing is that note. It's in Evelyn's handbag. Shows you arranged to meet her here. Jealous of some younger lover, I suppose.'

'But I *wasn't* jealous, I didn't arrange—' He stopped.

'Can't very well say it was for Liz, can you? Not when Evelyn turned up.' The door bell rang. 'Oh, I forgot to say we called the police when we found the body. Our duty, you know.' He looked at Oliver and said reflectively, 'You remember I said there was always a flaw in the Perfect Crime? Perhaps I was wrong. I suppose you might say the Perfect Crime is one you benefit from but don't commit yourself, so that nobody can say you're responsible. Do you see what I mean?' Oliver saw what he meant. 'And now it's time to let in the police.'

FIXATION

by Miles Tripp

It was Freddie, my oldest friend, who dragged me out of a sinking spiral of depression following my mother's death. He wouldn't accept my refusal to go out for a drink and when we were sitting in a pub he asked what the trouble was. I told him there was no trouble. He didn't reply. He simply rested his hand on the sleeve of my coat for a few seconds and then removed it. He still didn't speak. It was obvious he didn't intend to speak. 'I'm beginning to wonder if I'm quite normal,' I burst out.

He didn't laugh. He didn't look surprised. He said, 'Don't we all sometimes wonder whether we're normal?' and took a long drink.

It was difficult to believe the implication of his remark. What worries could Freddie have? He was happily married, he had three daughters, a splendid home and he was senior partner in a well-established legal firm. To all appearances he lived a full and successful life. 'You are certainly normal,' I stated.

'Am I? What is normal?'

'That's not easy. Not in a few words.'

'What is abnormal then?' he asked.

'Isn't it a bit abnormal,' I asked, 'for a man of forty-two to have spent all his life with his mother and when she has gone to realise that his life has been devoted to performing for her, to winning praise and approval? Is that abnormal or normal?'

'I'll answer that,' he said, 'by telling you of the time when I wondered whether I was normal.' And he told me of a period when he had quarrelled violently, and every day, with one of his daughters until the stage was reached when he felt unsafe to be alone with her in case he strangled her. Fortunately one of his clients was a psychiatrist who had told him the border between normality and abnormality would only be crossed if, once the daughter started going out with boy-friends, Freddie still continued the warfare. It was a certainty that the girl wouldn't continue once she had a boy-friend.

Freddie gave me a quick glance. 'It seems that fathers and daughters can have pretty complicated relationships under the surface, but these are quite normal. I was normal.'

It was astute of him to make the observation about fathers and daughters because there had been times when I had wondered – never very coherently and with thoughts quickly suppressed – about mothers and sons. References in books and newspaper articles to the Oedipus complex have always made me feel uncomfortable, particularly since my father's death was inadvertently caused by me when I was a small boy. I fell off a pier into the sea. My father, who couldn't really swim, jumped after me and was drowned. I was saved by a local lifeguard.

'So you see,' Freddie continued, 'we all get these times of doubt. You are as normal as the next man but I'd like to give you a bit of advice. It's free. No professional charge.'

'I know. I need a holiday. No thanks, Freddie.'

'Get married.'

I had to laugh. I know it was impolite, but I couldn't help it. What woman would look twice at a man of my age, whose face had never been his fortune, and who held a humdrum job as an executive in a firm of chartered accountants.

'I know of a marriage bureau,' he said, 'where they interview you very carefully and then get a computer to work out what sort of partner is likely to be compatible. I'm told it works very well.'

Sometimes, in the quiet of my flat, I had wondered about consulting a marriage bureau but could never nerve myself to take the plunge.

'Don't forget,' he said, 'you'll not only be doing yourself a good turn, you'll be doing someone else a good turn. Someone who at this very moment is probably sitting alone wondering whether her loneliness will ever end.'

Although it was a busy pub and there was noise and movement all around I felt as though I was sitting in a sealed capsule. I was an astronaut on a launch pad and it was for me, and only me, to decide whether the infinite sky should be explored.

'All systems go,' I said.

He grinned. 'That's more like it. I'll arrange the interview for you. Can't do more than that, I'm afraid.'

I had a snatch of awful hesitation. 'Not this week,' I said.

'I'll arrange it tomorrow and don't tell me you can't take a couple of hours away from adjusting other people's tax returns, because I know you can . . . Have another?'

'It's not Dutch courage I need at this moment.'

'You'll be all right. Damn it, what have you got to lose?'

I had no answer.

'You can only gain,' he said.

I was interviewed, documented, tabulated, coded and programmed into a computer.

Two weeks later I was looking at a photograph of Kay. A little white triangle of a face with big, staring eyes, and hair torn back from temples and forehead. I remember thinking, 'She looks quite pretty,' and then, 'Why has she found it hard to get married?'

She was thirty-five, an audio-typist in the personnel department of a London store, and her interests were reading, crocheting and walking. She liked to go on day trips to the country and would try to identify and name all the wild flowers and grasses she saw. She enjoyed listening to classical music, and cooking French regional dishes. She usually took her holidays in France.

The computer had done its work well.

We could have met in the bureau's office but it was suggested that I should ring her for a date for an evening meal. A particular restaurant was recommended where the service and food were excellent, and we could be sure of special attention if I mentioned the bureau when making the reservation. It was important that slow service or indifferent waiting should not spoil the evening.

A timid voice answered the telephone and when I announced my name and asked if we could have a meal together the voice became slightly breathless, but the date was made and two evenings later we met.

She was small and fragile and looked like a sparrow that might dart into flight if anyone came too close.

We shook hands and I asked if she would like a drink or whether she would prefer to go straight in for a meal.

'I'd like a gin and tonic,' she said.

We sat opposite each other at a small table. A waiter swooped and was an attentive parrot to my order. I began to feel more confident.

'It looks like rain,' I said.

'I listened to the forecast before I came out.' She paused and gathered breath. 'They expect a cold front bringing rain to reach London during the night.'

'The farmers need rain.'

'Yes.'

'Not that there are many farmers in London,' I said. It was meant as a little joke, but she gave the futile remark a sort of strained and serious attention.

'No,' she said, after a pause.

'What I mean is that the rain tonight in London won't mean much to farming communities.' Although the tiny joke was dead I was parading its corpse. And even as I spoke I realised the phrase 'farming communities' was one I had never used before. Hearing my own voice was rather like overhearing a pedantic stranger talking about the most boring triviality imaginable. And then my mind went utterly blank. All the conversational gambits I had rehearsed were scattered to the four corners of my unconscious mind. If she didn't speak we should sit here for ever, figures trapped in an engraving of embarrassment.

'Have you had a holiday this year?' she asked.

She had produced one of my lost gambits.

'Not yet. I suppose I should plan something but since my mother's death . . . We used to go on a cruise each August . . . How about you?'

'I used to go away with a girl-friend. But the last of my single girl-friends got married in March and . . . I don't fancy going on my own.'

The waiter arrived with our drinks.

I lifted my glass to her. 'Cheers.'

'Cheers,' she replied, and her hand was shaking so much as she raised her glass that she had to use the other hand to steady it. When she drank it was as though she was holding a chalice.

Then she put down the glass and said, 'Look, if you would sooner finish these drinks and say goodbye, we can. The meal hasn't been ordered.'

I felt as breathless as she sounded. Had she decided against me, having met and seen me? A voice which I scarcely recognised as my own said, 'I'm in no hurry to go. But how about you?'

She smiled for the first time, and if smiles were electrical discharges I should have become a pile of bemused ash. And when the enchanting, stunning smile faded, she said, 'I don't want to go. I like the view from where I'm sitting.' And she directed another smile at me.

It was at this moment we fell in love.

The following weeks were a dream but as the wedding date drew near I had misgivings, not about the marriage but about my competence. I was inexperienced.

Because this subject has some bearing on what follows I cannot gloss over it, but briefly, I had a word with Freddie about my fears and his advice was, 'For God's sake don't leave it to the first night of the honeymoon unless there's no alternative. Start now, and start slowly. Get to know each other gently. Don't worry if nothing happens on the first or second nights. It will. Leave it to Mother Nature, but don't try to push the old girl. Nothing good ever came of trying to push Mother Nature.'

Freddie's advice was absolutely right. What a splendid lawyer the man is.

By the time we went on honeymoon – to a little French village near the Pyrenees where the scent of flowers is so strong that it seems to pervade food and drink and even the pores of one's body – we were lovers, and completely attuned.

That was seven years ago.

Marriage didn't alter our lives. I continued to work in an accountant's office and Kay, after a six-month period of housekeeping, decided she preferred to be a working girl and went back to being an audio-typist. We changed physically, however. My scant hair accelerated its departure and within a year I was completely bald, and within two years I had a disgraceful paunch. Kay's appearance changed more dramatically. 'I used to be an undersized weakling,' she laughed. 'Now look at me!'

In her own words she was 'a tub on two match-sticks', and although this was a slur on her beautiful legs, she had certainly put on weight. Her face had filled out too; but I love her face and every surplus ounce on her. To someone looking at her objectively she would be a plump, ordinary, middle-aged woman, but I cannot be objective about her although, in retrospect, I can see that when the trouble started I did act with admirable objectivity.

She would usually come home to our flat an hour before me and prepare the evening meal. It was on a perfect June evening as we were clearing away the plates that she said, 'Have I ever mentioned Wilson to you?'

'No. Who's Wilson?'

'He's fairly new. In the Buying Department. He's only about twenty.' She hesitated. 'He seems to have a ridiculous sort of crush on me.'

I asked what she meant and I felt mildly amused.

'He makes all sorts of excuses to come into our room. And he hangs about looking at me. Josie and Pat pull my leg about it.'

'He hasn't asked you for a date, then?' I asked jokingly.

'No. He seems too shy for that. He just stands. And looks. It's getting quite unnerving.'

'It's your fatal fascination,' I said.

Kay wasn't amused. 'It's absurd,' she said. 'I'm old enough to be his mother. There are dozens of young attractive girls around the place. Why pick on me to make sheep's eyes at?'

'If it bothers you, you can tell him to shove off,' I said, but immediately I had spoken I knew this would be difficult. Kay is incapable of being rude to anyone.

'Oh well,' she said, 'I expect he'll get tired of it when he sees he's getting nowhere.' And that, so far as I was concerned, was the end of Wilson.

But one evening during the next week, just after we had switched off the television and were preparing to go to bed, she said, 'There's something I must tell you.'

An anxious note in her voice made me stop whatever I was doing and look at her.

'It's been on my mind all evening,' she said.

'What has?'

'You remember I told you about Denis Wilson?'

I had to think. The name 'Denis' wasn't familiar.

'You know,' Kay said. 'The boy at our office.'

'Oh yes. What's he been up to now?'

'On Monday he was waiting for me at the main entrance when we were all leaving. I know it was me he was waiting for. He said, "Goodnight." It was the same yesterday, Tuesday. Today he came across and said, "May I speak to you?"'

'What did you say?'

'I asked what he wanted. Do you know what he said?'

How could I know? 'I've no idea,' I said rather brusquely.

'He asked if I'd have a drink with him in the lunch hour tomorrow.'

This jolted me. 'And what did you say?'

'I said, "No thank you," and hurried off. He didn't try to follow, but I felt very upset. I know it sounds stupid but when I stopped at the Underground to get a ticket my legs were shaking.'

I put my arms round her. 'Don't think anything more about it, darling. He probably had to get it out of his system and now that you've given him the brush-off he won't bother you any more.'

'I hope he doesn't,' she said. 'There's nothing wrong with him. To look at, I mean. But there's something about him that frightens me. Josie says I'm an idiot to worry about it. She says he'll soon get tired.'

'I'm sure she's right.'

'But I think even Josie and Pat are a bit puzzled by it. There are so many young and pretty girls he could choose from but he doesn't seem interested in any of them. I'm twice his age and not a beauty by any stretch of the imagination.'

I told her my imagination didn't need to stretch an inch to find her beautiful.

She nestled against me. 'You're different,' she said, and she added softly, 'Thank God.'

The following evening I asked whether the young fellow had troubled her. She said she hadn't seen him. But the next day, Friday, she told me she had seen a medical certificate for Wilson on the Personnel Manager's desk. He was suffering from gastric enteritis but expected to return to work early next week.

'No doubt caused by frustrated calf-love,' I said, trying to make a joke of it.

Kay said, 'I hope not,' and I was surprised to see that she had taken my remark seriously. 'I'd hate to be the cause of anyone's – pain,' she said.

'He's probably eaten too many green apples,' I said, but this time, although I meant it to sound reassuring, I had the first intimation, or perhaps it was an intuition, that I should take the Wilson business more seriously.

I suppose it was about two weeks later when we were walking home from the cinema that I asked, 'How's the Wilson boy these days?'

We had been walking slowly side by side, enjoying the mild evening, but she quickened her step. 'He's all right.'

'Not giving any trouble?'

'Not here,' she said. 'Wait till we get home.'

Ten minutes later, as she was making coffee, she said, 'It seems to be getting worse.'

'How do you mean?'

'He hangs round the main entrance to see me arrive in the morning, he comes into our room on the most feeble pretexts and he hangs around in the evening to say "Goodnight".'

'He hasn't asked you out for a drink again?'

'No. But I think he might have tonight only I had Pat with me and I sensed he was disappointed. He gave her a sort of look.'

'What sort of look?'

'I can't describe it. But she noticed it too. She said it made her feel like a gooseberry.'

She passed a mug of coffee. 'He makes me nervous,' she said. 'I get a terrible feeling of panic inside me when I see him. And then I tell myself he can't help what he's doing. I ought to feel sorry for him.'

I snorted into my coffee. 'Don't waste your emotions on him. He isn't worth it.'

'But if he's . . . I mean . . . People do get fixations, don't they?'

I don't know why this question, and the use of the word 'fixation' should have made me suddenly very annoyed, but it did. 'Is that what you think this is?' I said. 'A fixation?'

She lowered her eyes. 'Josie said she read a letter in a woman's magazine some time ago about a similar sort of situation and the reply was that young men sometimes get fixations on older women. The thing is for the woman to give absolutely no encouragement. Eventually it fades or he gets fixated elsewhere.'

'You don't encourage him?'

She lifted her eyes, and to my dismay I saw they were filled with tears. 'Of course I don't,' she said. 'What sort of woman do you think I am?'

Rather unhappily we went to bed. That night our love-making lacked something, not in technique (to use the textbook word) but in mental harmony. Afterwards we lay silent. Then, out of the darkness Kay said, 'I wonder if he thinks about me all the time or just when he's at work.'

I didn't reply but her words stabbed me with an arrow of anxiety. Kay soon went to sleep but dawn was creeping into the eastern sky before I drifted into a shallow loss of wakefulness.

It was on the following night that the telephone calls started. Kay answered, and I turned down the sound of television.

'It is,' she said.

'Yes,' she said.

'What do you want?' she asked.

'Certainly not,' she said.

She hung up the receiver without saying goodbye.

'Not him,' I said incredulously.

'He must be mad,' she said. 'Ringing me here. He must know you'll be home.'

'What did he want?'

'I asked him.'

'I heard you. What did he say?'

Kay flushed. 'He said, "You know what I want. Will you come out with me?"'

'Well, your reply should have given him the message. You sounded very firm.'

'I need a drink,' she said.

I got her a drink without question but it worried me that she should be so upset by the call that her first thought was for alcohol to steady her nerves.

The telephone rang again the next evening and I answered.

The caller rang off.

He rang again an hour later. Again I answered. Again he rang off.

The third time he rang Kay answered and I stood beside her.

'Yes,' she said.

'It's me,' said a man's voice.

'What do you want?' she asked, and I took the phone from her.

'Please come out with me. Just for a drink. I need to talk to you.'

'Look here,' I said. 'If you don't stop troubling my wife I shall call the police.'

He rang off when I reached the word 'wife'.

Kay gave me an agonised look. 'We can't go on like this,' she said. 'Every time the phone goes my heart seems to lurch.'

I thought for a few moments. 'Tomorrow I'll come with you to the store,' I said, 'and if he's there I shall tell him in no uncertain terms what I shall do if he persists in his conduct.'

I don't know what reaction I expected from Kay. A look of gratitude perhaps. I didn't expect her to groan, 'Oh no!'

'Why not?'

'I'm sure he can't help himself. It's something out of his control.'
'But not out of my bloody control,' I replied.
That night we didn't make love.

Kay's store is in Oxford Street. At nine in the morning the street is a rush of workers scurrying from buses and trains, most of them looking as though they are late for an urgent, but somewhat unpleasant, appointment. At least, the older ones look like this; the younger ones are more casual. They wander and seem to get in the way of the dedicated clockers-in.

'That's him,' whispered Kay.

She was gazing at a tall, thin youth. His pale face was fringed with dark hair which fell in curls to his shoulders. He had what used to be called 'poetic good looks' and I felt a twinge of jealousy.

'Please don't be unkind to him,' said Kay.

She had tried to dissuade me from coming along, and this final plea was very annoying. Why shouldn't I be unkind to him? He had been unkind to us.

'You go along,' I said. 'I'll see you tonight.' Later I realised that this was the first time we had ever parted without a kiss.

I made straight for the young man and said, 'Your name is Denis Wilson?'

He looked startled. 'That's right.'

'And you have been pestering my wife. Asking her to go out with you.'

'I only want to talk with her,' he said.

'She doesn't want to talk with you.'

He flinched. 'I'm sorry,' he said.

'I'm sorry too. This thing is becoming a nuisance to both of us. My wife and me.'

'I'm sorry,' he repeated.

'So you've already said. It's got to stop. If you bother her any more, hang around for her, speak to her or ring us up, I shall report this to your manager and to the police. Is that clear?'

He nodded, and I felt a sense of relief. All he needed was a straight talking to.

'I have your promise that you won't cause any more trouble?' I asked.

'What do you mean? Trouble?'

He looked at me with soft brown eyes.

'You know exactly what I mean.'

He gave a sigh. 'I love Kay,' he said.

What I did was inexcusable, but I don't regret it. I grabbed his shirt collar intending to shake him as one might shake a naughty pup, but as I tugged the collar his tie, a scarlet bow tie, came away in my hand. I gazed at it feeling somehow off-balance.

'If you like it, you can keep it,' he said, and before I could give him back the tie he turned and ran into the building.

Kay was standing on the steps. Our eyes met, and then she followed him inside.

That evening she said she had felt humiliated when she saw me grab at his collar. I asked whether he had been waiting for her when she left, and she said, 'No.'

'In that case,' I said, 'your humiliation was worth it. He's obviously seen the error of his ways.'

A few minutes later the telephone rang. I picked it up. 'Yes?'

'This is Denis,' said a voice.

'I warned you this morning to stop this nonsense.'

'May I speak to Kay? Just for a moment?'

'You may not,' I said and slammed down the phone. Turning to Kay I said, 'He's asking for it.'

She was apprehensive. 'What are you going to do?'

'There's no point in making threats if one isn't prepared to carry them out.'

'No. Please, no!'

'I'm sorry, Kay. I've had enough. I'm involved in this too.'

'Please, please!'

There is no point in relating word by word, phrase by phrase, how I slowly weakened. Nor how our love-making reached a new height that night. It is sufficient to say that at this stage I did nothing more than fix an appointment to see Freddie. I didn't tell Kay.

As ever, Freddie was the cheery, solicitous friend. 'What can I do for you, old chap?' he asked. 'By the look on your face it's not advice on a fortune you've inherited.'

He listened patiently to my account of the absurd infatuation of Denis Wilson for Kay. And yet it wasn't a resigned patience. Once or twice (it might have been my imagination) I thought he was on the verge of smiling. When I had finished he said, 'All this is a great compliment to Kay, and indirectly a compliment to you for choosing Kay.' He seemed to be speaking with perfect seriousness. 'I can understand that you might be aggravated,' he said, and then qualified this statement by adding, 'In a way, I can see it.'

'Wouldn't you be annoyed, Freddie?'

He picked up his pen and began to peck at the blotting pad on his desk. 'Perhaps I should,' he said. 'But you know Cynthia.'

I did know his wife but the implication escaped me.

'How do you mean?'

'Obviously Kay and Cynthia aren't the same. We're all different. But Cynthia would have frozen him off within ten seconds.'

'Kay finds it difficult to be – cold.'

'I know. I appreciate that. And I'm not saying that she's actively encouraging him . . .'

'I should hope not!'

'But a woman of Kay's years . . . How old is she?'

'Forty-two.'

'Women of forty-two usually know how to handle these situations.'

'Kay doesn't,' I said doggedly. 'And I want it to stop. How do I go about it?'

Freddie frowned slightly. 'My advice is – do nothing. You've already done enough. Technically you committed an assault on him. Tell Kay not to speak to him if he speaks to her, and if she's always with another woman he's bound to give up in the end. No man can persist against endless snubs.'

'Wilson can. What about reporting it to the police?'

He shook his head. 'What can they do? He isn't guilty of threatening behaviour. There's been no breach of the peace. The police will dismiss it as a domestic matter.'

'I'm sorry, Freddie. I want some action. What about suing him for invasion of privacy?'

He continued to prod the blotting pad with his pen. 'Not in this country, old chap,' he said. 'It might be different in the States, but the courts over here don't recognise what you call "invasion of privacy".'

'Can't you do anything?' I asked.

He put down the pen and looked me straight in the eyes. 'The fellow is obviously a bit of a pest but I wouldn't be optimistic about obtaining an injunction to restrain him from molesting Kay. And that's your only legal remedy. Look at the facts. He has hung around for her at her place of employment – but it is his place of employment too. He has telephoned your flat a few times, and these are admittedly annoyances. But would they amount to a nuisance in a court of law. I doubt it. This isn't a case of obscene calls. He's been quite well-mannered and polite, as I understand it. Apart from anything else an action on the grounds of nuisance – which I don't think this is – happens to be a lengthy and expensive process.'

'In other words, you don't want to act for me.' I said huffily.

To Freddie's credit he didn't greet this remark with the chill it deserved. He said, 'You can always count on me, old chap, but you said something earlier about not making threats unless you were prepared to carry them out. I feel the same. I could easily write to this man and say that my client has instructed me with regard to the unwelcome attention being paid to my client's wife, and unless these attentions cease we shall reluctantly be compelled to institute proceedings against him. I can say that, but I wouldn't want to carry it through. I don't think you've got a case. However, if you're not satisfied with my opinion, I could take counsel's opinion.'

I felt as though I were banging my head against a brick wall. I knew and respected Freddie well enough to realise that he was giving good advice.

'Try to treat the whole thing as a joke,' he said, 'even if it's a joke in rather bad taste.'

I stood up. 'I doubt if I can do that. I'm a bit old-fashioned. But thanks for the advice, Freddie.'

'Now don't go doing anything silly, will you? And for God's sake don't grab hold of him again. If you can treat it as a joke you'll find that it's become a joke. And I'll bet, six months from now, you'll have forgotten his name.'

Looking back, I can see that the sensible course would have been for Kay to leave the store and find a job elsewhere. But she liked the work and I felt that for her to resign would be a sort of defeat. Too often in life the innocent suffer through the actions of irrational and selfish people. Why should Kay be another victim?

I decided to take advantage of the Personnel Department summer party to approach Kay's boss about Wilson. These parties, sociable without being exciting, were normally held in the private bar of a pub to the rear of the store. The formula was the same this year. Members of the staff were each allowed to bring one guest. I was Kay's guest.

Her boss was an extrovert who answered to the name of 'Mr Forbes'. He was in his early fifties and with erect bearing and trim moustache he looked like a retired army officer.

When Kay was busy elsewhere I went across to him.

'Hello there,' he said. 'No spot prizes today!'

This was a reference to a prize Kay and I had won during a waltz at the Christmas dance.

'I wonder if I could speak to you for a few moments, Mr Forbes. Off the record, as it were.'

His smile vanished and he assumed the air of a man accustomed to being entrusted with important confidences. 'Somthing to do with Kay?' he asked.

'Yes.'

'Happy here, isn't she? We're all very fond of Kay.' He was annulling in advance any complaint that she was unhappy through neglect.

'Oh yes. She enjoys her work and likes her colleagues in Personnel. But there is a fly in the ointment.'

He listened to the story of Wilson. At first his forehead was furrowed with concern but gradually this expression changed to one of slight hostility.

'Sounds like a storm in a teacup,' he said when I had finished. 'Wilson's a very good man. Excellent progress reports.'

'I was hoping you might have a word with him.'

He shook his head. 'Let's be men of the world,' he said, and paused.

I had no objection to being a man of the world. If I am not a man of this world, of what world am I a man? I said I didn't understand what he was driving at.

'A young lad finds your wife attractive. Nothing criminal in that. Flattering, if anything. He asks her out for a drink. Nothing criminal in that either.' He lowered his voice. 'There are hundreds of friendships made in office hours. You know that. I know that. Nothing harmful. Just a couple of people who get along well having a drink or a meal together in the lunch hour. They may be married to other parties, but what's the harm? Anyway, where's the opportunity, even if harm crossed their minds?'

'That isn't the point.'

Forbes straightened his shoulders and looked very military. 'This is not a departmental problem,' he said. 'I'm sure Kay, or one of her friends, is capable of treading on Wilson's toes if he goes beyond the bounds. And, as I say, he has an excellent record here. The sort of man we don't want to lose.'

He meant, 'I don't give a damn how many married women Wilson seduces so long as his work is first-class.'

'So you won't do anything about it,' I asked.

He made an impatient gesture with his hand. 'It's nothing to do with me. We're not living in the reign of Queen Victoria now, you know.'

That was the end of the conversation. Later, Kay said, 'What were you and Mr Forbes talking about?'

I knew the truth would upset her and, feeling a curious mixture of cowardice and kindness, I told her we were discussing London's transport problems.

'How dull,' she commented and mercifully the subject was dropped.

I doubt if Forbes said anything to Wilson, or to Kay, but from that night things began to improve. When I asked Kay if she had been bothered by Wilson she would say, 'I didn't see him at all today,' or 'He was around when I left but I'm not sure whether he saw me.'

There was a change in her which was probably due to the ending of a period of tension. She had lost some weight and this made her look younger. Her eyes regained their sparkle and her skin looked softer. But although she seemed happy, the memory of the ridiculous affair lingered in my mind and was reinforced by practically everything I saw or read.

Articles in newspapers and magazines which presumably I had sub-consciously avoided reading after my eyes had skated across the heading seemed preoccupied with 'the permissive society'. One couldn't turn a page without finding some reference to adultery, pregnant schoolgirls or 'the Pill'. I began to read the articles I had formerly ignored and when I was travelling I found myself examining posters on Underground platforms and escalators. Why hadn't I noticed before that everywhere there were invitations to the vacant-minded passer-by to think about sex. Had I been travelling in blinkers for the last decade?

And I began noticing the name 'Wilson'. It was on shop fronts, in references to the Labour leader, and most frequently of all in my local library. Whenever I glanced through the rack of recently returned books there seemed to be a work by one of the Wilson trinity – Angus, Colin and Edmund.

Sex and Wilson were inescapable. I began to wonder for the first time since my mother's death whether I was normal. I disliked what I saw and yet was strangely compelled to contemplate it. I was out of step with the times, but was I also out of step with normal behaviour? From what I read nobody seemed to care much if his wife committed adultery. Parties were even arranged where wives could be swapped like used postage stamps. It was commonplace for wives to conduct affairs under their husbands' noses and with their husbands' consent. This was inevitably referred to as 'civilised behaviour'.

And then I read a passage in a book which gave me comfort. It is from Aldous Huxley's *Brave New World Revisited*:

The really hopeless victims of mental illness are to be found among those who appear to be most normal . . . They are normal not in what may be called the absolute sense of the word; they are normal only in relation to a profoundly abnormal society. Their perfect adjustment to that society is a measure of their mental sickness.

I didn't fit in with modern society but this wasn't evidence of abnormality on my part. The abnormal ones were those who swapped wives because it was fashionable to swap wives, and who regarded the Pill as mankind's salvation. They were those who advocated promiscuity as a norm and found it necessary to sell cars, chocolate and even kitchen utensils by blatantly sexual advertisements. They were men like Forbes who said, 'What's the harm?' and like Wilson who with fantastic impudence could say 'I love Kay' to Kay's husband. These were the new sick born of the permissive society. Thank God I was normal.

And then there occurred the incident of the carnations.

Many months before, we had booked to go on a cruise in August. It was to be my first holiday afloat since my mother's death and the boat, a luxury liner, was scheduled to make calls at Lisbon, Madeira, the Canaries and Casablanca. A week before sailing we decided to catch an early morning train on Saturday and go for a tramp on the Sussex downs. Unfortunately when we woke it was raining heavily and the forecast was for continuing rain. Even so, we almost went, but Kay eventually decided the issue by saying, 'What if we catch colds? It would ruin the start of the holiday.'

So we stayed in the flat. If we hadn't been at home we shouldn't have heard the bell ring during the morning and answered it to find a messenger boy on the doorstep with a dozen deep red carnations.

'Who on earth would send me these?' asked Kay when the boy had gone.

I said it must be a mistake.

'It can't be,' she replied. 'It's my name and address. And here's a card.' Her eyes were shining and I wished I had sent the flowers.

She read the card. 'Oh,' she said.

I took it from her.

'TO KAY, WITH DEEPEST RESPECT AND ADMIRATION – DENIS'

'The bastard,' I said.

'Aren't they lovely?'

I wondered for a split second if she had gone insane and then I took the sheaf of carnations from her and hurried outside to the dustbin.

She ran after me calling, 'Have you gone mad?'

'I thought you had gone mad,' I said.

'What do you think you're doing,' she asked, retrieving the carnations from the dustbin. 'These are *flowers!*'

Dear Kay. She is so sensitive and sympathetic towards flowers. To her they are as much creatures as animals are. What I had done was almost equivalent to putting a child in the dustbin.

'I'll put them in water,' she said, and I followed her back into the flat.

'I'd prefer not to be reminded of their provenance,' I said. 'If you must keep them, would you mind keeping them in the spare room?'

'Why? They're lovely to look at.'

'They have come from a young fool who would, if he could, wreck our marriage. It's not asking too much to have them kept out of sight.'

She looked at me in a way I shall never forget. It is said that one remembers only the pleasant things in life and forgets all else. I can only remark that this may be true for the majority but it is not true for me. Kay's disdainfully cold look was photographed on my memory. 'Very well,' she said. 'We'll keep them in the spare room.'

'You do understand?' I asked.

'I understand,' she said. 'Perfectly,' she added.

And she put them in a cut-glass vase in the spare room. I didn't know whether to be angry at her disregard for my feelings or to find her love of flowers so endearing as to erase my annoyance.

The carnations remained in the spare room until we sailed.

On boarding at Southampton we were shown to our cabin. It was compactly designed with separate berths covered in green and blue tartan overlays and with a wide dressing table between the bed-heads. Piped music drifted into the cabin and we had a choice of different radio channels so that, if we wished, we could listen to non-stop classical music instead of the pop which was playing on our arrival. The cabin had its own small bathroom. Kay peeped out of the porthole by her berth and said, 'This is going to be fun.'

After unpacking some luggage we went up to the restaurant to obtain a table number from the manager. Then we went aft to enjoy the sunshine on the quarter deck. The first meal was tea which could be taken in one of the lounges. As we sipped from our cups we watched the shore of the Isle of Wight slide slowly past.

I am a fairly good sailor but on my advice Kay had been inoculated against sea-sickness and although by dinner time there was a moderately heavy swell in the Channel we went to the restaurant, happy and hungry.

It is said that one never realises when one *is* happy only that one *was* happy. Happiness is in the wake. As we entered the restaurant I wasn't conscious of being happy (although at that moment I was happy) but the moment we sat down I was acutely aware of being suddenly unhappy. Directly across the aisle and gazing at a menu was Wilson.

I said, 'Good God,' and the words emerged aloud although I had meant to keep them under my breath.

'What's the matter?' asked Kay.

'Look!'

She had been slightly flushed but the blood faded from her cheeks. 'I can't believe it,' she said.

At that moment he looked up from the menu, saw us staring aghast at him and gave a timorous half smile.

'Did you know he would be on board,' I asked in a lowered voice.

'No. How could I?'

'He must have known you'd be on board.'

'Well, lots of people at the office know about this trip. He could easily have heard about it.'

I said I was going to get our table changed.

'Please don't make a fuss,' she said. Kay dislikes fuss and scenes. 'Please!' she begged.

I looked around. Every table was full. It was unlikely that we could change now.

'Let's see what delicacies they have for us,' she said, trying to sound bright. 'I'm famished.'

My appetite had gone. I was thinking, 'Twelve days . . . Twelve days on the same ship with him!'

This was only the beginning. We should see him in the bars, as we moved around the decks, as we lay sunbathing, as we ate, as we danced, as we debouched at each port of call; we were all captives in the same prison and my only escape was in the cell of our cabin.

I was glad Kay wanted to turn in early. I could hear her breathing in sleep on the far side of the cabin as a succession of furious thoughts tumbled through my mind. If Wilson had walked in through the cabin door I am certain I should have strangled him with my bare hands.

If he spoke to us, even to say 'Good morning', I should have to restrain myself. And there were twelve days of this accumulating tension.

Eventually my immediate fury burned itself out and I resolved to exercise iron self-control and to ignore the fellow if he spoke to us. If you discipline yourself to ignore an unpleasant fact of life it can sometimes happen that, except when your nose is rubbed in it, you can succeed in ignoring it.

At first it wasn't quite as bad as I expected; we managed to eat at different times from him and although we saw him about the ship he made no attempt to speak to us.

'Why the devil doesn't he get a girl,' I said. 'There are enough around for a thousand and one shipboard romances.'

'I feel rather sorry for him,' said Kay. 'He looks awfully lonely.' She adjusted her sun-glasses and lay back on a reclining chair. 'Isn't this wonderful,' she said. 'I'm going to get as brown as a berry.'

In the distance I could see Wilson leaning forlornly on the rail gazing out at a blue expanse of water and sky.

At Lisbon we didn't join an organised shore excursion but took a taxi to the top of Parque Eduardo VII and then strolled down past the little bird sanctuary with its splendid peacocks towards the main part of town. The day was warm without being too hot and we wandered along pavements that were diapered in black and white stones observing the lottery ticket sellers, the plethora of policemen, country-women with panniers on their heads, the numerous blind, the numerous shoe-shiners, the well-stocked shops; and thus idling we reached the Praco Rossio Don Pedro IV in time for lunch. In the afternoon we went to look at the castle district with its warren of narrow streets and ancient buildings. It was a delightful day and I hardly thought about Wilson whom we had seen earlier departing, glum-faced, on a coach tour bound for Estoril via Quelez and Sintra.

Kay and I are used to walking long distances without tiring and although we must have covered more than a dozen miles we walked all the way back from the castle district to the dock where our ship was berthed passing through fish and fruit markets on the way. Kay hugged my arm. 'Not a tourist in sight,' she said. 'We really are away from it all.'

The ship pulled out while we were having dinner and we watched the Salazar Bridge and the illuminated statue of Christ glide past as we sampled *espalada*, a fish caught off the Portuguese coast. There was no sign of Wilson. Perhaps he had got lost at Estoril, Quelez or Sintra. I hoped so.

'There's a dance tonight,' said Kay. 'Let's go, or are you too tired?'

A Spanish proverb has it that a gentleman is never tired and I quoted it to her.

'Good,' she said. 'I'll wear my long red dress.'

But, a couple of hours later, we were no sooner on the dance floor than I saw Wilson standing on his own at the bar. His face matched the colour of Kay's dress and he was wearing an orange kipper tie on a bilious yellow shirt. His suit was bright emerald green and he looked like a garish advertisement for poster paints.

'Look who's here,' said Kay, fashioning her body to the rhythm of a quickstep. 'Hasn't his face caught the sun?'

'I've seen him. A walking Joseph's coat of many colours.'

We danced, and we sat out, and we danced again, and then we were in a waltz with spotlights dappling the dancers. Wilson had disappeared. Perhaps he'd gone to bed.

'Excuse me,' said a voice. I felt a tap on my shoulder.

The dance was a gentleman's excuse-me. I turned to see who had requested the pleasure of taking my place and before I could protest (or 'make a scene' as Kay would say) Wilson had whisked her into the splashes of moving light.

My first reaction was to re-excuse him, but I decided to ignore his unwanted intervention. I had planned to ignore him, and ignore him I would.

The dance seemed to last a long time. When Kay rejoined me she looked tense and I wondered what had upset her.

'Let me sit down,' she said. 'My feet are ruined. I don't think he's ever danced a waltz in his life.'

Shortly after this we left the dance, and while we were undressing in the cabin I asked what Wilson had talked about.

'He kept apologising for his steps. He needed to.' She gave a brief smile. 'He said, "They call me the octopus of the Buying Department – I've got four times the usual number of feet."' She gazed down at her own small and pretty feet. 'They don't look too bruised and battered, do they?'

I moved towards her but she turned away. 'I'm dog-tired, darling. And we've been on our feet all day.'

I shrugged. 'All right . . . What else did you talk about?'

She scrambled into her bed. 'Nothing really.'

'He just kept saying that he was an octopus?'

'I'm too tired to remember,' she said and she switched off the bed-head light.

I suppose a normal man by the standards of the permissive society would have dropped the subject, or even said, 'You were slow, dear. Why didn't you go to his cabin?' but I am not normal by the standards of a sick society.

I got into my bunk and persisted with the question. 'He must have done more than apologise for bad dancing. You were a full three minutes together.'

'Three minutes!'

'What do you mean,' I asked, 'saying "three minutes" like that?'

She didn't reply.

'Kay. What did he say to you?'

'Please. I'm dreadfully tired.'

I switched off my light. The cabin was in darkness.

'Kay?'

'What?'

'Answer my question.'

She sighed loudly. 'How do you expect me to remember anything when you were sitting glowering at us?'

'I wasn't glowering. I was ignoring the whole thing.'

She gave a laugh.

'What's so funny?' I asked.

She gave no answer.

'I was watching,' I said. 'Not glowering. And he was talking a lot. What did he say?'

'What does it matter?'

'It matters to me.'

'You just want an excuse to make a scene with him.'

'Look, Kay, I swear I won't make a scene. I shall ignore the whole thing, but I do want to know what he said.'

She gave another sigh. 'We talked about Madeira. He asked what plans I had for the day ashore.'

'What did you say?'

'I said I left the planning to you.'

'What did he say to that?'

'Oh, please, can't we stop this? I really am whacked out.'

'What did he say, Kay?'

'I don't remember.'

'Of course you do. What did he say?'

'It was a joke.'

'Tell me the joke, Kay.'

'It was just a joke. He asked me to ditch you.'

'He asked you to ditch me?'

'Can I go to sleep – please?'

'What did you say? Did you say, "Well, I don't like making scenes so you can take me out if you like."'

Suddenly she was furious. Her voice came across the cabin like a whiplash. 'Yes, that's what I said. And I told him I'd do my best to ditch you. Now are you satisfied? Can I go to sleep?'

It was my turn to make no reply.

Within seconds she was snoring.

As I lay miserably awake in the darkened cabin I realised that Kay would not have said this, and she was only pretending to have said it to stop my incessant questions. I didn't hold her snappish reply against her, but I did hold Wilson responsible for an argument between man and wife, and I couldn't forgive the suggestion he had made to her. No wonder she had looked tense and distressed after dancing with him.

What else would happen in the days ahead? It was plain that Wilson would never give up his obsessive quest for Kay and I was beginning to wonder if his obsession might not, in the end, win the day. How does one fight a man who is utterly preoccupied with obtaining a woman's affections? How do you deal with a man whose *idée fixe* is far beyond reason, persuasion, threats of bodily violence or (provided he doesn't overstep certain bounds) the reach of the law?

Wilson would pursue his objective ruthlessly, never doing enough to condemn him in a legal tribunal, but he would erode my marriage by gifts of flowers, unstinted devotion and indelicate suggestions. Kay would gradually be attracted to him against her will and she would begin to regard me, and not him, as the enemy. Kay is gentle; Kay is kind. She can't even refuse a street flag-seller. Her life has been sheltered and she doesn't know how to cope with the harsher realities. How long would she be able to stand Wilson's pernicious pressures? One day a situation would arise when her fidelity would be tested beyond the limit. It might happen at her office. Pat and Josie would be out at lunch and Wilson would walk in. He would lock the door. Only a typewriter on a desk would be between them. Silently he would push the typewriter aside, vault the desk, and she would succumb to his overwhelming desires.

It is said by some philosophers that to understand a problem is also to know its solution. I understood the problem and the solution was obvious.

On the following day Kay seemed very subdued and all my efforts to cheer her failed.

There is no point in charting the various twists and turns of my mind on that unhappy day; it is sufficient to say that I wrote a note in a fair imitation of Kay's hand and slipped it under Wilson's cabin door, having first obtained the cabin number from the ship's telephone operator.

The note said: 'Meet me at 1.30 a.m. tomorrow morning at Station 5 on the Boat Deck. Urgent. Kay.'

She was asleep when I slid, fully dressed, off my bed and stole out of the cabin.

The long narrow corridor was empty. I hurried to the elevator and ascended to the Boat Deck. As I stepped out, I looked around. Nobody in sight. I went to the door which opened on to the deck. It swung open silently. A cool salt breeze was blowing and the sky was milky with millions of stars. I walked to Station 5. I could see Wilson's outline. He was leaning on the rail and characteristically gazing out across the moon-washed sea.

I should never have a better opportunity. I crept up behind him. He didn't move. I bent down, pushed both arms between his thighs and bundled him over the rail. He let out a piercing, blood-curdling scream as he fell.

I heard the splash and was about to run away when I noticed a sandal on the deck. Somehow, one of his sandals had fallen off. It is very odd but that lone sandal looked more human than Wilson. I picked it up and tossed it over the side, but I knew I should always remember its shape and its feel.

Then I scampered back to the elevator, descended to our deck, ran along the empty corridor, tip-toed into our cabin, undressed and climbed into bed. The sheets were still warm. A moment later the ship's siren blew a long powerful blast.

I could feel a faint vibration running through the panels of the cabin. Was the ship stopping?

Kay woke and called my name. I gave a sleepy grunt.

'The siren's just gone,' she said. 'It woke me up. What do you think is happening?'

'Didn't hear it,' I mumbled.

A few minutes later she kneeled on her bunk, drew the curtain aside and peered out of the porthole. 'We've stopped,' she said.

'Stopped?'

'Come and look.'

She was right. The water around us was still. The ship might have been moored to a quay.

For half an hour we conjectured why the ship should have stopped in mid-ocean; then the engines started and we were on our way.

When the steward woke us with early morning tea I asked, 'Why did we stop in the night?'

He pulled a grim face. 'Man overboard, sir.'

'Good God. Was he saved?'

'They got a boat out to him with the ship's surgeon on board but he failed to respond to artificial respiration.'

'How did he fall?' I asked.

'No idea, sir.'

'Who saw him?'

'Someone on watch heard a scream, I think, sir. He looked over and saw what appeared to be a person in the water.' The steward edged towards the door. 'Very interesting manoeuvre the first officer made. Slowed the engines and did what we call a "Williamson Turn". Brings the ship back on a reciprocal course.' He left before I could ask more questions.

The day in Madeira was in contrast to the carefree day in Lisbon. Kay seemed unhappy and she didn't care for Funchal. She begged me to go sight-seeing without her; but I had to pretend Wilson was still alive and I said jocularly, 'Can't leave you alone with that young wolf around.'

She took a couple of aspirins and lay down on her bed. After a while she fell asleep and I went off to the coffee bar. I wanted to be on my own. Nobody could have seen me bundle Wilson overboard but they might find the note signed 'Kay'. But even if it was traced to us a hand-writing expert would confirm it wasn't in Kay's writing. There was nothing to fear. Wilson's death could not be attributed to me.

I felt no guilt or remorse. I had been provoked beyond endurance by a young man obsessively interested in my wife. I had acted as any normal man would. Only a permissive society could suggest that my action had been abnormal. Strangely, the single sandal worried me for a while. I knew Oedipus was a name meaning 'swollen foot' and I had an idea that this damned myth was haunting me. Did the oracle say that Oedipus would enter Thebes wearing one sandal? Luckily, the ship's library had a book on mythology and I soon realised I had been confusing Oedipus with Jason. It was Jason who lost a sandal in a muddy river and thereby began the fulfilment of an oracle.

To hell with Wilson; I had regained peace of mind.

If Kay hadn't been feeling so seedy I would have turned cartwheels all over the deck.

When she learned that Wilson had been the 'man overboard' she cried. I could understand her reaction. After all, she is a very sensitive woman and he was an office colleague.

Back in England her health did not improve. She went to a doctor who told her she had a mild depression and gave her drugs. The depression persisted. Physically she melted away and became an undersized weakling again.

I was at my wits' end wondering how to help her when, after a fit of crying, she let slip the cause of her depression. She had convinced herself that Wilson had committed suicide.

'What if he did,' I asked. 'That's not your fault.'

'But it is,' she cried. 'That night at the dance when he asked me to ditch you, I steeled myself and told him I wouldn't look at him if he was the last man on earth.'

I was amazed. 'That isn't what you told me.'

'I only said what I did because I was fed up with all your questions. I wanted to be left alone. I knew if I told you the truth you'd want to make love to me, and I couldn't bear the thought of being touched. Can't you understand?'

I shook my head. 'Not really . . . And you didn't make him commit suicide.'

She looked at me with tear-filled eyes. 'I finished by telling him he could jump overboard for all I cared!'

Kay's health is slowly improving. I couldn't let her suffer for my actions and so I told her the truth. When the shock wore off she said we couldn't live the rest of

213

our lives together with this secret between us. But if I gave myself up and took my punishment, she would wait for me, and one day we would start afresh.

Freddie has briefed counsel and has impressed on me that if we can make out that I was suffering from a temporary abnormality of mind the sentence should be less and the reunion with Kay will be speedier.

I can see the force of his argument, but it goes against the grain that I, a man who has given the extreme proof of his normality, should have to parade himself to the world as a specimen of abnormality.

Wilson was the one with an abnormal fixation, not me.

OK FOR MURDER

by *Michael Underwood*

'You will try and get home a bit early this evening, won't you, love?' Oscar said as he watched Oliver making his preparations to leave the house that morning. 'It *is* our anniversary,' he added as though Oliver needed the further reminder.

Oliver smiled. 'Of course. And don't *you* forget to book a table! Better make it eight-thirty.'

Oscar nodded. 'That'll give us time to have a little celebration here first. I'll put a couple of bottles of champagne on ice.' He opened the front door and gave Oliver an almost wistful look as he went out. 'Six years ago today, it was,' he murmured.

Oliver paused and glanced back. 'Wonder what we'll be doing in another six years,' he said with a faintly quizzical smile.

'One thing for sure, I'll still be the same age as I am now,' Oscar remarked. 'As from today I'm not getting any older.' He held up his left wrist from which hung the twenty-two carat gold chain Oliver had given him as an anniversary present. 'It's beautiful and I love it,' he said.

'Good, because it cost enough.' Then observing Oscar's suddenly clouded expression Oliver said, 'Don't get all sentimental, it's too early in the day. Save it for this evening.' With a final wave he got into his car and started the engine.

Oscar watched him out of sight before going back into the cottage. If everything went according to plan, it was the last time he would see Oliver alive.

The day was indeed the sixth anniversary of their first meeting which had taken place on the upper deck of a number 14 bus as it was passing Harrods. That in itself, they later agreed, had been a sort of omen.

Oscar had been casting interested glances at Oliver for two or three minutes before Oliver became aware of the fact. His return glance when it came, though less brazen, was sufficient for Oscar to get up and move into the seat next to him. By the time the bus reached Hyde Park Corner, they had exchanged telephone numbers and discovered, to Oscar's entrancement, that they had the same initials. Oliver Knight and Oscar Knudsen. To Oscar, who sought omens everywhere, this was the clearest possible indication that they were meant for each other. It was Oliver, however, who phoned that evening and suggested dinner the next day.

They met at a small Italian restaurant in South Kensington, not far from where Oliver had a flat. Oscar, at the time, had a bedsit in less fashionable West Kensington.

In the course of dinner Oscar learned that Oliver was thirty-two and therefore six years older than himself, that he still carried the scars of a failed marriage, and that he was the director of a firm of travel agents.

In turn Oliver learned that Oscar was of Danish extraction though he had been born and brought up in England and that he worked in the publicity department of a magazine where he was underpaid and generally miserable.

One week later Oscar moved into Oliver's flat and they had lived together ever since, moving to Maple Cottage, five miles from Dorking, two years ago.

Oscar had long since given up his job, leaving Oliver as the bread-winner. Not that there was any shortage of bread for the travel agent business had prospered, in addition to which Oliver had inherited £100,000 from his grandmother.

For a time it had been a perfect match, the temperamental, fickle and passionate Oscar and the good looking Oliver behind whose relaxed appearance lurked an acreage of insecurity. But whereas Oliver seemed prepared to condone his friend's infidelities, Oscar was apt to work himself up into a jealous rage every time he suspected Oliver of being unfaithful to him. And suspicion came as naturally to Oscar as rainfall to the western isles. Oliver had always accepted that Oscar's philandering involved no more than ships that passed in the night, except that mid-afternoon was their more usual time, when Oscar had the cottage to himself. When 'business' kept Oliver late in town he was careful to conceal from Oscar what he had been up to. Anything, but anything, to prevent his sinking into one of his foul moods.

As yet Oliver had not met Keith, the new lad who came twice a week to help in the garden. Oscar always referred to him in an off-hand tone and said he smelt strongly of compost.

'Thank goodness he doesn't work inside,' he would add disdainfully.

Thereafter, whenever Oliver enquired after him, Oscar was dismissive.

Nevertheless, it was Keith who filled Oscar's thoughts as he turned back into the cottage after waving Oliver goodbye that morning. Keith, with whom he had fallen head-over-heels in love. Keith, who was the pivot of the carefully laid plan that was to result in Oliver's death.

Oscar glanced at his watch. The morning, hardly begun, was already dragging. He felt anxious and ill-at-ease as he closed the front door and went upstairs to the bedroom. A quick shake of the pale mauve duvet and matching pillows and the bed was made. Oliver's pillow smelt of the Vidal Sassoon almond shampoo he always used and he buried his face in it for a sentimental moment. He was still very fond of Oliver and didn't want to hurt him; that's why a quick drastic solution was best. He was almost able to persuade himself that Oliver wouldn't mind being removed from life in such a good cause. And this time next year there would be a new anniversary in his calendar. That of Oliver's death.

Oscar reckoned that eleven o'clock was the earliest Keith would be back, but that lunchtime was a more realistic hour. After all, the logistics of the plan were formidable, involving the disposal of Oliver and the abandonment of his car, followed by Keith retrieving his own car and getting back to Maple Cottage.

In its essence, the plan was simple enough. Keith, his cropped blond hair hidden under a dark wig and with a matching moustache to complete his disguise, was to be waiting to thumb a lift as Oliver came along on his way to work. A rucksack on his back and a stout pair of boots on his feet would reinforce the impression of a genuine hitchhiker and exploit Oliver's weakness for offering lifts to lonely young men at the roadside. On a usually deserted stretch of the road where it passed through a dark wood Keith was to feign an urgent call of nature. When Oliver drew up he would be overpowered by the physically much stronger Keith and strangled. His body would be dumped in the back of the car and covered by a blanket, after which Keith would drive eight miles along by-roads to a disused gravel pit where he would dump the body in deep water. The car was to be abandoned elsewhere. Thereafter Keith would retrieve the bicycle he had hidden in advance and make his way back to where he had left his own car. After which he would be ready to make his way to Maple Cottage and report 'mission accomplished' to a nervously waiting Oscar.

That was the plan which Oscar reviewed in his mind as he moved restlessly about the kitchen. At one stage he had thought to ask their cleaning woman to change her day and come that Thursday to provide him with an alibi, but on subsequent reflection he decided this might arouse suspicion on the part of those investigating Oliver's mysterious disappearance. Moreover, the fact he had never learnt to drive a car himself was alibi enough in the circumstances.

He sat down at the table in the breakfast alcove with another cup of coffee and reached for his cigarettes. He glanced idly at the front page of the *Mirror* (Oliver always took the *Daily Telegraph* with him), but found it impossible to concentrate. His mind was too full of other thoughts. Thoughts of life with Keith. Sturdy, muscular, twenty-two-year-old Keith who had already served a sentence for GBH and to whom the prospect of committing murder was a normal progression – provided the rewards were sufficient. Oscar had not been slow to tell him that he and Oliver had made wills in each other's favour which meant that he, Oscar, would inherit a considerable fortune on Oliver's demise.

'If I die first, all Oliver will get will be a few old T-shirts,' he was fond of saying to their friends with a slight moue.

Obviously he and Keith would need to behave with circumspection at the outset, but once everything was settled and Oliver's estate was legally his, they would be able to make a proper life together. Meanwhile, there was no reason why he shouldn't dream about the day that lay ahead . . . Why, there was even a portent to be found in Keith's own initials. KO for Keith Offingham, and he was certainly a knock-out. Though Keith had shown no patience with Oscar when he purported to find special significance in their initials.

'For Chrissake,' he had said the last time Oscar had referred to it, 'who cares a bugger what your initials are as long as they don't spell bum or shit!'

Meanwhile Oscar lit another cigarette and continued to dream of Keith.

Around ten-thirty he decided to call Oliver's office. Oliver wouldn't be there, of course, but it would give him an opportunity to express concern and anxiety.

217

His car broken down? Or a pile-up on the Kingston by-pass? He didn't often call Oliver at work as Oliver had made it plain he should only do so in the event of urgency. But he and Ruth, Oliver's secretary, knew each other's voices and always exchanged pleasantries when they spoke.

As Oliver wouldn't be there, he didn't really have to think of an excuse for phoning, but, if necessary, he'd tell Ruth it was about their arrangements that evening. He dialled the number and waited.

'Suntravel,' a voice announced with a briskness that was apt to leave callers floundering.

'May I speak to Mr Knight, please?'

'Mr Knight's secretary, can I help you?' Ruth answered a moment later.

'Hello, Ruth, it's Oscar Knudsen.'

'Good morning, Mr Knudsen.'

'May I have a quick word with Oliver, please?'

'I'm afraid Mr Knight's not in.'

Oscar smiled into the receiver. 'I suppose he must have been held up in the traffic. It seems to get worse every day.'

'He's not expected in at all today,' Ruth remarked.

'Not expected in at all?' Oscar said in a voice that trembled.

'No, he's not been in since Tuesday and won't be back in the office till next Monday.'

Oscar's mind reeled, but after what seemed to him like several minutes of paralysed silence, he managed to stammer something about having obviously misunderstood what Oliver had told him and rang off, falling back into an armchair in a state of collapse.

If Oliver had not been at his office yesterday either, where had he been? He'd left home at the usual hour and returned in the evening as if he'd spent an ordinary working day. Oscar tried to recall whether he had said anything in particular about the day, but couldn't remember anything. He had been too eager to find out what Oliver had bought him as an anniversary present to ask him what sort of a day he'd had. And this morning he had again set off as usual, but where was he going? Oscar felt a sudden constriction of his throat muscles. Supposing Oliver had not taken his normal route. After all, if he was not going to work, was he necessarily making for London? But if not, where? Where? Might Keith still be waiting futilely at the roadside? No, that at least could be ruled out, for if their plan had been aborted that early on, he would surely know by now. Keith would have been on the phone.

It was now two and a half hours since Oliver had left home and Oscar felt suddenly angry and outraged. How devious and deceitful Oliver had become! He'd always believed he could read him like an open book, but after this morning's shock . . . The more his mind pored over events, the wilder became his speculation and the greater grew his anxiety.

He wondered whether to call Ruth again and see if she had any notion where Oliver was, but even as he reached for the phone he saw it as a rash move and shrank back.

All he could do was wait. Wait until Keith turned up. Pray God that he would – and soon! Albeit that it was now too much to hope that their carefully thought-out plan had succeeded. Indeed, such was his mental turmoil, it would hardly surprise him if Oliver came through the front door.

But as the minutes ticked laboriously away neither Oliver nor yet Keith appeared and one morbid thought chased another through Oscar's aching head. Supposing Oliver had somehow managed to kill Keith, instead of the other way about? Or, even worse, supposing the two of them had gone off together leaving Oscar high and dry and totally deserted? Oscar felt he had to do something to relieve the tension, but what? His nerves were in shreds and he'd already smoked more cigarettes that morning than he normally did in the course of the day.

And then just when he was about to surrender to a full-blooded bout of hysterics, a car pulled up in the lane outside and Keith got out. Oscar flew to the front door and flung it open, undecided whether to upbraid the approaching figure or fling his arms round his neck.

'Everything OK?' he asked tensely. Keith nodded. 'I've been worried out of my wits,' he went on. Then in a choked voice he said, 'Am I relieved to see you, love! I was expecting you much sooner.'

'I don't know why. This is my usual time for coming, isn't it?'

'Yes, but . . . '

'It'd have looked funny if I'd come earlier.'

'Yes, yes, of course. I didn't think of that,' Oscar burbled in his relief.

'Well, I did.'

'Come in and I'll make you a cup of coffee and you can tell me everything.' As he closed the door behind them, he wrapped his arms around Keith and hugged him tightly. Keith accepted the embrace without any show of enthusiasm, but then he never was one for overt emotion. His forte was the bedroom where he could be vigorous and physically exciting.

'Did everything go according to plan?' Oscar asked when they were in the kitchen.

'Without a hitch.'

'Oliver, where is he?' Oscar asked with a slight catch in his voice.

'In thirty feet of dirty water.'

'And his car?'

'Where we decided.'

'No problem getting him to stop and offer you a lift?'

'None.'

'What did you talk about before . . . while you were in the car?' Oscar enquired tremulously.

'He just asked me where I came from and where I was heading for.'

'He didn't try and make a pass at you?' Oscar said with a nervous giggle.

'At eight o'clock in the morning? He's not as randy as you are.'

'So it all went according to plan?'

'Like I've already said.'

'And you got rid of your disguise and rucksack without any difficulty?'

Keith gave a big nod. 'I keep on telling you, there were no hitches anywhere along the line.'

'I don't mind telling *you*, love, I almost had kittens at one stage. I phoned Oliver's office.' When he had told Keith what had transpired, he added, 'Did Oliver mention where he was going?'

'He said London.'

'Did he say he was going to work or anything like that?'

Keith shook his head. 'He said he was a travel agent, but that was all.'

'I'm still puzzled as to what he's been up to.'

'Whatever it was, he's not up to it now.' Keith drained his coffee mug and put it down.

'Shall we go upstairs for a little while?' Oscar asked hopefully.

'I'm here to do some gardening, remember? Your nosey neighbour will be wondering what I'm doing indoors all this time.'

'It's all right. She's away.'

'Even so.'

'Later then?'

'Perhaps,' Keith said with a wink that made Oscar's heart skip a beat. Observing Oscar's reaction he suddenly grinned, revealing a row of beautifully even, white teeth. Oscar felt he was going to swoon with anticipation. The day was only half over, but it was already one he would never forget for as long as he lived.

As soon as Suntravel opened the next morning, Oscar was on the phone, speaking to Ruth.

'I'm terribly worried about Oliver,' he said in an anxious voice. 'He never came home yesterday evening and I've not heard a word. Have you any idea where he can be?'

'I'm afraid not, Mr Knudsen. As I said when you called yesterday, he's not expected back in the office until Monday.'

'But didn't he leave any clue as to what he'd be doing?'

'No, he didn't. He simply said he had some private business to attend to and was taking three days off.'

'Where on earth can he be?' Oscar said in the agonized tone he had been rehearsing. 'We were meant to be going out to dinner last night. It was a special occasion and he just never came back. I'm sure something dreadful has happened.'

'It's certainly very strange.' Ruth said warily. 'Let me have a word round the office and see if anyone knew his plans. He may have said something to one of the other directors. I'll call you back in a few minutes.'

'I'd be most grateful if you'd do that as I'm getting frantic.'

'I'm sure there'll turn out to be some innocent explanation, Mr Knudsen.'

'I wish I could think so,' Oscar replied.

Ten minutes later the phone rang. Oscar answered it immediately so that Ruth would be aware he'd been waiting anxiously for her return call.

'No news at all I'm afraid, Mr Knudsen. I've spoken to both Mr Parker and Miss Satchell, but it doesn't appear that Mr Knight told either of them where he was going. Mr Parker suggests that, if you've had no news by tomorrow, you should inform the police. Mr Parker also said not to hesitate to contact him at home over the weekend if you wish.'

'Please tell him I'm going to get in touch with the police immediately. I can't go through another twenty-four hours not doing anything. Obviously something terrible must have happened . . . ' Oscar's voice trailed away.

'I'm sure there'll be a happy ending,' Ruth said stoutly.

'It was all Oscar could do not to giggle. It was in a small sad tone, however, that he thanked her for her help.

Later he telephoned the police and said he wanted to report a missing person. The officer at the other end of the line took down the necessary particulars, including the registration number of Oliver's car and assured Oscar they'd be in touch with him as soon as they had any news. Oscar thanked the officer profusely and repeated how worried he was for his friend's well-being.

That evening Keith picked him up after dark and they drove to a secluded spot where he parked the car.

'It's driving me mad only being able to see you in this furtive way,' Oscar remarked petulantly.

'No point in running unnecessary risks. We oughtn't to be seen out together until the dust has settled,' Keith said matter-of-factly.

'I'll go and see the solicitor on Monday and tell him to get things moving.'

'Not much he can do until the body's been found.'

'Surely the police'll have started dredging all the ponds and quarries in the area by then. Failing which, Oliver's death will just have to be presumed.' He rested his head against Keith's shoulder. 'Tell me you love me!'

'Don't say such daft things!'

'What do you mean?' Oscar asked in an offended voice.

'I'd hardly have gone through all that hassle yesterday if I didn't like you, would I! Commit bloody murder and you ask me if I love you.'

'But do you? Not just like me, but love me?'

'Oh, for Heaven's sake, stuff it!'

Oscar sat back sulkily. At the very moment he longed for a display of affection, Keith was in one of his funny moods. He quickly cheered up, however, when Keith suggested he should put in an extra afternoon's gardening the next day, Saturday.

The following afternoon Keith dug a flower bed while Oscar pretended to do a little weeding nearby, though his attention was more on Keith's rippling muscles than on the removal of any weeds.

Keith suddenly paused and glanced in Oscar's direction.

'The phone's ringing,' he said.

'Oh, I didn't hear it,' Oscar said, coming out of his reverie.

'It's still ringing.'

221

Oscar hurried indoors and picked up the receiver.

'Is that Mr Knudsen?' a male voice enquired.

'Speaking.'

'This is Detective Sergeant Claymore. You phoned yesterday about a missing person. A Mr Knight. I believe he lived at your address.'

'That's right. We've been at Maple Cottage two years.'

'We've found his car, but there's no trace of him.'

'Where was his car?' Oscar asked with the right note of anxiety.

'It was up a track in Effingham Forest. It was locked and my guess would be that it hadn't been touched since being abandoned there.'

'Was his briefcase still in the car?'

There was a slight pause while Sergeant Claymore apparently consulted a piece of paper.

'There wasn't a briefcase in the car.'

'Oh!'

'Presumably he took it with him which makes it look as if he's still alive and well. If he'd intended taking his life, he'd hardly have bothered to remove his briefcase.'

'He might have,' Oscar said tentatively.

'Most unlikely. Anyway, for the moment there's no indication that he's met a sudden end.'

'But what on earth can have happened to him?' Oscar burst out in an anguished voice.

'You're in a better position to answer that than I am, Mr Knudsen. You knew him, I didn't.'

'I'm sure something awful's happened. I mean, he left here to drive to work but never arrives and the next thing is his car's found abandoned off his normal route.'

'It's a not unknown pattern.'

'But it's totally unlike Oliver. He's the most orderly and systematic person you could meet.'

'Well, there's not much the police can do for the moment other than post him as a missing person.'

'Surely you'll initiate a search?'

'Not until there's some evidence of foul play. And there's none, I'm happy to say.'

Sergeant Claymore might have been happy to say it, but Oscar was anything but happy to hear it. He returned to the garden and reported to Keith.

'What did you do with his briefcase?' he asked.

'Weighted it and threw it in after the body.'

'It might have been better to leave it in the car. Also to have left signs of a struggle.'

'Bit late in the day to think of that now,' Keith observed in a not too friendly tone.

'I'm not criticising you,' Oscar said hastily. 'Somehow we've got to get the police to dredge that quarry. At the moment they obviously think Oliver's just walked out on me. I could tell from the officer's voice. Though goodness knows why he should have abandoned his car if that were the case! It may make sense to the police, but it won't to anyone else.'

'Go and put the kettle on,' Keith said after a pause, 'I'm ready for a cup of tea.'

'Perhaps you'll be ready for something else as well,' Oscar remarked with a leer.

'Perhaps.'

But as soon as Keith had departed later that afternoon, all Oscar's anxieties returned. Why couldn't everything work out as smoothly as he had envisaged?

Sunday was every bit as wearisome and frustrating as Oscar had expected. He felt it was never going to reach an end as he paced restlessly about the cottage, smoking endless cigarettes and drinking countless cups of black coffee, while his nerves became more taut by the minute.

Keith had driven down to the coast to visit his grandmother, who was his closest relative and who had brought him up. He had never known his father and his mother had abandoned him and gone off with an American airman when he was only a few months old. He had moved into the Dorking area after his release from prison and now lived at a hostel, earning his living as an odd-job man and casual gardener.

Oscar had suggested he should accompany him on the drive, saying that he would go and look at the sea while Keith was with his gran. But Keith had vetoed the idea and Oscar had to be content with his promise to phone him on his return.

The call came around eight o'clock, by which time Oscar's nerves had become so raw-edged he was ready to scream.

'Thank God it's you love,' he exclaimed with a small strangulated sound. 'I was going mad. It's been the worst day of my life.'

'Why? What's up?'

'It's just that I've had nothing to do all day. I've talked to nobody and I've missed you terribly.'

'Oh, is that all?'

'Isn't it enough?'

'I thought you'd have been phoning round your friends telling them of Oliver's disappearance.'

'I did try and call Desmond and Tony, also Patrick and Ian, but everyone seems to have gone away for the weekend.'

'Nothing further from the police?'

'Not a word.' Aware that Keith would ring off in a moment if he didn't keep the conversation going, Oscar said desperately, 'How did you find your grandmother?'

'Fine.'

'Pleased to see you, was she?'

'Yep.'

223

'What was the traffic like?'

'Not bad.'

'When will I see you next?' Oscar asked frantically.

'I'll call you tomorrow evening.'

'Why don't you come round for supper? You can park away from the cottage, so nobody'll know you're here.'

'It's a possibility.'

'I'll cook your favourite. Steak and kidney pie followed by chocolate mousse.'

'OK, but make it a steak, I had pie at my gran's today.'

'Anything you want, love.'

'A nice fillet steak with all the trimmings.'

Oscar purred with delight. 'It shall be done. When we're living together you'll be able to have steak three times a day.'

Keith chuckled. 'Let's hope Oliver's money holds out!'

The next morning Oscar phoned a solicitor friend. This seemed better than calling the London lawyer who looked after his and Oliver's affairs.

'It's Oscar, Peter. I'm turning to you for advice as a friend who's also a lawyer. I'm desperately worried about Oliver, he's disappeared. Went off to work last Thursday, never arrived and hasn't been heard of since. The police have found his car which had been abandoned, but there's no trace of Oliver. I'm certain something terrible has happened.'

'You mean, you're afraid he's dead.'

'Yes,' Oscar said in a faltering tone.

'Are the police making a search?'

'No, because they say there's no evidence of foul play,' Oscar said indignantly.

'So what advice do you want from me?'

'How long will it be before Oliver is presumed dead?'

'Seven years. The odds are, however, that if he *is* dead, his body'll be discovered before then.'

'But if it's not?'

'Then seven years is the period that must elapse before you can apply for a presumption of death.'

It was a stunned Oscar who put down the receiver and lit a cigarette with a trembling hand.

There was only one thing for it, Oliver's body had got to be found. And soon.

Four cigarettes and two cups of coffee later, Oscar decided to phone the police. He had conjured up a picture of a quite young Detective Sergeant Claymore, clean-limbed and dark-haired. This on the evidence of his crisp telephone manner. When Sergeant Claymore answered the phone, Oscar was jolted out of his reverie.

'I was wondering if you'd had any news over the weekend?'

'Nothing, I'm afraid.'

'I can't remember if I told you that apparently Oliver wasn't expected at his office the day he disappeared. In fact he'd not been in the previous day, either.'

'No, you didn't tell me that, Mr Knudsen,' Sergeant Claymore said more crisply than usual. 'But I found out when I spoke to one of his fellow directors.'

'Oh! I hadn't realised you'd been in touch with his office.'

'But naturally. It was a routine enquiry.'

'I believe I did mention that he'd been rather depressed of late,' Oscar went on.

'No, you didn't tell me that, either.'

Oscar let out a nervous laugh. 'I've been so worried about him, I don't know what I've said and what I haven't said. But it's one of the reasons why I think he may have . . . may have done something drastic.'

'Killed himself, you mean?'

'That's what I'm afraid of.'

'He'd hardly have needed his passport for that.'

'His passport?' Oscar echoed foolishly.

'Yes, didn't I tell you? His fellow director to whom I spoke said he must have taken his passport from the desk drawer in which he kept it when he left his office last Tuesday, because it was no longer there.'

'How strange!' Oscar said, feeling as if he had trodden on a missing floorboard.

'Strange or not, it doesn't look as if he was intending to do away with himself. Seems more likely he was planning a trip. But I gather he never mentioned that to you?'

'No, never.' Oscar gulped and wished the conversation could be brought quickly to an end, but Sergeant Claymore hadn't finished.

'I've also been in touch with his solicitor,' he now went on. 'It seems that Mr Knight had recently re-arranged his affairs. Made a new will, that sort of thing. Are you still there, Mr Knudsen?'

'Yes, I'm listening,' Oscar said, his head swimming.

'I gather you didn't know about that?'

'No.'

'All of which leads one to believe that Mr Knight is somewhere alive and well. So I shouldn't worry too much if I were you. I expect I'll be talking to you again before long.'

With which Sergeant Claymore rang off leaving Oscar feeling as if he'd been mugged.

'Now what's happened?' Keith asked when he arrived that evening.

The question was quite superfluous as nothing was going to stop Oscar giving him a blow-by-blow account of what he had been through that day.

While Oscar talked, Keith helped himself to a Scotch and dry ginger and sat down.

'Sounds like a right cock-up,' he said, when Oscar reached the end. 'And what's all this about his changing his will?'

225

Oscar gave a helpless shrug. 'I wish I knew. I can hardly ring the solicitor and ask him.'

'Why not?'

'Because he wouldn't tell me. It'd be a breach of professional confidence.'

'Even though you and Oliver were like husband and wife?'

'He still wouldn't.'

'Pity you didn't think of that earlier. Come to that, pity you didn't think of a lot of things, such as this presumption of death business. One thing for sure, we don't want the police finding his body.'

'But they must.'

'And see he's been murdered? You must be mad.'

'But there'll be nothing to connect either of us with it. And anyway it may look like suicide.'

'With marks on his throat and a load of hard rock in his pockets!'

'I could say he once told me that if he ever committed suicide, he'd drown himself.'

'The police would be on to you in no time. They'd squeeze you as if you were a tube of toothpaste.'

'They certainly wouldn't get anything out of me.'

'They would if they put enough pressure on. They're experts at it. Anyway, you'd be tempted to put it all on me.'

Oscar gave a cry of dismay. 'How can you say such a thing when all I want is to spend the rest of my life with you! Haven't I done all this just for you?'

'What about me? I'm the fall guy. I'm the one who's taken the risks.'

'We mustn't quarrel, love,' Oscar said in a tone of suppressed hysteria. 'It's all going to be all right, I promise you. It's no more than a hiccup in our plans.'

'More like a bloody great belch, if you ask me,' Keith observed as he got up and went across to pour himself another drink.

The meal that followed was not one of the most successful. In his distracted state Oscar overcooked the steaks and the chocolate mousse turned out lumpy, both an indication of the stress he had been through earlier in the day.

After dinner, Keith remained impervious to all Oscar's blandishments and the evening concluded on a generally unsatisfactory note.

After a restless night, Oscar drifted into a stuporous sleep around five o'clock. He was brought out of it by the insistent ringing of the front-door bell. He peered bleary-eyed out of the bedroom window and saw a blue saloon car parked outside the gate. Hurriedly combing his hair and putting on his kimono dressing-gown, he went downstairs and opened the door.

'Mr Knudsen? I'm Detective Sergeant Claymore, we've spoken on the phone a few times. It looks as if I've woken you up.'

'I don't even know what time it is,' Oscar said numbly.

'Just turned ten o'clock. May I come in?' Without waiting for an answer he entered and Oscar closed the door behind him. 'Why don't you go and get dressed and, if you'll show me where the things are, I'll make us a cup of coffee.'

Oscar nodded. Sergeant Claymore was almost exactly as he had pictured him, trim-figured and friendly in a detached sort of way. Maybe they could get on first name terms. That would make for ease, as well as being propitious.

Ten minutes later Oscar returned to the kitchen, dressed in a white roll-top sweater and a pair of purple cords.

'I've even had a quick shave,' he said, giving Sergeant Claymore a hopeful smile. 'If you don't mind my saying so you're exactly as I'd pictured you would be.'

'Oh!' Sergeant Claymore sounded momentarily nonplussed, but quickly recovered and said, 'I thought you'd prefer me to come and see you, Mr Knudsen, rather than get you along to the station.'

There was a touch of steel in his tone that had not been there before. Picking up the tray of coffee things, on which he had placed a plate of fancy French biscuits, Oscar led the way into the sitting-room.

'I'll come to the point straight away, Mr Knudsen,' Sergeant Claymore said while Oscar assumed an air of polite interest. 'I wonder why you're so certain Mr Knight is dead?'

Oscar blinked. 'It's just that when somebody with whom you've lived for six years suddenly vanishes, you're apt to assume the worst. I'm still stunned by what's happened. I can't believe he'd leave just like that.'

'It wouldn't be because you had some part in his disappearance?'

'Some part? I . . . I don't follow you,' Oscar replied, swallowing hard.

'That you'd planned his death, shall I say?'

'You can't be serious,' Oscar exclaimed, quickly putting down his cup which had begun to rattle in its saucer. 'I loved Oliver. You mayn't understand that, but I assure you that gay people are capable of the same sort of love as ordinary married couples.'

'And the same sort of rows and deceits, too, I've no doubt,' Sergeant Claymore remarked equably.

'Oliver and I never rowed.'

'But to get back to my original point, why are you so keen to persuade me that your friend must be dead?'

'It's just that I have this sense of foreboding.'

'Of the two of you, he was the one with the money?'

'Yes.'

'To put it crudely, Mr Knudsen, he kept you?'

'Only in the sense that a man keeps his wife. In every other respect our life together was one of total sharing.'

'What do you think has really happened to him? It's obvious you believe he's dead, but how do you suppose he came by his death?'

'As I mentioned on the phone yesterday he'd recently been depressed . . . '

227

'And so he decided to take his life, is that it?' Oscar nodded. 'How would you expect him to have done it?'

'He once told me he'd drown himself, as that would be the simplest and least painful way, should he ever be driven to suicide.'

'So he sets off as usual last Thursday morning, abandons his car in Effingham Forest and looks for a suitable stretch of water in which to drown himself. Is that how you see it?'

'Of course, we now know he wasn't intending to go to his office that day.'

'Naturally not, if he had suicide in mind.'

'And he'd not been in the previous day.'

'Maybe he spent it doing a recce!'

'It doesn't seem to me that the police are taking the matter very seriously,' Oscar said stiffly.

'Oh, but you're wrong, Mr Knudsen, I'm deadly serious. But forget suicide for the moment, what else do you think may have befallen him?'

'I suppose he could have been murdered,' Oscar said with a shudder.

'In what sort of circumstances?'

'He used to pick up people in his car. Young men thumbing a lift. I'd told him it was a risky thing to do as you never knew when one of them mightn't attack you and steal your wallet, but he continued despite my warning. He used to say that they were often interesting company and a change from the radio.'

'So you believe he may have been murdered by a hitchhiker?'

'It seems a possibility.'

'You think we ought to explore that line?' Sergeant Claymore said thoughtfully.

'I most certainly do.'

'Do you think it's more likely than the suicide theory?'

'Yes, I think it probably is,' Oscar said with a frowning nod.

'Would you see it something like this? Hitchhiker persuades him to stop for some reason or another, they both leave the car and walk off together, hitchhiker attacks and kills Mr Knight and disposes of his body, doubtless stealing any money he had on him . . .'

'Oliver never had less than two hundred pounds in his wallet,' Oscar broke in.

'There you are then!'

'I think it could easily have happened just like that,' Oscar observed, trying not to sound complacent.

'There is, of course, the alternative,' Sergeant Claymore said, fixing Oscar with a steady stare.

'What alternative?'

'The one I mentioned earlier on. The one that has you playing a part in his disappearance. In his murder, in fact.'

The room seemed to give a sudden lurch and Oscar gripped the arms of the chair. He stared disbelievingly at his questioner, but words refused to come.

'The police are not as simple as some people think,' Sergeant Claymore went on. 'We don't just accept everything we're told without question. We look around, then probe here and there.'

'You're making a monstrous . . . outrageous suggestion,' Oscar managed to say at last. 'What possible motive could I have had for murdering Oliver?'

'You've already told me that.' He glanced around the room. 'You inherit all this and more besides.'

'Incidentally, I have an alibi for the whole of last Thursday morning. I was here at home.' His tone was coldly defiant.

'I never said *you* murdered Mr Knight. I'm sure you *didn't* do the actual deed, but you certainly had a part in it. A big part. The major part.' Oscar tried to look scornfully dismissive, but his expression had become one of frozen panic. Sergeant Claymore went on, 'In the language of the law, Mr Knudsen, you conspired to murder Mr Knight.'

'Conspired? Conspired with whom, may I ask?'

Sergeant Claymore looked at him pityingly. 'You don't really want me to answer that, do you? You see, we picked up Keith Offingham when he left here last night. We've had a long chat with him and he's told us everything.'

'I don't believe you. Anyway, he probably told you lies.'

'Lies? How you worked out a plan which involved him disguising his appearance and thumbing a lift in Mr Knight's car. How you and he were going to set up home together once you'd got your hands on Mr Knight's estate. Lies?'

'He's just a little money-grabber,' Oscar shouted hysterically. 'Anything he did was his idea.'

'That'll be for a jury to decide, Mr Knudsen.'

At this point, Oscar covered his face with his hands and surrendered himself to a bout of noisy and uncontrolled sobbing, while Sergeant Claymore observed him impassively.

In the days that followed Oscar's prevailing mood was one of obsessive self-pity and vicious resentment, which was transformed into a destructive fury when he learned that Keith had turned Queen's evidence against him and would be a witness for the crown instead of standing at his side in the dock.

It was during this period that he received a letter. It bore a Florence postmark and read:

'Dear Oscar,
    You were certainly right about one thing, Keith does smell strongly of compost. I noticed it as soon as he got into the car. Whatever his qualifications as a lover, he has few as a potential murderer. Admittedly I held all the cards once I'd rumbled him and he was astute enough to realise just how vulnerable his situation was. Even so he accepted my counter-plan with a readiness that was hardly flattering to yourself. I would 'vanish' for a short while and he would pretend to you that he had done the deed. As a matter of fact I'd realised several weeks ago that he meant more to you than a mere tiller

of soil. You were always devious, Oscar, but on this occasion you were incredibly naïve as well. Your elaborate plan showed little attention to detail, but then you were always inclined to be slapdash in your eagerness to reach a goal. Anyway, I won't go on other than to say that my death would not have brought you the anticipated goodies as I had recently made a fresh will in which you're not mentioned.

I'll be back in England before your trial.

Yours still alive,
OK'

A WISE CHILD

by John Wainwright

It is almost a year, now, since I decided to kill my father. To murder him, as retribution for re-marrying after the death of my mother.

I knew what I was doing. Let that be clearly understood. A modern fifteen-year-old, with a good education, can never claim 'ignorance' on moral issues. I knew I contemplated murder. Patricide, in fact. And, because I was capable of appreciating the moral issues I was, equally, capable of reaching a moral conclusion.

He didn't deserve to live.

Until my mother's death we had been a happy enough family. Just the three of us. Mother had doted on me a little; allowed me the occasional excess while he, in turn, had frowned mild disapproval without openly objecting. Long before I reached my teens, I realised he was a weak man. Mother was the dominating partner and, if sides had to be taken, she was always on my side.

On the other hand, I cannot remember seriously misbehaving myself. Sometimes a schoolboy prank that went a little wrong, or was taken beyond the point of moderation. Now and again, the deliberate playing of one against the other, in order to get my own way. Those were the limits. In the main, I was happy enough to obey my parents, because I loved them and because I respected them.

They, in turn, loved me . . . I make no Freudian excuse of being a 'misunderstood' child.

Perhaps we were too close. Perhaps we were too interdependent. Other than when he was at work, they were always in each other's company. For myself, I was a solitary person and wanted it that way. I read a great deal. Books on every subject under the sun. Travel books and history books; biographies and autobiographies. I read fiction, too – even crime fiction – but always, at the back of my mind, there was the knowledge that fiction was merely the out-pourings of an over-active imagination. The concocted murders were too involved. The alibis were too easily broken. The culprit was far too obvious – or, if not obvious, far too ridiculous.

Most of all, I enjoyed reading about trials. Real trials. Real murderers, who were stupid men, because they'd been caught.

I think the Seddon trial fascinated me more than any of the others. Frederick Seddon. He was called 'the meanest murderer of them all', but I could never understand that. To suggest *that* implies a price on human life. A cash value. I read and re-read various accounts of the Seddon trial and, to this day, I can't accept the proposition that he poisoned Miss Barrow for her money. She had so little. More than that, she was as valuable to him alive as she was dead.

There was just no case to answer. Edward Marshall Hall knew that. So, I'm sure, did Rufus Isaacs, who was prosecuting. Oh, no – the man who put the noose around Seddon's neck was Seddon himself. He was too clever by half. Too fond of the limelight. Had he *not* given evidence – had he declined to take the stand – he'd have walked away from court a free man.

As it was . . .

We were a happy enough family. (*We*, I mean, not the Seddons.) Mother was no raving beauty, but she was pretty enough, in her own way. A somewhat middle-class way, I suppose, but that's what we were – *very* middle class. Father worked in a solicitor's office. He wasn't a solicitor, of course, but he worked in the closed environment of parchment and law books. He was, I think, something to do with the conveyancing side. Something dreary, and not too technical. It must have been a very boring job, but that didn't worry him. He was a very boring man. Not deliberately unkind. Merely monotonous – and *very* boring.

He had jokes and witticisms. An amazingly limited repertoire of jokes and witticisms. He would trot them out with a regularity warranted to make me cringe. Something would be said – some remark a comedian might have described as a 'feed line' – and I'd know *exactly* what that dull-dog of a father would say next. Mother would dutifully laugh. A quick, obliging touch of laughter, which never reached her eyes. And, sometimes, she would glance at me, almost appealingly, as if to say, 'Can't we *do* something to stop this irritating man from *always* saying the same ridiculous things?'

We couldn't. We could only tolerate him. I think that, tacitly, we both accepted the burden of toleration until such time as nature took its course.

Odd . . . there was an unspoken assumption that he'd go first.

I rather think the same applies in all families, large or small. In some subtle way, one member is earmarked as being the first to die. Nothing to do with age. Nothing to do with illness. A sort of herd-instinct which prepares the rest for the first shock of close-range bereavement.

I suspect life-style has something to do with it. Father, for instance, was never fully *alive*. Whenever you caught him in an attitude of complete relaxation, the first thing you noticed was that his mouth corners drooped. His natural expression was that of a sad man. An everlastingly serious man. Even a sombre man. Which was quite ridiculous. A fiddling little clerk in the office of some unimportant solicitor, and his attitude suggested that he carried an impossible burden across his shoulders.

Young as I am, I have seen many men of father's ilk. Grey, vaguely unhappy men, without even a splash of colour. And most of them (like father) suffer slight pangs of indigestion. The first signs of quite unnecessary ulcers.

Mother, on the other hand, was quite charming – or would have been, had she not had the millstone of father around her neck. She had a certain spontaneous gaiety which bubbled beneath the surface. On the few occasions when just she and I went out together – to a show, to a cinema, to a concert – she fairly sparkled. She was a changed woman, without him around. She was a delightful companion and (a couple of times, no more) I suspected her of mildly flirting with some man sitting next to her. Nothing serious. Nothing objectionable. Just a happy exchange of pleasantries, accompanied by the sort of smile she so rarely had the chance of using at home.

Then, she died.

I truly couldn't believe it, at first. The head sent for me, from the chemical lab. He made me sit down in his study, then told me. He did his best – but I suspect there's no *easy* way.

'I have some bad news for you, my boy.'

'Yes, sir.'

'Your mother collapsed in the supermarket, earlier today.'

'Oh!'

'It's serious, I'm afraid.'

'How serious, sir? Is she in hospital?'

'I'm afraid she's dead. They think it was a heart attack.'

There was an inquest, and there was a funeral, and not once did I weep. Nor, come to that, did father. With me, it was a hurt too deep for tears. With him, it was – nothing.

I had difficulty in bringing myself to believe she was dead. I think he had equal difficulty in remembering that she'd ever been alive.

In bed, at night, I used to stare into the darkness and wonder what sort of man he was. What sort of a human being. He wasn't evil . . . God knows, he wasn't *evil*. He wasn't even hard. I could have understood, had he been one of the 'manly' types, to whom tears are a sign of weakness. Had he been like me, with a grief too savage for mere tears. But, he wasn't that. He wasn't that, at all. He had simply erased her from his life. From his memory. Like a misspelled word on a page. She wasn't there any more . . . period.

I once took him to task.

'Don't you miss her?' I asked.

'Of course I miss her.' But, he mouthed the words – he didn't *mean* them.

'You don't show it,' I accused.

'I'm not very demonstrative,' he said, gently. Then, with a quick, half-smile, 'One day you'll know. There's nothing more lonely than a double bed.'

'Not *that*!' The quick spat of disgust made me almost shout the words.

'Not *only* that,' he corrected me. 'You're young, yet. You don't . . . ' He stopped, mid-way through the sentence and looked awkward and embarrassed.

'I don't "know".' I ended the sentence for him, then added, 'But one thing I *do* know. One thing I'm certain of. I miss her. I miss her terribly. Far more than you miss her . . . and in a different way.'

He didn't argue, and that was the end of the conversation. Nor did we touch on the subject again. There was this distance between us – this gap – and it couldn't be bridged. He was kind enough. He refused me nothing, within reason, and he gave me freedom which I, in turn, didn't abuse. There was a certain deference between us. But not love. Not even real respect, at least, not on my part.

I had no aunts, no uncles, no grandparents. My parents had been only children and I, too, was an only child. But that didn't matter too much. I was given a key to the house, let myself in when I arrived from school and often prepared our meal for when father got back from the solicitor's office.

I was quite able to live a satisfactory life, without the help of adults. Without the companionship of people of my own age. I counted myself in no way odd. In no way peculiar. I had no real interest in sport, I could see no merit in pop music, I found the bulk of television facile, but having completed my homework each evening, I had my books.

The woman was called Angelica. *Angelica!* Botany lessons had taught me that angelica was a garden plant whose leaf-stalks and mid-ribs were candied for use in Christmas cakes. A sweetmeat. A nothing. I think she had a most appropriate name.

I don't know how or when they met. Neither of them ever saw fit to tell me. They became far too besotted with each other ever to give much thought to simple civilities.

I recall (it was little more than a year after mother's death) that father arrived home from the solicitor's office and announced that he was going to a concert that evening. Some string quartet was performing at the local hall. Part of the local musical society's programme, I think. After the concert, he was having supper with some friends. I remember that quite well. *Friends* – plural – not *a* friend.

I was surprised. It was so out of character. I admit, I was not displeased. My preference was to be alone; to do what I wanted to do, without the slightly strained atmosphere which had gradually built up between us.

Just before he left, he said, 'Don't wait up. I may be a little late.'

Again, there was some slight astonishment on my part, but no complaint. As far as I was able, while still being dependent upon him for a home, I lived my own life.

Nevertheless, and although I was in bed, I heard him return. It was past midnight, and he was humming quietly to himself.

That became the pattern. Twice a week. Sometimes three times a week. A concert. The cinema. Some amateur Gilbert and Sullivan production. That sort of thing. There was always an excuse – always a reason – and always 'supper with friends'.

His character gradually changed, although not towards me. He became less serious. Less hangdog. His choice of ties, while not being flamboyant, became less drab, and he didn't *always* wear a white shirt. In a way difficult to explain, he became 'different'. Not flash – he could never have become in any way flash – but 'different'.

Then, about six months after that first concert, he brought her home, after one more concert. No 'supper with friends' this time. They arrived at about half past nine – shortly after I'd settled down to read one of the *Famous Trials* series –

and I heard the key in the lock and the door open and close without taking much notice.

I was a little surprised and a little disgusted, when he brought her into the front room and introduced us. But, in honesty, I kept my distaste to myself because (I told myself) he was a weak man. A basically stupid man. A contemptuous little man living his own contemptuous little life and, for a few more years, I'd have to tolerate him.

But, *after* those few more years . . .

Then, he said, 'I've asked Angelica to be my wife, and she's done me the honour of accepting.'

It caught me completely flat-footed. I was so unready for the remark. So unprepared.

I think the shock showed itself, because she gave a saccharine smile, and said, 'You don't mind, dear, do you?'

'Mind?' I struggled to regain control of myself.

'You see, dear, we don't want to . . . '

'Why should *I* mind?' I closed my book, then repeated the question, but with a different emphasis. 'Why *should* I mind?'

'Of course you don't mind.' The pompous little man thought that, because I was able to hide my outrage, I approved. 'You'll have a mother again . . . won't you?'

He married her two months later.

It was a quiet enough wedding. The registrar was a paunchy, fussy little man, with loose dentures. The two witnesses were complete strangers to me. I think one came from the office where father worked, and the other was a woman friend of 'the bride'. Everybody dutifully kissed each other, after the ceremony – but nobody kissed me!

'He's at that awkward age.' This, from the 'Angelica' woman, when I backed away from the female witness. 'He thinks it's weak to show any outward signs of emotion. Don't you, dear?'

That was another thing. She would insist upon calling me 'dear'. I didn't want to be her 'dear'. I didn't even want to *know* her.

They went away for a fortnight's honeymoon. Somewhere near Southport. They gave me the address, before they left, but I didn't write. They, in turn, sent me two 'wish you were here' postcards.

Perhaps they did, too – wish I was with them, I mean. They must have been very boring company for each other. The gushing, simpering woman, and the pathetic little man with his limited stock of funny remarks. Two weeks of each other's company must have almost driven them mad. Perhaps they spent most of the time going to 'concerts'. Or having 'supper with friends'.

I never asked, and they never told me.

While they were away, I planned the murder.

I decided upon arsenic. What was good enough for the Borgias seemed good enough for me. I also felt that it had a certain 'romantic' connotation. It is reputed to have aphrodisiac properties. I think some cosmetic preparations include it in their formula. In a typically cynical Continental expression, it is known as the Inheritance Powder, the *poudre de succession*.

Definitely arsenic.

It wasn't difficult to come by. It was there, for the careful filching, at the school lab. I called in at the reference section of the local library, and checked in Glaister's *Medical Jurisprudence and Toxicology*. Three hundred grains was more than enough. Much less than an ounce. I didn't steal it all at once. Four times, and nobody missed it.

Then I stored it in an empty pill box, and hid the box at the back of my books, on a shelf in my bedroom. Then I waited.

The waiting was the worst part. I knew him to be a worrying man, and I knew the worrying brought on the indigestion and the stomach pains. Strangely, his guts seemed not to be causing him as much trouble as they had done previously. He remained the same apology for a man, but seemed not to carry his petty concerns around so heavily. Or, come to that, so obviously.

Perhaps this new wife of his was good for him. If so, she was only going to be good for him for a limited period, and I loathed both of them that little bit more for that fact. He had no *business* being content. Mother had been his wife – morally, was *still* his wife – not this giggling, empty-headed female with a ridiculous name.

In retrospect, the waiting period worked in my favour. I'd stolen the arsenic from the school lab, and the science master was more than a little lackadaisical in his checking of equipment and materials. Nevertheless, three hundred grains *had* been 'lost'. When a new supply arrived and was added to the little left in the container, I breathed more freely. I had the poison. Nobody knew I had it. And now, nobody would *ever* know I'd taken it. I was quite safe.

Thereafter, Lady Luck walked alongside me.

He came home on the Friday evening holding his middle.

'What is it, dear?' She sounded quite distressed. 'Are you ill?'

'Indigestion. That's all. I've had quite a day.'

'Should I send for the doctor.'

'No, no.' He played the part of the brave little sufferer. 'It comes on, periodically. I have some capsules the doctor gave me. I'll take them for a day or two. They always do the trick.'

I knew those capsules. They were part of the plan. As much a part as the arsenic itself.

The GP was a busy man; too busy to be forever examining a patient with recurring belly-ache. There was a 'repeat prescription' arrangement. Added to which, father was the sort of man who hoards medicines. The bathroom cabinet bulged with bottles and boxes and, amongst them, there was a fine supply of capsules from past bouts of indigestion.

He said, 'Four a day. They'll put me right.'

He went to bed early and, privately, I determined to make sure he would never get up again.

The next morning, the woman Angelica said, 'I have the weekend shopping to do. I've given your father his capsule. You're not going out, are you?'

'Later. About noon.'

'I should be back by then. He's asleep at the moment. I'll give him his second capsule when I get back.'

That left me two hours, and I didn't need two hours.

I gave her time enough to ensure she wasn't returning for something she might have forgotten, then I moved cautiously into the bedroom. He was still fast asleep. I took the bottle of capsules and returned downstairs. I spread a newspaper on the kitchen worktop, then began the substitution. I did it, one capsule at a time. Emptying the contents down the sink, under a running tap, then carefully substituting arsenic. The capsules were green, and when the two halves were replaced they looked no different from when they'd held whatever it was they'd originally held. As I filled each with arsenic I dropped it back into the bottle. There must have been forty capsules – at least forty – and I doctored every one.

Then, I returned upstairs. Father was still asleep, and I returned the bottle to the bedside table.

On an impulse – a quite imaginative brainwave – I sought, and found, the woman's work-basket. It contained reels of cotton, needles, thimbles (the usual junk) and I pulled the stuff to one side and carefully scattered the barest hint of arsenic in one corner of the silk-lined interior. Then I returned the work-basket, folded what was left of the arsenic into the sheet of newspaper, took it out into the garden, stuffed it into the fire-basket and lighted it.

When the woman, Angelica, returned she said, 'How is he?'

'The last time I looked in he was asleep.'

'Good.' She dumped her basket. 'I'd better go up. It's time he took another capsule.'

It took him all weekend to die. It was very painful and very messy. All the classic symptoms of arsenic poisoning were there. A burning pain in the stomach. Severe vomiting and diarrhoea. The fools thought it was a worse-than-usual attack of indigestion and, because it was the weekend, hesitated about sending for a doctor.

Having been up all Saturday night, on Sunday morning she said, 'He has it bad, this time.'

'Really?'

She described the night's activity, then said, 'Go up and see him, dear.'

'It wouldn't do any good.'

'No. Probably not. He doesn't like to be disturbed.' She frowned, then added, 'I think I'll double the dosage of his capsules.'

'That might help,' I agreed.

I borrowed five pounds from her, took a bus into the country and walked a little. It was a beautiful day. I enjoyed a quiet lunch at an out-of-the-way café, walked a little more, then took the bus back home.

She was in something of a panic when I walked into the house.

'He's getting worse. I'm sure he's getting worse.'

'Indigestion?' I smiled.

'He's in pain. Terrible pain.'

'The capsules have worked before,' I murmured.

'I know,' she wailed. 'He keeps asking for them, and I keep giving them to him.'

'Do you think you should call a doctor?'

The suggestion had to be made, if only for the sake of appearances.

'I keep saying so.' She sighed, heavily. 'He won't have it. He doesn't want to be a nuisance. But if he's no better tomorrow . . .'

It was a 'tomorrow' that never came.

Because he hadn't attended him, the doctor couldn't issue a death certificate. Because there wasn't a death certificate, there had to be an inquest. Because there was an inquest, there was a post mortem examination.

It was all rather like The House That Jack Built.

The pathologist found traces of arsenic. The police took possession of the remaining capsules. Later that same day the police returned and made a clinical search of the house. Among the things they took away was the work-basket.

Early next morning, they arrested the woman Angelica.

Although I was questioned, and gave the appropriate answers, I discovered that I could watch all this with complete detachment. It was, of course, what I'd planned, and it went as smooth as silk.

I found myself thinking how like the Seddon case it all was.

The same poison. The same lack of real, or obvious, motive. The same outpourings of indignation when the suspected murderer was arrested, and the same continuation of that indignation at the trial. In so many ways, a perfect parallel to the Seddon case.

Like Seddon, she was convicted.

For myself, I tried to out-do *Mrs* Seddon – and succeeded.

That fine lady (if you recall) was jointly charged, with her husband but, unlike that husband, she made herself as inconspicuous as possible. She allowed her husband to hog the limelight and, from the shadows, defied the prosecution to overturn the Presumption of Innocence. Every scrap of evidence that convicted her husband *could* have convicted her. But it didn't. Figuratively speaking, she crept from the stage, while Frederick Henry made a fool of himself, and was hanged for his trouble. She was acquitted!

I built upon Mrs Seddon's wisdom. My profile was so low, they didn't even charge me. They asked a few questions and, as was becoming in the circum-stances, I bravely fought back crocodile tears and answered quietly, but vaguely. They were satisfied.

Even the woman Angelica didn't suspect. She ranted on about 'mistakes'. She

238

raved about the incompetence of the pharmacist. She screamed abuse at the police, and accused them of cooking the evidence.

Like Seddon, she virtually convicted herself.

She was convicted, of course, and, within the first month of her prison sentence, managed to commit suicide.

For myself, I managed quite well. I could (still can) live alone, without any real difficulty. I taught myself to cook simple meals and carefully organised the housework to ensure that keeping the place moderately clean was moderately easy. I had money, of course – not a fortune, but enough – and could take an occasional meal out when I felt like it.

I congratulated myself upon a remarkably efficient removal of certain annoyances. I assure you, I didn't suffer a single bad dream, nor yet the hint of a prick of conscience.

Then, some few weeks ago, the man from the office where father had worked called. He was obviously embarrassed, as he handed me a well-sealed envelope.

'We – er – we all liked your father,' he muttered.

'Thank you.'

'He left this with us. The envelope I mean. To be given to you, in the event of the death of himself and his wife.'

'What is it?'

'I'm sorry. I don't know. Just that he asked for it to be kept, and when – *if* – you were ever left alone . . . '

His voice trailed off, miserably.

'That's very kind of you,' I smiled.

'Just that – y'know – with all the upset of the trial, and such. We thought it better to wait until you'd had time to settle down a bit.'

'That's very thoughtful of you.'

Then, he left, and I opened the envelope.

I have the letter in front of me. It's from the man I'd called 'father' all my life. He *wasn't* my father . . . and, to be honest, I wan't too surprised. A little taken aback, that I'd poisoned the wrong man, I think, but not really *shocked*. My mother had been pregnant when he'd married her. He'd 'made her respectable' – his words, not mine. So like him. So much the action of a strait-laced ninny.

Mother had told him who the father was. My *real* father, that is. But the man hadn't known he'd impregnated her. That word – 'impregnated' – was his way of putting it. He was never told.

The name of my real father was there in the letter. And his address.

I made a few enquiries. It wasn't difficult. He'd moved house, and he's now happily married. He doesn't know, of course. He doesn't know how much I hate him, how much I've already learned about him. He certainly doesn't know what's going to happen to him.

I went up to London for the day. Talked to people in the offices of Macmillan Publishers. Convinced them that I had the germ of an idea for a short crime

239

story. They agreed to read it, to 'consider' it. Publish it, if it was good enough.

This is it. You've just read it. My father – my *real* father – likes anthologies of crime stories. That's something else I learned about him.

Hopefully, he'll read this anthology – read this story – then he'll know . . . won't he?

THE MAN FROM THE WHITE MOUNTAINS

by *Ted Willis*

In one sense, of course, murder may be measured in moments. It takes only a split second after the squeezing of a trigger for a bullet to enter the brain or the heart, and only a fraction longer for a knife to slice into the soft flesh of the throat or penetrate a breast.

But to say this is to say little or nothing, the equivalent of asserting that love is no more than the fleeting moment of sexual climax.

A murderer – and, for that matter, his victim – is not made in a moment. He is the product of a long process, a combination of genes, background, upbringing, circumstances; in short, of his or her entire life. Luck can also play a vital part. There are many people, living innocent, respectable lives, who, in certain conditions, could and would commit murder, but who probably never will. It is their good fortune to escape the sequence of events which could drive them to kill. Others are not so lucky.

If, for example, we are to understand why a man called Marcos Kolomenos committed murder in Adelaide, South Australia, on March 17, 1972, it will be necessary to go back over forty years in time. The actual crime took only a few seconds, its preparation was a matter of careful planning over a period of months. But the seed of murder was planted in Marcos Kolomenos many years before, and ten thousand miles away, in the high White Mountains of Sphakia, to the west of the island of Crete.

It was there in the tiny village of Nigrita, on October 8, 1931, that a married woman named Lilika Kollias was taken, with her lover, in the act of adultery.

In accordance with the age-old custom of the mountain people, the woman was driven from the village with stones and left to fend for herself. In the weeks which followed she was seen from time to time on the outskirts of the village, a pathetic, starving, half-mad creature, trying desperately to get a glimpse of her children. No one spoke to her, no one fed her, no one lifted a little finger to help her. Eventually she was seen no more, but it was strongly rumoured that she had found her way to Athens and was working there in a hundred-drachma whore-house.

The man, Angelos, with whom she had sinned was left, according to custom, to the mercy of the husband and the brothers of the husband. For such a man castration was normally considered to be an apt punishment, but there was a complication. Angelos was a relative of the husband, a first cousin on the maternal side, and this made his betrayal of the unwritten code all the more serious.

The husband and the brothers sought the advice of Stavros Kontas, the oldest and wisest man in Nigrita. It was, after all, a question of the honour of the family. Stavros had to think for a long time and search his memory before he could give them an answer, for the problem was an unusual one. In his long life-time there had only been two instances of adultery in Nigrita, and since relatives were not involved, the customary punishment had been meted out. Expulsion for the woman, castration for the man.

And then Stavros remembered that his grandfather had once told him of a case in which a wife had betrayed her husband with his own brother. In such severe circumstances, the code decreed that the man should be put to death. It was a savage and primitive judgement but some deep instinct, centuries old, told the people that without such strict moral sanctions their isolated communities would degenerate and perish.

The following morning, as the sun was rising, Angelos was taken from the village into the mountains. He was stripped naked and while the three brothers held him, the husband castrated him. He was still screaming in agony as they carried him to a ledge and threw him on to the rocks eight hundred feet below. Then the husband broke Angelos' knife on a rock and threw the pieces after him. They left the body for twenty-four hours and then covered it with stones.

Marcos Kolomenos was five years old at this time. He heard the outcry in the village when the lovers were first discovered, and he realised from the behaviour of his elders that something of great importance and seriousness had taken place. Although he had been ordered to remain indoors, he crept out and from a discreet hiding-place watched the grim-faced women, his own mother among them, as they stoned Lilika Kollias and drove her away. He was appalled, yet excited by this strange game.

The next morning he saw four men leave the village with a fifth man, whose arms were tied behind his back. He recognised this man as Angelos, a person whom he had always admired. Angelos was tall and handsome, with white flashing teeth and a fierce, manly expression. At first, Marcos had been afraid of him, but once Angelos had carried him on his shoulders up into the mountains for a long, long way and shown him the hidden entrance to a wonderful, secret cave; and on another occasion Angelos had made him a wooden knife, shaped just like the sharp, steel knife he carried in his own belt.

Marcos wondered what his friend had done to have his hands tied thus, and why he was being taken away. He wanted to call out to him but he was too frightened to do so. He was puzzled to see that Angelos was wearing his best clothes, just as though it were a Sunday or a feast-day, and to see the knife with its decorated handle in his belt. Angelos walked proudly, with his head high, looking neither to left nor right and Marcos watched until he was out of sight.

Marcos never saw Angelos again, but the incidents made a deep impression upon him. His life changed with the years, he became a different person, but there were times when the memory of Lilika and her lover echoed and surged in him like the sound of distant bells. Whenever he saw a man carrying a small boy on his shoulders, he would remember his friend. At such moments he imagined

242

that he could smell, across the years, the strong, masculine scent – a blend of wine and old leather – which was his first experience of Angelos.

It wasn't until he was twelve years old that the full significance of what had happened was revealed to him. He did not question the judgement or the sentence. Both were just, they followed naturally from the unwritten code of the Cretan mountain people.

It was, after all, a simple question. Every man had the right and the duty to defend his honour. If he failed to do so he betrayed not only a code which had lasted a thousand years, but himself. Such a man was not fit to live.

In May, 1941, when Marcos Kolomenos was almost fifteen years of age, the Germans carried out a massive airborne invasion of the island and succeeded in occupying the main towns and the coastal plains. But the Cretans, helped by remnants of the British army, retreated to the mountains and carried on the resistance. The Germans turned in fury against village after village, but they were never able to break the spirit of a people for whom honour was more important than life.

This was a crucial time for Marcos. In a few weeks, even a few days, he became a man; with his father and his uncles, he joined the partisan forces. He saw many of his comrades die, and there were times when death brushed his own shoulder. He learned the art of survival the hard way. Older men came to admire and respect not his courage, for that in a Cretan was taken for granted, but his cunning, resourcefulness and adaptability.

He learned, also, that there was another world beyond the White Mountains and his village. He became friends with an Australian sergeant, a former schoolmaster, and in the long intervals between engagements the sergeant taught Marcos English and the elements of arithmetic. He talked to him for hours of other lands and other peoples, but most of all, he spoke of his native Australia, holding the boy fascinated with his tales of that immense brown country. By a strange coincidence, they spent most of their time together in the big, secret cave which Angelos had shown Marcos years before.

'When the war is over, you must leave,' the sergeant told Marcos. 'There is nothing for you here. Australia is the world's last frontier, it's a young man's country. You could make your mark there.' He said it time and time again.

The idea of leaving Crete shocked and frightened Marcos at first. He could not imagine himself living in any other place. In the event, it was the Germans who, inadvertently, settled the issue for him.

His mother was caught by an enemy patrol in the act of smuggling ammunition to the Resistance. She was stripped naked and hanged on a gallows in the village square as a deterrent to any others who might be tempted to follow her example.

The death of his wife changed Marcos' father. Normally a careful, slow-thinking man, he allowed anger and grief to overcome caution. At noon one day he went down to the nearest town with a British Sten gun concealed under his cloak. He sat on a bench in the little square and waited in the hot sun until a detachment of German soldiers came marching by on the way to the local barracks; then, quite calmly, he opened fire. Fourteen of the enemy were killed and seven wounded before the father was himself cut down.

From that point onwards, his comrades noted a new depth of ruthlessness in Marcos. It was as though all human pity had been drained from his soul. He rarely took prisoners, and those few enemy soldiers who did fall into his hands longed for death.

When the war was over, there was nothing to keep him in Crete. He had a brother, Alexander, who was seventeen years his junior, but there was no one else towards whom he felt any responsibility. In March, 1946, at the age of twenty, he emigrated to Australia. He left Alex with an aunt, promising to send for him as soon as he had settled in the new land.

He was still only twenty years of age, but he had the look and bearing of a man fifteen years older.

Marcos settled in South Australia, near the city of Adelaide, at a place called Paradise. The name appealed to him. But for the first year, his life was something less than Elysian.

He was employed as a labourer by a farmer named George Smith, a harsh, humourless man, who had a contempt for 'New Australians' and regarded them as a source of cheap labour. He worked Marcos as one would work an ox, housed and fed him little better than an animal. The young Cretan seemed to accept this patiently, even willingly; but underneath the resignation his spirit glowed fiercely, waiting like a fire which has been momentarily dampened but remains unquenched.

During those twelve months Marcos learned another valuable lesson – that patience can also be a weapon, that there are times when a man must simply wait and watch and learn. He perfected his knowledge of English (though he never completely lost his accent or the Cretan rhythm of speech) and he took the measure of this country in which he had decided to make his home. He saw that it was, indeed, a land of opportunity, and he knew, after only three months, that he could and would succeed there. This inner knowledge fortified him as the days of back-breaking labour passed; he had no doubts, his self-confidence was complete.

Quite suddenly, one morning, he decided he was ready. He had been into Adelaide the day before and seen the opportunity for which he had been waiting. He packed his few belongings, told Smith that he was leaving immediately and waited for the reaction. He did not wish to go quietly, he had a debt to pay and he was hoping that the farmer would give him an honourable opportunity to settle it. He was not disappointed. Smith began to rant and rave, piling the old familiar insults one on the other. He was a heavy man of formidable strength, but Marcos was confident.

He dropped his worldly possessions to the ground, stripped off his shirt and faced the astonished Smith. His right fist thudded into the farmer's beer-ripened belly, and as the big man gasped in anguish and doubled-up, Marcos linked his hands together and chopped down with pulverising force on Smith's neck. Smith fell to the ground, tried desperately to raise himself, and rolled over on his back. Marcos was angry that it had been so swift and easy a victory. He felt cheated of his revenge. He looked down at the farmer and, for a moment, he felt himself back in the White Mountains, standing over a fallen enemy, his hand reaching automatically for the knife in his belt. Smith must have read the intent in the Cretan's face, for he rolled his blue eyes imploringly and cried in fear, 'No, Marcos, no! No, no!'

Marcos steadied himself. He was not in Sphakia, there was no knife in his belt, the blubbering man at his feet was not a Nazi. He lifted a heavy boot and Smith whimpered in fear, then screamed as the boot crunched home. Marcos gave a grunt of contempt and spat at Smith; the spittle rolled slowly down the farmer's cheek, but he did not attempt to wipe it away.

Mrs Smith, a thin, scrawny woman in a shapeless dress, stood watching the scene from the homestead, her face like a sallow moon in the dark shade of the verandah. She made no move towards her husband, her eyes looked at Marcos without expression.

He picked up his things and walked away from Paradise without regret, and without once looking back.

The first thing Marcos did after this was to buy himself a hole in the ground. It was about two miles from the centre of Adelaide, a stretch of derelict and neglected earth, just over an acre in size, almost entirely made up of this huge, yawning hole. He bought the site for £90, which was half of what he had saved, and the man who sold it to him thought he was mad. But Marcos had seen, with the fresh eyes of a stranger, that Adelaide was growing, and that trucks, loaded with rubble from the demolition of old buildings, were being driven each day to tips on the city outskirts. He posted a notice inviting the demolition companies to dump their rubble on his site. Since, by so doing, the companies saved themselves time and mileage, they were quite happy to pay Marcos the nominal charge of £1 per truck-load which he imposed.

Within six months the hole was full and the site more or less levelled. Marcos sold it to a developer for £2,500, and with most of this capital he bought a half-share in a small building and construction company. His partner was Andy Byers, a small, genial, happy-go-lucky Australian who knew a great deal about building but very little about business. Marcos waited again, learning all he could from Byers, and at the end of two years he bought him out. Byers was drunk when he signed the contract of sale and on the following morning his wife tried to get Marcos to tear it up. He listened without emotion to her frantic pleading.

'Your husband is a good bricklayer, Mrs Byers,' he said. 'If he wishes to come back and work for me as a bricklayer, I will find him a place. But the business is mine. From now on, it is mine, please understand this.'

'You cheated him!' she screamed. 'He didn't know what he was doing, he was drunk. You made him drunk.'

'He has no head for drink and no head for business,' said Marcos calmly. 'Take my advice. Keep him away from both these things.'

A few months later, when he had run through his money, Andy Byers

245

swallowed his pride and came back to Marcos for a job. He was made foreman-bricklayer on a big new development in the suburb of Springfield, a position which he accepted gratefully and humbly, and in which he served Marcos well.

It gave Marcos no satisfaction to take back his old partner on these terms. He valued pride in a man above all things, and the servile attitude of Byers offended him. Whenever they met – something he tried to avoid – Marcos found it difficult to conceal his contempt.

Shortly after taking over the construction firm Marcos Kolomenos changed his name to Mark Coleman. It was a difficult step to take, and one which he regretted, but he decided that it was essential to the success of the business. In any case, this was his country now, he knew he could never go back to the old life in Crete. When he had lived the statutory five years in Australia, he applied for and was granted naturalisation. He felt a surge of pride as he swore the oath of allegiance to the Queen and to his new country. He had left his old life behind forever, he was now an Australian, a man of substance.

In 1955 he built himself a new, modern house in Springfield, and sent for his younger brother, Alex, and his aunt, Amalia. He longed for their arrival, he wanted to have his own family around him, to show them what he had achieved. He had no interests outside the business, his one concession to his own nature was a weekly visit to a brothel in the port area of the town; but these cold encounters only served to sharpen his growing feeling of loneliness.

In the event, Aunt Amalia refused to leave Crete, and Alex, now a sturdy lad of twelve, travelled to Adelaide alone. He knew little or nothing of life outside Nigrita and the White Mountains and he was astonished by the sophistication and luxury which he saw around him. Most of all, he was enthralled by his brother, who seemed to be so much a part of this new environment, to be so confident, rich and successful. The house, the car, his bedroom with its own bathroom – the sheer space, the grandeur of it all took his breath away, it was like a dream.

But it wasn't a dream, it was astonishingly real. On that first evening Marcos said: 'All this is ours, Alex. Yours and mine. And believe me, it is only the beginning.'

Only the beginning? Alex was amazed. What could be better than this, how could a man want or have more? But he said nothing, only watched his brother with big, dark, wondering eyes.

'You will become an Australian like me,' Marcos continued. 'First, you will learn to speak the language. I've arranged all that. Then school, real school. And after that, university.' He spoke proudly.

'University?' It was a new word to Alex, he had never heard it before.

'You are tired. We will speak of it tomorrow – we shall have time enough to talk.' At the door, Marcos paused and looked back at his brother. 'Alex. Do you know what a millionaire is?'

'A rich man?'

'A very rich man. Like Onassis. I am going to be a millionaire, that is my plan. I shall achieve this in ten years.'

'Why do you want this?'

'Because it is important. Money is important.'

'But in this country it seems to me that everyone has money.'

'Not everyone. You will learn that. And it is the same here as it is back home. The rich give the orders and the poor obey. The greater the riches, the greater the power.' He moved in closer to the boy and put a hand on his shoulder. 'This is the way I see it, Alex. Our mother and our father did not die so that we should live for the rest of our lives taking orders from other people. I did not fight in the mountains for that either. Do you understand?'

Alex nodded, although he did not properly follow what Marcos was saying.

'The important thing is that you are now with me. We shall do well together.' Marcos embraced his brother and kissed him in the Cretan style. The boy was very near to tears but he held them back, knowing that it was unmanly to weep and that Marcos would not approve such weakness.

Marcos was as good as and better than his word. These were the lush, plush years when half the world seemed to be set on a course of endless growth, and whole nations nourished themselves on greed. Money made money and more money; the quick-witted and the corrupt fattened themselves on their easy killings. It was a time tailor-made for Marcos, a time for which all his background and experience had prepared him.

Within ten years he had expanded into real estate and mineral development; he had extensive interests in the wine districts of the Barossa Valley, he owned a television station in Adelaide, two radio stations in the country, and he was a major shareholder in several newspapers and leading industrial companies. He was a millionaire three times over, a powerful and influential figure, to whose views politicians and businessmen listened with respect, and even fear. Such was his reputation that he figured prominently in news stories and press cartoons; one satirical television programme (not on his own station) lampooned him at regular intervals.

This programme was to play an important part in later events.

What his critics did not understand was that Marcos seemed to take no joy from his success, no satisfaction from his conquests. Though few doors were closed to him, he found no pleasure in social life; he remained an enigma, a grim, solitary person for whom there was no existence outside his business. His one relaxation was an occasional weekend flight in his private plane to a small station he owned near Townsville, in North Queensland; but even on these occasions he took his working papers with him, and he was invariably alone.

This weekend hide-out was also destined to feature prominently in the unfolding pattern of the drama that was to come.

The force that continued to drive Marcos forward was disappointment. As Alex grew older it became clear that he shared none of his brother's character or ambition. The simple truth was that he had been spoiled. Marcos had pampered the boy, giving him all he asked – and more – without question. Content to enjoy the fruits of the harvest, Alex gave nothing in return. He became notorious as a rich dilettante who was only protected from the consequences of his irresponsibility by the power and influence of his older brother. He developed artistic and literary pretensions, and openly mocked Marcos, making no secret of the fact that he regarded him as an uncultured moron whose horizons were bounded by balance-sheets. He returned cynicism for affection, coldness for warmth. The two men reached a point where they could hardly exchange a civil word and Alex left home.

Marcos continued to pay him an allowance, for to do otherwise would have been to deny his own roots. He was the eldest brother, he was still responsible. But beyond this there was nothing, only the business, into which he sank his energy and his bitter sense of loss.

And then fate or luck (aren't they, after all, the same thing?) made the final move in its long, remorseless build-up to inevitable tragedy.

It was as though Kristina Ayres had been kept waiting in the wings until the stage was set, and the other protagonists in position.

Marcos met her at one of his rare social engagements, a dinner party given by the Premier of South Australia to honour a group of visiting businessmen. The hostess paired her with Marcos and within a few minutes he was completely captivated by his dark-haired, vivacious and beautiful partner.

'Kristina?' he asked. 'It is a Greek name. Are you Greek?'

'I am Australian,' she answered with a smile. 'My father was English and mother Greek. I am called after her.'

He nodded with approval. Throughout the evening he watched her, noting her poise and sophistication, her humour and bright intelligence; above all, the odd, shy moments of innocence which showed in her big, dark expressive eyes. For the first time he felt his own lack of the social graces, his awkwardness. In her presence he felt like a thick-fingered peasant.

In a sense, it was for him a rebound from the crushing disappointment he had experienced with Alex. He needed someone as the centrepiece of his life, someone to show off his glittering wealth and thus give it purpose and meaning. And there was something more. She could give him a replacement for Alex, she could give him children, the sons he yearned for. Alex had been a sort of son, but that was ended, Marcos could take no pride in his brother. But with Kristina he could be proud again; to possess such a woman would make him the envy of other men, she would be a magnificent confirmation of his success and position.

What he felt for her could hardly be described as love, though he admired her body and desired to take her. It was as though he had seen something of extraordinary beauty and value in a shop-window and was desperate to own it. But this was the man he had become and he could think in no other terms. It was the nearest approach he could make to the concept of love; sadly he knew no other way.

For weeks he laid siege to her, bombarding her with invitations and presents. She liked him, he amused her, and she was flattered to be courted by such a rich and famous man. And she was intrigued to find that, unlike other men, he made no sexual advances, there was no attempt to get her into bed. There were times when she wanted this herself, for she found him physically attractive; and she felt that only in this way, naked and in the act of love, would she discover the true Marcos, the man behind the image. But she held back, sensing that this would cheapen her in his eyes, that she was, in a sense, on trial.

Day by day, she saw herself coming more and more under the spell of his forceful personality. He wanted her, he was determined to have her, and any obstacles she erected were swept aside like so much chaff. He surrounded her, overwhelmed her, and she was helpless to resist.

They were married on August 2, 1970, a wedding of such magnificence that it made headlines in all the newspapers and was featured on television. Alex attended the reception, even putting on a suit for the occasion, and met Kristina for the first time.

'So you are his latest possession,' he said mockingly. 'Not bad, not bad. I've known him make worse bargains.'

She turned away from him in anger and distress, but she was to remember the words later, when the bitter truth they carried was stamped into her consciousness. Perhaps, in her heart, she had recognised some part of this truth from the beginning.

For truth it was. She was deeply fond of Marcos, she admired and respected him, and she told herself that this was enough, that she could build on this foundation and draw from him the response which would make her truly love him.

But it was a response of which he was incapable. He was generous and affectionate, proud of her, but that was all. She was, indeed, a possession, treasured as such and treated as such. And if the possession, at times, tried to assert her own individuality, to move beyond the mechanical role allotted to her, he rode over her with a ruthlessness which was frightening.

There was warmth between them, at least during the first year, but little tenderness. In bed, any veneer of sensitivity which he had acquired was left outside the sheets with his clothes; he coupled her as he had coupled the girls in the brothel, as though it was his right to do so, and he was only collecting what he had paid for. It was then that she felt most strongly that to him she was an ornament, an object, a possession.

Many women have suffered as much or more and have come to terms with their lives, content to accept half a loaf. It is possible that Kristina would have followed this path, for she was by nature an honest person with a strong dislike of intrigue or of anything that smacked of the underhand. Had she met and fallen in love with a stranger, her first instinct would have been to face Marcos with the fact, and to brave his inevitable wrath.

But almost inevitably, the man who came into her life was Alex. He began to call at the big house in Springfield again, it seemed that he was prepared to make some sort of peace with Marcos. Kristina was forced to amend her first impression of Alex; as time went on she found his company amusing and relaxing. Marcos was pleased that this should be so and encouraged them to see more of each other; it relieved him of certain social duties which he found irksome.

He liked to see them laughing happily together, like children. In a way, that was how he looked upon them both. The change in Alex made him happy also; for the first time in months he began to feel something of the old warmth for his younger brother.

This was a time of deep content for Marcos. His business affairs were thriving, there was some talk that he might be recommended for a knighthood; his marriage, though not perfect, seemed to have settled into a secure pattern, and Alex was once more back in the family circle. The one disappointment was that Kristina had so far failed to produce the sons he wanted, but there was time for that, he told himself.

The contentment did not last long. One evening, working in his study on the first floor, he happened quite by chance to get up and look out of the window towards the large flood-lit swimming-pool. He smiled as he saw Alex and Kristina sporting together in the blue water, and he felt a touch of envy also. Kristina was seldom as relaxed and carefree with him. Perhaps it was his fault? He used the pool for exercise only, grimly swimming a statutory ten lengths each morning; to him it was a tool, useful for toning the muscles, not a playground.

The trouble was that he had gone from boyhood to manhood in one step. He had missed his youth – the best time of all. He was forty-five years of age, almost old enough to be their father – and at that moment, he felt the weight of the years that separated them. He would try to relax more. There was the yacht, moored in the harbour, idle for most of the year. He would take time off, he would take Kristina and Alex away for a long cruise, he would show them that he, too, knew how to enjoy life.

It was then that the incident occurred.

Alex was helping Kristina from the pool, pulling her up out of the water. He could see them clearly in the amber light, their bodies striking long shadows on the paved surface behind them. As Kristina straightened up, she stood close to Alex, and he put up a hand and held it against her cheek. It was more than a gesture, it was a caress as intimate and full of meaning as if he had touched her breast. They stood there motionless for a moment, not smiling, simply looking into each other's eyes, his hand still resting gently on her cheek. Then she pulled away abruptly and threw a warning look towards the house.

It was no more than that, a small, trivial thing. But watching them, Marcos felt a sudden, inexplicable apprehension of danger, manifested as in the old partisan days in the mountains, by a chill stiffening of his neck and spine.

He tried to set the thought aside, telling himself that the gesture was no more than a sign of friendship, that they were children, that it meant nothing, but it was useless. Fear and suspicion filled his mind, spreading like a virus in the bloodstream. He dared not watch Kristina too closely, lest she in turn should suspect, but as the days passed his torment grew. He feared to learn the truth but he knew that without it he would find no peace of mind.

At the end of a week, he hired a private detective agency to keep observation on his wife and Alex. They came back in five days with their report. She had visited Alex in his studio-apartment in South Adelaide three times during that period, and each visit had lasted for two hours or more. On one of those occasions she had told Marcos that she was visiting her dressmaker; and on another that she had driven up to Elizabeth to visit a girl-friend.

He put the issue to a further test. That weekend he flew up to the house in Queensland on one of his regular visits. On his return, a new report awaited him. Kristina visited Alex at his apartment on the Saturday evening. They went out to dinner and then returned to his place. She left him at 5 a.m. the next morning.

Marcos paid off the detective and dismissed him. His instinct had proved to be right – Kristina had lied to him, she was deceiving him with Alex, his own brother.

He instructed his secretary to block all calls and cancel his appointments. He was surprised at his own outward calmness; in that sense, at least, the truth had brought a certain peace. It was only later, as he sat at the big desk, with the light fading behind him, that the anger and bitterness crowded in on him. From that moment on, it could be said that the balance of his mind was disturbed, that he ceased to be a rational person.

Or perhaps it would be more accurate to say that Mark Coleman became more truly himself, the new Australian became once again the old Cretan, Marcos Kolomenos. Centuries of history, age-old instincts and concepts of honour stirred in his blood. He remembered Angelos and Lilika, he saw again as in a film, his own mother as she hurled a stone at the guilty woman, he saw Angelos being led from the village. The sharp scent of leather and wine came back to him across the years.

But this was not Sphakia, he knew that; there vengeance could be simple and direct, everyone would expect him to redeem his honour, they would see it as something obvious and inevitable, as natural as breathing. It was different in this new land; here they would not understand his motives; quite simply they would call it murder and instead of being honoured for the deed he would be hunted down as if he were the guilty party.

It would have to be done, there was no question about that, but it would have to be done in a different way. For why should he suffer, why should he throw away all he had worked for and achieved? He had done nothing wrong, he had been a faithful husband and brother. It was they, Kristina and Alex, who had brought dishonour to the family, not he.

And now all the sharp cunning and talent for organisation which Marcos had acquired over the years came to his aid. When he left the office it was quite dark, but the main outline of a plan was already clear in his mind.

It was not until one weekend, almost three months later, when all the pieces were in position, that he began to put the plan into operation.

It was nothing new for Marcos to fly to Queensland to spend a weekend alone with his papers, but Kristina was worried, on edge. During the past few weeks she had sensed a new tension in her husband and it frightened her. There was nothing she could put a finger on, no positive evidence; it was simply that he seemed to be burning with some secret, inner fierceness.

Nino and Faustina Silone, the Italian couple who looked after them, had gone to Melbourne and would not be back until Monday. There was nothing unusual in that, they had relations there whom they visited regularly, but their absence added to Kristina's foreboding. Even the air was heavy and oppressive, it weighed on her skin, as though warning that a storm was about to break. At least, it seemed so to her.

Alex laughed at her fears. He saw in the absence of Marcos and the servants a wonderful opportunity for them to be together. He wanted to spend the night with Kristina in the house, under his brother's roof: the thought of it gave him a peculiar satisfaction.

'Oh, come on, Kris,' he said petulantly. 'What's wrong?'

'I don't know. I wish I did. It's just this feeling. I can't explain it.' She moved around restlessly. 'It's just – just that it is all too convenient. I mean – Marcos has a cold, a terrible cold, but he insisted on going. And then there's Nino and Faustina – they offered to cancel their trip, but he insisted they should go. He has been strange lately, Alex, he really has. I'm not imagining that.'

'You are! It's all in your mind!' Her attitude was making him irritable. 'Look, the main thing is – did he go or didn't he?'

'Yes,' she said listlessly. 'He left here at nine o'clock this morning.'

'Well, then!' he said as though that settled it. He tried to take her in his arms, but she eluded him with a frown.

'Yesterday,' she said thoughtfully, as though Alex hadn't spoken. 'Yesterday I was checking my make-up in the bedroom. Marcos came in, and I caught a glimpse of him in the mirror. It was only a flash, a moment, but the look in his eyes – it was terrible, Alex. I can't describe it – hate, madness, despair – all those things, but mainly hate.'

'Why should he suddenly hate you?'

'It could only be for one reason.'

'No,' he said firmly. 'Now you are imagining things. He trusts us. He goes out of his way to throw us together. This weekend is an example. He wouldn't go away if he suspected anything. Why, he even asked me to keep an eye on you! Which, of course, I said I would do with pleasure.'

He kissed her, but her response was cool. 'OK,' he said angrily, 'OK. If that's how it's going to be, there's not much point in my staying!' He moved to the door, and she made no effort to stop him. 'Listen,' he said, from the doorway, 'is that place in Queensland on the telephone?'

'Of course.'

'Then ring Marcos. Put your mind at rest. Speak to him. Find out once and for all if he is there.'

'What shall I say?'

'God, you're his wife. Ask him about his cold – say you're worried – anything.' He went to the phone and picked it up. 'What's the number?'

'Greenvale, North Queensland 274. Area Code 032.'

He dialled the operator, gave her the area code and number, and asked for a personal call to Mr Mark Coleman. She took the phone from him, and he kissed her lightly on the cheek. 'Don't be frightened,' he said.

Relief showed in her eyes as she heard Marcos answer. She nodded towards Alex, who spread his hands as if to say, 'I told you so.'

'Marcos, it's Kristina. I – I just thought I'd ring to find how you were feeling. How's the cold?'

'It's much the same,' he answered abruptly. She could hear the slight hoarseness in his voice. 'Is everything all right at your end?' he continued.

'Yes, oh, yes. I was only concerned about you.'

'There is no need. I'm not going to die. I shall be back tomorrow as arranged. Goodbye.' There was a note of irritation in his tone.

She put the telephone down slowly. 'Yes,' she said, 'he's there. He's there, all right. His usual polite courteous self.' She went to Alex. 'Come on, let's go to bed.'

She spoke with bitterness, it was as if the need to spite Marcos was uppermost in her mind. They went up to the main bedroom.

She found little enjoyment in their love-making. She felt ill-at-ease lying in the bed which she had so often shared with Marcos and regretted the bitter impulse which had led her to take Alex there. And there was something in his attitude which disturbed her. He had taken her fiercely, swiftly, and when it was over he lay back smiling as though in triumph.

'That was the best ever,' he said with a deep sigh, 'the best ever. Great! In this bed, in this room! Great!'

'In his room, in his bed. Isn't that what you mean?'

'You've got to admit, it adds an edge to the situation. A certain flavour.'

There was a smugness in his voice which angered her. A sense of disgust, as much for herself as for him, rose in her throat like bile. She got out of bed and put on a robe.

'Oh, stay here, Kris,' he pleaded and his voice sounded like that of a spoiled child. 'Come back to bed.'

'Alex,' she said quietly, 'when Marcos comes back, I am going to tell him.'

'Oh, yes,' he said with a smile, 'I can just see you doing that.'

'I mean it. I shall tell him everything, and then I shall leave him.'

'You're out of your mind!' He sat up in the bed. 'You don't know Marcos. He won't just sit back and accept it. Kristina, come back to bed and don't be foolish.'

'Alex,' she said quietly, 'what is more important to you? Your love of me or your hatred of your brother?'

'What the hell are you talking about? Kris, for heaven's sake, what's wrong?'

'Nothing. Only, perhaps, that I don't like being used.'

'Used?'

'By Marcos. And by you against Marcos. Because that's what you've been doing, isn't it? Oh, I daresay you love me well enough in your spoiled, little-boy

253

way, but that's not really what drives you, is it? You're using me to get back at Marcos. I'm just a—'

She stopped suddenly, holding her breath, listening. 'What was that?' she whispered.

'What?'

'I heard something. A door. Someone's in the house, Alex.'

'Oh, rubbish!' he said. But fear showed in his eyes and he rose from the bed quickly, reaching for his clothes.

'Listen! Listen!' she said urgently. He paused in the act of pulling on his shirt. Nothing at first, no sound, and then they heard it; the quiet, measured tread of someone mounting the stairs. Each step seemed to crack the silence like a footfall on ice.

Alex scrambled in panic for his jeans. 'Help me, help me, for Christ's sake!' he croaked. But Kristina was standing still and calm, as though she had anticipated this moment and was almost relieved that it had come.

The sounds stopped outside the door. A century passed, and then the handle began to turn. Alex, holding his jeans around his waist, his shirt flapping, snatched up the rest of his clothes and rushed for the bathroom, as the door opened.

'Marcos!' said Kristina, trying to keep the fear out of her voice. 'What is going on? I thought you were in Greenvale – I spoke to you on the phone only a half-hour ago. What are you up to?'

He looked at her in contempt and past her with the same contempt to the soiled and rumpled bed. His dark eyes glowed, he was breathing heavily; she caught in her nostrils a sour scent, as of an animal, and then he hit her. She cried out and fell across the bed. He looked down at her for a moment.

'Whore!' He ground out the word from behind his clenched white teeth.

'Marcos, please,' she whispered. 'Let me explain.'

'Explain? How do you explain this? And this?' He ripped the robe from her shoulder, tearing it to the waist; he plucked the blue sheet from the bed and tore at it with his great hands as though it were tissue. As he did so he kept repeating: 'Whore! Whore! Whore!'

He pulled her up, hit her again, and caught her as she fell unconscious into his arms.

In the darkness that surrounded her, Kristina heard the shot. It seemed to come from a long way off, and it took her a full minute to work out what it could be. She opened her eyes and saw that she was in one of the spare rooms. The full realisation of what had happened came as she looked at her tattered robe. She struggled painfully to her feet and stumbled to the door. It was locked on the outside; she wrenched at the handle, hammered feebly on the door-panels.

Quite suddenly it opened and she saw Marcos standing there. He seemed very calm now and when he put a hand on her arm his touch was gentle. She dimly registered the fact that he was wearing gloves.

'Now, Kristina,' he said evenly. 'Let us talk together for a moment or two.'

'Alex,' she said hoarsely, 'where is Alex?'

'Alex and I have reached an understanding,' he said, smiling. 'It was quite simple really. I offered him fifty thousand dollars if he would clear off. He stuck out for double, and I agreed. After all, he is my brother. He left you a farewell note.'

Still dazed, she took the piece of paper he held out to her. 'Dear Kris,' she read, 'It is impossible for us to go on like this, so for your sake, I am doing the only thing possible in the circumstances. Please understand, and try to forget me. Goodbye, darling.' It was signed *Alex* and she knew that it was his handwriting.

'No, no,' she moaned, 'it isn't possible.' Her head cleared suddenly and she remembered the shot; pushing past Marcos, she ran to the bedroom. The door was open, the bitter smell of gun-fire hung in the air, and Alex was lying on the floor at the foot of the bed. There was a spreading crimson stain on the white carpet and half his face and head was missing. She turned on Marcos in horror and began to beat at him with her clenched fists, but he held her easily.

'I wasn't lying, Kristina,' he said. 'I told you the truth. He agreed to take a hundred thousand dollars and go to South America. That was your price. That was how much he loved you. He was a coward, he was a cheat. He had no true feeling for you.'

She wrenched herself free and ran like a mad thing, trying to reach the telephone at the side of the bed, but he was too quick for her. She stared past him towards the body; he took her chin and pulled her face close to his own. A trickle of sweat ran down his cheek.

'It had to be done, Kristina!' he shouted. 'Listen to me, listen! He should have respected and cherished you as a sister, as if you were of the same seed. Instead, he lay with you, he took you into my bed, he did this – this – dirty thing with you. He had to die, there was no other way.'

'They'll hang you!' she cried. 'They'll hang you or lock you up in a cell for the rest of your life!'

'Oh, no!' he said smoothly. 'That is not the way I have planned it. You see, I am not here. Have you forgotten so soon? You spoke to me on the telephone. I am in Queensland.'

'Who was that? Who did I speak to?'

'An actor. A drunken out-of-work actor. Very good at impersonation. He took me off several times on TV – do you remember? He is in my debt – and we agreed that this would be a good way to pay it off. Please Kristina, you surely know me by now. I like to organise things properly, thoroughly. You think I am standing here – but I am not. It is an illusion.' He glanced at his watch. 'As a matter of fact, at this moment, I am on my way into Greenvale to collect some supplies. I shall be seen by several people – it is what they call establishing an alibi, I believe.'

'They know you up there! They'll know it isn't you.'

'You under-estimate the acting ability of my friend. He really is very good. I took care to put on a cold to help him with the voice. As for the locals – well –

they know I prefer to be alone. On my recent visits I've taken care to develop a reputation for surliness. Oh, I have no fears about that part of it, Kristina.'

She remembered the actor now although she couldn't put a name to him. His impersonation of Marcos on TV had been stunningly convincing, he had got the voice and the mannerisms exactly right. And he had managed to look so much like Marcos.

'The pilot!' she said suddenly. 'He knows you too well! You couldn't fool him!'

'Lockstey? Oh, he wasn't on duty today. He's on leave. I hired a temporary pilot. I went to the airport this morning. I met my actor friend in the gentlemen's lavatory, I gave him my coat and bag, and he took off in the plane while I stayed behind. All he had to do was pick up the car I keep at the Townsville airfield and drive to the house. He'll look after himself there as I always do. Tomorrow he'll drive back to Townsville, and take the plane back. I'll meet him as before, he'll hand back my identity and then disappear.'

'Suppose he decides to talk?'

'He won't,' he said blithely. 'I have, shall we say, strong reasons for believing that.'

'You blackmailed him!'

'It's a word. I prefer to think I persuaded him. So there you are, Kristina. It took weeks to perfect, but it was worth it. A good plan – I'm rather proud of it.'

'You haven't yet told me how I fit into it,' she said. 'I'm sure you can't have overlooked that.'

'Oh, not at all. The – what is the word they use? – scenario. The scenario runs as follows. You and Alex have been having an affair. You are madly in love with each other. Alex, my dear brother, is overcome by conscience. He feels that he can no longer go on betraying me. This fit of remorse comes upon him after he has made love to you in this room on his brother's bed. He tells you that the affair must be broken off. You argue, even fight – that will explain those bruises on your face. But you make up – and then go downstairs. He takes a sheet of paper from the drawer – there – a sheet of my paper and writes you a farewell letter.' He held up the note. 'It isn't a forgery, he really did write it – to my dictation. He thought it was a ticket to freedom and a hundred thousand dollars. To catch a jackal it is necessary to bait the trap, you understand. So – to continue – he writes this letter, then he takes your pistol from another drawer, and blows his brains out. Yes, it is your pistol, Kristina – the snake-pistol I bought you two years ago.'

He took it from his pocket and weighed it in his gloved hand.

'Then what happens?' he continued. 'Isn't it obvious? You hear the shot and come running upstairs. You see your dead lover, you read the note. You are overcome, you cannot bear the thought of life without him so you turn the pistol on yourself. Very romantic – like a lovers' suicide pact. And while all this is going on, I am quietly working on my papers in Queensland. I shall come home tomorrow afternoon and discover the tragedy. I shall weep for my dead wife and mourn for my dead brother. End of scenario.'

There was a long silence. Then in a small voice she said: 'Don't you ever frighten yourself? Don't you ever wonder if one day the luck will turn against you?'

'I don't believe in luck,' he said shortly. 'A man makes his own fate. Alex chose his own path, he knew where it must lead.'

'The Cretan code,' she said.

'Yes. A man is nothing without honour.'

'You call this honourable? This act of bloody murder! Oh, no, Marcos. That I will not take. You killed him meanly, for revenge, to satisfy your own vanity. There is no honour in it.'

'If this had happened in Sphakia,' he said coldly, 'you would have been stoned out of the village and left to die. The women would have done it. That is their way with an adulteress. It is not a pleasant thing. I shall be more merciful.'

'I don't think I want your mercy,' she said. 'In any case, it is too late. Think about that, Marcos. If you'd shown a little mercy, a little tenderness at the beginning, even after the beginning, we might have made it. I was prepared to love you, to be a good wife. But it wasn't in you. What happened to your human feelings? Did you leave them behind in the White Mountains?'

'I loved Alex, I cared for him. I loved you and cared for you also.'

'As you love this house, your position, your business. And that isn't enough, Marcos, it really isn't.' She was suddenly weary of it all. 'Give me the gun then. Let me get it over with. That's what you want, isn't it?'

She held out her hand, and at that moment the telephone rang, startling them both. It rang for a long time, shrill and angry.

'Aren't you going to answer it?' she mocked. 'Oh I forgot, you can't. You are not here, are you?'

He seized her arm and dragged her to the bedside table. He held the gun against her bare breast. 'Answer it!' he shouted. 'Answer it – and watch what you say!'

She picked up the telephone. 'Mrs Coleman speaking. Who is that, please? Police?' She felt him tighten at her side; the gun was pressed hard against her flesh. She listened for a long time, looking up at Marcos, her eyes widening. 'Yes. You're positive? Yes – yes – I understand. Yes – all the evening. Thank you. Yes, I'll be all right. Goodbye.'

She lowered the phone on to its cradle, sat down on the bed and a smile grew on her face like a flower opening; then came laughter, soft at first, but growing louder and crackling with hysteria. The tears ran down her face as he shook her fiercely.

'What did they want? What was that about!'

Her whole body was shaking and she got the words out only with difficulty. 'The Queensland police. Calling from Townsville. You're dead, Marcos.' She laughed again. 'Didn't you know? I thought you knew everything. You took the car out this evening for a drive. You'd had rather a lot to drink. You went off the road, and crashed into a brick wall. The car burned out, with you in it.'

'You're lying!'

257

She picked up the phone, and held it towards him. 'Want to check? Come to think of it, why don't you call them and say it was all a mistake – just some drunken actor who took your place so that you could do a little murder on the side. Chalk up another death, Marcos.' She crossed herself. 'Poor devil. I shouldn't laugh. God have mercy on his soul.'

Marcos knocked the phone from her hand and it fell on to the crumpled pillow, the dialling tone purring steadily. He lifted the gun and shot Kristina, the bullet entering the forehead between her eyes.

Once before in his life, when he had heard of the death of his mother, Marcos had howled like an animal in pain. The same cry swelled in his lungs now and burst from his throat.

He turned the gun on himself and fired.

HAZELL AND THE PATRIOT

by P B Yuill

On the Tube to Dot Wilmington's office that August morning I'd read over somebody's shoulder in the *Mirror* where another of our pop geniuses was moving out to dodge tax.

Reluctantly, of course.

'No, I'm not desperate for work,' I said to the short, dumpy woman with the dyed blonde hair. 'I got at least eighty quid in the iron tank and the garage only wants ninety for clutch work. Plus I got about a hundred and fifty owing to me on a job I did . . .'

'All right, you're desperate,' Dot said.

We stared at each other across her desk. The window behind her was open to let in a cool breeze but any air moving outside was hotter than three in a bed.

'Business is terrible all round,' she said. 'That was your mistake, not becoming a brewer or a bureaucrat.'

'Or a rocker.'

'There's an electrical wholesaler in Acton – somebody's weeding out the stock. How's your double-entry bookkeeping?'

'Nine times nine is . . . ninety-nine?'

'Didn't you make two grand out of the crook you saved from the heavies?'

'Paid off the motor, didn't I? A week in Jersey . . . soon goes. Anyway, it was you phoned me, remember.'

Outside on the ledge two pigeons muttered among themselves about the drought. It did just cross my mind that Dot was enjoying all this. I'd once been on the staff of her security consultancy, seventy-five quid a week on the muck and bullet line.

Then she brought up a file from the carpet.

'Bad debts,' she said, shoving it across the desk. 'I usually bung 'em to a smart cookie called Vinnie Rae on a split-commission basis. Penny ante stuff most of it, not even worth the small-claims court. As a favour to me she might let you take a couple – twenty per cent of anything you recover. I'll ring and tell her you're coming over . . .'

'Her?'

'Yeah – and a word of warning, lover boy. Karate was her best subject at Roedean.'

'All go with you women nowadays, innit?'

Sicilian Avenue is an arched passage off Southampton Row in the no-man's land west of Tottenham Court Road. Little businesses, a stamp-collectors' shop, a restaurant with outside tables, a touch of the Continongs if you didn't look too hard. Naturally the developers had wanted to destroy it a couple of years back.

One good thing about the country being bust – you can count on seeing the same buildings two weeks in a row.

Vinnie Rae had told Dot she'd be having coffee outside.

I spotted her partner first.

Jason. Black mostly, with a bit of brown, very sleek and shiny. Bit of a gay dog judging by the way his big eyes said hello.

She was cream mostly, what you might call a biggish girl, very healthy, in a pale blue denim suit and white shoes.

'Vinnie Rae?' I said standing well away from the hound. 'James Hazell . . .'

'Ah yes.' She squinted up at me. The dog checked my credit-rating and decided I wasn't worth burying for later. 'Do have a seat . . . it's all right, Jason only goes for the throat if I raise a finger.'

'What does he go for if you raise two fingers?'

'A lady never raises two fingers.'

I sat down and put the folder on the table.

'Had any experience of debt-collecting?'

'Collecting new ones every day.'

She smiled.

Up to the table came this second hound, mostly black, very sleek, very shiny. Only this one had a dry nose. And big shades.

'All hail,' he said dramatically, clicking his heels and sliding into a seat. He was wearing a black shirt open to the navel, with a gold ornament on a chain dangling down his hairy chest. From his flared jeans he brought out a bundle of readies, which he slapped down beside her coffee-cup.

'Four hundred and twenty-five, full settlement!'

'Well *done*, Roger,' she said. 'Never thought you'd crack it.'

'I knew it would take something special,' he said modestly, with a little wave of his hand. 'I steam into his reception . . .' He held both hands behind his back . . . 'I steam past his plush secretary and there he is behind his desk. "You again?" he says sarcastically. "Yes, me again, Mr Slippery" . . . then I go *whoosh!*' He brought his right hand down smack on the table. 'First axe – smack into polished cedar! "Better give me the doings or this one"' – he brought his left hand up – '"'is for your *skull*!" Paid up like a lamb!'

'Poetry in motion,' Vinnie murmured, starting to thumb notes off the bundle. She slung him around seventy or eighty fives and oncers. The way they disappeared into his skyrocket his jeans might have had jaws.

'And I had to buy two axes,' he said, quite reasonably I thought. Vinnie wasn't impressed.

'Deduct them.'

'*Tax*?' He stood up and gave her a clenched fist salute. 'Those about to die of Socialism salute you!'

His slimline buttocks jigged away through the tables. 'Roger's an out-of-work actor – he can make a bad debt seem like a death warrant.'

Then she came back to me. 'Oh yes.' She opened the file. 'All right – here's an old friend you can have a beginner's bash at.' She handed me the sheet of paper. 'A mere two hundred and thirty pounds but you only have to go as far as Oxford Street . . .'

'What's the . . . er . . . form?'

'Question of psychology really. No violence.'

'Yeah? What do you call smashing axes into desks?'

She smiled and touched the hound's chin. 'We call that applied psychology, don't we, Jason?'

I got away without being retrieved . . .

You'll find a lot of buildings like it in the West End, tucked away in odd corners. The notice-board listed everything from escort agencies to cut-rate carpets, cheap fares to Australia, palms read (crystal ball by special arrangement), a yoga health clinic, several secretarial agencies . . . and Mr Dornford's little conglomerate.

I went up to the fourth floor. On the way I passed three or four silent Indians. The businessman sort. Most of the doors looked a bit damaged – it's a safe bet any building like that in the pulsating West End echoes at night to the traditional sounds of splintering panels and jemmied hinges.

Mr Dornford was in Thirty-Nine. Judging by the number of companies with notices on his door his office had to be slightly bigger than the Vickers building. Travel and insurance mostly.

I knocked.

He was about sixty-five, dark suit, white hair combed back with a strict parting, a moustache the colour of old piano keys, a regimental tie with the kind of knot that makes fingernails yell for help.

A gentleman of the old school, no doubt about it.

'Mr Dornford?'

'He's gone. What's it about?'

Two silent Indians came along the corridor. He gave them a bit of a glare. They slid past me.

'Gone?'

'Knew what he was doing,' he said, quite viciously, staring at the disappearing Indians. 'I bought his businesses—'

'Gresham's office equipment reckon he owes them—'

'Sorry, can't help you.'

He was going to shut the door. For twenty per cent of two hundred and thirty quid I was willing to risk causing offence. I put my hand on the door.

'Where is he then?'

'He drops in occasionally to collect his mail – write to him. Now, unfashionable as it may seem, I have work to do.'

'They've tried writing – he never replies.'

'Can't blame him, postage rates these days. Now . . .'

'If you bought the business you'd be legally responsible . . .'

'I bought only the goodwill – the ill-will as it turned out.'

Behind him in the office a phone rang. He turned to look at it. On the wall I caught a glimpse of a framed photograph of a young geezer in uniform.

'If he comes in I'll ask him for his address – best I can do,' he said . . .

Half an hour later I was going into Vinnie Rae's office on the third floor above Sicilian Avenue. She was on the phone. The Dobermann was on the floor. The bundle of notes was on her desk.

I was on edge.

But the hound gave me the benefit of the doubt.

'Funny how people never complain about our forty per cent until the money's been recovered,' she was saying. She gave me a little wave, pointing me in the direction of a small purple sofa with wooden arms.

They say animals can smell fear.

Maybe Jason had a cold in the nose.

'Well, I have two hundred and fifty-five pounds here for you,' she said, thumbing the notes. I reached the sofa without provoking Jason. Vinnie laughed. 'Oh no no no no,' she said, giving me a wink, 'we deduct at source. Cash business, no cheques – and *no* bad debts . . . very good.'

She rang off.

'Well?'

'Bit hot.'

She stretched her arms. Her denim suit seemed a bit tight.

I dunno why, I looked quickly at Jason.

Oh yeah, he knew what I was thinking. He sort of sneered. There was only one dirty dog in the room and it wasn't him.

'Dornford's sold out to an old geezer called Telford,' I said. 'Telford's getting me an address for Dornford.'

She managed to frown and smile at the same time.

'And what're you going to do while you're waiting for the address?'

'I dunno . . . maybe try another one . . .'

She sighed. 'Dot did say you needed a bit of help.'

'I'll register as a charity I expect.'

'I *hate* to tamper with masculine pride and all that but . . . Telford – one of the old brigade? Seedy but a certain air of previous distinction? Pushing seventy perhaps? Moustache, white hair?'

It was paper-hat time. The kind with a big D.

She smiled ever so sweetly.

'We don't have time for looking and learning in this racket,' she said.

So back I went to Oxford Street.

This time it was Plan B . . . steam in like a fist with a smile on its face.

Knock knock.

'Who is it?'

'Hazell.'

'You're beginning to be a nuisance.'

I got down in a crouch and looked through his letter-box. He was on the other side of the room, looking at me over a desk.

'You going to let me in, Mr Dornford?'

'I told you – my name's Telford.'

'And mine's Lawrence of Bethnal Green.'

'Oh . . . oh very well.'

As he opened the door a teenage person came along the corridor. Hard to say what sex, pale face, green hair.

'Did you see that?' Dornford let his head fall. I closed the door. 'What *is* the country coming to?'

'To a halt. Anyway, this debt of yours . . .'

He snorted as if I'd made a bad joke. He went to the window. 'When I think of all the wonderful men I saw dying around me in the desert – the lifeblood of a proud nation seeping into the sand . . . *now*? Has it ever occurred to you – who would fly the Spitfires today?'

'Look . . .'

'Long-haired layabouts. Poofs. Hermaprodites with green hair. Thieves – in this rat-hole they'd steal the paint off the woodwork. The only ones that will work are these dusky devils – place is full of 'em. Is this the Britain we fought and died for?'

'You owe Greshams two hundred and thirty quid.'

He waved a gentlemanly hand. 'Is that the only motivation we have left – money, money, money?'

'Let me put it this way. You pay your debt and I'll buy British.'

'Haven't got it, old boy. Business is abominable.'

'You had an electric typewriter out of them . . .'

'Stolen. Burglars. Kicked the door down.'

'The insurance . . .'

'I insured with my own company.' He heaved with silent laughter. 'My insurance company's gone bust!'

I decided to cut out the social niceties.

'I think you're an old bleeding fraudsman,' I said heavily. 'Don't give me all that dying in the desert crap . . .'

He nodded and walked to his desk. He sat down, folded his arms and closed his eyes.

'Well, get on with it,' he said.

'Get on with what?'

'The rough stuff. That's what they pay you for, isn't it? Go on – you represent the new morality. Kick an old man whose only crime was to fall behind with his payments.'

'Fall behind? You never got under starters' orders!'

'They should never have encouraged a man of my age to incur such a debt. That's how they make their money, you know – tempting people into commitments with seductive blandishments and then . . .' He opened his eyes. 'Does your work make you feel *proud*?'

263

I walked across to his desk and thumped my fist down. It was supposed to make him . . . well, not exactly putting the frighteners in but letting him know.

I hurt my knuckles as it happened.

'Can't you pay *anything*?' I said.

He brought a wallet out from his hip-pocket and opened it wide. 'My daily entitlement,' he said, sliding out a solitary pound note. 'My own fault – I should've packed in years ago, but when you have a sick wife . . .'

I had the pound out of his hand.

'Let's talk about the balance.'

'I *could* break into a small building society account that my wife and I hoped would see us through . . . very bleak at our age . . . you young chaps never think it will happen to you . . .'

'Look, mate,' I said, wagging my finger at him, 'I want the money.'

He had a bright idea.

'Man in your line – how are you off for insurance?'

Honest to God. He was trying to sell me insurance.

'I'll act as broker – you pay me the initial premium and I'll give you back my commission – it won't cover the whole debt but it's a start, isn't it?'

The phone rang. He picked it up, still looking at me with his small blue eyes. His hand had blue veins and looked slightly warped. It shook a bit. His eyes were watery.

'Oh hello,' he said into the phone, 'how is my wife?' He listened. 'Oh . . . confirmed, is it? . . . Well yes, one has had to prepare oneself for the worst . . . yes, thank you very much for phoning.'

He put down the phone. Somebody knocked at the door. He motioned at me to keep quiet.

'Mr Dornford? It's Captain McInnes.'

'The block manager,' Dornford said, going to the door.

They'd have made a fine pair of book-ends, only the Captain was fatter.

'Just thought I'd tell you, old chap – two offices done over last night. I'm chucking out this damned security mob – oh, busy are you?'

'It's all right . . .'

The Captain gave me a look. 'No, won't disturb you, Dornford. You seem to be the only other white man in this teeming bazaar. May drop by later.'

Dornford shut the door. He shook his head. 'In a way I'm glad my time's about over,' he said cheerfully, 'this isn't what I was used to. Oh well . . .'

He went to the window.

He looked much older, standing there against the sunshine. Call me a naïve sentimental fool but there was something stopping me from putting the boot in.

I did have a spin through his wallet. Didn't even have a credit card, just junk.

'No, I don't envy you your youth,' he said. 'I had my best days in a much better world. Different class.'

'Oh ballocks.'

I got up and went to the door. I wasn't put in this world to terrorise old geezers with shaky hands, was I?

'Going?'

'Yeah.'

We looked at each other. I don't know why, I found myself laughing. I went back to his desk and put the pound note down. He nodded wisely.

'Thank you.'

I left with that good deed feeling. Sort of clean, you know what I mean?

'You got *what*?' Vinnie demanded.

She was back outside having coffee and a pastry.

'One sov.'

'One pound?'

'Yup.'

'Very good . . . you've earned twenty pee.'

'No I haven't. I gave it back.'

'What?'

'I don't think I got the stomach for this debt-gathering caper. Better send him, the old axe trick.'

'Dot said you were a bit of a romantic but . . . a debt-collector giving the money *back*? You might get in the *Guinness Book of Records*.'

I raised my hand. The waiter came over. I ordered a cup of tea. Jason was on the deck, tongue hanging out. A girl passed in a white summer dress. One thing about all this heat, legs were coming out of hiding.

'I like to think of myself as a professional,' I said. 'Enquiry agent I suppose you'd call it. You know – missing poodles, missing husbands, who stole the priceless eggcups? Some old guy living in a dream world . . .? I mean, he actually expected me to whack him about.'

'Drink your tea,' she said, 'we're going for a little walk. You can tell me about these lofty ideals of yours.'

Oxford Street on a hot August afternoon. All your foreigners and that, come to sunny Britain for a bargain. She had Jason on a chain. People do tend to dodge a Dobermann. Vinnie seemed amused by something.

I was sweating a bit by the time we turned into Dornford's building. On the stairs we met these two way-out characters, Indians – but something else. White surgeons' masks, white robes, little white mops over their shoulders.

'Jains,' Vinnie said.

'Who's Jane?'

'No it's a religious sect. They believe in the sanctity of life. The masks are to stop flies getting into their mouths. The mops are to wipe the ground in front of each step in case they tramp on an ant.'

'You'd learn that kind of stuff at Roedean I expect.'

'My father was Indian Army.'

'He could come here for a reunion.'

'He's having it in Heaven.'

'Sorry about that.'

'I'm not.'

When Dornford saw the hound he tried to close the door. Jason didn't exactly knock him down and trot all over him but he wasn't standing any nonsense.

'What's all this?' Dornford demanded, getting the desk between himself and our four-legged friend.

'I believe you've been giving our Mr Hazell a hard time,' Vinnie said.

'I explained to Mr Hazell . . .'

'I'm afraid Mr Hazell is learning our business. You can take this as a compliment.'

'Compliment?'

'I am the final sanction. Vinnie and the Dobermann.' She cocked a finger at Jason. 'Good dog.'

Jason did his imitation of the MGM lion. Dornford looked ready to get up on the desk.

'I appeal to you – as a man of reason,' he stammered.

'You don't appeal to me,' Vinnie said. 'Now – can we settle this matter once and for all?'

'I told Mr Hazell – I'm in no position to . . .'

'What a lovely view of dirty walls,' she said, looking out at the well behind the building. 'Are we going to be here long enough to get to like it?'

'I daresay I could make some kind of proposal . . .'

Vinnie took a deep breath, shaking her head.

'It's too late for proposals, Mr Dornford. I'm instructed to collect the whole amount. It's not the principle, it's the money. Do you like Dobermann pinschers? They have a bad reputation but by and large they're quite sensible. Jason can count up to ten. Talk, Jason, talk.'

The hound barked.

'This is outright intimidation,' Dornford said. There was a note of complaint in his voice. I began to think this Vinnie was a bit strong.

It took them long enough but once women find the way in . . . look out.

'No, it has to be a lot worse than this before it's intimidation, Mr Dornford,' Vinnie said.

'Bringing a brute like that in here? That's bad enough in my book. Are you willing to get yourself involved in this sort of thing, Mr Hazell?'

I shrugged. 'Better give the dog a bone, Mr Dornford.'

'Let me make two things quite clear, young woman. I am not paying you a penny and I'm also going to make sure Gresham's pay heavily for this gross intrusion . . . demanding money with menaces is the legal description.'

'False pretences is the legal description for assuming a false name,' Vinnie said.

The old geezer was beat.

Vinnie didn't wait till he was down.

'There's also an electric typewriter bought on hire-purchase . . .'

'The burglar took it.'

'Why didn't you tell Gresham's?'

'I don't know, I don't know.' He was really suffering.

'Look, Vinnie,' I began, 'he doesn't . . .'

Hope came into his face.

'Perhaps you're too easily gulled for our business, Mr Hazell,' she said. She turned on Dornford. 'Two hundred and thirty pounds.'

I cannot tell a lie, I was pretty sure I'd have to stop her putting the hound on him. Obviously he didn't have the money—

If my face had fallen any further I would have been tramping on my nose.

The old rascal sat down, pulled out a wallet, opened up a cheque book, and started to write.

A different wallet!

'To cash,' she said pleasantly.

He muttered something, then tore off the cheque.

Hardly looking at it she handed it back. 'You forgot the date.'

'Oh, did I? Terrible thing, old age,' he said. Somebody had just topped him up with oil. He gave her an old-fashioned smile this time.

She examined the cheque, then handed it to me.

'Jason and I will wait till Mr Hazell brings back the cash,' she said. 'You can ring the bank.'

It was twenty past three.

As I went out the door he started telling her about some package holiday deal he was promoting for the Greek Islands . . .

She drove me back that evening, after a couple of drinks. Aston Martin – of course. As a woman driver she was about as indecisive as Dirty Harry.

'Aren't you asking me in for a drink?' she said when we reached my gaff. I was kipping down in Paddington that month, short-term rental furnished till I copped enough for a proper flat.

'Will Jason be all right?'

'Give him a pint of milk, he'll be happy.'

'Couldn't we leave him out here? Give him a pedestrian to chew on . . .'

'I think you're scared of Jason.'

'I'm not too sure about you either.'

She patted me on the back.

'It has to be a lot worse before it's intimidation.'

As I say, now women have twigged to what it's all about they're *worse* than men. Not only did she say I couldn't expect more than five per cent, considering it was her who screwed the readies out of Dornford, she didn't muck about when it came to the old sack race.

'Don't you like aggressive women?' she asked sweetly. Her fingernails were making grooves on my back.

'This shirt only came back from the laundry yesterday. Do you mind?'

'Sorry.'

'That's better,' I said, taking it off. 'Can we blindfold Jason or something?'

'Once you've worked together a few times you'll get to love him.'

267

'I'll be a bit busy for a while,' I said.

'Yes, where is the bedroom?'

'My life – are you hinting at something?'

Jason watched us going into the bedroom.

I waited till afterwards to tell her.

'You did me a good turn as it happens,' I said, 'they've been having a lot of break-ins at Dornford's building. The manager reckons it's always the same bloke. Thirty quid a night we agreed on. Not bad, eh?'

'To catch a burglar? Stuck in that dump night after night? I can do better for you than that—'

'Anything I can do you can do debtor? By the way, maybe none of my business . . . but why *did* Dot send me round to you?'

'She'd told me a few things about you.'

'Such as?'

'None of your business. Why go touting for other work? I've a backlog of people like Dornford.'

'Women bosses? Dogs for partners? Terrorising old men? Enought shit in this life without making a career out of it . . . I always say.'

'If that's how you feel . . .'

She made a move to get out of bed. She was a big strong girl but . . .

Somebody's got to fly the Spitfires, haven't they?